THE STONE SKIMMERS

Typesetting and cover design by Formatting Experts

ISBN 978-1-8382227-4-1
Published by Volker-Larwin Publishing

THE STONE SKIMMERS

A NICK FISHER NOVEL

ALEX DUNLEVY

NAMED CHARACTERS

Adil MacKinnon . . . . Half-Syrian brother of Leila, son of Ian

Aléxandros Lékas . . . . Manager of Kalí Liménes oil terminal

Andréas Iliádis . . . . Lieutenant seconded from Athína drugs squad

Anna Vasilákis . . . . Police lieutenant from Iráklio prefecture

Anna Zerbákis . . . . Sergeant with the Chaniá police

Antónios Thánou . . . . Director of Enka

Captain Eliádes . . . . Police captain at Ioánnina

Chrístos . . . . Captain at Réthymno prefecture

Daric Hassan . . . . A GP from Somalia and father of Yasir

Darius Savvídes . . . . Greek Coastguard officer

Dimítris . . . . Bright constable from Chaniá prefecture

Doctor Pánagou . . . . Medical Examiner in Chaniá

Doctor Máras . . . . Doctor assigned to Paksima's care in Ioánnina

Dragan . . . . Serbian criminal

Farid Lohani . . . . Afghan junior doctor at Ioánnina

Ghislaine Saidi . . . . Bel's sister

Hari . . . . Sun lounger franchise holder at Soúda

Ian MacKinnon . . . . Father of Leila and Adil

Iphigénia Loukákis . . . . Administration manager with the Greek Coastguard

Isobel (Bel) Saidi . . . . Well-known French Moroccan journalist

Jamal Dunham . . . . Son of Oliver and Leila Dunham

Jason Buckingham . . . . Nick's son

Jen Buckingham . . . . Nick's ex-wife

Katerina Larsen . . . . Wife of Wilhelm

Kóstas (Kostí) . . . . Kafenío owner in Saktoúria

Lauren Fisher . . . . Nick's daughter

Leila Dunham . . . . Oliver's half-Syrian wife and mother of Jamal

Lena . . . . Swedish artist and sculptress in Saktoúria

Leonídas Christodoulákis . . . . Lieutenant with the Chaniá police

iv

Loúkas . . . . Technology geek with the Ioánnina police

Márkos . . . . Brother of Stélios, fisherman in Agía Galíni

Melody Schreiber . . . . VP of data security at Dropbox, San Francisco

Michális . . . . Lifeboat skipper with the coast guard

Michális (Mike/Mikey) Kallis . . . . Lieutenant with the Ioánnina police

Mr Kappas . . . . Andréas's undercover alias

Mrs Lékas . . . . Wife of Aléxandros

Náni Samarákis . . . . Sergeant with the Réthymno police

Nick Fisher . . . . . . Former DCI in The Met, now living in Saktoúria, Crete

Oliver (Ollie) Dunham . . . . English husband of Leila, father of Jamal

Osmanek Fahri . . . . Turkish criminal

Paksima . . . . Illegal migrant from Afghanistan

Razmik . . . . Turkish criminal

Stélios . . . . Brother of Márkos, fisherman in Agía Galíni

Tásos Ioánnidis . . . . Director of Enka

Thanásis (Thaní) Konstantópoulos . . . . Sergeant with the Chaniá police

Theodóros Diamántis . . . . Director of Enka

Valádis . . . . Constable from Chaniá prefecture

Vangélis Ioánnidis . . . . Founder of oil terminal at Kalí Liménes

Wilhelm Larsen . . . . Norwegian tourist

Yasir Hassan . . . . Illegal migrant from Somalia, son of Daric

Yiórgos . . . . Fisherman-philosopher in Saktoúria

CHAPTER 1
THE BOY FROM THE SEA

The night had already been endless, exhausting. The Wind-God Nótos had summoned one of his long, hot blasts from the south. Always inclined to understatement, Stélios referred to it as *the hair dryer*, but it was more like an evil curse. The air temperature rocketed as it drove all the freshness from the air and coated the deck with fine, red, Saharan sand that scrunched like grit beneath their boots. This was the wind that fanned the flames when the great palace at Knossos burned. Everyone knew it. When it blew, folk became irritable and fractious: friends argued; lovers fought. Even the dogs howled more than usual. By the third day, some were no longer thinking straight. There could be violence. Sometimes there were suicides, even murders …

Tonight, it was a Force 4 or 5 but gusting 6 or 7. It made the boat hard to handle, the work even more tiring. Stélios was relieved to be pulling in the nets now. His arms and shoulders were aching. Soon they could head back for breakfast and some rest. He and his brother were pulling sea bream and red mullet from the nets and dropping them into tall, plastic bins. Many were small, barely legal. About one in three had to be thrown back. Their night's catch filled just two and a half bins; no more than eighty fish. *But maybe the prize is yet to come*, he thought. He could feel weight in the net, still. There must be plenty more down there.

As he threw the winch handle for the last time, something flopped into the boat along with the cascade of silver fish. It was much bigger, and dark; a shape he recognised at once, despite the incongruity. He stopped, aghast, then looked at his brother. They were thinking the same thing, but Márkos was the first to put it into words:

"That's no bloody fish, Stélio. Let's get it out of there," he said, in Greek.

It was lying face down, not tangled in the netting. The fish were flapping and gasping but the body was still. It struck Stélios as an almost biblical scene, as if the hand of God had delivered this creature into their fishing-boat. Or, like Jonah, it had been spewed up by a whale. They cleared one of the side benches, then lifted the body clear of the nets and laid it there, face up. It was a young, black boy. No more than sixteen or seventeen, maybe less. His face was perfectly formed, innocent and calm. There were acne scars or perhaps tribal markings on each cheek. *And he was proper, matt black, like the chessmen at the kafenío*, Stélios thought. But the darkness of his skin was in stark contrast to the hideous grin of pink that gaped beneath his chin.

"The boy's been killed, Márko. Look. Some bastard's gone and cut his throat."

They looked at the young boy, the sodden, grey hoodie with the bright red Rolling Stones' tongue and lips logo, the black football shorts with the silver stripe at the sides, the open sandals.

"And not long ago, I reckon, Stélio."

"Why say that?"

"He's not bloated or discoloured, is he? More than a couple of days in the sea and he would be. Might even have a few bits chewed off."

"True." Stélios took a cigarette and tossed the pack to his brother who did the same, leaning across to share the flame from the lighter.

"How the hell did he end up here, I wonder?" Stélios asked.

"Well, no-one lives on these islands, do they? Not a soul. So, maybe he was brought out here to be dumped in the sea."

"Or he was dropped from a passing boat. Let's hope whoever did this is long gone, then."

"Shit. I hadn't thought of that."

Stélios saw his brother's eyes flit across the horizon before darting back, towards the mainland.

"Maybe we just chuck him back and get away, then?" he said.

"He's not some undersized mullet, Márko. The poor boy's been murdered. We must take him in, report it. He'll have a mum and dad somewhere. Put yourself in their shoes. You'd want to know, wouldn't you?"

"I'm not sure I would, to be honest. Might prefer to go on hoping. And we'll face a barrage of questions and paperwork from the bloody cops."

"Maybe, but we have no choice, do we? We're human beings and so was he, poor devil. Come on now. Let's pull these last few fish in and head on back."

CHAPTER 2
FATHERS AND SONS

Nick drove straight from the airport to the beach. He needed time to collect his thoughts and find some peace again. Soúda was a place he knew well. Seldom crowded. A good spot for a long, quiet swim, or to hire a sun lounger and read, or just watch the idle sea and think. And, if he got hungry later, as he often did, the Delfíni Taverna would provide sardélla, the excellent local sardines, or those delicious courgette balls, kolokíthokeftédes, and one of their special salads with the honey mustard dressing.

He parked the Jeep just off the road on the promontory that overlooked the perfect arc of the bay. He grabbed his beach bag and made his way down, through tamarisk trees and along wooden walkways to the centre of the shingle beach, the quietest part. The western side was dominated by Greek families with children who needed tavernas and toilets, the eastern side by a scattering of naked, older Germans who did not. Only three of the loungers in the more ambivalent, central section were occupied. He paid his five euros, had a chat with Hari about the global economic forces impacting the sun lounger business, and then settled down for the rest of the afternoon, undisturbed – other than by his regrets.

The week with his son did not go as planned, to say the least. It was a huge disappointment for them both. Was it even *relief* he sensed from him as they parted? Maybe he felt it too, for that matter. They should have done more together; walked a gorge or two, climbed some hills, driven east to Káto Zákros or Xerókampos or south, to Léndas. He should have realised: Jason needed to bond with his dad again before he could relax, open up, be himself. If he had come for three weeks, as originally planned, there would have been time for adventures too, but Nick had messed it up. And one week was never going to be enough.

And then there was the senseless argument. About Jason joining the police service. His son was looking for support and encouragement but was handed only scepticism and disbelief. Nick saw that now. *Do you understand what's involved? Do you really have the strength of character required for the job? Are you tough enough?* Jason thought it would please him to have a son follow in his footsteps. But dear old Dad came down on the idea with the size tens, poking his son just where it hurt while he was at it. *You can be such a stupid bastard, sometimes, Nick Fisher.*

He glanced at his watch. The plane was about to take off. He would not be coming back. If Nick wanted to see his son again, he would have to travel to England, and he might not be welcome, if he did. What a total screw up. They all reminded him: Jen, Lena, Kóstas, Yiórgos. *It's your last chance, Nick. Don't fuck it up.* And now he had done precisely that.

He took out his phone and composed a text message:

Happy landings, son. Great having you here. Lots of love, Dad xx

He hesitated, inserted a hopeful *See you soon* and then pressed send. Jason would see it when he landed.

Nick packed the phone away and stepped gingerly across the shingle to the water. Within a few seconds he was in and thrashing through a burst of crawl before rolling onto his back and gazing up into the deep blue, cloudless sky. Next, he set himself the task of making his way, breaststroke, the three hundred metres across the bay to the rocks. The rhythm of the exercise and the coolness of the water would start the healing process. His mind would go blank as he looked down into the depths or focused on the objective.

Ten minutes later, he grasped the sharp rocks at the far end of the bay and swung himself around. He would do a full crossing now, and then a third leg back to the centre of the beach. It was about twelve hundred metres in all, or forty minutes' swimming. He swilled out his goggles, reset them and kicked off.

He was about halfway across when he noticed the boat. It was not unusual to see the odd small craft here: a fishing-boat, a pedalo or the occasional, dreaded jet ski. There was the yellow boat from

Plakiás that brought tourists for the day sometimes. In the height of the season, there might be a smart day-cruiser owned by a well-to-do family of Greeks or Italians. But this was something else.

Anchored perhaps seven hundred metres offshore, it would be about twenty metres long, he reckoned. Sixty feet, at least. A motor yacht, ocean-going, sleek and white with darkened windows in its ample superstructure. There would be an extensive living area inside, with cabins and berths for six or eight below. The wheelhouse was raised, towards the bow. There was a large sun deck above that, with an alternative, open-air wheelhouse. Towards the transom there was a luxury seating area with striped cushioning. It looked like the kind of boat a big game fisherman would own in The States, maybe Florida. The kind of boat that oozed money – and chewed it up. *Like standing in a shower, tearing up fifty-euro notes*, he recalled someone saying. Nick would not have been surprised to see such a boat in Santoríni or Mýkonos or perhaps Chaniá, but here in Soúda it was a real eye-opener. He guessed that such a boat, even second-hand, might cost close to a million euros. Big money, for sure.

He ploughed on across the bay, watching the few tourists playing in the shallows. He saw a tanned girl manoeuvring a paddleboard with skill. As he turned for home, shoulders aching now, he ducked his head under, then again reset the leaking goggles. His son would have left Greek airspace by now and, like the vapour trail, Nick's guilt and regret were dissipating. The air was clearing, his natural optimism resurfacing. From now on, he would try harder to be a friend and a supportive dad. He would call often and avoid talking about himself. He would show interest in what Jason was doing, how he was feeling, what he was planning, and he would say good, encouraging things about it all. And, in the end, Jason might want to invest some time in getting to know his father. It was only natural, and it would happen, someday.

Just as Nick was returning to the shallow water, he flinched as a stone flashed close by his head and he looked up to see a long-haired, coffee-coloured boy of about ten, his hands covering his mouth in horror. A paler, blond-haired man raised a hand in apology and called:

"Sorry, chum. Bit awry that one."

It was an English voice, public-school educated, rather louche.

Nick waved and called:

"No harm done," and swam further to the right, out of the firing line. He hung in the shallows for a while, watching them.

He saw them scouring the beach for stones. After a few minutes, the boy presented a selection to his dad, if that was who he was. Dad allowed only the slimmest, roundest stones that would fit in the palm of his hand and flipped the rejects back onto the beach. Then he showed the boy the stones he had chosen and passed a few across. They came to the edge of the water with their prizes then, and the boy made a few, wild attempts before the man ruffled his hair and then held him from behind, talking and coaxing, getting the boy to bend lower so his hand was closer to the water, turning his arm in the flatter arc needed for a fast, level throw. The boy made a few more attempts, gradually improving.

And then the man took a black stone and washed it in the shallows before winking at the boy. He was waiting for the next, small wave to break. Then, he wound himself up like a baseball pitcher before swooping low to his right and firing the stone, flat, fast and low across the water. The stone flew four or five metres before skimming the surface of the water several times. With each touch the gap shortened, before a flurry at the end when it was hard to count the number of skips. Finally, gravity won, and the stone plunged beneath the surface.

"A sixteen!" the boy shouted, in delight.

"Gosh. Really? Not bad, then. Now, you have another go."

Nick made his way back to the sun lounger and grabbed his towel, but he kept watching as he dried himself. The boy was improving, his throw flatter now, if still rather wayward. The man's loving patience impressed Nick. Each time they gathered stones, filtered their finds, and then the boy would get to throw almost all of them with the man throwing occasionally. His throws were near perfect, ranging from eight to twenty skips and arcing out fifteen or twenty metres.

The man was attractive in the English way, thought Nick. He wasn't muscular but he was lithe. There was no fat on him. He was blessed with a naturally athletic frame rather than one built pumping iron in some gym. He would be in his early forties but showed few signs of ageing. His wheat-blond hair was still thick, his face not yet wrinkled, his stomach flat. And he exuded a quiet confidence. *This is someone from a privileged background. He knows he looks good, and he knows he is loved*, thought Nick.

The boy's dark, brown hair fell straight, all the way to his chest. He was mixed-race and skinny but full of energy and tactile. It was obvious to all how much he loved and admired this man.

Nick was a cauldron of mixed emotions as he made his way back to the Jeep. This was how a father should be with his son: loving, teaching, forgiving, building the boy's strengths. He wondered how he could have got it so wrong with Jason. Was there a time when it was like that? Probably not, if he were honest.

At the Jeep, he looked back. The skimming had stopped now and the two of them were watching a boat puttering into the beach, piloted by a dark-skinned woman. Once in the shallows, the man dragged it onto the shingle, helped the boy in and then kicked off again, rolling himself into the boat as he did so. The boat pivoted around then, and the woman gunned the outboard. Nick took a pair of binoculars from the glove compartment and followed them as they streaked out to the motor yacht.

CHAPTER 3
THE BAKER'S ROUND

By the time Nuri reached the northern end of the camp, his sack was half empty. He had given several loaves to the children seated in a semi-circle in the dirt, reciting English words in their toneless but happy singsong. He made a face and put his hands over his ears and their pretty, Egyptian teacher grinned ruefully.

The group of Afghan men practising martial arts took a couple off him with their mock threats and their backslapping and then he placed one in the hands of the small boy with the eyes that wanted to hide. He seemed to be alone, day after day. Withdrawn and wounded. Nuri did not know if he would eat it, if there was even room for bread in his wasted, little body.

*

A few minutes further on, he saw the Syrian widow with the soulful eyes and the secret smile she seemed to save for him. He handed her a loaf and she thanked him. He saw her tear off a piece and hand it to the silent boy in the bright orange life jacket.

"He's still wearing it then," Nuri said.

"He won't let me take it off him. Not yet."

"Did it save him, then?"

She jerked her head, and he followed her a few steps, away from the boy.

"He thinks it did, but it didn't. I don't know how to tell him. The life jackets don't work. That's why his father drowned."

"They don't work?"

"They just don't keep you afloat. They're useless. But this Turkish man said we had to have them, and he charged us twenty euros each for them."

Nuri shook his head in disgust.

"What kind of man does such a thing?"

The woman took it as a rhetorical question and said nothing. Nuri glanced back at the silent boy before turning back to her.

"Are you okay, Janiya? Are you coping?"

He saw her staring at the newly flattened acres of land to the north of the camp, where lorries and JCBs were gathering dust in the morning sun.

"When will they come, Nuri?"

"Soon, I'm sure."

"It's already September and all they have done is clear the land. They tell me it is cold here in winter. There are fierce winds and electric storms, and the sea is cruel. I am afraid, Nuri."

"They will come soon, and they will build a beautiful, new camp. Proper buildings again instead of tents. Bathrooms and toilets for everyone. You'll see. Bel told me. The European Union has much money for this. They will not let us down."

*

As Nuri made his way along, behind the beach, he heard shouts from the sea where two men were fighting. He saw one fall back into the water, then the other came storming through to the beach. He was a black man of about forty with bloodshot eyes.

"Fucking animals," he spat.

Nuri gave him a few seconds to calm down.

"You want bread, man?"

The man seized a loaf without thanking him and bit straight into it.

"What was that all about?" asked Nuri.

"You know how it is, Nuri," the man said. "Twenty showers for eight thousand people – and six of them don't work. So, we wash in the sea, right? I do. I expect you do. My wife and my little girls do. So, there I am, washing the mud off and I turn round to see this bastard taking a dump, for Christ's sake! Totally fucking unacceptable."

Nuri glanced back to see an older, Arab man scurrying across the shallows, clutching his trousers at the waist.

"He's running away now," he said.

"Good. He won't do that again in a hurry," the man said, raising his voice to call: "stupid bastard," almost as an afterthought. Then, he looked at Nuri with a wicked grin.

Nuri dug out another loaf.

"Here," he said, "take this, for your family."

The black man took the bread and grasped Nuri's shoulder.

"You're going straight to heaven, man," he said.

"Not just yet, I hope," said Nuri.

*

The central part of the beach still bore the markings, he saw. The Greeks had shovelled sand on it in their haphazard way, but it was still obvious to those who knew.

Nuri was remembering the stillness of the young woman sitting cross-legged on the bare sand, the calm of her mysterious ritual, the almost ceremonial pouring of what they assumed to be water on that stifling day. How she raised her head to face forward in proud silence, placing her left hand on her womb, then using the right, without hesitation, to flick the lighter. He would never forget her gasp, the shudder at the instant, ravenous fury of the flames, the sudden stench of burning robes, and those white eyes staring, as if in accusation, even as her flesh puckered and blackened. And then, the silence of the crowd broken by isolated, screams of terror from the first to understand what their eyes were telling them. And then, afterwards, the terrible, endless wailing.

"Are you okay, Nuri?"

He looked up to see the kindly, broad face of Kuma.

"Just remembering. I can't help it."

"Nor me. It's hard to forgive what she did."

"Is it?"

"Not so much for herself, but the child."

"But you know how the child came about, don't you, Kuma?"

"I know what they say, but a child is still a child."

Nuri said nothing. He was shocked at the lack of sympathy from this otherwise big-hearted woman. Despite himself, he took a loaf from the sack and pressed it into her hands. When her little girl came over to join them, he gently pinched her nose between his index and middle fingers before pulling back, pushing his thumb between the same fingers, then raising his hand and staring at it in mock alarm.

"Don't be such a silly," she cried. "It's not my nose."

"Have you checked?" he grinned.

He gave them a wave as he picked up his sack and went on his way. He heard Kuma say:

"Now, take these bottles, girl, and get yourself into the water queue. Then, in a while, we can enjoy a drink with our bread."

*

Back at the makeshift bakery, his brothers were packing up for the day.

"Ah, Nuri. About time. We've had a message," said one.

"Seems your girlfriend, the journalist, is coming back," said another.

"She can't stay away," teased the youngest.

"I don't think it's my charm or my irresistible looks, unfortunately," said Nuri. "But at least she will listen. And then she will tell the world."

CHAPTER 4

THE BOY ON THE BICYCLE

The boy swung away from the harbour towards the town, raising his bottom from the saddle as the bike morphed into a bucking bronco on the stretch of cobblestones. Then, reaching the tarmac, he saw the shop right there, at the foot of Archoléontos. *But it would be more fun to do the circuit, like before,* he thought.

He swung left down Kallergon, accelerated past the Venetian stone arsenals, and raced by the pink villa where the ground floor was mysteriously boarded up. He swung right into Rianou, swerving to avoid an abandoned motorbike and, after a hundred metres, right again past Jasmine studio into Sifáka. Now, he felt his mouth watering as the rich smell of frying meat reached him from the café on the corner. He could see people already enjoying a gýros píta with their morning coffees. But he was concentrating now, repeating the shopping list to himself: *milk, matches, bread, olives. M-M-B-O. Hmmm. B-O-M-M would be easier to remember. BOMM. Oh – and Dad's tobacco. Mustn't forget that. Golden Virginia. Five things, then. BOMM-T. BOMM-T-BOMM, BOMM-T-BOMM.* He went on reciting the mantra, and stretched for the back pocket of his shorts to make sure the twenty-euro note was still there before the final run in.

He was standing tall on the pedals now as he swung right again, into Daskalogiánni to complete the square. The bike frame jagged from side to side as he raced away down the straight stretch to the grocery shop. He could see boat masts again now, framed by the glorious, blue sky. The tourists crowding the pavement were a blur as the gradient took him faster still. He thought of showing off with a wheelie, but you needed to be on the flat for that and not going quite so fast. He was a Maserati now, breaking free, engine yowling from his mouth, head thrown back, ponytail streaming in the wind from the sea.

There was a split second when he saw the dark shape swerve into his path, felt the front wheel slam into something, heard a clattering of metal, a woman's shriek. And then he took off, like Icarus. Soaring blind into the sun, then tumbling into blackness.

*

By the time Sergeant Anna Zerbákis arrived, a crowd had gathered around the stricken boy. They seemed shocked and were arguing about what to do. There was no sign of the vehicle.

"No, don't move his head!" the sergeant cried in Greek, and a middle-aged woman backed away from the boy, raising her hands. The boy was on his back, eyes closed. A little, bright blood had spilled onto the road. *Please, God, let it not be a fractured skull*, she thought.

"Has anyone called for an ambulance?" the sergeant called, but her question was met with shifting looks and uncertainty. She moved in close, crouched down and made the call. Then, she grasped the boy's hand.

"It's all right," she whispered in Greek, though she had no idea if he could hear, "you've been in an accident, but you're going to be okay. Just stay still for a bit."

When the paramedics arrived, the sergeant moved among the bystanders, asking them what they had seen. It was a dark pick-up, they said, perhaps a Toyota or an Isuzu. Black, maybe dark blue. Most agreed, it looked *hot* or *souped-up* with a tuned engine and fat tyres. Some thought there were darkened windows. Another mentioned a bull-bar on the front. No-one could make out the driver and no-one thought to get the registration number. *Surprise, surprise*, thought the sergeant.

There was general agreement that the truck swung right into the path of the fast-moving bicycle. Some thought the driver might have fallen asleep or been lighting a cigarette, maybe changing a CD. Others ridiculed such suggestions. No way. It was deliberate. You could see. No question. He pulled across into the path of the bicycle, then reversed over it before speeding off. A hit and run. On a child. Shocking. Such things don't happen; not here in Chaniá.

The older paramedic stood and walked over to the sergeant:

"He's a very lucky boy," he said. "He has bruises all over and nasty scrapes on his right arm, and he may have a mild concussion, but nothing seems to be broken."

The sergeant saw the boy propped against the wheel of a nearby car. He looked groggy and shaken but his eyes were open now. Some of the onlookers were on their haunches, chatting with him, others were moving away now, relieved that the boy seemed to be okay, after all.

"But there was blood," she said.

"From the arm, not the head. It would be an automatic reflex to use the arm to protect the head, then roll into the fall. He's fortunate not to break his arm, at the very least. And his skull seems to be intact. I suggest you take him home. Get the parents to keep a close eye on him. If he gets severe pain or dizziness, or if his vision is affected, they must take him to the hospital right away and get them to do a scan. There is a slight risk of a blood clot."

"That's it?" said the sergeant. "Shouldn't he be scanned *now*, as a precaution?"

"Boys are very robust, Sergeant. I don't think it's necessary."

"And what about shock?"

"I've given him a mild sedative. Some hot, sweet tea when he gets home, and he'll be just fine."

"Nothing else?"

"Catching the bastard who did this, I would suggest."

"Oh, we'll do our best, don't worry."

"And getting the poor lad another bike."

She followed the paramedic's gaze to the bicycle, crushed and mangled on the road: a total write-off.

The boy was sitting up straight now, wrapped in a silver blanket. He looked about ten, she thought. The sergeant thanked the paramedics and moved over to him, looking him in the eyes with warmth and curiosity.

"What's your name?" she asked, in Greek.

"Signómi. Den katalavéno."

"What is your name?" she asked again, this time in English.

15

"Jamal," said the boy.

"And where is your house?"

"It's not a house. It's a boat."

"Is it here, in the harbour?"

"Yes."

"And are your Mummy and Daddy there?"

"Yes."

"All right. Let's go and find them, shall we?"

She helped Jamal up, looked him over and dusted him down, then took his hand. The remaining crowd responded with a ripple of applause, and he gave a little bow and grinned, showing even, white teeth. For the first time, the sergeant noticed what a beautiful child he was.

*

"Did you see the car that hit you, Jamal?" she asked, as they walked along the paved area towards the harbour. "Was it anyone you recognised?"

"I didn't see anything. It was all so quick. Just a black blur."

"Black?"

"Yes. It was black – and big."

"Did you see the make, the driver?"

"No. It was just there, all of a sudden, and then whack; I was flying. That's all I remember."

They were entering the harbour area now. She saw perhaps one hundred and fifty craft: fishing boats painted in bright colours, sleek sailing yachts, ostentatious motor cruisers. Water lapped hulls, shrouds clinked against masts, house martins were flitting in and out of a row of ancient, Venetian arsenals to their right.

"It's third from the end," Jamal said, pulling her hand.

They made their way along the left-hand quay, past a variety of substantial boats. The sergeant was wondering how honest people ever afforded such things, then Jamal was waving and running towards one of the larger boats. She saw the name on the stern. Destiny would have to be twenty metres long: a white motor yacht with smoked glass windows. Not new, and perhaps a touch old-fashioned in style, but still very smart indeed. She was stern-in to the dock but, as they came closer, the sergeant could see the sleek lines, the glistening upper deck, the chrome rails. *This is one expensive boat,* she thought.

A dark-skinned woman responded to Jamal's call and started waving, then did a double-take and concern flashed across her face. She ran to the stern to meet them.

"What's happened, Jamal? Are you all right? Where's your bike?"

"I'm okay."

"He had an accident, Mrs ...?"

"Dunham. I'm Leila Dunham, Jamal's mother."

"He was hit by a car, but the paramedics think he's all right. No serious damage. The same can't be said of the bike, I'm afraid."

The sergeant noticed an attractive, blond-haired man appearing behind Leila.

"Not wheelies again, Jamal?" he asked, in a sarcastic tone.

"The boy was not to blame, sir," countered the sergeant. Then she turned to Leila. "Why don't you take Jamal below and look him over, Mrs Dunham? Maybe give him some sweet tea for the shock. Make sure he's okay. The paramedic says you must take him straight to hospital if he gets a bad headache or any dizziness, or if his eyesight is affected."

Leila stared back for a second longer than was necessary, but then did as she was told. When they were out of sight, Zerbákis turned to the man, who was now rolling a cigarette.

"Mr Dunham?"

He raised his eyebrows as he was sliding his tongue along the paper. Then, he rolled the cigarette in his fingers and tapped the end on the bulkhead before placing it between his lips, pulling a silver Zippo lighter from the pocket of his shorts and lighting it. All the time, he was appraising her. As he exhaled a shroud of blue smoke, his face broke into a regretful smile.

"Always getting into scrapes, Jamal. I'm sorry for your trouble, Sergeant."

"Do you have enemies, Mr Dunham?"

"Why on earth would you ask me that?"

"Because we have reason to believe the boy was targeted. It appeared to be a hit and run."

"Surely not."

"Do you?"

"In Chaniá? No, of course not. We're just visiting."

"Where are you based, then?"

"We don't have a base. We travel around the islands. I have a charter business; we often have paying guests on board."

"Any aggressive business rivals, disgruntled guests?"

"None who would do anything like that, I assure you."

"Do you know anyone with a dark pick-up, a Toyota or an Isuzu, maybe with darkened windows, perhaps a bull-bar?"

"Sounds like one of those young, Cretan farmers. No-one I'd know. Are you sure it wasn't just a stupid accident? Maybe the driver drank too much rakí and fell asleep?"

"With respect, I'm not sure you realise how serious this was, sir. Your son could have been killed in what looks like a deliberate attack on your family."

"I hear you, Sergeant, but I think there must be a less dramatic explanation. I can't imagine why anyone would want to do that."

The sergeant handed him a card.

"Well, perhaps you could let me know if anyone comes to mind, Mr Dunham. We will be opening an investigation into this incident but, to be honest, we don't have a great deal to go on."

Dunham took the card and smiled again. *He's disarmingly handsome*, she thought.

*

When Leo scanned the sergeant's report the next day, something didn't smell right. As she pointed out, the man seemed cool, blasé almost. Leo put himself in the man's position and imagined himself incensed. He would be desperate to know more. He would want to pursue the owner of this truck and tear him limb from limb. And yet Dunham asked no questions, almost tried to excuse the attacker, by the sound of it. *Perhaps it had been an accident.* He even suggested the boy himself might have been to blame. *Maybe it was the difference between a Greek's reaction and an Englishman's? That famous, cool reserve. But surely*, he thought, *a father is a father, no matter what …*

Later that morning, Leo decided to get out of the office, take a stroll down to the harbour. He wanted to meet this family for himself, see what made this guy Dunham tick. When he reached the berth, he called in to check.

"You're in the right place, sir," said the sergeant, "third from the end of the left-hand row. There was a smaller, pale blue boat next to it, I remember."

The lieutenant glanced to his right.

"Okay. The blue boat is here. But *Destiny* is not."

When he checked with the harbourmaster, the man was surprised. They had booked and paid for a week's stay just three days before and, for a large boat, it was not cheap.

"Perhaps they're just having a day on the water," he said.

Leo handed him a card.

"Call me right away if you see the boat again. All right?"

The man gave him a sideways glance, then nodded.

Outside, Leo called the sergeant again.

"Okay, Anna, I want you to alert the other ports on the island: Réthymno, Iráklio, Eloúnda, Ágios Nikólaos, Sitía, Ierápetra, Paleóchora. Make sure the harbourmasters let us know if they see this boat. Then, check with the hospital. Did the Dunhams take the boy in for a check or a scan before they left? And keep me posted on your search for the driver. I'm not sure what it is, but I think we're missing something."

CHAPTER 5
LUNCH, INTERRUPTED

The lunch had been arranged for some time. The excuse for it: a thank you to Nick for helping Leo's former protégée Náni Samarákis with the missing Swiss lad – a grisly case that had ended in drama and tragedy, two months before. Nick was to choose a favourite venue and the bill was on Leo (to be charged to Réthymno Prefecture, if Nick knew Leo). A constable called that morning to confirm, and to check that Nick had not forgotten. He had not. And so it was, this Thursday morning, that Nick was trundling along the Spíli-Réthymno road, through Arméni and down the hill to the city.

The choice of restaurant had been a no-brainer. Nick adored the place. It looked across the water at the Venetian Fortezza from its peaceful spot on the rocks, to the west of the small city. The menu was an inspired mix of gourmet Greek and Japanese with an obvious fondness for fish and seafood.

Nick was the first to arrive and was shown to a table under an awning, close to the sea. The waiter brought a jug of iced water with lemon and Nick ordered a small beer. Leo arrived ten minutes late, looking harassed and haggard. It was around ten months since they last met but Nick thought he looked three years older, at least until he smiled as he was doing now. They shook hands and the smell of tobacco smoke engulfed Nick.

"Sorry to be late, Nick," he said. "I drove as fast as I could."

"No change there, then. Anyway, not to worry, I started without you," he said, nodding at the beer glass.

"So, I see." He turned to the waiter. "Bring me a Coke, would you?"

The waiter half closed his eyes and tilted his head in acknowledgement before leaving. They sat down and grinned at each other.

"Not drinking?"

"I'm on duty, Nick. Sorry. I will have a little wine with the meal."

"So much for the big blowout."

"*You* can drink as much as you want. You are my guest."

"To be honest, I've been drinking less. Jason was here, of course."

"Of course! How did it go, Nick?"

"Ah, difficult … no, awful, to be honest. My fault. I tried too hard to make everything right in a week and just made everything worse."

"A week? I thought he was coming for three."

"He was, until I put him off, back in June. He thought I was putting work first again, like before."

"And you weren't?"

Nick pulled a sheepish grin. "You know how it is, Leo. And he'll find out for himself one day. He wants to be a copper now."

The waiter had placed Leo's tall glass of Coke on the table and was setting out some amuse-bouches.

"Some appetisers from the chef, gentlemen," he said as he placed the menus on the table. "Let me know when you're ready to order."

"Another cop in the family. How do you feel about that?" asked Leo, as the waiter moved away.

"It's his life, Leo. He knows what it's done for me – and *to* me, over the years."

"But he is not *you*, Nick."

"No, he's not. I expect he'll find a role that suits him."

"We can drink to that."

They clinked their glasses together.

"It's good to see you, Nick. You're looking well."

"Thanks. Been looking after myself a bit more. How are *you* doing? How's work?"

"It's the same as ever, Nick. Too much to do, too few resources. I still have Thaní, thank God, and Dimítris, but then, as if we didn't have enough to cope with, a couple of weeks ago we were given an unsolvable murder."

"Surely, no murder is that."

"This one appears to be. Let's get some food ordered and then I'll tell you about it. Maybe you'll have some ideas."

21

Leo lit a cigarette, and they studied the menus in silence for a couple of minutes before ordering a tapas-style selection of five dishes: a ceviche of raw fish, some smoked eel with truffle oil and an egg, a beef carpaccio with rocket and two plates of sushi, to be washed down with some floral, white wine by Lyrarákis.

"Good choice, Nick. Unusual."

"And damned good."

They watched as the waiter uncorked the wine and poured a little for Leo to taste. After a sip, he raised his eyebrows and smiled at Nick, then nodded twice at the waiter and the man filled both glasses to the halfway mark, placed the bottle in a cooler and left.

"So, tell me about this murder of yours," Nick said.

Leo toyed with his knife for a moment, frowning, and then turned his eyes on Nick's.

"The sixth of August, almost three weeks ago, fishermen from Agía Galíni found a body in their nets, near the Paximádia islands. Do you know where that is?"

"Those are the two islands you can see from just about everywhere on the south coast, right?"

"Right. They're a few kilometres offshore, between Agía Galíni and Triópetra. Uninhabited. The body was a young, black boy. His throat had been cut."

"How young?"

"The ME says only fourteen or fifteen."

"Jesus. How did he get there, of all places?"

"Dumped from a boat, presumably – either a local boat or one on its way past."

"ID?"

"We don't know who he is or where he came from, Nick. The fishermen didn't recognise him and there have been no sightings of any black boy his age in the nearby coastal towns. His pockets were empty. Any ID or money – if he had any – had been removed. His clothes were westernised stuff you can buy at any bazaar for forty or fifty euros."

22

"Identifying marks?"

"No scars or tattoos, just some markings on his cheeks."

"So, he's African?"

"We're assuming that."

"DNA?"

"No match with any database we have access to."

"What else have you done?"

"We sent photos to all the African embassies in Athína and to the Greek and British embassies in all the North African countries with a Mediterranean coastline. They're telling us he looks *East* African."

"So, you've narrowed it down to about a hundred million possibles," Nick said with a wry grin.

The waiter arrived with their food, and they were silent as he arranged the dishes.

"Any thoughts, Nick?"

Nick already had a forkful of ceviche in his mouth but managed a grunt as he savoured and swallowed the delightful mixture.

"The boy seems very young to be caught up with a criminal gang. But the manner of his death suggests the killer *was* from a criminal, or perhaps military, background. Your average citizen doesn't go around cutting throats, at least not where I come from. It also implies that the killer was older. A kid of his own age – a rival for love or leadership, perhaps – would have just stabbed him, you'd think."

"Sounds right."

"So, why was he killed, execution-style? Revenge or punishment for something he did? Was he in the wrong place at the wrong time? Did he see or hear or learn something that had to be suppressed? Was he mistaken for someone else, even?"

"Could be any of those, I guess."

"This might be reading too much into it, but could that western style of dress indicate a wish to become westernised himself, to get into western Europe?"

"Clothes like those are worn everywhere now, though. Global brands."

"If you can afford them. I'd guess they're not cheap, somewhere like East Africa, compared to a local sarong or whatever. Perhaps the boy comes from a relatively well-to-do family."

Nick was tackling the smoked eel now. Leo seemed happier with the beef, he noticed. He saw him put out his hand to block the waiter's attempt to top up his glass.

"All good input, Nick, but I don't know what to do next. The ME has the body in cold storage until we come up with something, but I doubt we will. Most likely, he will remain a mystery and the murderer will get away with it."

"A blot on that spotless record of yours, Leo."

"You know I don't care about that sort of thing, Nick. But somewhere there's a devastated mother and father wondering what happened to their boy. With modern technology, I feel we ought to be able to find them. Put them out of their misery, at least."

"You need a global DNA database for that, and we'll struggle to get one with so many bleating about their privacy being violated, not to mention the enormous task of getting the technology up and running, the procedures followed. It could be quite a while, my friend."

They chatted for several more minutes about the Utopian vision, for police forces at any rate, of everyone in the world having a computerised DNA record and an identity card, and how much easier it would be to detect crime or terrorism. Leo allowed the waiter to give him an extra half glass of wine at the second attempt and Nick let him drain the remainder of the bottle into his. The conversation turned to people they both knew and cases they had been involved in. Then, Leo asked him if he would stay in Crete now and Nick said he didn't know. He gazed out over the water.

"There are many things I love about this place, Leo, but also some I hate. I guess it evokes strong emotions in both directions for me."

"What do you find to hate?"

"Those things that make it feel less civilised, more *third world*. The people mean well, I think, but there is an amazing lack of consideration, compared to the UK. Here, if you feel like operating your road digger or chainsaw at seven in the morning, you just get on with it. Tough shit on everyone else. In England, you'd hesitate to use a lawn mower before ten on a Sunday morning for fear of offending the neighbours. There might even be a law against it, come to think of it."

"But that works both ways, Nick. We are not so constrained here."

"And you park wherever the hell you want, with no regard for other road users. In England, that's all controlled with a bit of common sense."

"How boring."

"Then there's the treatment of animals, the failure to control fly tipping, the erratic supply of water and electricity, the blasted concerts that don't start till eleven and then go on till five in the morning. I could go on …"

"You must move to Réthymno, Nick. You've been living in the sticks too long."

The waiter moved in to clear the plates and leave the dessert menu. Leo noticed the red light on his phone flashing and excused himself to take a couple of calls. Nick sat there chuckling to himself. Maybe he was being rather ridiculous. What were these minor gripes when set against the astonishing beauty of this island, the warmth and fierce independence of its proud people, the glorious climate, the mountains, the sea, and the low cost of living? Not to mention food like this. No, he would be staying. If not for ever, at least for several more years.

Leo reappeared, but he didn't sit down. He looked apologetic, awkward.

"I'm sorry, Nick. That was a fine meal, but I'm going to have to pass on the dessert. I have a window of opportunity to check on something, over in Ágios Nikólaos."

"You party pooper. Is it a lead on the African boy?"

"No. It's something else. Something that happened in Chaniá a few days ago. My gut is telling me to follow it up, and now I have a second chance. Get yourself one of those delicious desserts and relax. Shall I order you a Metaxá or some rakí to go with it?"

"I'd rather come along for the ride."

"It's quite a way, Nick."

"I know where Ag Nik is."

25

"Well, I have to come back this way, more or less, so why not? You can leave your Jeep here. Give me a minute to settle up, then I can tell you about it on the way."

*

"I thought the harbour was in town," said Nick as they turned away from the centre.

"The inner harbour? This is a twenty-metre boat, Nick. It'll be in the marina on the south side. We're almost there."

Nick saw a gathering of straw parasols on a triangular beach to their right and then Leo swung the police car into a parking spot in front of a grassy patch. They got out and stretched. The marina was modern and functional, with four or five concrete jetties extending from the apron, protected, and almost encircled by a substantial harbour wall, also concrete. A dozen or more boats were moored either side of each jetty so there must be room for at least one hundred and fifty, Nick reckoned, and then there was the harbour wall itself, which was used for some of the larger boats. It might not be an attractive structure, but the boats compensated for that, and it must be a great spot to be, he thought, with the clear, blue, Cretan Sea just beyond the harbour wall, yet just a short stroll from the centre of town and the tavernas that clustered around the buzzing, inner harbour area.

"I think that's her," said Leo, pointing to a large, white, motor yacht moored about halfway along the harbour wall, bows to the entrance. "We will have to walk all the way around."

They strolled around three sides of the marina, past the slipway and dry dock area where a handful of boats were out of the water for repairs. It was the ninth boat along the harbour wall, Nick counted. He saw the name Destiny on the stern, above the name of the port, Larnaca. As they stopped, they saw a youngish man leaning down from the sun deck, watching them.

"Can I help you gentlemen?" he called, in English. The voice sounded familiar to Nick and then he made the connection. Of course. The stone skimmer. *That* boat.

26

"Are you Oliver Dunham?" asked Leo.

"That would be me. Ollie to my friends."

"I'm with the police in Chaniá, Mr Dunham. I need to ask you a few questions."

"I'll come down."

They saw him swing down the stairs, disappear into the main cabin and then emerge in the brown and cream striped seating area towards the stern. He invited them to join him by crossing a gangplank from the quay.

"Wait a minute," he was looking at Nick. "I know you. You were on the beach the other day, near Plakiás."

"Soúda, yes. Well remembered."

"You two know each other?" asked Leo, incredulous.

The other two looked at each other, uncertain how to respond.

"We spotted each other on the beach. Nothing more," said Nick, as Ollie beamed.

"My son almost killed your colleague with a wayward stone, I'm afraid," he said to Leo, "though he has nothing against policemen, as far as I know. Now, please have a seat, gentlemen. How may I help you?"

"I am Christodoulákis, Lieutenant. This is Mr Nick Fisher."

"Ah. So, not a policeman, then. But you are English, Mr Fisher," said Ollie.

"I am, but I live here now. I used to be a policeman in England."

"So, on the beach that day. Were you on assignment? Were you watching me, Mr Fisher?"

It was a sharp-edged tease. Light-hearted banter.

"No. Of course not. I'm retired, anyway. It was just one of those things."

"Quite a coincidence," observed Leo. "So, was that the son who was knocked off his bicycle in Chaniá?"

"Jamal, yes. He's our only son. Our only child, in fact."

"And how was he, afterwards?"

"A bit subdued that day, but he said he felt okay. And the next day he was fine. Back to his usual, precocious self. But I'm guessing you didn't drive across the island to inquire about my son's health."

"You left Chaniá in rather a hurry, Mr Dunham. That seemed an odd thing to do when your son might need access to a hospital, and you had paid for a week's mooring."

"Well, the others had gone by then and I had a call about a possible charter. It's worth wasting a few days' mooring fees to win a fortnight's charter, I assure you."

The expression on their faces told Ollie that his words needed some clarification.

"Leila's dad hasn't been well. Emphysema. Forty a day for forty years didn't help, I'm guessing, and now the old bastard's on his last legs. They've gone to be with him."

"Where is that?" asked Leo.

"Glasgow."

"A flight from Chaniá?"

Ollie nodded.

"And did you?"

"Did I what, Mr Fisher?"

"Win the charter?"

"Jury's still out. I'll know in the next day or two. But they wanted to look around the boat, so I agreed to sail her over here."

"Do you have a base for this charter business, Mr Dunham?" asked Leo.

"Our base is the eastern Mediterranean. We can be anywhere that works. Anywhere we can pick up business. Anywhere our customers want us to be."

"Aren't you based in Cyprus, then?" asked Nick.

"No. Destiny is *registered* in Larnaca, for tax reasons. But we move around."

"And Jamal? His education?" asked Leo.

"He's home-taught, so far. We're always travelling. He sees so much, asks so many questions. He knows far more about things that matter than most ten-year-olds."

"But I'm guessing you had a more formal education yourself," said Nick.

"Oh God, yes. Daddy saw to that. Prep school, then boarding at Winchester."

"And university?"

"Edinburgh, till I dropped out in the second year."

"I did the same. Manchester."

"Ha! All the best people do, Mr Fisher."

"And Destiny is *your* boat, Mr Dunham?" cut in Leo.

"She belongs to a Cypriot company; I'm a shareholder."

"Meaning you paid for it?"

"Lord, no. My father is the majority shareholder. He put in most of the capital. With that, the company was able to get a marine mortgage. One of his other companies acts as guarantor for that, I believe."

There was an awkward silence before Ollie continued:

"Look, I'm happy to answer your questions, Lieutenant. Really, I am. I'm an open book. But I'm struggling to understand what any of this has to do with my son's bicycle accident."

Leo asked if it was okay to smoke. Ollie said it was no problem and started rolling one for himself.

"There are three reasons why I came here, sir," said Leo, blue smoke escaping with each word. "The first is that Jamal seems to have been the victim of a deliberate attack, *not* an accident, and your reactions, as reported to me, were not what I'd expect from an enraged or horrified father. I did not understand."

Ollie raised his eyebrows and drew on his cigarette but said nothing.

"The second is your rapid departure from Chaniá. It looked like you were running away from something or someone, perhaps connected with this alleged hit and run."

Ollie was shaking his head now, forehead crinkled.

"And thirdly, to be frank, my sergeant was suspicious of a family living in a million-euro luxury yacht with no obvious means of support. We wanted to know more."

"What, she thought I was a pirate or something?" Ollie was chuckling. "Well, as I said to your sergeant, when you find the driver of that pick-up, I'm sure we'll discover that he just fell asleep or something and then drove off in a panic. Perhaps he'd been drinking at one of those all-night concerts. Such things are not unknown here. Why on earth would anyone target Jamal? God knows he's irritating sometimes, like any curious child, but most people seem to adore the boy. And I've explained why I left Chaniá – not in a rush at all, but early the *following* morning. And now you know that my career is rather more mundane; that I have a struggling charter business, largely financed by my father. Case solved, and I am sufficiently embarrassed, I think."

"If you could give me the name of your company, I would be obliged, sir."

Another awkward pause.

"These things are in the public record if you care to waste your time digging, Lieutenant. Now, shall we bring our little meeting to a close? I know I have better things to do, even if you gentlemen do not, though it has been a pleasure to make your acquaintances and to see you again, Mr Fisher."

Ollie stood, making it clear it was time to leave.

"Where might we find you, Mr Dunham, if we need to be in touch again?"

"Right here, I should think, unless this charter comes through. Take one of these, anyway. It has the mobile number on it."

He handed Leo a business card.

*

"You're leaving it at that?" said Nick as they walked away from the boat.

"A tactical withdrawal," said Leo. "I'm not in a position to accuse him of anything, but now I have information to verify. We'll do some research on Mr Dunham and his family: the generous father, the Cypriot company, and the expensive boat. What is your gut telling you, Nick?"

"Not very much, to tell the truth. He's from a privileged background, a bit posh, as we say. He seems very relaxed."

"What means *posh*, Nick?"

"Someone perceived as coming from the upper classes: inherited wealth, silver spoon, private education. The whole shebang."

"Your famous class system."

"Infamous, more like. The bright and the beautiful. Except they're the same as the rest of us, just with more to spend on education, clothes and cosmetics."

"Anything else you noticed about him?"

"Maybe a bit of resentment towards Daddy?"

"Why would he resent him?"

"Sending him to boarding school, pushing him to be a big achiever when he's not made like that? Maybe Ollie had to go cap in hand to Daddy to finance the boat – and now Daddy owns more of this Cypriot company than Ollie does – and therefore Destiny. I'm guessing, of course, but I sensed something there."

"Interesting. Do you think he's gay, Nick?"

"Did he strike you that way? No, I think it's just an English public-school thing. He's a very good-looking man but he's not a macho man. He's *in touch with his feminine side*, as they say. He seems to be devoted to his family. Maybe wobbled a bit at that boarding school of his, but I'd say he's fundamentally straight."

They were back at the police car now. It was ten past five.

"It's been a long lunch for you, Nick."

"That's okay. It's been interesting, and with seeing him and his son on that beach, it seems like I was destined to know him better."

"Yes, that was strange. Anyway, I'll keep you posted if you like."

"Please. I'm quite curious about Mr Oliver Dunham."

CHAPTER 6
A JOURNALIST'S THEORY

The next morning, Leo was summoned to the captain's office.

"Good morning, Leo. It must have been a good lunch; I gather you didn't make it back."

"It was an excellent lunch, Captain, but I had to cut it short. I needed to check something out. I'll let you know if anything comes of it."

"Something on the African boy?"

"Er … no."

"Where are we with that, Leo?"

"Nowhere, sir. We've not been able to identify him; we don't know where he's from and we've no idea who cut his throat – or why."

"Hmmm. That's what I thought you'd say. Well, I may have a lead of sorts. While you were indulging yourself yesterday, I agreed to meet with a rather famous journalist: Isobel Saidi."

"The Syrian woman? I've seen her on television."

"She's French Moroccan."

"Ah. Well, every time I see her, she's complaining about Assad."

"She has taken an outspoken position against the Assad regime, it's true. She was a war correspondent before, of course. Covered the second Gulf War."

Leo was nodding.

"So, why come to you, sir?"

"She has a theory – and it comes with a warning attached. She freelances now, focused on pieces aimed at television and the news magazines. She's been researching the crime business in the eastern Mediterranean: the smuggling or trafficking of arms, drugs and people."

"Brave woman."

"Indeed. She's based in Beirut, but she came to me when she heard about our black boy."

"She has good ears."

"Press contacts. Everywhere. That's how she pulls it all together."

"So, why does she care about an unknown, teenaged, black kid found off the south coast of Crete?"

"Because it might – just might – give credence to this theory of hers. A theory no-one has taken seriously, so far."

"Go on, sir."

"She thinks the smugglers are using a new route, further south, as a result of our clampdowns on the Southern Balkan route."

"You've already lost me, Captain."

"Okay, Leo. A brief history lesson."

The captain took out a large sheet of paper and started drawing.

"Asia. And here is Turkey."

He drew a thick line coming from one to the other.

"Ancient trade routes, established centuries ago, bring goods to Europe from Asia and vice versa, through Turkey. These routes are still used today, not only for legitimate goods but also for hard drugs, particularly heroin."

"Marco Polo has a lot to answer for."

The captain gave him a tolerant smirk, before drawing an arrow, pointing from Turkey, up through eastern Europe.

"The main route out of Turkey to Northern Europe was the Balkan Route. It meant you could avoid entering the EU for longer and go through states with, shall we say, less rigorous enforcement."

"Easier to bribe your way through."

"Indeed. But all that changed after the EU's big expansion. Now, the likes of Romania and Bulgaria are part of the EU. The traffickers found life much more difficult. In response, they developed two new routes …"

He drew a second arrow, above and to the right of the first one and then a third, almost due west, from the Bosphorus to the Adriatic.

"… one further east, starting from the north coast of the Black Sea. This is the Caucasus route, heading to Germany, The Netherlands, and the UK. And the other – the one we're interested in – across Northern

33

Greece to Italy, and then France. This is the so-called *Southern* Balkan Route. So, now they had a choice of three routes, and they could vary the amount of traffic through each depending on the degree of enforcement they encountered."

"How did they get from Greece to Italy?"

"Various ports along the Adriatic have been used. We know of a couple in Albania – Durrës and Vlorë – and our own Igoumenítsa. They put trucks on the ferries or use their own boats. It's almost impossible for us to police and they know it. What we *were* able to do, though, with some success, was raise the level of spot checks on the roads crossing Greece."

"So, the cartels responded by channelling more through the other two routes."

"To some extent, yes. Maybe they started to supply France from the northern route, through The Netherlands? We don't know. But what we *do* know is that neither the original Balkan route nor the Caucasus route is a practical way to reach Italy – and Italy is a prime market for these guys. This is where Bel's theory comes in. She'd have us believe that, because of our interventions on the roads across Northern Greece, they've now established a new, southern route to serve Italy."

"Makes sense."

"In theory it does, but, until some seizures are made, we can't be sure."

"Does she have a route?"

"She thinks it could be way south, but still in Greek waters."

"Involving Crete?"

"Yes. From Turkey, passing Crete and then swinging north to the heel of Italy."

"That's a hell of a long way, sir, and the winds are treacherous."

"I know. But such a route would bring advantages, too. There is far less traffic in those waters and almost no police or coastguard presence. And, for people smuggling, you could start from *southern* Turkey, close to the Syrian border. Many of these refugees are from Syria, of course, fleeing the war. For them it's a quick escape. No overland trek to northern Turkey."

"And this Saidi woman thinks our black boy came from a smuggler's boat, does she?"

"She does. She thinks he fits the profile of a migrant, but she doesn't know why he was killed."

"Even if she's right, it doesn't take us much further forward."

"Not in solving this boy's murder perhaps, but, if she's right, we have a chance to put an end to this new operation before it's fully established, and before boatloads of migrants have to die. Listen, Leo. I took this woman – Bel, she calls herself – to meet with the Investigating Judge. We're going to set up a short-term task force to investigate this and I want you to head it up. A lieutenant from the drug squad in Athína is flying over to join us. You might know him, Andréas Iliádis?"

"I know Andréa, but I thought we were talking about *people*, not drugs, sir."

"Bel believes there's overlap. Some of the same people are involved in both, particularly the smaller operators. And often using the same routes. Andréas will be familiar with those."

"Arms, too?"

"Less likely. There's a lot of arms trafficking going on, as you know, but it's a more specialist area. They tend to be bigger operators with political nous who deal only in arms." He paused before leaning forward. "Pick your team, Leo, then meet with Bel. She'll tell you everything she knows, then it's up to you. See if you can find any truth in her suspicions. I'm giving you a month."

"What about everything else on my plate, sir?"

"Delegate all you can. This has to be your priority."

"Sir, with respect, this is a massive task. I don't know where to start."

"I have every confidence in you, Leo. You'll work it out. As you learn more, I'm sure you'll develop a plan. And, by the end of the month, I'm looking for evidence that this new route exists and, if it does, an outline plan for closing it down. I realise you'll need more resources at that point."

"I'll do my best, Captain."

"I know you will. Succeed in this and you'll be the natural choice for the new captain at Réthymno. Chrístos will never make it back now, poor guy."

"I hadn't heard."

"Well, you must have heard about the cancer. Metastasized. Poor bastard is riddled with it. Just a matter of time, now. Weeks or months, not years."

"Sorry to hear that."

"When the time comes, I'll put your name forward."

Leo tried to look appreciative, but he was not sure he wanted a promotion. Nor was he sure he wanted to head up this task force. Since when did the police set up task forces at the instigation of journalists, anyway? The captain's intuition must have picked up on this.

"I know this is a challenging assignment, Leo, and it's possible that you'll get nowhere or discover that it's all nonsense – something from a journalist's imagination. That's okay. But we *must* respond. You've seen the boatloads drowning, the dreadful scenes on the islands in the north-east, the encampments, the squalor. We don't want that here on Crete, do we?"

"No, we don't, sir."

"Then let's do everything we can to stop that."

*

The next morning, Leo called his principal sergeant into the office and told him about the new assignment.

"I'm not asking you to join the team, Thaní."

"That's okay, sir."

"Not because you're not up to it. Of course, you are. It's just that I need someone I can trust to deal with everything else, while I'm swallowed up by this."

"I understand, sir."

"Good man. Let's schedule an hour or so to walk through the outstanding cases this afternoon."

"May I mention one thing, sir?"

"Of course."

"You asked me to follow up on Dunham, the Englishman with the boat?"

"Anything of interest?"

"He's been lying to us."

"Has he now?" Leo moved forward in his seat, all ears.

"Leila Dunham's father was a man called Ian MacKinnon."

"Was?"

"He died four years ago."

"A bit late to rush to the man's bedside, then."

"Indeed. Someone bought tickets to Glasgow for Leila and Jamal, and they were checked in online. But they didn't show up for the flight."

"Which begs the question, where the hell are they?"

"They could be back on the boat by now."

"So, why did he lie? Why don't you get the local police to have another chat with Dunham, or get over there yourself?"

"Because the boat's gone again, sir. I called the harbourmaster at Ágios Nikólaos and he told me. The boat left the morning after your visit. So, I rang the mobile number on Dunham's card several times, but it just goes to voicemail."

"Perhaps he won that charter, then. If so, he'll be away for a couple of weeks, at least. If Destiny shows up again in Crete, we should be informed. Until then, there's not much we can do. Come back at five, Thaní, and we'll go through these files together."

CHAPTER 7
AN OLD FRIEND APPEARS

Nick had just dipped the roller into the paint tray again and lifted the long, giddy pole with the roller attached all the way up to the top of his wall. The paint had not dripped, this time, and the roller had not fallen off the pole. Success. He started to move the roller up and down the wall, seeing the paint carve a swathe of fresh cream through the grey. That was when the mobile rang. Cursing, he hurriedly lowered the four-metre pole and laid the roller on the edge of the paint tray where it fell off the pole again and buried itself deep in the paint.

"Oh, sod it!" he cursed, painty hands groping in his pocket for the phone.

"Hello!" he said, a little too loudly.

"DI Fisher," said the voice, "as I live and breathe." It was a voice accented and husky. It took Nick right back to the streets of London, nine or ten years earlier.

"Bel? Can it be?"

"They said you were here, hiding from the world. I didn't believe it."

"There's a lot you don't know … But you said *here*. Are you in Greece?"

"Better than that, I'm in Chaniá and I have a car. I thought I might buy you dinner. Is there anywhere remotely civilised over there? And do you have a spare room?"

"Not what *you* would call civilised, but I can do convivial, and I can do great food at good prices, with some excellent wine and rakí. And yes, I do have a spare room." *Should it be required*, he almost added.

"Then that will have to do."

*

She arrived at six forty-five in a rented, gunmetal Mercedes, wearing a glamorous, orange, white and silver dress that complemented her brown skin and flashing, black eyes. Nick had pressed his best shorts but was still pulling paint off his fingernails.

"Your house is so small! I missed it altogether the first time!"

She stepped out and looked at it, and then at Nick.

"But now, I see that it is a very pretty house and that you are not looking ten years older, damn you, Nick Fisher."

She would be in her late forties, he reckoned, and looked it now. The strong features seemed stronger still: the full lips, the curved nose and the dark eyebrows that defined her youthful beauty now took her halfway to caricature when she grinned, as she was doing now. But only halfway. She was still a stunner; clever, dangerous, and sexy.

"Neither are you, my dear," he said.

"We both know that's bullshit, but I thank you for it anyway." She opened the boot and took out an overnight bag. "Now, shall we have one drink here and then I'll drive us to this restaurant of yours? But first, you must show me your darling, little house."

"Well, that won't take long. Then we can have a glass of wine on my new roof terrace."

"Perfect."

*

Bel was one of those people who got you to open up. Nick supposed that was what made her so successful. It took less than one glass for her to learn about his promotion to DCI and then the departure under a cloud after the Kitchen case. Then it was the death of his father, the break-up with Jen and his decision to come to Crete. By the second glass – the one they were not going to have – she confirmed that he had worked with the local police on a couple of murder cases.

"I find it amazing, Nick, that the Greeks would let a retired, British cop get involved in serious, local cases with them."

"Well, it doesn't cost them much," he said, with a rueful grin. "But I know what you mean. It happened because it was *my son* accused of murder in that first case. And then, after the early turf wars, Leo and I found that we liked and respected one another and worked rather well together. It was him that put me forward for the second case, and that also involved a foreigner. I suspect I'm limited to that – helping out when a serious crime involving a tourist occurs."

"Or there's a British angle of some sort?"

"Maybe, yes."

They saved the remainder of the bottle for their return and left in the Mercedes. As they roared past the kafenío, Kóstas was standing there in a grubby vest, scratching his considerable belly and staring, but his face broke into a huge smile when he spotted Nick in the passenger seat, and he yelled something in Greek. Bel saw him waving in the rear-view mirror.

"Who was that man?" she asked.

"That's my friend, Kóstas. He owns the kafenío. He's also appointed himself my counsellor in all matters of the heart."

"So, it's him I need to win over."

"I think you already did. He loves your car."

Nick directed Bel up, over the hill, to the Spíli road and then through Acoúmia, Spíli and Koxaré to the Kourtaliótiko Ravine. Bel gasped at the rock walls towering above them, either side of the road, buzzards circling.

"Is this safe, Nick? It doesn't look it."

"It's safer than it was. Stunning though, isn't it?"

Bel was silent, willing the car through it as quickly as possible.

*

At the restaurant, Nick was welcomed like an old friend. Knowing looks and raised eyebrows passed behind Bel's back as Nick followed her down to their table by the water.

"What an impossibly romantic setting, Nick," she said, looking across the windswept water to the rocky promontory, where the sun was beginning to set, "Who'd have thought we'd meet again, somewhere like this?"

"I didn't think I'd ever see you again, Bel. Now, I know we're kind of fond of each other, but I don't believe you came to Crete just to look me up."

"I might have, if I'd known you were single these days."

"Don't give me that old flannel. What are you here for?"

"Let's order something, then I'll tell you."

Fresh fish was the obvious choice. Nick went for the swordfish, Bel the sea bream. Then the waiter brought a jug of iced water, a basket of fresh bread and a half-litre carafe of local, white wine. Nick poured the wine and raised his eyebrows.

"Well?"

"Cheers, Nick." She raised her glass to clink with his.

"Yeiá mas," said Nick.

When she had taken a sip, she placed the glass on the paper table-cloth and started to explain.

"I am here as a journalist, Nick. I'm following a story. There's been a murder here – a body found at sea – and I'm trying to find out who he is and why he died."

"You mean the black boy who had his throat cut?"

"Yes. How do you know?"

"I'm in touch with Christodoulákis. He told me."

"Did he tell you what I'm investigating?"

"No. He said nothing about you."

"Okay. It's recent news."

She went on to tell him about the exposé of smuggling operations she was working on, and her theory that a new route had been initiated.

"If this boy was a migrant, Nick, it could prove my theory."

"But why kill him? In that scenario, he's the customer. You don't get far in any sort of business if you murder your customers."

"We don't know, yet. I have friends asking around, in the camps. Something might turn up."

"Sounds like a dangerous game you're into this time, Bel. I hope you're being careful."

"I always am. I'm followed most of the time now, in Beirut."

"Who by?"

"I think it's just Assad's goons."

"Just?"

41

"I doubt they'll do anything, Nick. I'm too high-profile and I'm just words when all's said and done. There's nothing I can do to bring down his government, I'm sorry to say."

"There must be a reason to follow you."

"Just keeping tabs on me, reporting back to Bashir. Trying to put the frighteners on me, maybe."

"That's not going to work, if I know you."

"No. I'm not going to stop, Nick, but I do get scared sometimes, these days."

At that point, two waiters arrived with their food and the conversation turned to lighter things. It was not until Nick's request for the bill triggered the arrival of a dessert of halva and a small carafe of rakí, all on the house, that she became serious again.

"What do you know about people smugglers, Nick?"

"Only what I see on the news. Flimsy boats, crammed with refugees, trying to make it from Turkey to Greece or whatever."

"Did you know that at least fifteen thousand have died, trying to cross the Mediterranean, in the last seven years?"

"I didn't realise it was so many."

"Or that Europol reckons the smuggling and trafficking businesses have a combined turnover of between three and six *billion* euros?"

Nick shook his head in disgust.

"Many of the refugees are from Syria. That's why I got interested, of course. Assad has caused this. Many of these people are professional, educated people but there is no life to be had in the beautiful country he has destroyed."

"Almost all seem to be young men."

"Not those from Syria. They are families and displaced children. There are also so-called *economic* migrants from places like Afghanistan and Somalia. Most of *them* are young men, looking for a future."

"Most are being helped though, aren't they?"

"No. Really not, Nick. There are still thousands in camps, many in appalling conditions, waiting for decisions. Will they get asylum, or will they be sent home? And the EU kicks the can down the road, as usual. The decisions are too difficult to make, so they don't make them. They just move people around. They throw more money into building better camps so people like me have less to criticise, instead of finding ways to make the camps unnecessary. Meanwhile, many, many fine, upstanding people are being allowed to rot or die of frustration. It's terrible, Nick."

"Surely, it's not as bad as it was a few years ago."

"Less come now. Perhaps the horror stories are feeding back? But it's still a huge problem, Nick. We have so much in the west and these people have so little."

"What are you hoping to achieve though, Bel, by writing about it?"

"Awareness. People need to know, Nick. We can't let the authorities sweep stuff like this under the carpet. These people are being ripped off, put in extreme danger, and then dumped, forgotten, in camps. Thousands of them. It's not their fault, Nick. None of this is their fault."

Nick saw raw emotion now, on Bel's face. Tears were not far away.

"And then what?" he said, more gently, "when people *are* aware, I mean."

"I hope they'll get angry, put pressure on their governments to act and take some responsibility. Get this terrible, bloody mess sorted out."

"You need to get cameras in there, let people see the suffering."

"Oh, I will, Nick. But first I need a story to sell to the television networks."

Nick topped up their glasses.

"You're doing good work, Bel. So much more worthwhile."

"Than being The Independent's crime correspondent in London? Yes, things have moved on, I guess. They were good times, though."

They fell into talking about their times together in London as they finished the rakí. Nick had always been attracted to this woman and the few extra years made no difference. She was brave, feisty and fun. Life was a dangerous game to her. She did not take her own life too seriously, though she was deadly serious about her work and her efforts to right the wrongs of the world. She was not the marrying kind. He knew that. But she was a passionate woman; no doubt about it.

Nick asked her if she was okay to drive.

"What do you think, Nick?" she replied. "Don't worry. I'll get us home."

*

They stumbled up to the roof terrace with the last of the wine. The Milky Way was an explosion of cloudy nebulae scattered with a trillion stars; the night air heavy with jasmine. The background throbbing of the crickets was punctuated every so often by a solitary dog barking on a distant ridge.

"I don't suppose you see this very often, in Beirut."

"No. And it's wonderful, Nick, but it makes me feel so small. Insignificant."

"You, insignificant? I don't think so. People like you make a difference, Bel. The world needs you."

"I'm not so sure. I try, but it's hard and sometimes I think it's getting harder. There's a world of entitlement out there. People think, because they're lucky enough to be born in a prosperous country, they're *entitled* to all that, even as millions starve. I don't understand, Nick. I don't understand why higher taxes or generous foreign aid budgets are resented, when they can do so much."

"I suppose many people believe charity begins at home. They don't want to look beyond the problems of their own countrymen."

"Don't get me started, Nick. Fucking nationalism. We're all citizens of the world, aren't we? Whatever happened to that notion?"

"People don't believe these issues can ever be solved. Not really. *The poor will always be with us.* And many think there's corruption in the charities themselves, or in those who receive the charity. They don't believe their money will get to the right places where it will do the most good."

"And yet, there can be such outpourings of generosity when the public's sympathies are energised. Look at Live Aid, for instance."

"A specific cause. Beautiful Ethiopian children starving. A fixable problem. And, in Geldof, a champion the public believed would make sure their money got to the cause. Also, some bloody good music, apart from The Boomtown Rats, obviously."

"Woah. I *loved* them!"

She started singing *I don't like Mondays*. Nick raised his hands in protest.

"Anyway, my point is, all that's a world away from setting up a blanket donation; a standing order to Oxfam, for example, or inviting governments to take a bigger slice of one's income, when people think most of it will be used to bribe foreign potentates."

"You're an old cynic, Nick," said Bel.

"Not me. I'm an idealist. Or, at least, I was born that way. I'm just telling you how I think the great unwashed feel."

"Perhaps I need to get Geldof over to the refugee camps, then."

"You could do worse. Or some Greek equivalent."

They fell silent then and sipped their wine as the atmosphere of the night enveloped them. After a while, Nick felt Bel's hand on his.

"We're too nice to find ourselves alone in this world, Nick Fisher. Take me to bed now. Just cuddles. I'll sleep better with your body next to mine."

He looked into her dark eyes, glinting in the starlight.

"Sex would be a challenge, anyway," he said, picking up the empty bottle as they shuffled inside, his hand on her shoulder.

*

The next morning, Nick stretched out for her but there was nothing there. For a moment he thought it had all been a dream, but then he smelled her scent on the pillow and spotted one or two stray, auburn hairs. *There's no way it would have stayed platonic this morning*, he thought, and wondered if she had done a runner to avoid complicating their lives. He found a note on the dresser:

Great to see you, Nick. I'll be in touch soon was all it said.

All very grown up and sensible, he thought, as he bashed around the kitchen, slamming cupboard doors, and yelling at the stray cat that seemed to have adopted him.

*

It was late morning the following day when Leo called.

"Hello, Nick. How are you fixed?"

"I'm good. Just pottering about, painting the outside."

"I have a job for you, if you're interested."

"Another murder?"

"Have you heard of a woman called Isobel Saidi, a journalist?"

"Of course, hasn't everyone? I know her as Bel. She's an old contact of mine."

"Ah. That explains a lot. She's convinced the captain to investigate her theory that there's a new people smuggling operation here. I've been asked to set up a team, initially for one month. I'd like you to be part of it, Nick."

"Why me, Leo? I have no expertise in that area."

"We have a smuggling expert already, a guy from the Athens drugs team called Andréas. I'm looking for an experienced, old hand, someone who can use his head, think on his feet."

"What's the objective?"

"To see if we can substantiate this theory – or not. If we can, we put together a plan for taking the bastards down."

Nick was not convinced the case against these people smugglers was so clear cut. Were they unmitigated bastards or just entrepreneurs, stepping in where governments had failed? But he kept his opinions to himself.

"Are you in, Nick?" said Leo.

There was a pause.

"I don't know, Leo. I'm not sure this is up my street. I think I'd rather finish the painting."

"It'll be just you, me and Andréas," Leo went on, "with Bel feeding us information, and with some admin support from the office, of course. I'm authorised to offer you twenty-five hundred euros for the month, payable in arrears. And I'd appreciate your support on this one, Nick."

"Oh, go on, then. The package is irresistible. I'll help if I can."

"Great. Come in tomorrow, then. The team is getting together at nine thirty."

Later, it dawned on Nick. Bel must have pushed for him to be part of the team. As far as he could see, there was no other reason for him to be involved.

CHAPTER 8

A CALL FROM LÉSVOS

Just before seven that evening, Nick took a video call from Bel.

"Hello you. What have you been up to?" he asked.

"I'm in Lésvos."

"Where's that?"

"You must have heard of Lésvos, Nick. It's hardly been out of the news for the last few years."

"Ah. Is it one of those islands near Turkey that gets all the refugees?"

"Right. I thought I'd see if things have improved."

"And have they?"

"Not a great deal, no. The EU has allocated funds for a new camp, but nothing seems to be happening and time is running out. But it never ceases to amaze me how resilient some of these refugees are. One of my guys is operating a bakery in the camp, with his brothers. They're making four hundred loaves a day now."

"Your guys?"

"My contacts, Nick. People I can call on to keep me in the picture. I've been in touch with Nuri since before the fire."

"Sorry, what fire?"

"You must remember what happened at Moría, Nick."

He looked uncertain; she saw.

"Last September, some of the refugees burned the place down. They weren't being listened to. The place was crammed; it had reached four times capacity. Four times, Nick! And there were over four hundred unaccompanied kids. Can you imagine? God knows what was happening to them. And then the bloody virus. Some tested positive and, in those conditions, it spread like crazy. When the firefighters came, the refugees *fought* them. It was so disgusting, they wanted it to burn, even though it was all they had. Twelve thousand of them were suddenly pitched out into the open."

"Desperate stuff," agreed Nick.

"The tent camps that followed were no better. Children have been molested. There have been rapes, suicides. A pregnant, Afghani girl set herself on fire in February. Covid hasn't helped, of course. The lockdowns meant they could never escape the damned camps."

"So, what have the authorities been doing?"

"The EU put up a heap of money for five new camps, including one on Lésvos."

"Won't that just *institutionalise* the problem, though?"

"It needs time to be resolved, Nick. Maybe a lot of time. Meanwhile, people are dying. This is a stopgap; *the containment model*, they call it."

"Well, the EU needs to up its game. Grant asylum or send them back. Not leave the poor sods stuck in camps forever."

"Easier said than done, Nick. The migrants pour over the border and Turkey can't cope. They plead for help from the EU, but they're not in the EU and some of Erdogan's policies are tough for the EU to swallow. So, there's a limit to what they will do. Result? Turkey turns a blind eye to refugees moving on, mostly to Greece. Erdogan is playing pass the parcel, in political terms. If you won't help us, here's the problem. *You* deal with it."

"Understandable, I suppose. It's too big a problem for one country to solve."

"And Turkey and Greece hating each other doesn't help."

"No, I'm sure. What's the answer, Bel?"

"Easy. Stop the wars and share the wealth."

"You're dreaming."

"I know. But it doesn't stop me being right."

"Sounds like you need a drink, Bel. Is there a bar there?"

"I'm in a basic hotel in Mytilíni, Nick. It has a bar, but I'm not going to be seen dead in it. I took the precaution of buying a quarter bottle of whisky and some chocolate at the local supermarket."

She brought a small bottle of Johnnie Walker into view.

"Attagirl."

"Well, I need a little something after today. It's heart-rending stuff,

Nick. And I heard some news today that got me mad. Not only are the Greeks building a twenty-seven-kilometre wall along the Évros river, complete with observation towers, night vision cameras and drones, they've started using LRADs at the border with Turkey."

"LRADs?"

"Long range acoustic devices."

She turned her iPad towards the camera, and Nick saw a police armoured vehicle with something like a large scanner mounted on it. She then played a video which showed the scanner being switched on and rotated, after which a high-pitched sound like a car alarm on steroids was transmitted in the direction it was pointed.

"These things are as loud as jet engines, Nick. Deafening for anyone trying to cross the river. And frightening. They're untested, pretty much. Who knows what impact they will have on nearby residents and wildlife, let alone the migrants themselves – and how will *they* respond? This is just raising the ante – with the migrants, but also with the Turks. This sort of thing doesn't help at all."

"And this is being funded by the EU?"

"The wall is, for sure, perhaps the acoustic devices too, through the back door. Who knows?"

"So much for citizens of the world sharing the wealth."

"It's just deferring the problem, Nick. And making it bigger. There's so much anger building in the third world now. With the spread of television and the internet, they see what we have now, and they don't understand why we have so much, and they have so very little. We need to be tolerant with them, help them build up their own countries, create opportunities for their young men and women. Locking people up in camps, building walls and now deafening people – it's inhuman. These *can't* be the answers, can they – or am I going mad?"

"I think you might be the only one who isn't, Bel."

"Are you getting angry, Nick?"

"Anger is only part of what I'm feeling. It's desperate, Bel. An organisation of twenty-seven countries and getting on for half a billion mostly decent people and they can't or won't provide something better? It's appalling. And it's depressing, actually. You bet I'm angry."

"I want you to be, Nick. I need you to be. Then perhaps we can get these bastards."

"But I'm angry with the inhumanity, the bureaucracy, the inertia. I'm not especially angry with the smugglers. They're just providing a service, aren't they?"

"They're selling a road to nowhere, Nick. A mirage of hope. They can charge thousands of euros for a very dangerous trip in an open boat. You've seen them on the news. These boats are often not fit for purpose and overloaded. One in ten of the migrants will drown. I've even heard of smugglers selling life jackets to them at exorbitant prices. Only most of them don't work. Some are even labelled as such, but most of the migrants can't read the English warnings. If they survive the trip, they're intercepted by the coastguard or arrested on arrival, and then they face many months, often years, in the camps, at risk from disease, not knowing if they will ever make it to their chosen country or will have to make do with somewhere else or even be sent back to the horrors they risked everything to escape. Be in no doubt, Nick. These people are the smugglers' victims. Those guys are evil and have to be stopped."

She excused herself for a moment. When she returned, she poured herself a whisky into what looked like the hotel tooth mug.

"Listen, Nick. I'm not coming back to Crete tomorrow."

"What about the team meeting?"

"I have a lead to follow up, in Igoumenítsa."

"Where the hell's that?"

"It's a port on the mainland next to Corfu, near the Albanian border. My contact tells me a girl was taken off a boat there; a drug overdose."

"Something else you're working on?"

"No," she said. "I think it might be relevant to our inquiry. You see, she's saying she came all the way from Turkey by boat with quite a few other people."

"Our route, are you thinking? It's quite a distance though, isn't it?"

"Indeed."

"You wouldn't attempt *that* in an inflatable dinghy."

"Hardly. So, I want to know more. She's on the mend now. They've agreed to let me have half an hour with her."

CHAPTER 9
THE INTERVIEW

It was a long haul for a short interview, but a telephone call would not do it. She needed to get under the skin of this girl, find out everything she knew and be sure she was telling the truth. And all in half an hour.

The hospital was not in Igoumenítsa, Bel discovered. The girl had been taken seventy-odd kilometres inland to the General Hospital at Ioánnina, the capital of Epirus. This proved to be a blessing, as Bel could fly direct from Athína to Ioánnina in about an hour. It was a little after three when she arrived at the neat, regional airport backed by mountains and named after King Pyrrhus, famous for his costly victories against the Romans. Everyone pronounced it *Yánnina*, she soon discovered, which was a little easier.

The bedside meeting had been arranged for five pm. She didn't need to get a cab for forty-five minutes, so she bought herself a coffee and settled in the airport lounge to catch up on emails. After a few minutes, she noticed a middle-aged man doing something similar in the far corner, his laptop balanced on a tan briefcase. Bel thought she remembered him from the flight.

*

Nick arrived in Chaniá that morning. He called into the police station at nine thirty, but Leo was tied up with something and Andréas was out somewhere. So much for the team meeting. He figured he might as well make a start. And, with any murder, even an insoluble one, the investigation starts with the body.

"What? You are working again, and so soon?" said Pánagou, on the telephone.

"It's just a month, this one, at least to start with," said Nick, and went on to explain his new role.

"So, you want to see the body of this boy? I still have it."

53

"I was hoping you'd say that. I'm on my way."

The two of them shared the same gruff, direct manner and a similar sense of humour, though hers was macabre in the extreme, at times. Today, however, she seemed a little morose.

"Hello again, Doctor," said Nick. "How are you?"

"I am the same, Nick Fisher. But today I am sad."

She had just completed a post-mortem on a six-year-old, she explained.

"Such a pretty little girl, from your country."

"An English girl?"

"Her family are from Mon-mouth," she said the name as if it were two words.

"Welsh, then. What happened to her?"

"Another one pulled from a hotel swimming pool. Hit her head and drowned, poor little thing. Her parents had no idea. They were fifteen metres away, enjoying a drink while their daughter was unconscious, underwater. Tragic."

"Where was the lifeguard?"

"The law says they must have one, but like so many laws here, it is not enforced. There was no lifeguard. The hotel put up a warning sign purporting to exclude liability, but they won't get away with it."

"God, then the parents must feel responsible."

"They *are* responsible, Nick. The hotel might be negligent, but the parents are responsible."

"I feel for them, though. You can't watch your children every minute of every day."

"She was only six, Nick, and playing on her own. They were reckless. Anyway, you didn't come here to hear about my troubles. Let me show you the boy."

Nick followed her to the cold storage room where she slid open one of the heavy drawers to reveal the naked form of a very black teenager.

"Tell me what you know, please," said Nick.

"This will not take long. He died because his throat was cut. He was picked out of the sea in a fisherman's net, but there was very little water in his lungs. He did not drown. I would guess he is fourteen or fifteen years old. No more. His DNA does not feature on any database, but the *pattern* of the DNA tells me his family is East African."

"I see he's circumcised. Does that tell us anything?"

"Very little. Many religions do this – Jews, Muslims, and a few others, I believe. Or it could have been needed for medical reasons."

"What about those markings on his cheeks?"

"Acne scars. Nothing tribal if that's what you were hoping."

"Any other marks on the body?"

"Apart from the throat, you mean. No. He is as God intended."

Generally, it amused him when she attempted her English idioms, but right now he was preoccupied with the hideously scarred throat.

"I see you stitched him up, then."

"When the police let me, yes. It seemed the right thing to do."

"I didn't realise you cared, Doctor."

"He is a beautiful, young black man, Nick. One day his parents may see his body. It took a few minutes only."

"Could you glean anything from the wound?"

"Glean? What is that?"

"Did it tell you anything?"

"Well, it was neat, wide and deep. A sharp knife, not small, used by someone who had done such things before, I would say."

"Do you still have his clothes?"

Pánagou crossed back into the main room and went to a tall, wooden cupboard and extracted a plastic bag containing four bagged-up items.

"Help yourself," she said, stood back and lit a cigarette.

"I thought you were giving those things up," said Nick.

"I am. It takes time."

"The secret is not smoking."

"Yes, I have heard this," she said.

Nick laid out the items on the table: a pair of black football shorts with a silver stripe to the sides, purporting to be Adidas but maybe a good fake, a pair of blue and grey underpants with a repeating elephant pattern, a pair of sandals, size forty-one, and a hooded grey sweatshirt with a Rolling Stones' logo.

"Anything else you can tell me, Doctor?"

"There is nothing else, Nick Fisher."

"Any thoughts, guesses you'd like to share?"

"Most people have things in their pockets. This boy has nothing."

"What does that tell you?"

"Perhaps he had a bag? Maybe someone empties his pockets so he cannot be identified – or maybe *he* empties his pockets because he does not want to be identified?"

"Because he's engaged in some illicit activity?"

"Your speculation, not mine."

"What would yours be, then?"

"I am trained *not* to speculate."

Nick shook his head in frustration.

"Someone suggested he was an illegal migrant," she went on. "This is possible, I think, only there is a difference."

"What do you mean?"

"He does not look as poor as one might expect. He is well-groomed. His clothes are not expensive, but they are quite new, quite good quality."

"So, he has a little money, perhaps from criminal activities."

"Or, more likely, at his age, he comes from a well-to-do family, at least by East African standards."

Nick sifted through the clothes but there were no name tags, no markings and only ubiquitous brand names. The sizes were consistent with the boy and there was nothing whatsoever in the pockets.

"Have you checked for foreign DNA?" he asked, finally.

"Bring me samples and I can try to isolate any DNA that matches the sample. There is no point in trying to make sense of all the DNA otherwise. It takes forever and is likely to be inconclusive."

"Surely it could lead to identifying the culprit, if he's on a database somewhere."

"You are dreaming, Nick Fisher."

"Fingerprints of any use?"

"You show me a database of East Africans' fingerprints and I'll try to match them. But some of these guys are not even registered at birth."

"But *he* would be, if he's from a well-to-do family, you'd think."

"That doesn't mean he's been *digitally* fingerprinted, though."

"What about dental records?"

"The boy has perfect teeth. No fillings, no caps. If he ever saw a dentist, he never needed any work."

*

When he got back to the office, Nick scanned the file Leo had left for him. He thought about interviewing the fishermen who found the body, but their statement seemed comprehensive, as far as it went, so he decided it would be a waste of his time. Could anyone else have seen what happened? Did anyone live on the Paximádia islands? He doubted it, but that needed to be checked. Had the coastguard been informed – and were they aware of any boats in the area in the previous day or two? He remembered Andréas was tasked with bringing the coastguard into the inquiry. He needed to speak to him. There was legwork to be done, there were bases to be covered, and it seemed to be down to him. He had better get on with it.

*

The doctor was a woman in her thirties, Bel guessed, dark hair pulled back into a bun and wearing glasses. She seemed distracted, overwrought.

"Ms Saidi?"

"Hello, Doctor."

"I know you. You are journalist, I think."

"I am."

"What is it you want with this girl, please?"

"Just a short interview. I am writing a serious piece on people smuggling in the Eastern Mediterranean. I want to highlight the plight of the victims, draw attention to the crimes."

"You think she is migrant?"

"Isn't she?"

"I don't know. My concern was to save her life. I leave everything else to police, immigration authorities."

"What happened to her?"

"A heroin overdose."

"Is she an addict, then?"

"There is no evidence of this."

"So, what was she doing taking heroin?"

"She was not taking it; she was carrying it. In her body. She was a drug mule, Ms Saidi. We found fifty-five capsules in her digestive system; each had contained powdered, white heroin. But two of them split, poisoning her. If it had been three, she would be dead. No question. She is a lucky girl. The weight of drug in the fifty-three intact capsules was one point three kilogrammes."

"My God. How is she now?"

"She recovers from a serious operation but still there is poison in her. We will keep her under observation for some more days. Then we see. The police are waiting."

"Can you tell me her name?"

"She is Paksima, from Afghanistan. How is your Dari?"

"My what?"

"It's Afghani Persian, her language. She has little English. You will need interpreter. Maybe you are lucky. We have another Afghan here, a young man whose English and Greek are both excellent. He is junior doctor, here in the hospital. You will wait while I see if he is free?"

The doctor showed Bel into a small, rather warm, waiting room while she went in search of her colleague. After a few sweltering minutes, a small, eager-looking man in horn-rimmed glasses appeared at the door. He was wearing a white coat, with a stethoscope dangling from a bulging pocket. He was smiling, as he did most of the time, she would discover.

"I am Farid, Ms Saidi. I think I can help you. My home language is Pashto, not Dari, but I think I can make myself understood."

"You must be quite a linguist, Farid: Greek, English, Pashto and some Dari."

"I like people, Ms Saidi. I suppose that's why I became a doctor. And, if you want to talk to people, you must make an effort. I also have some Italian."

He beamed over his glasses.

"I can give you half an hour now, if you are ready," he said.

"Do you know where to find Paksima?"

"Of course. You will follow me, please."

*

She was in a room to herself. Out of intensive care but still connected to drips and monitors. Bel had not expected her to be so young. She looked about sixteen. Farid introduced himself to the girl in a very gentle way, speaking softly and smiling a lot. She was not smiling.

"I'm just making sure we can communicate well enough," he said, over his shoulder.

"And can you?"

"I think we'll be okay."

"All right. Well, I'm going to record this on my phone if that's okay with her. Saves me writing everything down and helps me get it right."

He explained to the girl, pointing to Bel's iPhone but she started shaking her head emphatically.

"Tell her it's just for me. No-one else will hear it and I'll delete it within forty-eight hours."

Farid spoke some more, looking anxious. Finally, the girl acquiesced with a shrug, and he was beaming again.

"She is frightened of the people who did this to her but okay, she says she will trust you."

Bel took the girl's hand and looked straight into her eyes.

"I want to stop this happening to other people, Paksima."

Farid went to translate but Paksima was waving her hand.

"It's okay," she said. "I understand her. I want this, too."

Then she spoke some words of Dari to Farid, sat up a little more and took a drink of water.

"You may ask your questions now," he said.

CHAPTER 10
THE AFRICAN DOCTOR

Leo was waiting with the taxi drivers at Chaniá airport. When the crowds started to come through, he held the cardboard sign a little higher and looked around uncertainly. Was this the flight from Athína or one of the many other internal flights? Then, just as the crowd was thinning, and Leo was trying to check his phone with his spare hand, a large, dark form appeared, right in front of him.

"I am Daric Hassan," he said in perfect English, nodding at the card.

"Christodoulákis," said Leo, fumbling with the placard and the phone, while extending his hand.

"I didn't expect you to meet me in person, Lieutenant."

"It is nothing; a twenty-minute drive. You have come all the way from Mogadishu. It was the right thing to do. How are you feeling, Dr Hassan?"

He meant, how had he coped with the journey, but it was the wrong thing to ask. Leo studied the black face, the bloodshot eyes, the firm line of his mouth.

"Have you ever lost a child, Lieutenant?"

"I have, in fact."

"Then you know something of what I am feeling."

"Of course. I am sorry, Dr Hassan. It was a thoughtless question."

"Please, call me Daric."

"Let's go to the car, then, Daric. My name is Leo. We can talk on the way. Let me take that for you."

He took charge of the medium-sized suitcase, leaving the African with just the rucksack to carry as they left the airport concourse for the waiting police car. Once inside the car, side by side on the rear seat, Leo handed him a cold bottle of water and nodded at the constable's eyes in the rear-view mirror.

"Is it okay for you if we go straight to the mortuary?"

There was a pause before Daric answered.

"All right, yes. Let's get it over with."

Leo sought to take his mind off what was to come by getting him to talk. "I'd be fascinated to know how you found us, Daric."

"It's a bit of a story, Leo. After Yasir went with the smugglers, we heard nothing for a few days. I texted him. No response. Then I rang his mobile several times but was diverted to voicemail every time. We were worried then. We had no idea where he was, or if he was in trouble. I called the number they had given me, but it was unobtainable. Either I wrote the number down wrong, or, more likely, it was a bogus number. That got me alarmed.

"I started making calls, and my wife began trawling the internet. She was searching for news stories on accidents or murders involving Somali boys and there were hundreds of them, from all over the world; stories where the boys were victims, some where they were the perpetrators. I showed her how to narrow the search to the Mediterranean area and then, after a few days, she found it. It was an article on a news website called ekathimerini. It didn't pick up on the whole phrase, but the article said something like: *Could the murdered boy be Ethiopian or Somali?* That was enough for the search engine to locate the article. A body had been found and the authorities were struggling to identify it. The boy's face looked East African, it suggested, but there was no picture. Then we went back through their website, chronologically. Just a few days earlier, we found the initial report. And there was Yasir's face, staring at us."

"That must have been a huge shock for you both."

"It was the end of our world, Leo. Yasir was our only child. And murdered? Why, for God's sake? He was just a boy; a sweet, kind boy who never harmed anyone."

"Almost there, sir," called the constable, and Daric's face registered sudden apprehension.

A stern-looking woman of about fifty was outside, waiting for them. She extinguished a cigarette with her shoe as they approached and thrust her hands into the pockets of her white coat.

Leo made the introductions and she nodded at Daric.

"You are a medical doctor?" she asked.

"I'm a GP in Mogadishu, Somalia," he replied.

"Then, I imagine you've seen a lot of violent death," she said as they entered the building.

It was the wrong thing to say. Daric stopped in his tracks and stared at her.

"I have, but none where my only son was the victim."

Pánagou shot a glance at Leo for help but there was nothing either of them could think to say. As they entered the mortuary, Leo saw that Pánagou's orderlies had taken the body from the cold drawer and placed it on a trolley, where it was covered with a sheet, leaving only the boy's face exposed.

Daric approached, Pánagou's eyes not moving from his face. She saw the apprehension overcome by compassion. He touched the boy's face with a trembling hand.

"It is Yasir. It is my son," he whispered.

"We'll give you some time with him," said Leo, and signalled to Pánagou to join him outside.

"Wait, please," said Daric. "I must wash my son's body. And afterwards, I must wrap him. Can you bring me soap and water, towels? And do you have any white cotton? Even bandages would do."

*

During the short drive across to police headquarters, Leo remained silent, out of respect. The sight of his dead son seemed to have left Daric empty and defeated. He followed as Leo led him up to a meeting room near his office and asked one of the constables to organise hot, sweet tea and some biscuits.

"Thank you for the identification," said Leo. "I am sorry to make you do this."

He poured the tea and pushed a mug over to Daric. He saw he had covered his face with his hands and his shoulders were shaking. Leo found a box of tissues and placed it on the table. After a minute, the big man grabbed a fistful of them.

"I'm so sorry, Leo," he said.

"Don't be. You have to grieve."

"It's all my fault, though," he sobbed. "He was just a boy and I sent him to his death."

"You mustn't say that, Daric. You were trying to find a life for him. You did your best and you had no way of knowing it would end like this. Someone else took your son's life. Not you."

"But now I feel *relieved* that it is him. How can this be?"

"I understand this. It's the removal of tension, nothing more. You must not feel guilty about it. Now, you are sad, but you no longer have the terrible uncertainty. We fool ourselves all the time, Daric."

The big man was nodding slowly. After another minute, he took a sip of tea. Then the conversation became more pragmatic.

"As you probably realised, my family is Muslim, Leo. It is important to us to deal with things quickly, normally within twenty-four hours."

"I understand, Daric. I will tell you when we can release Yasir's body. I don't think it will be much longer."

"Thank you."

"I am sorry, but there are no cremation facilities in Crete."

"We don't cremate; we bury. But there are certain procedures that must be followed. There are many Muslims in Crete, so I imagine your funeral directors will be familiar with our customs."

"They will be, of course. We can help you find a good one nearby."

"Thank you."

They lapsed into silence. *Perhaps the pragmatic aspects of the burial process had distracted Daric from the horror of burying his only son,* Leo thought.

"Tell me about *your* child, Leo," said Daric, after a few moments.

Leo was taken aback. Except for his wife, he had never talked to anyone about her. And now a stranger was asking him. A kind-looking man, waiting. A man who, given the shared experience, might feel he deserved an answer. Leo began, hesitantly:

"We were in Athína then – Athens. Right in the city. My daughter started mixing with the wrong sort of friends. Drugs. We didn't know, at first. She was only sixteen, but she started to stay out very late – and she became deceitful. She agrees to return at midnight, but she has no intention of doing this. Steals money from us and takes items from the house to sell. Even things she or other family members care about. What is the word? – *cherish*. That is when we knew. But we didn't know how far she was gone. Or that it was heroin. And by then, it was already too late."

Leo stared out of the office window at the windswept car park, the boiling sea beyond and the barren mountains, iron grey in the distance. Daric looked at him sadly.

"Tragic," was all he said.

A few seconds passed, then Leo turned back to him with forced brightness:

"I don't want us to talk about me and my problems, Daric. Tell me *your* story. You and your boy – how he came to be here."

Leo sat down again and watched as Daric drained his tea.

"What do you know of Somalia, Leo?"

"What I see on the news: religious conflicts, armed militias, famine, corruption, pirates."

"You forgot the droughts and the suicide bombers. We've had thirty years of civil war, border conflicts and famine. Many are living on food aid in makeshift tents. It's an ongoing disaster and various ideologies try to feed off that, but all they do is inspire more violence, more fragmentation. My beautiful country has been shot to pieces and I no longer know how it can be put back together.

"It's no place to bring up a boy, Leo. One lives in constant fear of what may happen. Will he be killed or maimed? If he survives, will he be radicalised? And how to get a decent education for him? In the end, we decided we had to get him to England or Germany, if possible. If we succeeded, he would be safe there and have a future. Maybe we could even join him, in a few years."

"This is not just a plane ticket, though," said Leo.

"No. We knew the authorities would not let him in. So, we had to investigate other possibilities."

"Meaning smugglers."

"It wasn't difficult. People know who they are, if you ask around. Small-time crooks, opportunists. I met a few, but I was not impressed. They ran seat-of-the-pants operations, disorganised, under-funded. Dangerous. My boy was only fourteen, Leo, I wanted something better for him, something much safer.

"I made it clear I was prepared to pay more for the right people. It took a while but, in the end, I received a call from a man who called himself Adil. He told me he was Syrian, but he spoke English very well. He told me a new route had been started. Because it was new, the chances of a successful trip were much higher and there was no danger to life because it was a large boat in excellent condition. Also, it left from the south of Turkey, near the Syrian border. All we had to do was help him get false papers organised for Yasir and then he would be driven to the port of Mersin at the appointed time. He would organise everything for us."

"And what was the destination of this boat?"

"Somewhere in Italy. I didn't need to know where, he said, but there would be road transport laid on from there to the UK, a people carrier, or a lorry of some sort. The ultimate destination was to the west of London, not far from Heathrow. It sounded good. The man gave me confidence that he knew what he was doing, unlike the others. He seemed to have a professional team behind him. The only drawback was the price."

"How much did he want?"

"For the whole trip, including the forged documents: fifteen thousand US."

Leo whistled.

"But you agreed?"

"It was more than I expected, and it took all our reserves. I don't make much money these days, I'm afraid. Many people cannot pay for treatment. And this would take every bit of our savings. But it was to give my son a life, so I swallowed hard and said yes, okay. He told me it would take two weeks to put the false papers together and, for that, he would need me to provide passport photos of my son. After that, he would give me a firm date for Yasir to be collected – not from our house, but from a busy part of the safer side of the city. The date would be within a month, he said."

"And the money?"

"I had to pay half when I gave him the photos and the rest when the documents were presented. In cash."

"You can get US dollars in Mogadishu?"

"There are ways, Leo, at a price. The whole, damned country is a black market."

"So, what guarantees did you have that he would do what he said?"

"None. He made it clear. That was the deal; take it or leave it. It's a sellers' market."

"Do you have any more information on the boat?"

"Nothing."

"Hmmm. Maybe the port authorities at Mersin can help. Yasir made it to the boat, obviously."

"And he must have been killed by someone on that boat, Leo, but why?"

"I don't know, Daric, but we'll try hard to get an answer for you and find whoever did this to your boy."

"I am grateful for that."

"I'll make sure you are kept informed of developments. Now, can I have someone drive you to your hotel?"

CHAPTER 11
CONTACT IS LOST

The following day, Leo circulated an email to the task force team, letting them know the boy had been identified as Yasir Hassan, a Somali migrant from a once prosperous family. He had been on a smugglers' boat out of Mersin, Turkey, but there were no clues as to why he had been murdered.

Nick was home in Saktoúria, checking his emails. He had never heard of Mersin and had to resort to Google Earth to discover where the hell it was. He spotted a message from Bel, addressed only to him, he noticed:

Hi Nick. Amazing interview with the girl, who is Paksima from Afghanistan, and is recovering in the G. Hatzikóstas General Hospital at Ioánnina. I can't believe how evil these bastards can be! I've recorded it, so I'll send you a link. I'd like to talk it through before I share it with the others. Speak soon.

There was one of those emoji things – a rather lusty grin – at the end of the message.

Ioánnina – another place he had never heard of. It sounded like it was in Italy but no, Nick found it was a town in northern Greece.

Later in the morning, his daughter Lauren called. After the usual exchange of mild insults and updates, he asked her a question:

"So, hun, what does it mean when someone sends you a *link*?"

"Oh, Dad. For Heaven's sake! They're going to send you an email with a computer address embedded in it where you'll find whatever they want to share with you."

"That's what I thought, so there'll be another email."

"Very likely. Could be a text or a WhatsApp or something."

"Can't find one."

"Have you looked in junk?"

"Sorry?"

There was a sigh of exasperation from his daughter.

"If your computer doesn't recognise the sender, for whatever reason, the message could end up in your junk folder and you have to dig it out from there."

"Why would it put the second message in junk when it didn't do that with the first one?"

"I don't know, Dad, but you need to check. Can you see the tab for the folder?"

"Got it … wait … God, there's a lot of crap in there, but nothing from Bel."

"Is Bel your new girlfriend, Dad?"

"Don't be daft, she's just someone I'm working with, a journalist."

"Not Bel Saidi?"

"You know her?"

"I've seen her on TV, here and there. She's very smart, a rather attractive woman, too. Might be a bit out of your league, but you could do a lot worse."

"You cheeky bint. Look, just help me with this, can you, Lauren? If I ever find this link, what will it link me to?"

"All right. What's the context, Dad? What is she trying to send you?"

"A recording of a conversation involving two or more people."

"How long a conversation?"

"Around half an hour, I should think. That's all the doctors would allow her."

"And she recorded it on her phone?"

"I imagine so."

"Then it's going to be quite a big file. Maybe too big to email. She would have uploaded it to the Cloud and sent you a link."

"Any particular cloud? There aren't any in the sky right now."

"Now you're being silly. As I'm sure you know, there are services that store files for you. You can grant access to others by sharing a file with them, on the internet."

"By sending them a link."

"Yes. I do it all the time. I use Dropbox, but there are others, I'm sure."

"So, I guess I have to wait for the email with the link."

"Yep. Sounds like she hasn't had time to upload it yet. Maybe she's still working on it."

"All right. That makes sense. Thanks, Lauren."

They chatted for several more minutes, about the results of her finals, the unfortunate week Nick had spent with her brother, and how his ex-wife Jen was getting along with her second husband, The Creep. When the call ended, Nick felt good, as he generally did after talking with Lauren. And maybe she was right about Bel. *I could do a lot worse,* he repeated to himself. Then he remembered the *out of your league* bit.

*

Nick checked his emails for the rest of the day but there was nothing from Bel, even in the junk folder. Still thinking he might have misunderstood something technical, and curious to know about her interview, he called her at six but was directed to voicemail. He left a message, saying he hadn't received the link and suggesting they have a quick update anyway. He would be in all evening.

Nick's mobile rang at seven thirty-five, but it was Leo, not Bel: "Good evening, Nick. I'm sorry to disturb you."

"Hi Leo, how are you? Well done on identifying our body!"

"It was a stroke of luck, Nick. The father found us. But I am not sure it takes us much further forward. Now, we have a name, and we know he was a migrant, and we have the alleged port of departure, at least. Andréas is checking this out."

"I've never heard of Mersin."

"Nor me. Have you heard from Bel? We have our rescheduled session tomorrow and I've heard nothing since she left for Lésvos."

"Oh, so you don't know about Ioánnina?"

"We say *Yánnina*, Nick. What about it?" A note of irritation had crept into Leo's voice.

Nick explained how a girl who was taken ill on a boat from Turkey had been taken there from Igoumenítsa and that Bel had gone to interview her.

"Sounds like a long shot. Was it worthwhile?"

"I don't know yet. The girl was from Afghanistan, so she might well have been a migrant, too. Her name is Paksima. Bel seemed excited about what she'd heard."

He explained about the email and the missing link.

"All emails must be shared to the whole team. I will stress this tomorrow."

"I'll try her again this evening."

"Yes, do that. And let me know – or rather, let us all know – as soon as you have something."

Leo rang off and Nick put the phone down and stared into space for a minute. Then he picked up the phone and dialled Bel's number again, with the same result. This time he left a more urgent message, asking her to call as soon as she had an opportunity. As he put the phone down, he wondered what to do next, if she did not call. Was she staying in a hotel in Ioánnina that night? Would she need to, or was she planning to fly back to Athína or Chaniá that evening? Perhaps she decided to follow the trail back to Igoumenítsa? He realised, with a jolt, he did not even know in which city to start looking. And why had he not received the link? With the team meeting now scheduled for tomorrow, she must have been planning to discuss the contents of her file with him this evening. Something was wrong. He had a feeling in his gut and thirty years' experience told him not to ignore it.

He told himself to calm down and think. The last place she was likely to have been seen was the hospital. Ioánnina could have only one general hospital, surely. He would find the number and call them. If he could speak to the girl, Paksima, and her doctor too, he might find some clues as to where she was staying or heading.

"Kalispéra sas," Nick said when the hospital eventually picked up. "Miláte aggliká?"

"Of course," said a female voice, "How may I help you, Mister …?"

"My name is Nick Fisher. I'm working with the Greek police."

"But you are not Greek, I think."

"No, I was born in Britain, but now I'm living here and working with

Lieutenant Leonídas Christodoulákis from the Chaniá prefecture."

"One moment, please."

She put him on hold. *Perhaps she was checking that Leo existed,* he thought. It must have been four or five minutes before the line was opened again. Iit was a different voice this time, a more authoritative tone.

"Ioánnina General Hospital."

"It's Nick Fisher. I was …"

"Yes, Mr Fisher. What is it you want?"

"You have a patient. A girl from Afghanistan called Paksima?"

"Do you have a family name?"

"I don't, but surely there can't be many Afghani girls there. She was brought in from a boat at Igoumenítsa, I believe."

"One moment."

The line went dead again. Nick started tapping his fingers, but this time it was less than a minute.

"What is it you want with her, Mr Fisher?"

"I'd like to talk to her, please."

"I'm afraid that won't be possible."

"Look, I know I'm not a relative or anything, but this is not a request, it's a police matter."

"The police here are already concerned with this girl."

Nick assumed this was the immigration authorities.

"I don't have an issue with the girl. I'm trying to find the woman who interviewed her yesterday, Bel Saidi."

"One moment."

He found himself on hold for the third time, got to his feet and started prowling around the room. After two more minutes, she was back:

"I can put you through to her doctor."

"Okay, who …?"

She was gone again, but then a different voice, female, professional: "Marás."

"Are you Paksima's doctor?" asked Nick.

"And you are?"

71

Nick went through it all again, trying to keep a lid on his rising temper. When he had finished, there was a pause before she spoke again:

"Well, I am sorry to tell you, but Paksima died last night."

"She what? I thought she was recovering."

"So did we, but there was a sudden relapse and her heart failed. I am sorry."

"Do you know the cause?"

"It could be a number of things. There were toxins in her body."

"So, you're investigating the cause of death?"

"Of course, but her system was poisoned, and she was still very weak, Mr Fisher. These things happen."

"What poisoned her?"

"The heroin, of course."

"Oh, I didn't know. Can you tell me *when* it happened?"

"She was found at two minutes past six, yesterday evening."

Just half an hour after the interview ended, thought Nick.

"Found? You mean she was unattended?"

"That would be normal, at this stage of recovery. A nurse would go in every half an hour or so, checking vital signs, changing drips."

"Listen, doctor, I understand she was interviewed just a few minutes before her death, as it turned out. I'm looking for the woman who interviewed her, Bel Saidi. Can you help? Do you know where she was going? Was she planning to stay somewhere?"

"I'm sorry. I don't have any idea. But I know you are not the only one looking for her. The police also want to talk to her."

"You mean, about Paksima's death?"

"Of course. The relapse occurred so soon after the interview. They are concerned."

"Were you at the interview yourself?"

"I was not, but a colleague of mine was."

"Could I speak to her?"

"It's a him. He was acting as their interpreter. His name is Farid Lohani. He is not on shift this evening, but I can ask him to call you tomorrow?"

"That would be very helpful. Thank you. As soon as possible, please."

Nick gave her his mobile number and, ending the conversation, then scribbled down her name, Marás, and that of the interpreter guy, Lohani. He tried Bel's mobile once more, but it was still going to voicemail. He sent a text instead:

Hi Bel. Struggling to reach you. Please get in touch as soon as you see this. Sorry to tell you this, but it seems Paksima died soon after you left.

CHAPTER 12
STRUGGLING WITH TECHNOLOGY

The meeting went ahead as planned this time. Even though Bel was absent, Leo figured she might get in touch, and it would be better to be together if she did. Anyway, there was a lot to catch up on, with or without her.

Andréas was a well-rounded man with a dark shadow of a beard, Nick saw. He would be in his mid-forties or so. Despite his bulk, he was surprisingly nimble on his feet and, though reticent and softly spoken, he seemed sharp.

"When were you last in contact, Nick?" he asked.

"She phoned from Lésvos, early evening, the day before yesterday. She told me she was going to Ioánnina the next day, to interview this girl, rather than coming back here. She'd have to go via Athens, so she arranged it for later in the afternoon. Then I got this message."

He showed them the message on his mobile phone.

"So, she did the interview, at least," said Leo.

"She did. But I learned from the hospital that the girl died shortly afterwards. And I have no clues to Bel's current whereabouts."

"Did you get the link?" Andréas asked.

"Not yet, no."

"A link to what?" asked Leo.

"I would guess Dropbox," said Andréas. "Too big a file to email, so she put it in there and sent a link."

"Except she didn't," said Nick.

"She didn't send the link yet. She *might* have uploaded the file."

"But she knows about this meeting. She'd have sent the link and she'd be here if everything was okay. I'm sure she would."

"We need to find her, gentlemen," said Leo, "and we need to find that file. Where was she last seen by anyone, Nick?"

"At the hospital in Ioánnina. There was a guy interpreting for them, name of Lohani. I'm expecting a call from him today."

"Okay. Please follow this up. And I assume the hospital has CCTV? We need to get recordings from the cameras near the exits and elevators, and any near the girl's room for, say four thirty to six thirty pm. I'll speak to the captain at Epirus, get the local boys moving on that right away. I'll also brief them to look for Bel, of course."

"Can't we run a trace on her mobile?" asked Nick.

"Sure, if it's switched on. Otherwise, the best we can do is ask the network provider to tell us where it was when it was switched off. I can get on to this."

Leo paused the meeting for fifteen minutes then, so all actions to locate Bel and her phone could be put in motion. When they resumed, he asked Nick to summarise the Lésvos conversation, then shared with them his encounter with Daric and the identification of the body.

"Is he still here, the father?" asked Nick.

"I believe he is," said Leo. "Daric wanted to take some time, visit the place where his son was found, talk to his wife back in Mogadishu."

"Poor sod. I feel for him. From what you say, he spent all their money on this trip. All the family's hopes travelled with Yasir. But instead, it got him killed. How must Daric feel? And now, he and his wife are broke, condemned to this dangerous mess of a country, with no hope of escape. What a shitty world it is, sometimes."

The others were nodding, sad-eyed, lips compressed.

"Are we at least ready to release the boy's body to him?" Nick asked.

"I don't see why not," said Leo. "I'll chase Pánagou. Getting it back to Somalia isn't going to happen, though."

After a pause, Leo switched focus to Andréas. The coastguard had agreed to help, he confirmed, and were keeping half an eye on the route from Mersin, but they had no knowledge of boats in the south Crete area around the time of Yasir's death.

"What do you know of Mersin?" asked Nick.

"It's quite a big place. Over a million people live there, so it's bigger than any Greek city, even Athína," said Andréas.

"And we never heard of it."

"No, and yet it's Turkey's biggest seaport. It's near Tarsus, where Saint

Paul came from, right in the south-east corner of the Mediterranean. Very hot there, over forty in the height of the summer. There are solar panels everywhere these days."

"Have you been there then, Andréa?" asked Leo.

"No. This is just research. I was curious."

"How far is it from Syria?"

"A little over five hundred kilometres, by road. Seven or eight hours, maybe."

"I want you to get yourself over there. Put a cover story together. Ask around, pretend you're looking to be smuggled out yourself."

"Okay, boss, but I'm not Turkish or Syrian."

"No. Maybe you have a friend or relative who needs to get out? Use your head and you will learn things, I think. Try to find out who's behind this. We need you there. Anything you find will help the team."

Andréas looked a little taken aback, and it sounded like a tough brief, but he said nothing more.

The meeting was about to end when Nick said:

"What if we don't find Bel, or her phone?" It was the elephant in the room, the unspoken question, and no-one wanted to answer it. "I think I need to get over to Ioánnina and see what I can do to help."

"I'm not sure that's a great idea, Nick," said Leo. "Give it a day or two. See what the local cops come up with. Talk to your interpreter guy."

"Bel is an old friend of mine, Leo. I *have* to do more. She might be in danger. At least have them send me the security footage. I'd like to check it out myself."

Leo gave him an odd look, like he was wondering what *old friend* might mean, but then he said:

"All right. I'll see what can be done."

"And this file of hers," said Andréas, "is there any way we can access it without her account number and password?"

"We can try," said Leo. "I'll put in a call to Dropbox, assuming it's them, and see how we get on."

Nick felt dispirited after the meeting. He was worried about Bel and concerned about Paksima's sudden relapse. He wanted to be in

Ioánnina to make a judgement about the hospital's security systems and the integrity of its staff, but it was a different jurisdiction, and he was required to let them handle things, at least to begin with. That didn't stop him getting contact details from Leo, then calling to introduce himself and make sure they knew the urgency of getting the CCTV footage to him. They did, they assured him, and would have a disk couriered within twenty-four hours.

By mid-afternoon, Lohani still had not called, so Nick rang the hospital again. This time he was put through, and it was picked up right away.

"Lohani."

"Kýrie Lohani? It's Nick Fisher. I think you were asked to call me?"

"Mr Fisher. I was about to call. I have been very busy, as usual. Sorry."

"I'll come straight to the point. I'm looking for Bel Saidi, the journalist who interviewed Paksima. You were there, I understand."

"Yes, I was."

"Can you tell me what time she left and where she went?"

"She left at about twenty to six, I think. I assume she left the hospital, but I don't know where she went then, Mr Fisher."

"Was she planning to stay in Ioánnina, do you know?"

"I'm sorry. I don't know."

"And you know Paksima died soon afterwards. Did that surprise you?"

"The girl was not my patient, Mr Fisher. I'd prefer not to comment."

"But, as I understand it, she was able to be interviewed for half an hour and was described as recovering, and yet half an hour later she's found dead. That surprises *me*."

"Such things happen when the body has been abused to such an extent."

"Could you give me a summary of the interview, please, Mr Lohani?"

"It's *Doctor* Lohani. And no, I'm not sure I can, Mr Fisher. I was asked to interpret a private conversation. I'm thinking it should remain private without the permission of the people concerned."

Nick saw red.

"Well, one of them won't give a damn now, will she? And the other is a very good friend of mine who has gone missing – and I need this information to help me find her. So, come on. Doctor, for Heaven's sake."

There was a protracted pause while Dr Lohani struggled with his ethics. Then, he spoke again:

"I can tell you Paksima was suffering from a heroin overdose."

"I know that."

"She was carrying the heroin in her body, in capsules. Paksima was an illegal migrant from Afghanistan, Mr Fisher, on her way to Italy. I understand she agreed to carry drugs to make up the fare. She could not have afforded it, otherwise."

"Who was this agreement with – the smugglers or someone else?"

"I can't say."

"Bel must have asked the question."

"Not that I recall."

"And how did Paksima get to Igoumenítsa? That must have been discussed."

"On a boat from Turkey, I believe. I know nothing more."

"The police will be questioning you soon, Dr Lohani. I suggest you take out your moral compass and give it a good shake before then. It sounds like you're trying to protect your colleagues from a negligence claim *and* refusing to divulge vital information on people smugglers and drug dealers. The Greek police will not be sympathetic to your crises of conscience, moral dilemmas or what have you. And your immigration papers had better be in order or you might find yourself on a flight back to Kabul. No doubt the Taliban will be delighted to welcome you back."

"I don't appreciate being threatened, Mr Fisher. I'm just trying to respect confidences."

"Just think how many more lives will be blighted if these bastards get away with it, Doctor. Isn't that a wee bit more important than your woolly ethics?"

Nick ended the call and only just resisted the urge to hurl the phone against the wall. This man was a perfect example of someone who took his so-called principles from rules and textbooks rather than common sense or humanity. If there was no rule to follow, he found himself out on a limb and froze with inertia. *Pillock!* Nick decided to call the Epirus team again and ask them to pay particular attention to Doctor Lohani, who he believed to be an immigrant from Afghanistan. The extra pressure should unfreeze the good doctor. If not, he might be taking a flight to Ioánnina himself.

*

Nick remained in Chaniá until early evening, when the desk sergeant dropped a padded envelope onto his desk.

"Urgent package, courtesy of DHL, sir."

"Aha," said Nick, his face coming alive with anticipation, "that was good going." He looked at his watch; it was five past six.

He just about knew his way around the police headquarters' computer system now, so he logged on and loaded up the disk. His face fell as he saw about a dozen numbered files with a variety of suffixes. He clicked on one at random and received a *cannot open file* message. He checked the envelope again to see if there was a note explaining what to do. There was not. He ejected the disk and checked each side for any handwritten information but all it said was *G. Hatzikóstas* and the date, two days before. He could feel his frustration building as he loaded it once more, He tried three more files but none of them would open. Then he made the call.

"Leo? Hi. Look, do you have an IT whizz here somewhere? I've received a load of CCTV files from the hospital, but I don't know which is which and I can't seem to open any of them."

Five minutes later, he was apologising to a geeky young man called Loúkas with spectacles and thinning fair hair, unusual for a Greek.

"I hope I haven't ballsed anything up. I don't know what the hell I'm doing, to be honest."

"Don't worry. CCTV is big problem, always. There are no universal protocols."

"What the hell does that mean?"

"Everyone makes up their own rules. Unless you know the software the camera manufacturer used, it's difficult. Even when you do know, it's not so easy."

"Terrific."

"And people install the cheapest systems."

"Why?"

"Because any rubbish system will give them the discount on insurance they're looking for. They don't expect to need the footage and they don't think about how well the system works until there's a problem. And then the problem lands on us, the police."

"What a bloody mess!"

"So, let me see what I can do."

Nick moved to one side and let the geek sit at the screen.

"Let's see how big these files are," he said, and pushed a few keys. "You see, here? These four files are much bigger than the others. These will be video files from the cameras."

"What's all the other crap then?"

"Log files and such like. You don't need them."

"Well, why did they send them, then?"

Loúkas answered his question by spreading the palms of his hands and raising his eyebrows. Then he pushed a few more keys and his face lit up.

"Good news. They're AVI files. The codec should be in the file header, with luck."

"Let's hope so," said Nick, not knowing what on earth he was talking about.

"Eureka!" he said, a couple of minutes later. "Now I just have to download this piece of code and we should be good to go."

Nick went to get himself a cup of coffee. When he returned, the geek was looking pleased with himself.

"All done. Now, when you click on the file, it will find the code and open itself in Media Player. I have opened each of them to make sure everything works. You can fast forward or go back, like this. And you must use the fast forward, or you will be watching TV for eight hours." He checked his watch. "Until two thirty in the morning!"

"You're a genius, Loúka. I'd have been lost without you."

The young man scribbled his name and extension number and grinned.

"Call me if anything goes wrong. I'll be here until nine, at least."

"Wait. How do I know which file is which camera?"

"It's obvious when you start watching, but they put a header in for you too, in Greek. This one is the front entrance to the hospital. There's one for the rear entrance, one for the car park and one for the second-floor corridor."

"What about stairs and elevators?"

"No, this is all you have. Maybe they don't have cameras there?"

"All right. I'll start with these. Thank you."

When Loúkas left him to it, Nick took a swig of his coffee. It was going to be a long night.

*

Leo, meanwhile, succeeded in identifying Bel's network provider and asked them to run a trace. They told him the phone was inactive. Why would Bel switch her phone off, he wondered? To take a flight. To avoid being disturbed by it for some reason. Or perhaps it had been switched off by someone else. That was a much darker scenario.

Less than twenty minutes later, the company was able to provide coordinates for the location of the phone the last time it was switched on. It was still in Northern Greece, then. Leo passed the information to the Epirus team and went in search of the police lawyer.

"In a word, yes, they will," the lawyer said, in response to Leo's question. "But I think we'll need a subpoena issued by a US court. It's important to follow the correct procedure, and it'll help if we can limit our request to one person and only the relevant part of their stored information, if possible. The more specific we are, the more likely we'll get what we want without too much hassle. Dropbox will resist us if we don't follow due process and they'll try to narrow our request if they consider it too broad. If they agree, they'll notify the user, then send us an encrypted file."

Leo sat down with him, and they drew up a request explaining the circumstances and requesting copies of any files on Bel Saidi's Dropbox account which had been accessed in the previous three days.

"They may try to limit that, depending on the number of files," said the lawyer.

"But we don't know the relevant file, so we must resist any limit. Of course, if there's one labelled something like *Interview with Paksima,* it would be all we need."

*

Nick started by taking a quick look at each of the video files to determine the location of the camera and the likely usefulness of that particular file. The one facing the car park was a waste of time, he decided. It was set too high and covered a very wide area. It might just be possible to identify a type of car, if one knew what one was looking for, but little else. Number plates or the identity of drivers or their passengers would be next to impossible unless they happened to be very close to the camera.

The cameras at the entrances were more sensibly positioned, but there was a lot of activity, particularly at the front entrance. It would take time to trawl through this lot. He decided to start with the second-floor corridor. There would be less traffic, and this was where Paksima's room, number 208, was located. With any luck, he would be able to skim through and get an early sighting of Bel to confirm what they thought they knew.

He settled on triple speed. This was as fast as he dared go to be sure he would spot all the people. He started at the beginning, at four thirty. Nothing at all happened in the corridor for the first twenty minutes and Nick was wondering if there could be some fault, if it was stuck somehow, but the timer kept moving on. Finally, at four fifty-two, an old couple appeared, bickering, and searching in a bag for something before moving on towards the lift, still bickering. Three minutes later, a female nurse entered room 207, opposite. He slowed the replay to double speed. She left again five minutes later, at five pm but did

82

not go into 208. However, Nick saw her greet a female doctor, who looked to be in her mid-thirties, walking along the corridor towards the camera. *She* then entered room 208. Nick paused the recording and scribbled down the time, as he did again, when she left, just two minutes later. Maybe it was Doctor Marás, he thought. Then, at six minutes past five, he saw the familiar figure of Bel, ambling towards the camera in conversation with a young male doctor who did not look Greek. That must be Lohani, he concluded, as they entered Paksima's room together. He knew they would be in there for half an hour or so, so he moved back to triple speed but then, a moment later, hit the stop button. Just twelve seconds on, a thickset, older man with a tan briefcase hurried past the camera, head down. He did not look at the door or the camera. Nick wrote down the time again before moving on.

It was five forty-three when Bel and Lohani left the room together. Nick saw Lohani move his right arm up and down, the hand vertical, the arm extended, as if giving Bel directions. Then, he beamed and shook her hand before they went their separate ways, the young doctor passing the camera while Bel walked away towards the lift. As soon as she was out of sight, Nick moved back to triple speed, but again had to hit the stop button as he saw someone entering room 208. He reversed the recording. There was a man in a white coat, and he had a stethoscope around his neck, but he was older than the other doctors Nick had observed. His hair was iron grey and thinning and the coat was a little tight on him. And he was carrying a tan briefcase. Nick paused the recording at five forty-five and called Loúkas's extension number:

"Loúka? Sorry, mate. Can you spare me another minute? I need you to show me how to take screenshots."

*

By eight thirty, Nick had assembled a small stack of screen shots from the corridor file, showing everyone who came and left room 208. These included the mystery man with the tan briefcase leaving the room just four minutes after entering it and striding away from the camera, and a nurse entering at two minutes past six to find Paksima dead.

He turned his attention to the front entrance file, skipping through to five forty-five. This was much slower going as there were so many people, but he remembered Bel's distinctive dress and it did not take long to spot her making her way out of the entrance at five fifty-one. *Well, at least we know she was okay when she left the hospital,* he thought to himself. But then his heart sank as he watched her walk off towards the car park. A man was following. He reversed the recording again and saw a man of about forty leaning against a pillar near the entrance, smoking. As Bel walked past, he straightened up, stubbed out his cigarette and ambled off, about twenty metres behind her.

At ten past nine, he called Leo:

"I think we have a problem, Leo. Two guys. It looks like one of them got to Paksima and the other followed Bel away from the hospital. I need resources Leo. I can't do all this myself. Find me some constables to go through the rest of this stuff, try to match these guys to known thugs. We have two murders now, by the look of it, and a high-profile journalist has gone missing. We've only just started and It's all going tits up."

"All right, Nick. Calm down. Paksima is an Epirus case. Send them everything you found. I'll speak to the captain again, make sure they're giving it their full attention and, if you like, I can tell them you are coming to help them."

Nick thought for a minute.

"My heart says join the search, but my head's telling me the last thing they need is an emotionally compromised stranger with limited Greek. I think my time is better spent trying to find out how Paksima died before the autopsy gets closed down."

"How will you do this?"

"I'll start by talking it through with Pánagou. I'd like to get her involved."

CHAPTER 13
A CONVENIENT DEATH

The cemetery was on a hill just south of the city between urban sprawl and orange groves and vineyards. In the distance, the snow-free White Mountains were a dusty pink-brown. The arrival of the morning sun had stirred the cicadas into a rustling whistle, not yet the screech of midday, and a light but persistent breeze was providing endless fun for irreverent, joy-filled swallows that swooped and chattered in and out of a pair of giant walnut trees.

The grave was open and waiting, Leo saw, but there was no coffin. The boy's body had been brought on a stretcher and laid nearby. It was wrapped in a cotton shroud. Daric greeted Leo and thanked him for coming. There were no other mourners, just the imam and a small team from the funeral directors. The boy's mother and all his other relatives and friends would be in Somalia; a sad affair made sadder still by their collective absence.

While the imam read from the Qur'an, Daric excused himself and went to the loose earth where he fashioned three balls, each about the size of his fist. Then, with the aid of two sturdy men, bit by bit they lowered Yasir's body into the grave. Everyone moved to the graveside then, to see Daric position the body on its right side, with a ball of earth supporting the shoulder. He then placed the remaining balls under the boy's neck and, lastly, his head, before they helped him out of the grave and he wiped his hands on a handkerchief. The imam then switched from readings to prayers, parts of which Daric echoed in his sonorous voice. Finally, he took a handful of earth and trickled it into the grave, inviting Leo to follow suit.

*

"Will you go home now?" Leo asked later, as they reached the cars.

"Tomorrow," he said. "There is one more thing I need to do, for my

85

peace of mind, and then I will return to my wife. I think we will need each other to get through this."

"You know we will do everything we can, Daric."

"Thank you, Lieutenant," he said, pressing a business card into the policeman's palm, "and please keep me updated with any developments. I feel like I need to know, but not for vengeance or retribution. I'm surprised, but I don't want these things. My son has gone, and nothing will bring him back. I need to understand how and why it happened because that knowledge might help us put these dark thoughts to rest, in time. But that is all."

They shook hands and then Leo found himself watching for a long time as the big man said a few words to the imam before getting in his hire car and driving slowly away.

*

Nick knew it was against Pánagou's principles to work this late, so he sent a summary of his findings to the Epirus team and then decided to call it a day. He might still be able to grab some dinner on the way home.

On the drive back, he could not stop thinking about Bel. He sensed she was in danger – or worse. If she were not already dead, God forbid, perhaps she was being held captive. If so, there would be a ransom request, some kind of exchange – unless they were just trying to suppress information. Perhaps Assad's agents had pursued her here, looking to stifle opposition to the Syrian regime. But then why kill Paksima? She was just a young girl from Afghanistan, no threat to anyone. Except, of course, to the people who used her as a drug mule or the people who smuggled her into Greece on a boat from Turkey.

The more Nick thought about it, the more convinced he became; it must be all down to the interview. Information Paksima revealed that Bel wanted to share with the world. Information the traffickers could not allow to escape. Information young Lohani must have interpreted, word for word. He had been too soft on him. He would call the Epirus guys in the morning, make sure they put the screws on the young doctor.

*

In Nick's dream, he was lost, panic rising in his throat as he struggled to find his way out of a vast, ramshackle building. It was a building he thought he knew, but there had been changes. Nothing made sense. The gardens were landscaped, though the building itself was derelict. He was naked and struggling up a pile of large, white stones that were near vertical when he saw commuters from all directions converging on a railway station. Now, he realised, this building *was* the station. They had not spotted him yet, but his nakedness prevented him from crying out, and he knew he was in trouble now. Deep trouble. He could hear the emergency services coming. Then he woke with a start, sweating. The landline by the bed was ringing.

"Nick Fisher."

"Sorry to call so early, Nick. It is not good news."

It was Leo. Nick glanced at his watch on the bedside table. It was ten past seven.

"Lohani has been found dead in his apartment."

"Oh, shit!"

"Suicide, by the look of it."

"That's a bit convenient."

"Yes, I see that, too, but I think it might be genuine. It seems he was working illegally. His papers were forged. In the medical profession, above all, this is unacceptable. Perhaps someone threatened to expose him?"

Nick felt nauseous, a sinking feeling in his stomach.

"How did he do it?" he asked.

"Hanged himself. Nylon rope."

"Oh, Jesus."

Nick's mind flooded with dark memories. A boy dragged from a river after a hard interrogation by an ambitious and obsessed police officer.

"That's not all, Nick. Sorry. We found Bel's iPhone in a waste bin not far from the hospital. The SIM card has been removed and I'm sure they'll have wiped the phone but we're testing for prints, anyway."

87

"We need to identify those bastards at the hospital and get after them."

"The Epirus team worked all night on your footage. The guy with the tan briefcase and the other guy – the one who seemed to be following Bel?"

"What about them?"

"The camera caught them *arriving together* at the main entrance. They are a team, Nick."

Nick was struggling to stay focused. This did not sound good.

"Identifiable?" he managed to ask.

"It's a fair image. They are working on it. There's also a shot of the killer, leaving by the side entrance, but he's hiding his face. Same guy though. Same briefcase. No question."

"So, with Lohani gone and no SIM, it's all down to Dropbox. Let's hope to God she had time to upload that file."

There was a long moment of silent tension before they exchanged pleasantries and disconnected. Neither said, *Let's hope to God she's still alive.*

*

After the call, Nick was shaken. He sat on the sofa and stared out of the window at the mountains where a solitary, white cloud was anchored. *Would they kill her, these bastards? Just like that? Dump her body somewhere? They'd already killed Paksima, it seemed, so why not Bel, too? Could they have taken her hostage, instead, or hidden her somewhere? There had been no demands, though, no messages. Why the hell not?*

As he made himself some coffee and toast, he grew angrier. If this magnificent woman, this brave and beautiful woman, had been taken out by some low-life migrant smugglers, just to protect their grubby, little business, he was going to have these bastards. He was going to close them down, lock them up and throw away the key. And, along the way, some rather painful injuries could prove unavoidable during capture and interrogation. But none of this would bring her back, he realised, a pit forming in his stomach. When he tried to resume his breakfast, the coffee was cold, the toast had lost its flavour and he felt very much alone.

*

As soon as Nick made it to police headquarters, he called Pánagou.

"There's an autopsy being carried out in Ioánnina," he said. "Would you have any influence over that?"

"Influence? Yes, of course," she said. "Every medical examiner is their own boss, in their area, but, in practice, we are professionals. We consult each other, listen to each other, and learn from each other. At least, most of us do."

"Do you know the ME for Epirus?"

"Not well, but we have met a few times, at conferences or whatever. He seems okay."

Nick went on to explain who Paksima was, and the circumstances of her death.

"To me, this sudden relapse seemed suspicious, anyway," he said. "But then we checked the camera footage in the corridor. An unknown individual, posing as a medic, spent four minutes alone with her in her room. Now, Doctor, if you wanted to dispose of someone in four minutes and make it look like a medical relapse, what would you do? Any ideas?"

"Was she wearing a catheter?"

"I don't know, but I'd think so. She was still taking fluids, I believe."

"And was she sitting up or lying down?"

"I don't know, but I assume she was sitting up for the interview, so I expect she still was. No nurse had been in, to help her change position."

"And how much did she weigh?"

"I don't know, but this is a sixteen-year-old migrant from Afghanistan. I doubt it was very much."

"Okay, then. Well, there are many ways to kill someone. But, if I have only four minutes and I want it to look like heart failure? I would induce a VAE."

"A what?"

"A venous air embolism. I'd take a large hypodermic, empty it, then draw in air and inject it into an AC vein. Once might not be enough. I'd do it two or three times, to make sure."

"AC?"

"Accessory cephalic. It's a vein in the forearm that joins the cephalic and axillary veins. People are often injected there."

"Wouldn't it be more effective to inject into an artery?"

"Absolutely not. Veins carry blood *to* the heart; arteries take it away. Inject into an artery and the drug, or in this case air, would go into the body tissue, limbs. It could cause serious damage. It might lead to an amputation, but it would be less likely to kill. On the other hand, if I were to inject, say, two hundred or more millilitres of air into the girl's blood, it would cause a VAE that would almost certainly be fatal."

"A fifth of a litre? Wow. That sounds like a huge amount. I thought even small amounts of air were dangerous."

"They *can* be, but only if the patient has certain rare conditions or if the air bubble makes it to the brain, where it can cause a stroke. That's why you see nurses flicking the syringe to get the air to the top and then squirting a little liquid out before they inject you. It's good practice and disperses any air bubbles, but most of us can cope with some air in the blood. It depends how much, relative to body mass, how quickly it gets in and where it goes. A two hundred millilitre air bubble reaching the heart of a girl who weighed sixty kilograms or less would be certain to kill her, I would say."

"How would the victim know?"

"The symptoms are sudden onset respiratory distress, coughing and chest pain, accompanied by a sense of impending doom."

"She wouldn't be able to breathe, and she'd feel panicked."

"Panic and dread. Feeding each other. Then you die."

"Poor thing. And afterwards, how would *you* know?"

"She died alone in her room at the hospital, I think you said, so there was no-one to observe the symptoms. After the event, it would look like unexplained heart failure. Given the earlier overdose of heroin, it would be easy to assume that her struggle to overcome that proved too much. It's not unusual for patients to show improving signs in the run-up to a critical relapse."

"But, if you suspected a VEA, is there anything you can do to prove it, after the event?"

"It's VAE, Nick. Venous air embolism – an air bubble in the vein. There is something called Richter's Technique, if I remember right – but I've never done this. Once you have the chest cavity open, you fill it with distilled water, incise the heart and use something called an aspirometer – or perhaps gas chromatography, these days – to measure the proportion of air. If the reading is significantly higher than normal, then a VAE may be the cause. Then you'd look for needle marks, though with a drug user that might prove problematic."

"Oh, but she wasn't a drug user, Doctor. She was a mule who had an accident with heroin capsules bursting."

"Oh, I see. Well then you might find something, unless of course the killer was able to use the catheter."

"I don't understand."

"Do you know what a catheter is?"

Nick nodded, rather uncertainly.

"Well, the nurse inserts a catheter over a needle, which is then removed, leaving direct access to the vein for any drugs administered by drip. If your killer was able to replace the drip with his own device and use the catheter, there would be no need for him to make an injection. The pathologist would only find the hole made by the needle used to put the catheter in place."

"Is this why you asked if she was wearing a catheter?"

"Actually, no. That was because most cases of VAE are caused by nurses making a mess of *changing* the catheter. It's a very dangerous process if you don't know what you're doing, or you're not paying attention."

There was a pause. It seemed Nick had run out of questions, so it was Pánagou's turn:

"So, this girl's post-mortem: will it be carried out by the hospital or by a forensic pathologist?"

"Does it matter?"

"It matters a great deal. Hospital post-mortems are looking to confirm a medical diagnosis. Any external examination is cursory, at best. Sounds like we need a forensic pathologist on the case, and fast. One who has been urged to use Richter's Technique or whatever the modern equivalent is for detecting an excess of air in the heart."

"Would you be available to assist, if I'm able to swing it?"

"With respect, that's not the way to do it, Nick. Let me have a quiet word with the local ME. Now, let me have the exact details for this girl and when and where she died."

*

After the call with Pánagou, Nick walked around to Leo's office to update him. When he'd finished, Leo lit a cigarette, then took his glasses off, leaned back in his chair and blew smoke at the ceiling.

"I think maybe you should go there after all, Nick."

"To Ioánnina?"

He nodded, the tip of his cigarette glowing as he inhaled. Then he leaned forward and stared at Nick.

"Make sure they're doing all they can to find Bel. I don't want you on the ground, getting in the way. I want you where the decisions are made. You were a very senior police officer in the UK, and you have a personal involvement in what is now a high-profile case. I'm sure I can get them to listen to what you have to say, Nick, and I think you'll feel a whole lot better if you're involved in looking for your friend."

"You're right about that."

Leo stood and opened the window to flick out his cigarette end.

"And while you're at it, you can help catch the evil guys behind this."

"Amen to that," said Nick as Leo sat down again.

"There's also the question of Lohani. This supposed suicide. Was the man ill? Was he depressed? It does seem like an extreme reaction to the threat of being deported, and, as you said, for the murderers of

Paksima, his death was rather convenient and well-timed. It needs to be investigated, Nick. Make sure it happens."

"Count on it."

"The captain's name is Eliádes. His English is better than mine. Find him and get yourself involved. Let me know if he gives you any trouble, but I don't think he will. I expect he'll be glad to have someone to help in such an important case."

"And someone to blame if everything goes pear-shaped."

"Pear-shaped?"

"Pear-shaped, tits up, kaput. If it all goes horribly wrong, Leo."

"Hmmm. Well, I hope not. He can't avoid responsibility."

"Perhaps not, but the press is another matter."

"The journalists will be on your side, Nick. You're trying to save one of their kind."

"They will, if things go well …"

He gave Leo a wry smile.

"I'll keep you posted," he said. "How are you getting on with Dropbox, by the way?"

"Stuck with the lawyers, for the moment. A subpoena should be heading their way in a couple of days."

"Can't they at least tell us if such a file exists? We could be wasting our time."

"They won't divulge any information right now. Not even that. As soon as the subpoena is live, we can push hard for answers."

"So, it could be a few days."

Leo compressed his lips and nodded.

"And Andréas?"

"Settling into rooms in Mersin. We should have a video call, the three of us, in two- or three-days' time. I'll sort that out. Now, I suggest you have a break for the rest of the day, Nick. Get yourself an early flight in the morning."

Nick took Leo at his word. It was coming up to two pm. He could book the flight now, then head down to Plakiás for a swim and an early meal and still have time to sort out clothes and documents when he got home. It would be sensible to grab a refresher, though relaxing would be out of the question, given Bel's situation. It might be the last chance for a while. He had a feeling the investigation was about to change gear.

CHAPTER 14
A POIGNANT MYTH

As soon as Daric reached the village, the road dropped and wound and twisted past small hotels and shops. There were more tourists than he had expected, ambling along the road or spilling out of shops and tavernas. They were all white, he noticed. When he reached sea level, the road narrowed and the traffic ground to a halt as a truck was unloading ice cream. Cars were hooting, Greeks waving their arms and shouting, motorbikes weaving either side of the hire car. He eased the car forward, around the truck, and found himself with a clear run to a flat, harbour area. He was relieved to see a car park, right in front of him.

As he stood and stretched, he looked back at colourful houses, hotels and tavernas tumbling down the hill to the harbour. Steep, stone stairways led to broad pavements where tourists were making their way between the crammed tables of competing tavernas. It was a rather pretty town, he decided.

In the other direction, the harbour was filled with brightly painted boats, some advertising tourist trips, others clearly working boats. Above the harbour, a small amphitheatre had been cut into the rock face, and he saw two white statues. Beyond the promontory, the islands were waiting. He walked to the end of the harbour wall and stared at them for a long time.

Stélios had noticed the large, black man in the lightweight, pale blue suit as they sat on the boat, mending nets, and he was watching him now.

"What do you make of that, Márko?" he asked his brother, jerking his head in the direction of the end of the harbour wall.

"Don't get many like him around here."

"No, and he's been there for ages. You know what?"

"What?"

"I reckon he's something to do with our boy."

Just as he stopped speaking, the man turned his head to the right, looked straight into Stélios's eyes and appeared to nod, very slightly, almost as if he had heard. Then he started walking in their direction.

"What did I tell you? Now, he's coming over."

Both men put down their work and made their way to the side of the boat. Now the man was standing on the quayside, looking at them.

"Do you speak English?" he said, in a rich, deep voice.

"Óchi," said Márkos.

"Lígo," said Stélios. "A little bit."

"I remember the name of your boat. From the news report."

"Where have you come from?" asked Stélios.

"My home. It is in Mogadishu."

"Is that in Africa?"

"Somalia, yes."

Stélios spoke a few words of Greek to his brother and saw the astonishment spread to his face.

"I have come to Crete to bury my son, but today I wanted to come here, to thank you for pulling the boy from the water. And I would like you to take me there."

He was pointing towards Paximádia. Márkos started to shake his head. Stélios saw and let fly a torrent of Greek vitriol. Then he spotted Daric pulling a leather wallet from inside his jacket.

"Óchi. You no pay," said Stélios. "It is honour for us to take you, sir. We are sorry we could not do more for your boy. Please, you will come aboard."

Daric stepped gingerly onto a plank leading to the deck and felt it give a little as he made his way across. They introduced each other and shook hands vigorously, then Daric removed his jacket and Márkos took it from him, folded it and laid it with reverence on the bench below decks.

When he returned, he was holding a one-litre, plastic bottle and three small glasses.

"Ah. Good idea, Márko," said Stélios. "You will take rakí with us, Daric?"

Daric hesitated. It had been several years since he had touched alcohol. It was prohibited by the Muslim culture in Somalia, though available if you went looking and were prepared to take the risk. He had never felt the need to do so and, as a doctor, he advised his patients against it. But now, he looked from one to the other and saw the eagerness and warmth in their faces, warmth they wanted to share. And he was a long, long way from Somalia.

"I would be delighted," he said, and smiled for the first time, showing a splendid set of very white teeth.

Márkos disappeared below again and returned with a package wrapped in kitchen paper and a small, plastic tub. When he unfolded the paper and took the lid off the tub, some Cretan rusks and chopped cucumber were revealed.

"Parakaló," he said, gesturing for Daric to help himself and then, lifting his glass, he said more words of Greek to Stélio.

"My brother says it is important to drink it quickly."

Márkos nodded and grinned, revealing several gaps in his crooked teeth, and then clinked glasses with the others and downed his rakí in one. Stélios followed suit but Daric was more circumspect. He took a large sip and started coughing as the others fell about laughing.

"Óchi! You must drink all," said Stélios, topping up his glass so he could have another go. Daric was not at all sure about this. The firewater had quite a pleasant, nutty flavour but there was also a hint of vomit in the aftertaste. He wondered just how much of the plastic container had leached into the liquid. *What the hell*, he thought. *In for a penny ...*

His second, more determined effort was met with cheers. Daric blinked several times and then reached for a rusk which almost broke his beautiful teeth. But the cucumber he found to be soft and sweet. He grinned ruefully and they slapped him on the shoulders.

A few minutes later the boat was chugging around the rocky headland beyond the harbour walls. Daric could see the white statues, lit by the evening sun. One looked like an angel.

"Who are they?" he pointed, shouting above the rumble of the engine.

"It is Greek myth," said Stélios, indicating Daric should move closer. "These two are father and son. The father, Daedalus, is famous craftsman in Athína, but he worry. His apprentice, Tálos, is getting better than him. In a jealous rage, Daedalus tries to kill Tálos, but he makes a mess of it. Now, he must escape Athína with his son. This is Icarus – the other statue. They come here, to Crete, and Daedalus goes to work for King Mínos. The king asks him to build a cage for the Minotaur. You have heard of this? It is monster: half-bull, half-man. Nobody knows about this beast and Mínos, he want to keep it that way. It's like his secret weapon. Instead of a cage, though, Daedalus has clever idea. He will build a maze so complicated that no-one could find a way through to the Minotaur. When he has built it, the king is pleased, but he want to keep his secret safe, so he puts Daedalus and Icarus in prison."

"Not a nice way to say *thank you*," observed Daric.

"No, but this man Daedalus is idiot. He should see this coming. Anyway, he make an escape plan. He and Icarus gather bird feathers and make wings for themselves, held together with wax. The wings work well. Daedalus tells his son to fly above the waves but not too high. But, when they set off, Icarus is showing off. He flies way too high, so close to the sun that the wax melts, the wings fall apart, and he fall into the sea and drown."

Daric turned back to look at the statues then and was silent for quite a while until they disappeared around the headland. Stélios saw him pull a tissue from his trouser pocket. He squeezed his shoulder, then left him to his thoughts.

The islands seemed as one from this angle, as if a giant elephant lay part-submerged, just the top of its body, head and ears visible, trunk extended.

"Eínai eléfantas," cried Márkos, pointing, and Daric lifted his head, puzzled.

"The top of the creature, you see?" said Stélios, and Daric did see and nodded and smiled, in recognition.

As they came closer, he saw there were two islands. The nearer was less than a third of the size of the forbidding, larger island with its barren rock faces.

"Nobody live here," said Stélios, rather unnecessarily, as Daric could not imagine how anyone *could* live on these giant rocks. "But here is born Apollo and Artemis." He gave Daric a quizzical look which said: *and, if you believe that, you'll believe anything.*

Then, Daric heard the engine note fall and felt the boat start wallowing. He grabbed the top of the little cabin to steady himself and saw they had motored up the channel between the islands and were now on the side facing away from the Bay of Messará; the side that faced across the Libyan Sea to the coast of Africa.

"It is here," said Stélios.

"This is where you found him?"

Both fishermen nodded, though Stélios was not sure if *found* was the right word for what had happened. He decided not to argue the point.

Daric stared at the forbidding beauty of the place, the colours in the rocks, the crystal-clear sea. As the setting sun flickered over the water, for a moment he thought he saw the white feathers of a large bird floating face down, but then the shadows moved, the surf rippled and the illusion was gone, and he found himself wondering why he had come here. Perhaps the psychologists would say he was seeking closure. *That dreadful word.* Or perhaps Yasir had drawn him here. Was this somehow a farewell message from his son?

He felt a nudge to his elbow and saw Márkos offering him another glass of rakí but this time he declined with a sad smile. Márkos put down the glasses and gave the big man a salty hug.

*

When Andréas agreed to take his chances in Mersin, he had not reckoned with the nightmare of just getting there. Mersin was without an airport, which he found surprising. The nearest was somewhere called Adana. The short hop from Chaniá to Athína was easy enough, but then there was an hour and a half's wait for the flight to Sabiha Gökçen airport at Istanbul, followed by an almost two-hour wait for the third leg to Adana. When he got there, it would still be eighty kilometres to Mersin, so at least an hour's taxi ride. It would be four pm before he could check in. He reckoned he would be ready for a shower and a beer or two by then.

*

The day after Andréas arrived in Mersin, Nick was on his way to Ioánnina. It was a much simpler trip: the Sky Express to Athína and then a wait of an hour and three-quarters for the Olympic flight direct to Ioánnina, which took a further hour. By mid-afternoon, he had grabbed some lunch and was entering the police headquarters. A cream-coloured, pillared ground floor with barred windows supported a tired-looking, five-storey office building. Air-conditioning units clung untidily to the outside of most of the windows, seemingly as an afterthought, and a ragged Greek flag billowed blue and white from a pole protruding from the second floor. He tripped up the stairs and went through the rotating door.

"I'm here to see Captain Eliádes," he said to the desk sergeant.

"Your name is?"

"Nick Fisher."

"One moment, Mr Fisher. You will please take a seat over there."

He indicated a sofa covered in a shiny, blue material. Rips exposed the yellow foam interior and there were cigarette burns despite the *No Smoking* signs on the wall. Nick did as he was told, sat down, and waited. After almost ten minutes, a dark-haired man who looked to be in his mid-thirties stepped out of the lift and came over.

"Mr Fisher?"

Nick got to his feet, grabbed the extended hand, and shook it.

"I am Lieutenant Kallis," he said, in English.

"I thought I was to see the captain."

"He is busy today and has asked me to welcome you and tell you about the case."

"Are you involved, then?"

The lieutenant tilted his head and raised an eyebrow.

"Rather more than the captain, Mr Fisher, if you know what I mean."

100

Nick knew exactly what he meant, and grinned. They were going to get along just fine. He followed him back into the lift and they rode up to the third floor, down a corridor and into a meeting room without windows. A constable was ordered to bring coffees and water.

"The first thing to say, Mr Fisher, is that we respect the team at Chaniá, and are pleased to welcome you here to work with us."

"Well, that's good to hear."

"I understand Ms Saidi is a good friend of yours, so you have our condolences."

Nick's heart missed a beat.

"Oh, you've found her, then," he said, trying to keep his voice steady.

"No. Just her phone. And no trace of the SIM card, yet."

Nick breathed again.

"So, is there still room for hope, Lieutenant?"

"Please call me Mike."

"Mike?"

"Michális, but Mike is easier, I think."

"Okay, and I'm Nick. Is there hope, Mike?" he repeated.

"I'll be straight with you, Nick. Until we find a body, there is always hope, but we know she was followed by these guys, and they seem to be killers."

"Could they have kidnapped her?"

"They could, but we must ask ourselves why. There have been no demands from any kidnappers, no contact, so far."

"Maybe they need to find out what she knows about them ..."

... *before they kill her* was the unspoken end to the sentence and both men knew it. The likeliest scenario was torture, then death. They exchanged bleak looks.

"We will hope for the best but prepare for the worst, Nick," said Mike.

"Okay, but I want to do a lot more than sit around hoping. Will you take me through what you guys have done so far?"

Mike listed all the usual missing person procedures. Ports and airports had been alerted. Local snitches probed. Announcements made in the press and on both radio and national television but so far, they had yielded nothing. The hospital car park and grounds had been searched.

"What about her car?" said Nick.

"We don't know what she was driving."

"Come on, Mike. It must have been a hire car, so check with the hire companies for a contract in her name. And what about the footage from the car park camera? Which cars were still sitting there at four in the morning?"

"It's not a great camera position."

"Are there other cameras? Is the car park a franchise? Does the company running the car park have cameras at the pay stations or the gate? I bet they do, to catch vandals or accidents with the barrier or people trying to abscond without paying."

Mike was sitting up straighter now, Nick noticed.

"My guess is you'll find the hire car is still there, running up a bill. If they kidnapped her, it would be much easier to do so in the car park than on the road later."

"We will check this."

"In that scenario, the kidnappers would also have a car in that car park, which then left, with Bel in it. See if you can spot them on any available footage – from the hospital or the car park company – or, if that doesn't work, get a list of registration plates from them – all the vehicles leaving within thirty minutes of Paksima's death. I'd guess there's less than a hundred. You can then try to match those plates with your traffic cameras to track their movements."

"So, if they kidnapped her, where would they go?"

It was far too early to speculate. Nick ignored the question.

"What else do we know about them, Mike?"

"We ran the images of them at the hospital past our national database but couldn't find a match. We're waiting to hear from Interpol."

"So, they are likely to be foreign nationals. Logical, then, to assume they came to Greece to do their dirty work and now they are ready to leave, with or without Bel. Airports are out, if they have her with them so, unless they have a private plane or helicopter, we are looking at an escape by road or sea. Start with the car once you've identified it. Where's the nearest port?"

"Igoumenítsa. It's about an hour's drive."

"The port Paksima came from, right?"

"Right, but we assumed they were following Bel, not Paksima."

"Do we know, for sure?"

"Bel has been watched and followed, in the past."

"Assad's men, I know. Suppose, instead, these guys were after Paksima. Maybe they followed her here to keep her quiet."

"And just happened to encounter Bel?"

"Perhaps, or they heard Paksima was going to meet up with Bel."

"How would they know that?"

"There would have to be a leak from within the hospital. Anyway, let's start by identifying their car, then we can focus on Igoumenítsa and the motorways heading out of Ioánnina, particularly those heading out of Greece."

"Well, from here, the quickest way out of Greece is north, on the E853. Going south gets you nowhere and going east takes forever, just to leave Greece."

"And west?"

"That's the Igoumenítsa road."

"Where do you get to heading north, then?"

"Albania."

They paused to drink their coffees and reflect on the road map of Greece which was tacked to the office wall.

"Do you want to break for ten minutes and get your team focused on the search for the two cars?" said Nick. It was an instruction, not a question, Mike understood. "And then we need to talk about Paksima."

When Mike returned, Nick cut straight to the point:

"Where's her body now, Mike?"

"Still at the hospital, as far as I know."

"You're not sure?"

"I believe she's in the hospital morgue."

"Has the post-mortem begun?"

"I don't know."

"All right. I want you to call the hospital right now. Check if the body is in the morgue and stop the post-mortem or prevent it from starting."

Mike looked askance, so Nick continued:

"We suspect foul play, do we not?"

Mike was nodding.

"Then a hospital post-mortem isn't going to do it. We need a forensic pathologist to go through the body with a fine-tooth comb."

"A tooth comb? What the hell is that?"

"I mean, to use sophisticated forensics to test for criminal activity. We don't want the hospital to carry out a post-mortem that will destroy evidence and make certain techniques impossible afterwards. They'll only confirm Paksima died of a heart attack after a heroin overdose. That might be the case, but I'm betting it's not the whole story."

Mike was reaching for the phone, but Nick was still talking as he dialled:

"The body must be moved into the care of the medical examiner for Epirus right away and I need him to have a conversation with Pánagou, the ME for Chaniá before he starts the PM. She has a theory I'm sure he'll want to explore."

Nick suspected the conversation may have already taken place, but there was no harm in pushing from this end, too. Mike was talking now and meeting some resistance. Nick could hear only his side of the conversation.

"No, I most certainly *do* have the authority. This is police business … Because we suspect foul play. The girl may have been murdered in your hospital … No. Absolutely not. You must stop right now and wait. Do not touch the body … All right. I appreciate it's irregular … Good. Thank you. The ME will be in touch. Do nothing until then."

Mike disconnected and looked at Nick.

"We were just in time," he said, "she had the body prepared and was about to make the first incision."

"Bloody hell," said Nick, "that would have been a disaster."

"She wasn't happy, but I think she'll wait."

"She'd better."

"I'll call the Medical Examiner."

The ME for Epirus was on another call, but Mike was able to leave a detailed message. He stressed the importance of taking control of Paksima's post-mortem as a matter of urgency. He also mentioned Pánagou, Nick heard, in the stream of Greek.

Afterwards, Nick said:

"Turning to Lohani, could that be murder, too? Could the same guy have pursued the good doctor to his home and strung him up while his mate was abducting Bel?"

"My first thought too, Nick, but I don't think so. It looked like a genuine suicide to me."

"But the timing is so perfect for the bad guys."

"I know."

"Did he have a history of mental problems, depression?"

"No. Nothing like that."

"Would you mind if I took a look at the crime scene, snooped around a bit? I'd like to be sure we've got this right. If we're unable to prove Paksima's murder, we might get them on this one, after all."

"If it *was* murder."

"Why would a successful young man working hard in his chosen profession top himself, just like that?"

"You know his immigration papers were forged?"

"I did hear something, but surely that's not enough to string yourself up?"

"I don't know, Nick. It might be. It really might. It could destroy his life."

It was not what Nick wanted to hear, and the sick feeling surged back into his gut.

"But by all means take a look," Mike was saying. "A second opinion is always welcome. I'll get you a copy of the file."

*

The apartment was in a small, three-storey block in Mavroyiánni, an area in the north of the town, just inland from Límni Pamvótida, the lake which forms the eastern border of the town. There was a card entry system, and normally Nick would wait for someone to come out and then pat his pockets, proffer a rueful smile, and they would hold the door for him. Just like the murderer if there was one. Today though, none of that was necessary. He knew there was a police presence, so he rang the one labelled *Flat 8* and a constable buzzed him in.

Nick could see no signs of forced entry at the door to the top-floor apartment, *so perhaps Doctor Lohani let his killers in, on some pretext,* Nick thought.

"That's where he did it, sir," said the constable, pointing to a beam which traversed the vaulted ceiling. "Stood on that chair, which was on its side when he was found, and used that."

He was pointing to a coil of thin rope, lying beside the chair.

"It's five-millimetre nylon rope, sir. Very strong. You can buy it at any hardware store. We found a receipt in the kitchen bin. Made himself a hangman's knot of sorts. He must have known something about knots because it worked all right. Poor devil was purple and black when we found him."

"Any note?"

"We haven't found one, sir, and no messages on his laptop or phone."

"Have you spoken with the neighbours?"

"All very shocked, as you would expect, sir. No-one saw it coming. Nervous guy, excitable perhaps, but he worked hard. A great sense of humour, some said, but kept to himself, as a rule."

Nick looked around the place. It was minimalist, functional, not much in the fridge. It was the apartment of a single man who worked too hard and had no time to build a balanced life. There was no sign of any female visitors, few comforts.

Nick thanked the constable and started knocking on the neighbours' doors with a copy of the image from the hospital entrance. He asked if they remembered seeing either of these men or letting them into the building. No-one did.

The general hospital was in the same direction and not far from the apartment. Nick decided to walk there and discovered a modern, white and cream building with forest green windows. It had three principal floors, each set back, so as to find shade from the overhanging roof. A row of dormer windows in the terracotta tiled roof suggesting a fourth. The building was less than fifteen years old, he guessed, but it had not been maintained and was already looking shoddy, here and there. That irritated Nick because it seemed to be an attractive and well-designed, functional building. It was in a pleasant location, too, in the far north-west of the town, with wooded areas on three sides and a dual carriage-way on the fourth. There was a distant view of the mountains.

Assuming the role of a visitor, Nick soon found room 208 cordoned off with yellow tape. That was not a problem, he had no need to view the room. He was more interested in talking to people. He made his way to the reception area nearest Paksima's room and felt for the photograph in his pocket.

*

When Nick made it back to the police station, he went straight to the office of Lieutenant Michális Kallis. Unlike most of the Greeks, Mike did not smoke, and his office was air-conditioned. Nick welcomed the cool air after his sweaty walk back from the hospital.

"I've got something," he grinned.

"Go on."

"I found a witness. At the hospital. An orderly on the first floor recognised the picture of our killer. Said he seemed to be harassing our young doctor."

"Lohani?"

"Yep."

"But our girl was on the top floor, wasn't she?"

"Yes. Room numbers starting with two are on the second floor. This was the floor below; the floor where Lohani worked."

Mike leaned forward in his chair.

"When did the orderly see this?"

"He says he was on mornings that week, so his shift would have ended at two pm. He thinks it was Tuesday or Wednesday. Said Lohani looked humiliated, but also scared."

"So, this is either three or twenty-seven hours before the interview, at least."

"Right. Paksima had been admitted but Bel had not arrived."

"Did the guy hear what was said?"

"No. They stopped talking when they saw him."

"We'd better get this guy in for a formal statement."

"I told him to expect a call."

Nick handed him a slip of paper.

"This is his name and mobile number."

"What's your take on it, Nick?"

"Sounds like Lohani was being threatened, doesn't it? Maybe these guys had something on him. Perhaps they forged his papers for him, or they knew he was an illegal, somehow. Whatever it was, they had him between a rock and a hard place. I assumed they were after information: Paksima's room number, maybe also security arrangements. Did Lohani also tell them Bel was due to visit if he knew? Then, I remembered the drugs."

"What drugs?"

"The drugs Paksima was carrying, of course. I read it in the file. When they took the heroin out of her, there were fifty-three intact capsules totalling one point three kilogrammes. By my reckoning, a street value of around one hundred and seventy thousand euros. The hospital didn't give that a thought. Just popped the capsules in the back of the drugs fridge, at the bottom. I asked Doctor Marás to show me. And guess what?"

"Gone? Oh, shit! We were told that the medics had destroyed them. We weren't too pleased, as you can imagine."

"Sounds like that message came from Lohani. During his conversation with the killer, I'm guessing Lohani was tasked with getting the drugs back for them. These guys weren't about to drop that kind of money. Two burst capsules were bad enough, but the other fifty-three? No way.

"Earlier, I went to Lohani's place, and I agree with you; it looks like a genuine suicide. If it was *his* information that led to Bel's disappearance, the loss of the heroin and Paksima's death, it could have been too much for him. And these guys would always have this hold over him. He'd lost control of his life and disgrace was looming, with probable repatriation – to the Taliban. Too much to bear."

"Sounds right, Nick. How terrible for the young man."

There was a pause. Nick could almost see the cogs and wheels spinning in Mike's brain.

"But how on earth did you find this guy, the orderly?" he said.

"Just tedious legwork and a bit of luck. I asked pretty much everyone I saw. Not so much the doctors and nurses, more the administrative staff: the cleaners, receptionists, orderlies and so on. I figured they might have a little more time to spot things. Also, if I pestered the medical staff, I was more likely to get moved on."

"It must have taken a while."

"I was there for three hours."

Mike's admiration of his persistence was evident from the raised eyebrows and the slight turn of the head.

"Also, I just had a call from Pánagou."

"Your ME lady?"

"Yes. She's been asked to join a video call with your ME during his forensic examination of Paksima, later today. They're going to pool their knowledge on some tricky procedures."

"That's good."

Nick moved to stand but Mike waved him down again.

"I have progress to report, too. You were right, Nick. Bel hired a white Suzuki Swift at the airport and was supposed to return it by eight pm the same day. We found it in the car park with the keys in the ignition. I doubt she would leave it like that, so it sounds like the kidnappers bundled her out of that car and into theirs. We found nothing of hers in the car."

"What about identifying *their* car?"

"We struck gold. The barriers have ANPR cameras that record the time and registration plates of all cars entering or leaving the car park. We have a list of forty-seven plates: vehicles leaving the car park between six and six thirty. I have a team liaising with the traffic police to see which plates we can match with motorway footage on roads out of Ioánnina."

"Especially those heading north or west?"

"Indeed."

"Brilliant. Put everything you've got behind this, Mike. It looks like Bel was in that car. The sooner we trace them, the more chance she'll still be alive."

*

Later, Nick brought Leo up to speed with the vehicle tracing and their latest theories about Lohani's role.

"Good work, Nick. How are you getting on with Kallis?"

"He's not the sharpest tool in the box, but he's catching on fast."

Leo chuckled.

"They must be mortified at losing the drugs," Nick went on. "They should have seized them soon after they were extracted from Paksima."

"Perhaps no-one told them."

"Well, right after her death, then. They must have been aware then."

"That might already have been too late."

"And they don't seem to have got the hang of tracing vehicles."

"I think they have now, Nick."

"I've seen nothing of the captain."

"You won't, if things go well."

"Isn't that always the way?"

"Hotel all right? Are we looking after you?"

"It's fine. Functional, comfortable. Ioánnina's quite a nice town."

"Good. So, I have updates, too. I believe the post-mortem is under-way up there. We should hear the results first thing in the morning."

"Excellent."

"And our subpoena will be served this evening at seven pm. That's nine am in San Francisco."

"How do you expect them to react?"

"Oh, I think they'll be co-operative as soon as the legal process is completed."

"And they've covered their arses."

"Data security is everything in their business, Nick. Their reputation depends on it."

"When will we get the files?"

"Given the time difference, they'll have all day to get them to us before we wake up."

"Big day tomorrow, then."

"With luck, yes."

Nick disconnected and flipped through the hotel room service menu in search of inspiration. Minutes later, he was walking out of the hotel in search of a beer and a good taverna.

CHAPTER 15
OUR MAN IN MERSIN

By the end of his second day in Mersin, Andréas was familiar with most of the bars around the harbour area and feeling a little worse for wear as a result. He developed a routine, which he used if the place looked at all suitable. He would sit at the bar with a beer or maybe a rakí or a Turkish coffee and do his best to look worried and depressed, with the aid of a newspaper. As a rotund and naturally cheerful, if undemonstrative, fellow, it was not the easiest of roles for him to adopt. But it had the desired effect. After a while, the owner, or in some cases a fellow customer, would ask him if everything was okay. He would then make some general comment such as: *The world's going to shit. It's all getting me down.* He needed to bolster his limited Turkish with some broken English at times, but most of them seemed to understand him perfectly well.

The responses were either a general: *How do you mean?* or quite often a specific guess as to the source of his concern, as in: *You mean climate change?* That was quite a popular suggestion with temperatures hovering around forty degrees Celsius most afternoons and alarming reports hitting the press from other parts of the world. Others wondered if it was the exchange rate crisis, the economy or the pandemic getting to him. *No,* he would cry, waving his newspaper. *It's the goddamned refugee crisis. These poor bastards from Syria.*

That was guaranteed to get a reaction, he soon discovered, though not always a helpful one. Some resented the refugees and made general statements about them without foundation: how crime rates had soared, women were being molested, their children were begging on the streets, jobs were being stolen by the few who were prepared to do any work. And Turks were having to cope almost single-handed with the problem.

Others were more empathetic. There but for the Grace of Allah go we. Either way, Andréas would bring his imaginary brother into the conversation at an opportune moment.

"Your brother is there – in Syria?" they would ask, concerned, and he would respond:

"He's an engineer, been there on contract for three years now, but it's all turned to shit. They won't let him leave, but they haven't paid him for months. Now, he's afraid for his family."

By now, there would be a small crowd of Turkish men gathered around him, keen to help. Okay, the guy was Greek, but he was in a spot and, like men everywhere, they needed to come up with a solution for him.

"Can't you help him?"

"Does he have money?"

"Where is his family?"

After the usual barrage of questions, Andréas would appear to go through agonies of soul searching before saying:

"I think the time has come to get him out of there. He has money. Somebody said a guy called Adil might be able to help."

This brought shrugs or suggestions of other names. Mobile phone numbers were offered. More often they demanded Andréas's number, saying: "Don't worry. My guy will call you. Very soon."

Andréas had no way of knowing if these were genuine contacts for people smuggling operations or just some cousin who would do anything for a few thousand euros. Of the contacts he was given, only one ever called and soon the guy was bluffing answers to Andréas's most basic questions.

On the third day, however, it was different. He tried Borsa Atatürk and noticed a younger man amongst the group this time. When he mentioned the name, the man became agitated.

"Where did you hear this name, Adil?"

"A friend of a friend."

"What friend? You will tell me, please."

The words were polite enough, but insistent. Andréas could see there was danger here. He would have to think on his feet. The other men were moving away. They did not want any trouble.

"I don't know his name. I met him here, in Mersin; a young man, like you. This Adil helped his sister to escape Syria – a boat from here, I think."

"From Mersin? Are you crazy?" he hissed.

"I thought it was Mersin. A long sea trip to Italy. It was not cheap."

The young man took his elbow.

"Come."

Outside he looked around him and then put his mouth close to Andréas's ear.

"We do not talk of these things. Do you understand?"

He moved back to look straight into Andréas's eyes and receive a brief nod.

"You will give me your number."

Andréas scribbled it on a page in his notebook and tore it out.

"It might be a day, maybe two, but Adil will call you."

The young man searched his eyes again for some acknowledgement and then turned and walked away, disappearing around the corner into the crowd of shoppers. Andréas breathed a sigh of relief, at least for now. But he knew this was when it would get dangerous.

CHAPTER 16

WADING THROUGH TREACLE

Leo's optimism was premature. The email from Dropbox listed all file names attached to the account of Isobel Saidi and asked the police to identify which they needed by ticking a box next to each file name. Leo was furious. This could have happened yesterday. A whole day had been wasted. They would be asleep in California now. Nothing would happen till mid-evening, Greek time.

He scanned the list. It was a hierarchy of over thirty folders, each with sub-folders and files. He saw from the *last updated* record that many of the files had not been accessed for several years. Some related to her time in the second Iraq war or when she worked for The Independent. After fifteen minutes, he had narrowed the search to just six possible folders. All had been updated in the last two months. He went down through the levels and scanned the file names for anything named *Interview with Paksima* or similar. There was nothing. His heart sank. *Has this all been a waste of time? Did they get to Bel before she was able to upload the file?* He clicked on each of the six folder names and returned the email to the company. He wanted to send a stinging rebuke along with it but knew that would only make matters worse. He resolved to call them, mid-evening, to make sure they released the content without further delay.

An email from the Medical Examiner for Epirus also arrived early. There were several technical attachments, he saw, and it had all been copied to the captain and lieutenant at Ioánnina as well as Pánagou. The text of the email made things crystal-clear:

I concluded my examination of the body of Paksima X (surname unknown) last evening with the valued assistance of the ME for Chaniá, Doctor Pánagou. We cooperated on a technique to determine the volume of air in the heart tissue, and concluded it was between two and a half and three times higher than might have been expected, given the medical diagnosis of her death (see attachments for process and conclusions). This led us to suspect a VAE (venous air embolism) may have developed in Paksima's blood system. The most likely cause of this would be either (a) a poorly managed change of catheter or (b) a deliberate injection of air from a hypodermic syringe. In pursuit of (b) I then removed the catheter from the patient's left arm and micro-examined the tissue surrounding the AC veins of both forearms and was able to detect damage caused by the inexpert use of a large needle to the right forearm, close to the inside of the elbow (see attachment).

By eight twenty-five, Leo was calling Nick's hotel. Nick listened for two minutes, then responded:

"So, whoever these bastards are, they murdered Paksima, stole back the heroin, caused Lohani's suicide and kidnapped Bel, all in the space of a day or two."

"It looks like it, Nick. At least, we hope they kidnapped her …"

*

When Nick made it to the police station, Mike was looking excited.

"I think we have their vehicle," he said.

"The killers' vehicle?"

"We took the list of forty-seven plates and ran the numbers against footage from the motorway cameras."

"Footage?"

Mike gave him a pained look.

"We don't have ANPR cameras everywhere like in the UK, Nick. There are a few on the busiest stretches but not around here. These are traffic flow cameras."

"Doesn't that mean you have to look at all the cars, try to see all the registration plates at the same time as remembering forty-seven numbers to watch for?"

"Yes, pretty much. Not practical on very busy roads, but these are not so busy. It's possible to see almost all the numbers and, if you have a narrow time window, it's not quite as onerous as it sounds. But forty-seven is too many to remember so we had four constables memorise a dozen or so numbers each and sat them in front of footage from the traffic flow cameras on the E90 Ioánnina-Igoumenítsa highway and then the E853 Ioánnina-Kalpáki-Kakavijë route into Albania. We knew it wasn't perfect because the boys might forget their numbers or fail to spot them on the screens, but we got three hits."

"Wow! So, these are vehicles recorded as leaving the hospital in your time window and then spotted on one of these roads afterwards."

"Right. And spotted within ninety minutes of leaving the hospital. When we looked at the three, something became obvious. One of the vehicles had a foreign plate: two letters, a space, then three numbers followed by two more numbers. Greek plates are three letters, a space then four numbers. It was hard to see, but there might have been a double-headed eagle to the left of the plate with the letters AL, all in white on blue."

"Albania. So, was this on the E853, headed north?"

"It was. We zoomed in on the footage, but the quality was not so good. It was a black 4x4, though, and we could see a badge. Our best guess is it's a Hilux; definitely a Toyota."

"Great work, Mike. Can we track it in Albania?"

"No. They have no cameras. I'd have been tempted to call up a helicopter but, of course, they were long gone."

"No cameras? This *is* the twenty-first century, right?"

"Yes, but forty years ago, those guys were still using horse-drawn ploughs. They've come a long way in a short time, but cameras might take a few more years."

"But we can trace the registered owner, at least, from the plates."

"The Albanians can, yes. We're waiting to hear. I'm hopeful it won't be too long."

*

Nick was staring out of the window. The very first hints of autumn were appearing after the long, dry months. Leaves were yellowing on some of the trees and the fierce heat of midsummer was starting to wane, the evenings getting shorter. The swallows would return to Africa soon and, in a few short weeks, there would be mists on the surface of the lake, snow on those mountains. Perhaps it was his British heritage, he wondered, that made him feel sad at this time of year. In England, it would soon be time to say farewell to the sun for another year and face the dreary greyness and chill drizzle of six long winter months. Here, there was often an Indian Summer right through to Christmas. January and February were always grim, with howling gales, thunder and lightning, monsoon rains and sometimes heavy snow on the higher ground; a short, sharp shock of a winter, but still with frequent sightings of the sun. Not too much to dread. And yet …

The knock on the door was brief, then Mike opened it.

"Nick? I have news. Some good; some not so good."

They sat on either side of the desk.

"Tell me."

"The Albanians have traced the vehicle registration details. It *is* a Toyota Hilux, black with darkened windows and other modifications. About four years old."

Mike paused for a moment. *All as expected so far*, thought Nick, *so this must be where the not so good news arrives.*

"The owner lives in a suburb of Tirana and owns a tyre franchise." Another pause. "He reported it stolen three weeks ago."

"Bugger."

"It gets worse. They found the vehicle in Sarandë. It's been torched."

"Was there …?"

"There was no-one inside, Nick."

"And Sarandë is where?"

"It's an Albanian resort, just north of the Greek border."

"On the Adriatic?"

"Yes, Nick, of course. It's just above Corfu."

"So, not far from Igoumenítsa."

"Fifty or sixty kilometres. What are you thinking, Nick?"

"Would there be a harbour there?"

"I think there's a marina. Pretty small."

"We were asking ourselves if the killers were connected with the boat Paksima came from. Perhaps they went back to meet the same boat at Sarandë."

"Could be."

"This guy, the owner of the vehicle. Are they sure he's not involved, and the theft of the vehicle was genuine?"

"Seems so. He's a family man who seldom leaves Tirana."

"Bit of a flash vehicle for a family man."

"Yes, but he's in the motor trade, isn't he? You get that sometimes, don't you?"

"I guess you do. How long since they torched it?"

"It happened Tuesday night. The police were already aware. They assumed it was joyriders till we got in touch."

Three weeks is a lot of joy, Nick thought. *Do these guys know what they're doing?*

It was Friday lunchtime now, so the bastards had a head start of two and a half days. Should they be looking for a boat now, or another road vehicle? Would they be in Albania, Greece or somewhere else? Italy, maybe? Did they still have Bel with them, or had they dumped her body somewhere? They could be a thousand miles away by now, Nick realised.

"We're fucked, Mike." he said.

*

Leo put in the call to California at seven fifteen pm. The Americans should have been at work for a little while. He was directed to Melody Schreiber, VP of data security. She sounded about sixteen and had a singsong voice with a placatory tone that put Leo's back up:

"Oh hi, Mister Crysto-doo-la-kiss. Is that right? Is that how you say it?"

"It is Lieutenant, in fact, but call me Leo. It might be easier for you."

"Oh, pardon me. Of course, you're a police officer, Leo. In Greece, right?"

"That is correct, Melody. I wanted to make sure you received my email."

"You mean your folder selections? Sure, I have them right here."

"So, can you release the content of the folders to me now?"

"Almost. We have certain protocols to follow. First, we'll copy these files to a new folder which we will then encrypt. Then, I need my boss's approval to go ahead and release the information and, before we do, I'll need to notify Ms Saidi that we are going to share some of her data."

Leo wanted to be certain this time.

"You don't need Ms Saidi's *approval*, as I understand it."

"You're quite right. We don't. It's like a courtesy? You made your case and now we're cooperating with the police in a legitimate investigation. So, we must share the minimum, relevant data, as required by law. But we also have a duty to keep her informed."

"And your boss's approval – is that going to be a problem?"

"Should be a formality, Leo. I've been doing this for eight years now and I know the process, but he has to confirm that I've followed our security procedures to the letter. We take client confidentiality very seriously, here at Dropbox."

"So, when can I expect to receive the folders?"

"All being well, later today."

"In the next hour or two would be good. You see, it's nearly eight pm here, Melody. I can work on it tonight if you're quick. And it might help me find a woman who's in danger."

"All right, Leo. That sounds real important. I'm gonna see what I can do for you, okay? Don't go to bed just yet."

The email arrived at ten thirteen. Leo was home by then but checking his emails often. There was a password protected procedure to unlock the files and then he was in. Bel Saidi's private files in six sub-folders. He poured himself a mug of strong coffee and started trawling through.

*

Andréas heard nothing from the mysterious Adil the next day and realised he had no way of contacting the young man from the bar other than drinking endless coffees at Borsa Attatürk in the hope he might reappear. That was not a great idea. Some of those other guys might be regulars and the young man did not want any attention drawn to him. Instead, later in the afternoon when it was a little cooler, he decided to check out the port and the marina. A call with Leo and Nick was scheduled for the following morning and he wanted to make sure he had done his homework.

It soon became obvious that a stroll between the two was impractical. The distances were too great in this spacious, urban sprawl of a city and anyway, it was still far too hot. He took a cab to the port to begin with, a seven-kilometre ride as it turned out. From the dual carriageway, he could see steel containers in muted, matt colours stacked six-high behind wire fencing. He asked the cab driver to wait half an hour while he took a stroll around. Containers were everywhere, hundreds of them. There were half a dozen dockside cranes for lifting them on and off ships and two ships were in the process of loading, he saw. Another five or six ships were docked nearby, along with some sort of naval gunship with a helipad towards the stern. There were functional offices and warehousing and rows of silos containing God knows what. Altogether, a much larger, more industrial enterprise than he had imagined. Why had he expected anything less? It was a little like Piraeus without the ferries and rather more organised, he had to admit.

They drove up the coast then, to the west of the city. The dual carriageway ran past palm trees and advertising hoardings to an area of modern apartment blocks, ten to twenty stories high: quite smart, functional buildings in cream or pale terracotta. They would not win any design awards, but this pragmatic style of living must suit the Turks, he thought. It did not appeal to him at all. He loved his garden behind the small house in the suburbs of Athína with the shady walnut and fig trees and the sound of running water dribbling from the stone fountain.

The marina was tucked behind a line of trees and greenery. Andréas paid off the cab and strolled past a parking area onto a concrete apron. The harbour wall circled two-thirds of the way around, anti-clockwise, and a quarter of the way clockwise, providing a good measure of protection while leaving a narrow entrance. The setting was not a natural harbour; the structure was built into the water from a straight, featureless coastline. Andréas counted six jetties extending from the apron, with boats moored either side of them. There would be capacity for two hundred, maybe two hundred and fifty boats. *Their boats are like their apartment blocks,* he thought, *functional rather than pretty.*

Would either the port or the marina be a good place for embarking a boatload of illegal migrants? Andréas's answer would have to be an unequivocal *No.* There had been metal towers with security cameras at the port and no provision for smaller boats, which would look out of place there, anyway. Here, at the marina, there was nowhere to hide, no quiet shady corners. Everything was open and bright and would be well-lit, even at night. It was hard to imagine a small crowd of foreigners going unnoticed, unless they used a careful system of boarding one every few minutes over the space of an hour or two.

He had seen enough. He would head back to the hotel, cool off in the pool and grab some dinner, then write up his notes. Maybe he could find a map of the wider Mersin area.

*

The video call was set for ten am. Leo was in a meeting room at the Chaniá police headquarters with an iced coffee and a cigarette. Nick was in a room at Ioánnina police station with a Nescafé and a fresh spanakópita and Andréas was in his hotel room in Mersin with a bottle of water and the air conditioning on full. Once they overcame the technology, it was Leo who spoke first.

"Well, gentlemen. Kaliméra sas. I hope you have good news for us, Nick?"

Nick took them through the successful identification of the Toyota 4x4, then the revelation that it had been stolen and torched.

"So," said Leo, "we don't know *who* the killers are, we don't know *where* they are, and we don't know where Bel is, or whether she is alive or dead."

"About right, I'm afraid," said Nick. "We know they were in Sarandë on Tuesday night, but they could be in Timbuktu by now. We know what they've been driving for the last three weeks, but we don't know what we're looking for now – a different car, a boat or something else, and we don't know where to start looking."

"Did you get anything from Interpol, Leo?" asked Andréas.

"Our guys are not known to them, based on these images, but they are happy to try again if we can get better mugshots."

"Like that's going to happen," said Nick.

There was a despondent pause.

"This Toyota. Was it a pick-up truck, by any chance?" asked Leo.

"Yep. It was a Hilux, black, about four years old," Nick replied.

"Tinted windows, fat tyres?"

Nick looked back through his notes.

"Er … it had darkened windows and *other modifications*, so maybe, yes."

"You remember that hit and run – the boy in Chaniá?"

"Ollie's lad, Jamal, you mean?"

"Of course, you met Oliver Dunham."

"The day of our lunch, yes."

"I was just wondering. A long shot, but it sounds like a similar vehicle."

"True, but Sarandë is a hell of a long way from Chaniá," said Nick.

They saw Andréas raise a hand.

"You've lost me, guys."

"Sorry, Andréa. A young boy was hit by a similar vehicle in Chaniá a couple of weeks back. It looked like a hit and run. His father, Oliver Dunham, has a motor yacht and says he operates a charter business."

"The boat's called Destiny," added Nick, "registered in Larnaca, Cyprus."

"Well, long shot or not, I can ask around in Mersin," said Andréas.

"And I can get the Albanian cops onto Sarandë. And I can get over to Igoumenítsa myself," said Nick.

"What else have you got, Andréa?" asked Leo.

Andréas went on to tell them about the linkman he had found and how he was waiting to hear from the man himself, Adil.

"Do you think he was genuine, this young man?" asked Leo.

"Yes, I think so. Maybe they're checking me out, before getting in touch."

"You're using a false name, aren't you?"

"False everything. Don't worry. They won't be able to trace me back to the police."

"They'd better not, for your sake."

Andréas continued by telling them what he had discovered at the port and the marina.

"It doesn't feel right, Leo. I can't see a boatload of illegal migrants boarding a motor yacht in either location, even at night. It would be impossible to achieve covertly."

"So, what next?"

"I'm going to explore the area nearby and see if I can come up with any ideas. I'll go back to the bar if I don't hear from Adil in the next twenty-four hours, and I'll start asking around about this boat Destiny, starting with the harbourmaster. Do you have pictures?"

"No, but we can do some research and send you something similar, I'm sure."

"What about this guy, Dunham?"

"I'll send you what we have on him."

"Watch yourself, Andréa," said Nick. "These are dangerous bastards."

There was a pause, then Nick spoke again.

"What about the Dropbox files, Leo. Any news?"

"I have the data, at last. Six folders containing a total of forty-five files, mostly Word documents. I worked through them last night and I have constables going through them again right now."

"And?"

"It doesn't look good, Nick. If there was a file of the interview with Paksima, I don't think she uploaded it."

"Shit. So, they got to her first."

"We're still checking, just to be sure."

"What about the other folders, the ones you didn't even ask for?"

"We're double-checking those as well. If there's any doubt, we'll go back to Dropbox for them, too."

"Jesus," said Nick. "We don't have much, do we? Two murders that might or might not be linked, a suicide that appears to have been provoked and a kidnapping – at least we hope it's a kidnapping – and we've got bugger all to go on for any of them."

"Let's think about what we *do* have," said Leo, trying to sound positive. They saw him move over to a white board in his office and raise his voice. He wrote the number one.

"First, we have two bodies, Yasir and Paksima." He wrote: *Two Bodies*. "We *know* they were murdered. Yasir didn't slit his own throat and the medics are as sure as they can be that Paksima was injected with air." He wrote the number two and *Proof of Murder* beside it.

"We don't know who killed Yasir, but we know it happened on a boat that left Mersin, maybe the same boat that brought Paksima from Mersin to Igoumenítsa. If she were alive, she might be able to tell us. Or, if we had the recording of her interview with Bel, *that* might tell us. We *do* know who killed Paksima – at least we have their pictures from the security footage – we just need to *identify* them. It seems probable they are Albanians, maybe known criminals." He wrote the number three, and beside it: *Killers of Paksima – visual evidence*.

"I just had a thought," said Nick. "We haven't checked any footage from the hospital cameras on the *first* floor. They never sent that, but surely, they will have cameras on the first floor if they have them on the second. Why wouldn't they? Maybe we could get a better sighting of the perp who talked to Lohani?"

"Good thought, Nick. Follow it up. You never know your luck."

"God knows, we need some."

Leo was writing the number four.

"We also know the vehicle they've been using for the last three weeks. We know it was stolen in Tirana, we know it was at the hospital in Ioánnina, and we know it was destroyed in Sarandë. We are now wondering if it was also in Chaniá, earlier." He wrote *Known Vehicle*.

"And, regarding the people smuggling operation, Daric said someone called Adil is organising things in Syria and Turkey, and we know the boy Yasir left Turkey from Mersin. We also believe Paksima came on a boat from Turkey to Igoumenítsa and she paid for all or part of her trip by agreeing to carry heroin capsules in her body. We don't know if that agreement was with the people smugglers or someone else." He wrote the number five and *Adil: smuggles people – and drugs?*

"What about the boat?" said Nick.

"I'm coming to that," said Leo.

He was writing the number six and *From Mersin to Igoumenítsa?* "We suspect the boat or boats leave Mersin or somewhere nearby, but we don't know the destination. It might be Igoumenítsa, or that might just have been somewhere to drop off Paksima when she got sick. It could be somewhere in Italy or Albania. We do know a powerful motor yacht of some kind was used."

"How do we know that?" asked Andréas.

"It's a long way, Andréa. Under sail, it could take a week, maybe more, and the arrival time would be hard to predict. Also, the winds are treacherous to the south of Crete. No, it needs to be motor-driven, and it needs to be ocean-going, I believe."

"A hydrofoil, maybe?"

"That would be quick, Andréa, but too conspicuous for our guys, I think."

"A motor yacht, then."

"A far cry from the usual overloaded dinghies," observed Nick.

"Yes, I'm getting the impression this is a five-star service targeted at those who still have some money; a chance to get out quickly and in safety."

"Why do you say that, Leo?"

"Because it's designed with the customer in mind. And it must be expensive. I did some research."

Leo was back at the white board.

"How far do you think it is, from Mersin to Igoumenítsa?"

"A hell of a long way."

"It's almost eighteen hundred kilometres – nine hundred and seventy *nautical* miles. But some of these boats cruise at over twenty knots."

"You wouldn't want to go so far at that sort of speed, though, would you?"

"Why not, Nick?"

"Drawing attention to yourself?"

"Who's going to see them on that route?"

"Fuel cost?"

"It's true they would use much more fuel than at lower speeds, but who cares? These guys have money."

"Damage to the boat?"

"No. These boats are designed to do that sort of speed. Often more."

Nick was nodding, slowly.

"Exhausting for the crew though, you'd think," he said.

Leo acknowledged the remark with a shrug before continuing.

"Okay. A knot equates to a nautical mile, of course, so, with a refuelling stop, it would take at least fifty hours at twenty knots. Some of the beasts I've been looking at have massive twin engines. Combined horsepower of around two thousand seems likely, which means they would burn through at least five hundred litres of diesel every hour."

"Jesus!"

"A fuel cost alone of something like forty thousand euros for a one-way trip."

"Bloody hell!"

"And the fares need to cover the cost of the return trip plus a fat profit for the risk, no doubt."

"Plus something for forged documents," added Andréas.

"True," agreed Nick. Leo went on:

"The boats I've been looking at have between four and six berths. Perhaps, with a little modification, you could squeeze fifteen or twenty people below in acceptable comfort – and you'd want them below, out of sight, if any customs or coastguard launch came near."

"Where are you going with this, Leo?" asked Nick.

"I think they would want the price of a ticket, door-to-door, including documents, to be at least fifteen thousand euros. If I'm right, a trip with every place booked would net the smugglers two hundred thousand euros between them, best guess. Possibly more."

"Easy money," said Nick.

"I'm picking up something else," said Andréas, tapping his pen. "If the trip takes so long, Paksima could not have swallowed her capsules before she left Mersin."

"Because otherwise she'd poop them out before getting through customs."

"Right, Nick. But it tells me something else significant, too. If I'm a drug trafficker *unconnected* with the boat, I'm not going to let Paksima take fifty-five capsules with a street value approaching two hundred grand from me in the hope she swallows them rather than running off with them. I'm going to be there when she swallows them. Then, I know she's on the hook."

"So, what are you saying?"

"The drug trafficker must have been on the boat and supervised her swallowing the drugs when they were at least halfway through the trip."

"Meaning the people smugglers are also drug traffickers."

"Yes, or at least doing their work for them."

"Up go the trip profits," observed Nick.

"And maybe Paksima wasn't the only one paying this way, just the only one who got sick."

"That would drive the profits into the stratosphere."

"Indeed."

They took a break then, to grab a coffee, and Nick finally got to eat his spanakópita. When they resumed, five minutes later, Leo switched tack.

"Right, gentlemen. As you observed earlier, Nick, we don't have a huge amount to go on, but we can take some comfort from these six points. Let's use this session to work out our next moves."

CHAPTER 17
AN ALBANIAN ADVENTURE

It was an unpleasant, grey, steamy day; the sort when even a short stroll makes you break out in a sweat and your shirt clings, clammy, to your back. *But Igoumenítsa would struggle to look attractive on the best of days,* thought Nick. *True, the view across to the islands of Corfu and Paxos would always be beautiful, but the town itself would not. To be fair, it was a port, first and foremost, and ports are seldom pretty …*

He was trudging across town now, in search of the marina. The new port, with its massive concrete apron, was where the ferries came in. He had started there, at the air-conditioned passenger terminal which resembled an airport lounge. A constant murmur of Greek conversations echoed in the hall, pierced by a single child screaming. There were various franchises operating there but most were closed for some reason on this quiet Wednesday morning. Only the Carte d'Or coffee and ice cream stall and the ANEK Lines ticket office seemed to be doing any business. Huge, glass doors gave out onto the quay where the massive ferries from Piraeus or the Italian ports of Brindisi, Bari, Ancona, and Venice docked, on their way to Pátra. It was no place for a smaller boat, he had concluded, even one twenty metres in length.

The marina was no more than a fishing harbour, about two kilometres north of the port. It formed a sideways U shape, concrete walls ending in a jumble of rocks. And it was small. There might be room for forty craft, no more, and the boats themselves were not large; a twenty-metre motor yacht would stick out like a sore thumb, if it could squeeze in at all. It was close to a busy road, choked with slow-moving traffic, but there were open-air restaurants and cafes to either side. Nick saw the names Sympósio and Alékos. The tables already sported red and cream tablecloths, the colours complementing baskets of shrubs and red flowers. There were opaque, white globes on green pillars that would light the kerbside at night and Nick figured this must be a convivial spot when the sun shone. But today, the water looked green and choppy, the hills on the nearby islands formed blue shadows against a leaden sky.

He retraced his steps and found a long quayside area at the end of the port, where massive bollards provided mooring points. A large tug was already in situ, but there was room for other boats. Could this be the place? It would be easier for a large boat to negotiate than the poky marina and it would allow for a speedy entry and exit. On the other hand, it was close to the customs house and the coastguard office. That would make it a high-risk enterprise. But what was it like at night, he wondered? There was nothing right here, no cafés or restaurants. If the offices were closed, it could be an ideal spot to unload a sick girl, right under the noses of the authorities, and then get the hell out.

Nick walked back through the car park towards the fishing harbour. He found a pretty, waterside restaurant called Líthos shaded by neatly pollarded lime trees with white-painted trunks. Bright hibiscus and oleander grew in tubs, and baskets of pink and white flowers dangled from poles. He ordered coffee and a pastry and stared out across the water at the island of Corfu, contemplating his next move.

*

Andréas sighed and sat back. He pushed the map to one side and reached for his laptop. In a few moments he was using Google Earth to race along the coast, east and west of Mersin, but it only confirmed what the map had told him. There were no suitable coves, no natural harbours within fifty kilometres of Mersin. It was a very flat, straight coastline, featureless apart from the occasional man-made harbour. He searched from Karataş in the east to Kizkalesi in the west. There was a cove just west of Kumkuyu that seemed a possibility from the paper map, but when he swooped down on Google Earth, he saw sun loungers and high-rise apartment blocks backing the beach and dismissed it as any kind of remote smugglers' cove. However, the area from Kizkalesi out to Atakent, about fifty-five to seventy-five kilometres west of Mersin, seemed less developed and there were several coves and inlets. It was a fair way from Mersin, but a good, fast road hugged the coast all the way up. It would only take three quarters of an hour. Within a few minutes, he concluded: if the departure point was Mersin, as Daric believed, then the smugglers were unlikely to have used one of the rather exposed harbours or marinas within fifty kilometres of the city. They were much more likely to have used a secluded cove, further out. He would need to be systematic about this. A process of elimination. He had started to make some notes when the phone rang.

"Hello?"

"My name is Adil."

"Ah, yes. Thanks for getting back to me."

"You need my help, I think."

"For my brother, yes."

"You will come to Fraternity Park at six pm."

"Where is that?"

"It is near your hotel. You will find it."

The phone line went dead. Andréas was excited by the breakthrough but, at the same time, he felt the hairs on the back of his neck rise. They knew his hotel. What else did they know?

*

Fraternity Park proved to be a patch of green in a sea of concrete. A playground area featured green and orange slides. There were benches, palm trees and privet hedging. It was dull, suburban and incongruous, surrounded as it was by high-rise apartment blocks. A woman in a yashmak was pushing a pram along a concrete walkway. Further away, three teenage boys were kicking a football to each other.

The place may have been banal, but Andréas's heart was racing as he settled to wait on one of the benches. He wondered if he was being watched from one of the many apartments. He wondered if the woman with the pram was their accomplice. He looked around every few seconds, but he only became aware of a presence when he felt the bench seat give and turned to find a dark man sitting there, unsmiling. He must have approached from behind, across the grass. The man would be about forty, perhaps a little more. He looked tired and he needed a shave, but he was still a good-looking man. When he spoke, the voice was deep and husky.

"I am Adil, Mr Kappas," he said, in English. "Please, tell me your story."

Andréas gave him the prepared story of his brother, the engineer trapped in Syria, no longer being paid, and now fearing for his life.

"Why does he not just take a plane?" asked Adil. "The airport at Damascus is still operating, I believe."

"They would stop him and bring him back. And then they would punish him. This is what he believes. He just wants to get back to his family in Thessaloníki."

"He is there alone?"

"His family *were* with him, but he moved them back a year ago. He could see the way things were going."

"Why did he not leave himself, then?"

"He should have. He sees that now, but the work was interesting, and the money was good. He thought he'd give it a few more months."

"Money is only good if it is paid."

"Quite."

"I am a businessman, Mr Kappas. I am Syrian, but I'm not a humanitarian or an idealist. I offer a service for money. The service is safe, swift, and comfortable. After two or three weeks of preparatory work, we will collect your brother from near his home in Syria and take him to a town in the south of Italy, door-to-door, in three or four days. The price is fifteen thousand dollars. If he needs false papers, these can be arranged, within the price. Transport from Italy to his desired end destination can also be arranged, but this may be extra, depending on where he wants to go."

It was what Andréas expected, but he feigned shock at the price.

"There are many cheaper services available to your brother," Adil continued, seeing his concern. "They take longer, and they are not reliable. Most likely, he will end up stuck in a refugee camp or be one of the ten percent who drown. It is your choice."

132

"Can you tell me more about the route, the mode of transport?"

"An SUV on land, a motor yacht over the sea. Luxurious, fast."

"Does it leave from Mersin?"

"Close to here, yes."

"Is there any way to reduce the cost, pay less?"

The man looked askance. Andréas extrapolated.

"Something we could do for you, other than cash, perhaps?"

A flash of danger may have appeared in Adil's black eyes. Andréas could not be sure.

"An expat engineering consultant, Mr Kappas? I think your brother can afford it, to save his skin, even if he hasn't been paid for a while."

He stood up and handed Andréa a slip of paper.

"Take your time. Speak with your brother. Call this number in the next forty-eight hours if you want to move to the next stage. Do not call for any other reason."

Adil stared at him for a long moment, then turned and walked away.

*

Nick's conversation with the harbourmaster had been awkward, he reflected, as he took the spectacular motorway back through the mountains to Ioánnina. The man's English was poor, and Nick's Greek was still limited. He was not quite hostile, but he was not helpful. He took a defensive stance from the outset. No, there was no record of a boat called Destiny having docked at Igoumenítsa and yes, while it was possible in theory, it just would not happen without him knowing, not within a few yards of the customs house. And no, not even during the night would it be possible. They worked twenty-four hours, around the clock. The man was taking the mere suggestion that a boat may have docked without him knowing as a personal affront. Nick concluded there must have been incidents in the past that put him so much on the back foot. Maybe he felt his job was at risk.

The bearded skipper of the tug took a very different view. The harbour officials were lax, and, though their offices were open at night, they were lightly manned. How would they know if a boat came and went in the middle of the night, particularly a smaller one? And, if these guys came in a twenty-metre boat, they would have a tender. Maybe they used that instead of bringing the larger boat in? If it was not a hazard to their precious ferry lanes, the port authorities would not give a damn.

"There are no cameras here, so yes, my friend, I'm sure it happens all the time," he had concluded, with a pronounced wink.

When Nick arrived in Ioánnina, he drove straight to the G. Hatzikóstas general hospital. Rather than join the queue of cars waiting to enter the car park, he parked on the side of the dual carriageway as others had and strolled past the security hut without being challenged. At reception, he asked for security but, apart from the man on the front gate and a few cameras, they had none. When he explained he was working with the police and wanted to check their camera footage, they told him an outsourced service company maintained the cameras. The hospital staff paid no attention to them. After fifteen minutes, they were able to give him a scrap of paper with the address of the security firm.

Nick realised the address was just a few minutes' walk from the police station, so he dropped the car off there and walked, despite the heat. He found the office tucked down a shady side street, between a shop selling religious artefacts and an ice cream parlour. The door was opened by an obese, young man who must enjoy the proximity of the latter, Nick thought. When he explained what he needed, the man agreed he could help, but warned it would take a while.

*

Leo was running out of ideas. He had just met with his constables and concluded that the Dropbox data did not contain an interview with Paksima. And there was no point in requesting data from the other folders. They were just not relevant or had not been accessed for years. Damn it. He lit a cigarette and stared out of the window. The captain was expecting an update, but he had very little to give him. And everywhere they turned seemed to be a cul-de-sac. Just as he was grinding the cigarette into the ashtray, the telephone rang. It was Nick.

"Leo, I'm sending you a photo, or at least my friend here is. It's the perp talking to Lohani. The older guy – the killer. It's quite a good headshot, much better than the previous one."

"Great. Well done, Nick. I'll get straight on to Interpol."

"Trace him and we get a lead to Bel. The other trails have pretty much petered out."

"I hear you."

"She's been missing five days now, Leo."

"I know."

*

Nick ran out of ideas too, that afternoon. He decided to take a break and clear his head a little. He was less than impressed with the urban sprawl of Ioánnina, but the area around the castle and the lake was pleasant enough. He strolled along the side of the lake, where benches alternated with modern sculptures in the shade of plane and chestnut trees. He sat and stared across the water at the island of monasteries and the mountains beyond. The plaque told him that, two hundred years before, the Ottoman assassins caught up with Ali Pasha there. But he was not thinking about history. He was thinking about Bel. Was she alive or dead? Had they missed something? She had vanished from the hospital car park, maybe bundled into the stolen Hilux and driven to Albania, but then what, after Sarandë? There was no news from the Albanian cops. The trail ended there. Why would they keep her alive? She would be a millstone. A greater risk alive than dead. They might try to discover what she knew, but then what? She would be killed and dumped. She must already be dead. Nothing else made sense. These guys did not know the meaning of compassion. Her body would be in the Albanian countryside or floating in the Adriatic.

It was close enough to six pm. Nick moved to a waterside café and ordered a large beer. He was thinking about the times with Bel: the sharpness of her wit, the moments of laughter, the feel of her body and the loneliness deep in those dark eyes. A long friendship was burgeoning into romance, at last, only to be snuffed out, obliterated by these bastards. He looked around him at the other tables. Couples everywhere. He saw the touches of their hands, the warm, amused looks in their eyes and he felt alone. He ordered another beer.

By mid-evening, he found a dark, old restaurant and ordered a fillet of veal with vegetables and a special bottle of smoky, red wine. Later, at the end of his solitary, but delicious, meal, the waiter asked him if he would like the cork back, so he could take the rest of the wine home.

"Don't worry," he said, "there won't be any left."

*

In his dream, Nick was on a boat. It was a crowded rowing-boat, but he was not rowing. He was looking back over the stern at the island they were leaving, and Bel was on the shore, waving in desperation. Her face was clouded with disbelief. *Could he not hear her? Why was he deserting her?* As he looked, she seemed unaware of the small band of armed men, approaching her from behind. Then an ambulance siren started clanging in the other direction, the way they were headed. He turned and woke up.

The phone in his hotel room was ringing. He saw it was four forty am. *What the hell?*

"Mr Fisher? I am so sorry to disturb you, but I have an urgent call for you."

Before Nick could respond, he heard a different voice: older, female, stressed.

"Is this Nick Fisher?"

"Yes. Who is this?"

"I am Ghislaine, Bel's sister. She asked me to contact you."

"Meaning she's alive?"

"Yes. She's in hospital, in Albania. A place called Gjirokastër."

"Thank God. How is she?"

"A broken arm, exposure, exhaustion, cuts and bruises, but they say she'll be okay. She spent several days wandering the countryside before they found her."

"I'll get over there."

"Let me know what you think, Nick. I'd be there myself but I'm working in North Carolina. I could come tomorrow, maybe ..."

"Sure. I'll text you from the hospital. You'll have something when you wake up and you can decide then."

"That's kind. Give her my love, won't you? Let me have your cell number and I'll text you the location."

Nick noticed he still reeked of alcohol and felt disgusted with himself. He ran his head under the shower and towelled himself dry before scrubbing his teeth. Next, he threw a few things in an overnight bag, just in case, grabbed his passport, a bottle of water, a banana, and a cereal bar. He noticed his heart was beating faster. Was it the alcohol, or just burgeoning excitement? She was alive! He did not understand why or how, but it was enough. He checked out Gjirokastër on the map software and was surprised to find it was only an hour and a half from Ioánnina. He would be there by six thirty.

*

As Leo drove to police headquarters, he was feeling morose. The case was getting nowhere, and the captain was not impressed. The media were getting involved now, and the captain had been obliged to host a press conference where he had been non-committal in the face of furious challenges from journalists. One of their own was missing and the police were not trying hard enough to find her. Now, below a photo of the captain, the main paper featured an angry piece about police stonewalling and it was all Leo's fault.

When he made it to his desk with the customary Greek coffee and cigarette, there were three messages waiting. They would change his mood in an instant.

The first was from Andréas, informing him of the meeting with Adil. That cheered him a bit, though he was not sure how far they could go without putting Andréas in mortal danger.

The second was from Interpol. The new photograph matched a forty-seven-year-old Turkish national by the name of Osmanek

Fahri. He had served time for robbery with violence and supplying drugs, but not yet for murder. Not yet. Leo's smile tightened into a thin-lipped grin as he replied, thanking them, and requesting a list of known associates.

The third and final message was from Nick. Leo scanned it, then banged the table with relief and threw his head back, eyes closed. Then he looked at his watch. It was seven fifty-five. He should be with her now. He called Nick's number, but it went to voicemail. He left a message asking him to call as soon as he had further news, then lit another cigarette. In an hour, he could call the captain. Better news might get the press off his back. And it might just keep Leo his job.

*

The Omer Nishani regional hospital was a good deal more civilised than Nick expected. The car park was surrounded by lush lawns and a variety of trees, and the young receptionist looked bright and efficient, her hair swept back, brown eyes bright behind dark-framed glasses.

"It's a little early for visitors, Mr Fisher," she said, in response to his opening gambit.

Nick explained he was a close friend and was working with the Greek police to find out who had done this to her.

"She will want to see me, I assure you," he said.

"Wait, please. I must check with her doctor."

A few minutes later, the young doctor appeared, and offered to escort Nick to Bel's room. As they walked, he summarised the situation.

"She needs rest, Mr Fisher. We have set the arm and tended to her cuts and bruises. She is on a drip to restore her vitamin levels and I have given her some strong painkillers. She may appear a little drowsy. You can help me by persuading her to remain here long enough to complete the healing process. I need three or four days, at least."

"I can try, Doctor, but this is a strong-minded woman on a mission."

"I understand, but rest is very much in her longer-term interests. You will please help me by stressing this."

"I'll do what I can."

"And the press. I appreciate Ms Saidi is a well-known journalist, but we do not want to be under siege while we are trying to do our work here. I'd appreciate it if we could suppress news of her whereabouts for the time being."

"That might be beyond my control, Doctor, but I do understand your concerns."

They were at the door now, the doctor's hand on the handle. He turned to Nick and looked him straight in the eyes.

"At least make sure my concerns are voiced, Mr Fisher. Now, you may have half an hour with Ms Saidi. No more please. You may return later in the day if you wish. Regular visiting hours are between four and seven pm."

Nick nodded, followed him in and was shocked by what he saw. The right-hand side of Bel's head was swathed in bandages, the left side covered in purple and yellow bruises. Her right arm was strapped tight across her body in a foam wrapper that could have been pipe insulation, for all he knew. The doctor checked her drip, made sure she was awake and comfortable with her visitor, then left.

"Boy, am I glad to see you," Bel said, trying to push herself up. Nick got her to lean forward so he could plump up the squashed pillows, giving her left arm a gentle squeeze as he did so. She leant back and gave him a rueful smile. "Got any cigarettes?"

Nick patted his pockets and took on a look of pained regret.

"Thirty years ago, I might have. Anyway, you can't smoke in here."

"The nurses do. All the bloody time. I smell it wafting in from outside."

"How the hell are you, anyway?"

"I've been better, but honestly? I'm so glad to be alive, Nick. Thought I was going to die this time."

He sat down on the edge of the bed and took her left hand in his.

"I'm glad you didn't."

"Me too. It took me a while to realise. You see, it wasn't about me. It was *Paksima* they were after, and I think I know why. I was just in the way. And they had no idea who I was, or that I'd interviewed her. They must have thought I was a friend or relative."

"And they got to Paksima, right after you left, I'm afraid."

"No! Oh, God. The poor girl."

"The guy dressed up as a doctor and injected her with air. She wouldn't have suffered for long. And the guy who interpreted for you, Lohani?"

"What about him?"

"The bastards compromised him. After Paksima's death, he hanged himself."

"Oh, no. Jesus."

"And they kidnapped you, didn't they?"

"I think I must have seen something, or someone. Or they thought I had. One of them just dragged me out of my car and bundled me into theirs. He had a knife. We waited, then the other one arrived."

"A black Toyota Hilux?"

"If you say so. And then we raced to the Albanian border. Not a word to me the whole way. And I couldn't understand what they were saying, but then I have no Albanian."

"At least one of them is Turkish, we believe."

"I wouldn't know the difference. I don't speak either. I thought they were taking me somewhere to kill me. I was trying to reason with them, but they were ignoring me. Or they didn't understand me. About twenty minutes after we crossed the border, they turned off the motorway and a few minutes later they threw me out. Quite literally. They slowed down but they didn't stop. And they were laughing. Bastards."

"And you broke your arm in the fall?"

"All this is from that. When I came to, I was screaming with pain but there was no-one to hear. I had no idea where I was. I couldn't have been more than ten kilometres from the motorway, but I couldn't hear it, so I had no way of knowing which direction it was. I was in a rural wilderness, and it was getting dark. I managed to walk a few hundred metres, found a hedge and curled up underneath. I lay on my left side and cried myself to sleep."

"You didn't have your phone, of course."

"No. They rifled through my bag at the start and took it. Never gave it back, but then I think the whole idea was just to get me out of the way and out of contact for a while, rather than kill me, though they didn't seem to care much either way."

"We know they drove to Sarandë later and torched the vehicle. Perhaps they left the country soon after."

"Sounds right. Just needed me out of the way while they made their escape."

"So, what happened next? How did you end up here?"

"When I woke the next morning, the pain from the arm was worse, if anything. And I could feel dried blood on my face. And I was hungry. I started walking west. I know there are only three or four million people in Albania, and I figured most of them would live near the coast. I knew that was west, though I had no idea how far. But it was away from the rising sun, which was easier, anyway.

"The problem was the mountains. I was in a wide valley, but there were mountains both ahead and behind. I knew I wouldn't make it over them. I needed to find help before I got there, but there was nothing. Just fields and forest. I walked most of the day, but in short bursts. It was so painful. I remember seeing a farmer in the distance at one point, but he couldn't hear me shouting and then he got in his pick-up and drove away. I was heartbroken. Then I found a pear tree, then a fig tree and then a stream, so I was able to eat and drink something at last. I picked a few for later, too.

"That night, I slept in an old, concrete shed. I think it must have been used for sheep at one time, but it was abandoned. But I didn't sleep much. I was getting scared now. Would my wounds get infected? Would I lose my arm? Would I die there?

"The next morning, I noticed a good-sized hill two or three kilometres away and decided to make my way there. I struggled to the top and surveyed the area. In the distance, I saw a smallholding, just in the foothills of the mountain. And there was smoke. I guessed it was another eight to ten kilometres, mostly uphill, but I decided to try for it. There must be people there. Perhaps they would look after me.

"Maybe I got the distance wrong or maybe I was too feeble by now, but I didn't make it that day, so I had a third night in the open. The following morning, I could see it was less than three kilometres away. When I got there, my spirits fell because I saw how poor they were. They were Romany, I think; father, mother and three kids. I hesitated to impose myself on them, but then the mother saw me and took me in. I must have been a sight because the young girls recoiled from my face, but the boy, who was older – perhaps nine or ten – said hello and tried to talk to me in English. The mother fed me some sort of soup and dabbed my face while the boy talked with his father. Then he came back and said they had a phone, but it needed electricity. I must wait. Then they would call for an ambulance."

"Thank God they had a phone," said Nick.

"Yes. It was a crappy, old, pay-as-you-go thing, but it just about worked, after they charged it. The boy was able to explain where to come and the ambulance was there in about an hour. I must have passed out on the way, or perhaps they sedated me. Next thing I know, I'm lying here, and my arm has already been set. They told me they had found my passport and contacted my sister."

"You still had your passport?"

"Yes, I still had my handbag. Everything except the phone, in fact. They didn't even take my money. I used the bag as a makeshift sling and a fruit basket. Hermès would be proud."

Nick chuckled and squeezed her hand.

"You've been very brave, Bel. I'd expect nothing less, of course. Now, I want to let Leo know you're okay and Ghislaine wants me to report back."

"Oh, don't worry about her. I'll call her in a few minutes, before she goes to bed."

"She's worried; wants to know whether to rush over here."

"I'll call her, okay?"

"Okay. Now, before I call Leo, and before the doctors throw me out, I need to ask you a few questions if you're up to it?"

"Fire away."

Nick told her about their attempts to find a recording of the Paksima interview.

142

"Dropbox gave you my stuff?"

"A limited selection, with great reluctance. Don't worry."

"The recording is still on my phone, which they dumped. I was going to upload the file when I got to the car, but then I got myself kidnapped."

"And we found the phone later, but the SIM had been removed."

Bel looked puzzled for a moment.

"The SIM doesn't hold *data*, though. It only has what you need to access the supplier's network. It's like a pass key. The data are stored in the phone's memory, backed up to iTunes or iCloud."

"You mean the interview recording was there all the time?"

"You'd have to do a workaround without the SIM, but I think you can do that quite easily these days. And then you'd need my ID and password, but I guess Apple might have helped you out, in the circumstances."

Nick was shaking his head.

"We didn't know that," he said.

"Didn't you give the phone to the cops' techie guys?"

"I don't think we did. Without the SIM, we thought we were stuffed. Stupid, with hindsight. Did they take the phone to get the interview recording, do you think?"

"No. As I said, I don't believe they knew about the interview or even who I was. I'd guess they took it to stop me calling anyone when they dumped me. It would be standard practice to remove the SIM when they chuck a phone away. Anyway, you don't need the phone now. You've got me."

"Hang on. If they didn't know who you were, or that you'd interviewed Paksima, why go to the trouble of kidnapping you?"

"I've been asking myself that, Nick. Perhaps I saw something, or they thought I did."

"When we get back, I'll show you the photos from the security footage. Maybe something will jog your memory." Nick looked at his watch. "So, what can you tell me about the interview in ten minutes?"

Bel was blowing her nose and wiping her eyes.

"I'm sorry, Nick. I didn't expect to be the sole survivor of that interview. And they were so damned young."

"I know. Take your time."

"So, Paksima. I think she was a sweet girl, before all this, but she was orphaned in Afghanistan. Her father died fighting the Taliban and then her mother was killed in a suicide bombing. Carnage. That was on Paksima's sixteenth birthday. Her mum was out buying ingredients for the birthday cake, she said. Can you imagine what that would do to the girl? Paksima struggled to survive on her own for a while, but it was hard. I won't tell you the awful things that happened to her, but, after a few months, she decided to leave."

"No brothers or sisters?"

"No. She was alone. She had saved up some money from a job in a café. When she left, she took buses through Iran to Turkey, then looked for people smugglers to get her out, to Italy, if possible. But they told her she needed to be in the north of Turkey, where she could only get to Greece and, if she didn't drown, she'd be locked up in a refugee camp and forgotten about. Just as she was giving up hope, she met a young man who said someone called Adil could help her. There was a smuggling operation going from Turkey to Italy, but it was expensive."

"Just as you suspected."

"But, by now, Paksima had only two thousand euros left. The young man said the normal charge was fifteen thousand dollars, but there might be a way to bridge the gap."

"By being their mule?"

"Yes. The minders told her she would have to swallow capsules of white heroin and carry them into Italy inside her. It was quite safe and, if she did that for them, the fare would be just three thousand euros."

"But she only had two."

"Correct. This was their little con. The minders made it clear that a special price of just two thousand might be acceptable if sexual favours were also provided."

"Dirty bastards. She was only sixteen, wasn't she?"

"They said: *We're good Muslims, we're not going to take your virginity. We just need your hand and your mouth, whenever we feel stressed.*"

"Good Muslims. Right. And she agreed to this?"

"What choice did she have, Nick?"

He walked to the bedroom window. There was a breeze now and yellow leaves were falling from silver birches onto the unkempt lawn by the car park. He felt anger building in his chest. These bastards had used this girl like she was nothing: an expendable vehicle for their filthy drugs, a teenage virgin made into a whore to satisfy their lust. And now she was dead. Murdered to prevent her exposing their sordid, evil ways. Well, they weren't going to get away with it. Not on his watch. If he had felt ambiguity about this case before, he didn't anymore. He would not allow this to go unpunished. He would do everything in his power to nail these bastards, for Paksima and all the girls like her in this God-forsaken world.

Bel was speaking again, and he turned back to face her.

"The night they left, she said they drove along the coast for a while, away from Mersin."

"East or west?"

"I'm sorry, Nick. I don't know. But they were taken to a cove where they had to climb down and wait on a beach. There must have been another SUV, she said, because there were about eighteen or so people on the beach, at one or two in the morning, she reckoned. They ferried them out to a larger boat and put them below decks in a few different cabins. Paksima was in a cabin with three other people and then this black boy arrived, making it five. He was exhausted and fell asleep right away, but he was about the same age as her and later they got talking."

"Did she get a name for the boat, or describe it in any way?"

"She said it was rather grand. She hadn't expected to be travelling in such style. But no, she didn't see a name. It was dark, of course."

"And the black boy – did she get a name for him?"

"I don't think she ever knew his name, but she learned he was from Somalia and hoping to make it to England. They drove him

145

up through Africa to Egypt, then through Israel and Jordan to Syria, then Turkey. It took five days."

"She didn't mention the name *Yasir* to you."

"The boy who was killed? No. Do you think it could have been him? Anyway, Paksima and this boy swap notes. He told her his father paid for his trip. She told him she was having to do stuff to subsidise her fare, but she wasn't specific. He seemed like a sweet, innocent boy, she said, and she didn't want to upset him. Later in the afternoon, they came for her and took her to a different cabin, somewhere near the stern. When she saw the bag of capsules, she almost fainted. They told her there were fifty-five for her to swallow, but not to worry, it was the normal amount for a woman. But, before that, they wanted her to help with their stress levels."

"Meaning?"

"It was a euphemism for oral sex. They wanted her to suck their dicks."

"Oh, Christ."

"It was part of the deal, they reminded her. She knew she had no choice and, somehow, she got through it. She threw up afterwards, she said, and felt like throwing herself off the boat, she was so ashamed."

"And *then* she had to swallow the capsules."

"Yes. Two at a time. Twenty-eight swallows. And then they threatened her. Told her she must tell no-one or there would be severe consequences. But they didn't know she'd already told the boy."

"She wasn't specific though, you said."

"No, but the boy wasn't stupid. Maybe he followed and found a way to watch or hear what was going on? Anyway, when she was brought back to the cabin, the other women looked at her like she was filth, but the black boy was kind and solicitous. He told her she would be okay. They would be in Italy the next day. But it wasn't long before she started to feel ill. She wasn't surprised to feel some indigestion after swallowing all those capsules but, within a few minutes, she knew it was something much worse. She was getting shooting pains in her stomach and couldn't think straight. She was sweating and starting to hallucinate. The boy is getting anxious and asks the others to get help, but they ignore him. The women were smug bitches with *told you so* looks on their faces, she said. By now, she's slipping in and out of consciousness. The boy is no longer there. The other man says he's gone for help.

"Paksima didn't remember anything more until she was being lifted off a boat by two men – one of the ones who had given her the drugs and another guy, a fair-haired man she hadn't seen before. He went back to the boat after they laid her on the quayside. She was very scared then because she thought the one who remained was going to kill her. She saw a knife glint in the moonlight but then the blond man was hissing angrily at him and signalling with his arm, ordering him back to the boat. The guy didn't move, but, in that moment of hesitation, she heard an outraged voice cry out, and then a big man sprang from the shadows and attacked the guy. He must have landed a couple of good blows because she heard the knife clatter onto the quayside and then the guy ran off, back to the boat. Then a woman's face appeared and said: 'It's okay. We're going to help you, my dear.'"

"Who the hell were they?" asked Nick.

"We don't know. Paksima didn't know. She passed out soon after and the next thing she knew was waking up in the hospital, after the operation."

"So, these people must have called an ambulance."

"I guess."

"Or just driven her to Ioánnina."

"Good Samaritans."

"You're not kidding! But all for nothing, as it turned out. I need to find these guys. They might be able to identify the men – or the boat."

At that moment, the door opened, and the doctor reappeared.

"I'll have to ask you to take your leave now, Mr Fisher," he said. "It's time for Ms Saidi to take her medication and get some rest."

"No problem, Doc. I need to be heading back to Greece now, anyway. And you," he turned back to Bel, "need to get yourself better and re-join the hunt, but only when you're ready."

As the doctor held the door open for him, Nick signalled with his head for him to follow.

"What is it, Mr Fisher?" he said when they were in the corridor.

"Your patient is at risk, Doctor. The people who did this didn't realise she was a high-profile journalist. If they find out, they'll come back to kill her. They already murdered a young girl in a hospital in Ioánnina, we believe. We need to step up your security, keep her whereabouts as secret as possible. Maybe use a different name for her – a pseudonym – can you do that?"

The doctor looked nervous, Nick thought, but he managed to muster his reassuring bedside manner:

"We'll take good care of her, Mr Fisher. And that includes keeping her safe from any intruders. Don't worry."

Minutes later, Nick was calling Leo to update him on what he had learned at Bel's bedside. He finished by asking Leo to organise a police presence at the hospital, Albanian or Greek. Just someone to protect Bel. She'd been through a lot. They didn't want to lose her now.

CHAPTER 18
THE NORWEGIANS

Andréas used the next day for exploring. He had forty-eight hours before he needed to get back to Adil and he would use them to try to locate the smugglers' pick-up point. On the morning call, Nick shared what he had learned from Bel. Now, Andréas knew the passengers had been taken from a beach to a larger boat, moored offshore. It helped. He needed to focus on the coves. The location would have to be near the road and there would have to be a walkable road or track so the twenty or so people could make it down to the shore. It would have to be out of sight of any houses likely to be occupied. And west of the city would be nearer the ultimate destination, though that was less of an issue.

He returned to Google Earth and to the string of coves between Atakent and Kizkalesi. The geography looked helpful. In some cases, it would be possible for the main boat to moor around a headland, out of sight of the cove, and send in a smaller boat, probably a rigid inflatable boat, or RIB, to collect the passengers.

There was some tourist development, here and there, but it looked avoidable and maybe it would be unoccupied anyway, in late September. There was only one way to be sure, he thought, finishing the rest of his coffee. He would have to narrow his focus.

*

It was early afternoon by the time Nick made it back to the G. Hatzikóstas hospital at Ioánnina. Once again, he parked on the dual carriageway and strolled past the pointless security hut. Then, he headed straight for emergency reception.

"Kalispéra sas," said a dark-haired woman in her forties. "Can I help you?"

"Kalispéra. My name is Nick Fisher. I'm working with the Greek police on the murder of the girl, Paksima, which took place in this

149

hospital." He placed an old card on the counter which she glanced at.

"I am sorry. I know nothing of this."

"She was brought into emergency with a heroin overdose. This was at night, about two weeks ago."

"One moment," she said and left the desk for the back office.

She was gone for four or five minutes, and Nick felt impatience and frustration building, but then she was back with an unexpected smile and an orange file.

"I am sorry, Mr Fisher. Without a surname it is more difficult, but then I realise we do not know it either and so it is filed under X. Paksima X. What do you want to know?"

"Did she arrive by ambulance, do you know?"

"Ah … one moment." She was scanning through the file and then separated two pieces of paper from the rest.

"No ambulance. She was brought to the hospital by these people."

Nick realised he was staring at photocopies of two passports, Norwegian.

"It is normal," she went on, "to request ID and contact details in such cases. We or the police might need to ask questions later."

"How very sensible," said Nick. "Might I have a copy of those? I need to contact them."

"Of course."

Nick could not believe his luck as he walked away with the passport copies and even a mobile phone number in his pocket. This might just be the breakthrough they needed. As soon as he returned to the police station, he found himself a small office and made the call.

"Is that Mr Larsen?"

"Yes, I am Wilhelm Larsen."

Nick explained who he was and why he was calling.

"I expected someone to call before, Mr Fisher. How is the girl?"

"I'm sorry to tell you, Wilhelm, but she died."

A pause. Nick sensed mild shock, regret.

"Oh, that is sad," he sighed, "but I am not so surprised. She was in a bad way, poor thing."

Nick decided not to complicate things by mentioning murder.

"What you and your wife did was very brave and kind, Wilhelm. You gave her a fighting chance, but she had been forced to swallow many capsules containing drugs and two of them burst inside her. I want to catch the people who did this to her. Will you help me?"

"Of course, I will do anything I can."

"Great. Now, if you could cast your mind back to that night, and tell me in your own words what happened?"

"One moment." Nick heard muffled conversation in the background. A woman's voice and then a small wail of despair. "I'm sorry. My wife is here. The news has upset her."

"No problem. Take your time."

Wilhelm muted the call for half a minute to comfort his wife, then clicked the phone back to life.

"Sorry about that. And so, my wife Katerina and I were holidaying in Greece, as we often do. It was the last day of this particular holiday and we had driven to Igoumenítsa. We were scheduled to catch the ferry to Ancona the next day, but we arrived early so we could enjoy an evening there and celebrate our thirty-fifth wedding anniversary. We dined at a restaurant near the little harbour, rather late, and we were walking back to the car when we saw a man and a young girl on the quayside. He would have been in his late thirties, I guess, Southern European or Middle Eastern. She was much younger, and she was on the ground and seemed to be in trouble. She was doubled up in pain or maybe this was to protect herself from him. I couldn't tell. Then I saw he had a knife. I called out something. Was it: *What the hell are you doing?* Something like this. I just wanted to distract him.

"He was shocked to see me there but started coming towards me. I pushed Katerina to one side and whipped off my jacket to use as a foil for the blade. I'm over sixty now but I keep myself fit and I'm quite strong, I think. I feinted with my right arm – the one wrapped in the jacket – and distracted him for a moment. I was then able to grab his right arm with my left and twist it, hard. I am left-handed and he could not have known this. The knife fell to the floor. Then I hit him in the face a couple of times. He was stunned, I think, to find an old boy could be so powerful. He didn't fall, not quite, but he staggered. Then, there was an urgent-sounding call from some boat, a man was waving, and he ran off, leaving the girl. My wife was tending to her by then, but the girl was in very poor condition, maybe delirious. We didn't know what was wrong, but it seemed very serious. She was in great pain. Then, I saw the boat pull away from the quay, into the dark. I was relieved because I thought they might come back for me."

"Could you see the boat, or any other people?"

"It was one of those modern dinghies, pale-coloured, and the engine sounded powerful. I could see two people on board. The guy who called out was paler, fair-haired. The other – the one I fought – was darker, not so tall."

"Was it a rigid inflatable boat?"

"I don't know what you call it. It was about three metres long, flat-bottomed, with rounded bows and sides like torpedoes."

"And the guy you fought. Would you recognise him again?"

"I can't say. Maybe. It was dark, remember."

"Then what happened?"

"Katerina said we must take this girl to the hospital, so I jogged back to the restaurant to ask where it was. They told me there is no proper hospital in Igoumenítsa and we would have to drive to Ioánnina, which would take about an hour. It would be quicker than calling an ambulance. I had not drunk too much wine and the road was good. At the hospital, they wanted information before they would accept the girl. Who were we? How did we get involved? What had happened to the girl? We told them all we knew and then they asked for our passports and took copies for their records. We asked if she would be okay. They were non-committal, of course. Said it was too early to say but they would do everything they could for her. It was all we were going to get, so we took a note of the hospital's phone number, thinking we would call in a day or two to check on her. In fact, we never did. My wife was afraid we would find out she died. If we did not call, we could hope for the best. I know; the logic is flawed, but that's how it was for us. And we were surprised the police didn't call the next day, or after we got back to Stavanger. Nobody called."

Nick thanked him for his time and asked if it would be okay to call again if there were any developments, perhaps someone to be identified.

"Yes, of course. We will be here, and we will help if we can."

"Thanks, Wilhelm. You've been most helpful already."

Nick ended the call and realised he was starving. He would grab some lunch and then he needed to catch up with Leo.

*

Leo's feet were on the desk, the room filled with blue tobacco smoke. He was thinking about opening the window when the phone rang.

"I need to run something by you, Leo."

"Sure, Nick."

"An off-the-wall idea. I want you to shoot it down, play devil's advocate."

"Okay."

"Did we trace Destiny and our friend Ollie, after Ag Nik?"

"You think I would call out the coastguard because the man irritates me, Nick? No, of course not. He hasn't been back to Crete, so we assumed he won that charter and headed north, to sail around the islands."

"My Scandinavian friend Wilhelm caught a glimpse of the boat that dumped Paksima at Igoumenítsa. He says it was a pale-coloured RIB, and there were two men on board. One was a fair-haired man with a North European complexion. I think Destiny had a tender like that. Do you remember?"

"A RIB. In case you haven't noticed, Nick, these things are everywhere."

"Yes, but this –"

"Had a fair-haired man on board. Yes, I heard you. Probably some rich German."

"Can we just pursue the theory?"

"What *is* your theory, Nick? That Oliver Dunham, privileged son of one of the richest men in Britain, is smuggling drugs across the

Mediterranean and killing people along the way? For a hobby or a diversion, perhaps?"

"I didn't know there was a rich Daddy."

"We have researched. His father has a title and a massive estate in Norfolk, England. Not only that, but he is one of two partners who founded a large and very successful investment management firm. It now has over eighteen billion pounds in funds under management, and they still own it. If they take just half a percent commission, that's a cool ninety million a year. Even if it costs them forty million to run the business – a ludicrous amount for a firm with no more than twenty or thirty employees plus a bit of marketing – they would still make twenty-five million pounds each, every year. Oliver Dunham is not short of money, Nick."

"Assuming Ollie has access to Dad's cash."

"We know Dad paid for a very expensive education for his son. We know Dad paid close to half a million euros for his share of the charter business."

"A business that might be struggling. Maybe Dad lost patience with him."

"The man is rich, Nick. He's not going to alienate his only son because the guy needs a little more cash."

"Maybe it's not about money, then."

"You mean Dunham just wants to be an evil man, for some reason?"

"Maybe he has no choice, Leo."

"What do you mean?"

"Remember, when we went to see him, he lied about the whereabouts of his wife and son. Why do that? Why weren't they with him?"

"They could be anywhere."

"They weren't in Glasgow. I'm guessing they're still in Crete. But why aren't they on the boat, wherever it is?"

"They might be."

"I don't think they are."

"Perhaps the people who chartered the boat didn't want them on board, taking up space."

"Or perhaps *Ollie* didn't want them on board."

"Who knows?"

"My point is, we don't know where Leila and Jamal are, nor do we know where Ollie and Destiny are, at a time when a witness is telling us a man and a boat fitting the description of Ollie and Destiny's tender were dumping a sick migrant chock full of heroin at Igoumenítsa."

"*Fitting the description* is a hell of a stretch, Nick. Could this Wilhelm of yours identify Oliver Dunham?"

There was a pause, then Leo heard a note of resignation enter Nick's voice.

"I very much doubt it. The guy was at least twenty metres away, I should think, and it was dark. He wasn't even sure he could identify the one he fought with."

"It's very thin, isn't it, Nick? Andréas found no trace of Destiny at Mersin, remember. We have no reason to suspect Dunham and no sightings of Destiny."

"The attack on Jamal. Suppose that was a threat. Do as we say, or your family pays the price. How would *you* react?"

"If I believed the threat was serious, I'd have to comply, but I'd try to get my family out of harm's way first."

"So, Ollie hides his family somewhere safe, or worse, they are being held somewhere by the smugglers. Either way, he has to do whatever they want of him."

"Okay, that's a possible motive for him to be involved, but why him?"

"He has the right sort of boat and the skills to sail the thing."

"Yes, but how would a gang of people and drug smugglers operating out of Turkey latch onto this British dilettante wandering around the Greek islands?"

"I don't know, Leo, but I think that's the key piece of information we're missing. There has to be a connection of some kind, if I'm right."

CHAPTER 19
LEO CALLS THE COASTGUARD

Andréas was working on a process of elimination. There were too many possible sites. It would take more than a week to visit them all and he did not have a week.

Meanwhile, he put in a holding call to Adil. His brother was interested.

"Would he be in a position to leave tomorrow, Mr Kappas?" Adil asked.

"No. I am sorry. This is too soon. He told me he would need a week to tie things up at his end and to organise the money."

"Then we will try to call you later."

And that was it. Another brief conversation. Adil must have meant they could collect the imaginary brother tomorrow, in Syria. It would take a full day, at least, to drive him the six hundred or so kilometres to Mersin. Today was Friday. It looked like the next embarkation would be Saturday, or more likely Sunday night. He hoped to God it was Sunday. Then he might have a chance, if his logic worked.

He spread out the A3 sheets landscape on the hotel room table. He had identified six points crucial to choosing the pick-up site and listed them down the left-hand side:

1. Accessibility for the migrants (from the road)

2. Lack of occupied housing/development

3. Accessibility for a RIB (from the sea)

4. Proximity to ultimate destination

5. Availability of cover for the main boat

6. Absence of risk to the main boat (water depth? rocks?)

Some of these were more important than others, he realised. The ultimate destination was thought to be eighteen hundred kilometres

156

away, in Italy, so whether the pick-up point was fifty kilometres west or east of Mersin was almost immaterial. He started a column headed *weighting* and wrote the number one against item four. On the other hand, item one was vital. If the weakest passengers were unable to get to the site from the road, it was a non-starter. And item two was all about risk of discovery. They would be sure to view it as important. He wrote the maximum weighting of five against both items. Item three was less important, because a RIB would be able to get to most, if not all these places. If it was inaccessible to a RIB, it should not be on his list, in fact. On reflection, he scrubbed out item three altogether and renumbered the last two. Some of the possible sites were very open. Maybe it would matter less at night, but Andréas felt the skipper would prefer a coastline that afforded an opportunity to tuck the main craft behind a headland or something, out of sight. Preferable, but maybe not essential. He gave it a weighting of three. The last point would be more difficult to assess without access to marine charts of the area, but it was important, nevertheless. This was probably an expensive boat on a dangerous and illegal mission. They would not want to risk snagging on a rock or running aground. That would mean a wrecked boat and a prison sentence in Turkey. He gave it a weighting of four.

He stood back from his work. *That might do it*, he thought. A framework for comparison. Now all he had to do was give each possible site a score out of five on each of the five remaining points and then apply the weightings to come up with a weighted total for each site. It would take a while but, if it worked, it would give him a ranked hit list, and should cut his twenty-six possibles into something more manageable, saving a huge amount of time.

Two hours of jumping from Google Earth on his iPad to the coastal maps he had bought, to the A3 analysis on the table and Andréas was sweaty and exhausted. And, all this time, doubts were nagging at him. Was there a twenty-seventh possible he had missed altogether? Was his thinking flawed, was the whole idea a nonsense? And, even if the process were valid, would it establish a clear difference or would they all score the same, meaning it had been a complete waste of time? He wouldn't know until he applied the weightings and worked out the numbers. He set out to do that now with the aid of a spreadsheet to make sure he got it right.

At last, he was there. And thank God, the message was clear. It might not be correct, he had to admit, but at least it was clear. Only five of the possible sites scored more than sixty-five out of a possible ninety, and then there was quite a gap. These were the places on which he must focus his energies. He wrote out the names from west to east and looked at them as if something might spring from the page, some magic in the name, some divine guidance perhaps, that would help him know which:

- Yaprakli Koy, near Altinforz
- Calamie Beach Club
- Müze Beach, Kizkalesi
- Queenaba Beach Club, Kumkuyu
- Magarsus coves, south of Adana

There was an outlier. Magarsus was well east of Mersin. The other four were within a few kilometres of each other, a fair way to the west. The eastern one had the attraction of relative isolation. He hesitated. Should he go straight to the more likely area and hope like hell it was not the other one or should he try to eliminate the outlier before focusing on the other four. He checked his watch. It was already two forty-five, Friday afternoon. He should call Leo and update him on his progress. Then, armed with the reassurance that comes from collective responsibility, he would head east.

*

Nick had been thinking for some time that his work in Ioánnina was done and he should head back to Chaniá. The killers were long gone, the hospital issues resolved, and the task force team felt a little disjointed now. He wanted to get closer with Leo and make sure they stayed on track, with Andréas's help. He was on the point of wandering round to Mikey's office when the phone rang.

"Mr Fisher? It's Ghislaine again. You didn't call me. Are you still in Ioánnina?"

"Er, sorry … yes, I am, for now. Why do you ask?"

"I just tried to call Bel. You're not going to believe it."

"Try me."

"She's checked herself out of the hospital. Already."

"I *am* going to believe it, Ghislaine. It's typical, I'd say."

"Well, it's bloody stupid of her. That's all I can say. Look, it's one in the morning here and I have a big meeting tomorrow. Could you try to get in touch with her for me, find out where she is, what she's up to?"

"I'll do my best, but don't worry, all right? I saw her the day before yesterday and she wasn't too bad, considering. She was going to call you, she said."

Nick was grinning as he put down the phone. He knew what was going on. She did not call her sister because she knew what she would say. She had sent the doctor packing; told him she was getting back into the fray. And she was on her way right now, in all likelihood. He would go and sign off with Mikey and then he would get ready to head back to Crete, maybe with Bel by his side.

*

Soon after four pm, Andréas was hammering the hire car, retracing the route past Tarsus to Adana. It was a long trek inland but hugging the coast was not an option. Soon after leaving Mersin, the main road swung inland and, instead of endless tourist resorts, the flat hinterland became an arable patchwork of fields through which the Tabak River meandered. There were no significant main roads and Andréas did not have time to get himself lost, so he stuck with the D400.

At Adana, he turned due south on the D815 road to Karataş. Already, he was thinking it was taking too long. By the time he reached the coast, it had been almost two hours and his enthusiasm for this option was already waning.

He found a string of three, seemingly quiet, beaches before the tourist developments sprang up again, heading east. In fact, the farthest east of the three did feature a low-key development to the east of the beach which overlooked the whole bay, and they looked to be still busy. On those grounds, Andréas deemed it a non-starter. The other two were connected to one another, quieter, and more interesting on the face of it, but the route down was challenging. There was a small, crumbling cliff which Andréas negotiated with difficulty and a good deal of perspiration. When he reached the beach and looked back, he concluded it would be too much for a bunch of twenty people to tackle at night, especially if some were weakened by their recent experiences, as seemed likely. He stared out from the beach, listening to his inner voice, but heard nothing but the wavelets caressing the sand. This was not the place, he concluded. Too long a drive from Mersin, too difficult a descent and the wrong side of the city for the boat's destination. Nevertheless, he spent a further fifteen minutes searching both beaches, checking for signs. There were none. Cursing himself for backing the wrong horse, he clambered back up the cliff and got back into the car. It would be dark within the hour. Maybe he would find a restaurant in Adana. He had, at least, eliminated the outlier. It had to be done. And it was not nothing. No need to deny the inner man, he concluded, brightening at the thought of a lamb kebab.

*

Leo was deep in thought when the coastguard returned his call. He was surprised to hear a woman's voice.

"Lieutenant Christodouláki? I am Iphigénia Loukákis. I am the administration manager for the coastguard at Iráklio. I understand you have questions for me."

"Yes, thanks for getting back to me. I have a case which involves a motor yacht and I know very little about navigation or sailing. I wondered if you could help me understand a few things."

"Such as?"

"How would you go about finding a particular boat if it disappeared somewhere in the Mediterranean? Is there a requirement for the skipper to file a travel plan, anything like that?"

"You said a motor yacht, but can you tell me more?"

"I don't have much, but it would be a pleasure craft, quite big, perhaps twenty metres in length."

"How old?"

"I don't know, but I would guess it's less than twenty years old."

"Okay, Lieutenant. There is no legal requirement to log any kind of travel plan for such a craft, any more than you have to tell the road authorities where you are heading in your car, but these days, vessels of that size would have an AIS."

"What's that?"

"An Automatic Identification System. It's a piece of electronic kit not unlike a small laptop and it's normally found on the bridge. A VHF transmitter is built into the transponder. It sends out signals on the VHF mobile maritime band or via satellite to warn other vessels of your presence and receives signals from other AIS users in the vicinity."

"A bit like radar, then?"

"It's a different technology. Radar is about sending out a pulse and getting it echoed back. It helps you find land and any obstructions, including vessels of all types in the sweep area, even those not emitting an AIS signal."

"How far can radar see?"

"Depends on your set-up. The best navy sets – up to about fourteen nautical miles."

"And AIS?"

"A good deal further, in theory, over fifty nautical miles if you have a proper mast. But, in practice, this capability is seldom used. As a navigator, you don't want to be confused by signals from miles away. You want to focus on immediate threats, things you must avoid, so you might limit the display to, say, five nautical miles and use radar alongside for the bigger picture."

"That makes sense."

"So, where is this boat of yours, Lieutenant?"

"Right now? I have no idea."

"No sightings? No expected routes? Nothing?"

"Only conjecture, at this stage."

"Well, the only way to search a large area is by grid, breaking it up into smaller pieces that can be patrolled, either by boats equipped with the best radar systems or spotter planes, if you have them. It's resource intensive and expensive and often involves cooperation between different services and countries. Complex."

"So, I would need to give you a goodish shot at a location before we could even start."

"An approximate location, a likely route, a destination; any of those things. If we can narrow the search area to a box, say, fifteen hundred square miles or less – I'm talking *nautical* miles – we have a chance of finding her, but we'd need a minimum of four suitably equipped boats."

"That big an area?"

"It's not so big, Lieutenant. It's less than forty by forty. A fast yacht could be through it in under two hours. But the Mediterranean is three-quarters of a million square miles. This is just one five-hundredth of that."

"That puts things in perspective. What about satellites? Can't they be used to track the vessel, or its AIS signal?"

"AIS signals are collected by satellites and the vessel can be identified by its AIS signature, its system ID. It's not always as easy as it sounds, though. I don't think the technology is quite there yet. Also, on a pleasure craft, the skipper can disable the AIS, if he likes; go dark."

"You're joking. He can choose to be invisible?"

"If he has the right equipment, transmitting is optional."

"Wouldn't it be dangerous?"

"It's a little less safe, of course, but you can disable the transmitter without switching off the receiver."

"So, you can see them, but they can't see you?"

"Correct. You'd be well-advised to keep a close watch on the screens if you go down that route, particularly near the shore, but it's possible and it's not illegal for smaller craft."

"So, if he switches off his AIS, all we have is radar?"

"Yes. And with this boat, the signal is going to be weak."

"Why do you say that?"

"Because it won't be steel-hulled, unless it's older than you think. It will be GRP, glass-reinforced plastic. You may know it as fibreglass. Metal reflects the pulse better."

"There'll still be some metal on board, though, surely?"

"Yes, guardrails, shrouds, lights, comms equipment and so on. They may help us a little, but the best signals come from a solid, flat piece of metal like a steel hull."

Leo thanked her and put down the phone. He shook a cigarette from the pack, lit it and went to the window. In the square, three uniformed constables were laughing and smoking. An old woman, doubled up with arthritis, raised her head with difficulty as she passed, and whatever she said caused a pantomime of reaction. A bell was tolling somewhere, and the light was beginning to fade. Leo was lost in thought. It sounded like the only way they would find this boat would be if Andréas could discover the departure point in Turkey. He was a good man, but it was a hell of an ask.

When the phone rang, it was Nick. He was on his way back, he said, and he had Bel with him.

"That's good," said Leo. "I've a feeling something is about to happen. Let's meet tomorrow morning at ten. We can catch up and see if Andréas is getting anywhere."

*

Nick almost asked him if he knew tomorrow was a Saturday. Almost, but not quite. Leo knew all right. Bel still looked a bit of a mess, even with the foundation, and her arm was in a light sling now.

"Are you sure you want to do this?" asked Nick.

"My body's not sure, but my brain has no choice. We have to get these bastards, Nick. And I'm here now. I'll be fine. Let's get checked in."

On the plane from Ioánnina, Nick suggested they get a hotel in Chaniá rather than traipsing all the way to Saktoúria, then back for the morning meeting.

"You think I want to be seen like this, Nick?"

"I'm sure we can smuggle you in. Then we call room service."

*

In the night, she came to him. She was soft and warm. All her extroversion was gone, leaving a feminine, fragile creature. She even cried a little as he held her. Later, though, she pushed herself less gently against him, and he felt warmth and dampness. His response was instantaneous. This time would not be platonic, he realised, and his heart leapt with both joy and consternation. It felt right, but it was four years since he had made love with anyone, and over thirty years since it was someone other than Jen …

This time, she was still there in the morning, sitting up in bed, checking emails on her laptop as he lay beside her. She was wearing her stylish, green glasses, he noticed, the lights from the screen reflecting in them. Her auburn hair was a tousled mess. She turned to smile at him. It was a new smile, different somehow.

"I ordered breakfast while you were asleep," she said, putting her laptop to one side and taking off her glasses, "but it'll be at least half an hour, they said. They were most apologetic."

"Hmmm. We'll have to think of something to while away the time."

"I already thought of something," she said, and climbed onto his chest.

*

Later, as they were tucking into breakfast, she said:

"You do understand, Nick. We're just friends having sex, right?"

"What, you mean you're not planning to marry me, after all?" he said, slicing the top off his boiled egg with studied savagery.

"I wouldn't wish that on my worst enemy, and you're certainly not that," she said.

"Well, thank the Lord for that," he grinned. "I wouldn't know how to tell the kids I was marrying a Moroccan wild cat."

164

CHAPTER 20
ANDRÉAS HESITATES

Leo's meeting was a damned nuisance. With four more locations to check out, all *west* of Mersin this time, Andréas wanted to be on the road. He was not sure how long it would take or even how long he had, but he felt it would be tight if he could not get away soon. And an hour had already been lost in the time difference: ten o'clock Greek time was eleven, here in Turkey. *Still, he is the boss, and he needs to be kept in the loop and, who knows, maybe I'll learn something important,* he thought.

He slipped around to the café and bought himself a coffee and a pastry to take back to the hotel room. When the call came through, the faces of Leo, Nick and Bel appeared together on the screen. He could see Bel was still bruised and there were scrapes to one side of her face, beneath the make-up.

"Hi Bel. Great to see you back," he said. "Are you okay?"

"I'm on the mend," she responded, lifting her sling into the view of the camera. "This will take a while, though."

"I am sorry for you. Do we know who these guys were?"

Leo cut in:

"One was Osmanek Fahri, a Turkish criminal with a violent history. We've just received a list of his known associates from Interpol. Quite a few are Albanians. There's a Serb he did time with. I'll walk through them all with Bel."

Bel was staring at the photograph in Leo's file.

"I know this guy already. He's one of the kidnappers."

"We know that. Did you see him at the hospital?" asked Leo.

"Maybe, I'm not sure. No, wait! I remember now. I recognise that briefcase. I saw him at the airport. We were on the same flight, from Athens. We were both sitting in the airport lounge after the flight. There was no-one else there."

"Maybe he saw you at the hospital, too," said Nick. "Perhaps you were kidnapped in case you made the connection. Just until they got away."

"Maybe."

"He's not a nice man. You're lucky to be here, Bel," said Leo.

"I'd like to know if this Adil guy shows up as an associate of his," said Andréas.

"Of course, you would. We'll let you know if we turn anything up. Now, tell us what you've been up to, Andréa."

He told them about the further brief contact with Adil, how that led him to believe another run was now imminent and how he was trying to find places suitable for the covert boarding of migrants.

"How would you even start, Andréa?" asked Nick, prompting Andréas to go through his logic: the criteria, the weightings, how he had identified twenty-six possibles and narrowed it down to five, now four. There was general acknowledgement that his approach was pragmatic and thorough.

"That doesn't mean I'm right, though," he said. "It could be some-where else altogether."

"And you reckon it could happen as soon as tonight?"

"Tomorrow night, if we're lucky."

"But the remaining four are in the same general area?" asked Leo.

"They're all west of Mersin. Some are further west than others. Just give me a minute … Okay, they're all along a stretch of about twenty kilometres of coastline, from Kumkuyu to Atakent, between fifty-five and seventy-five kilometres from here."

"Is that consistent with what Paksima said, Bel?" asked Nick.

"She just said something like *along the coast for a while,* so I guess that's consistent, as far as it goes. I'm sorry, I should have tried to nail it down."

"Don't beat yourself up. It was dark, she was in the back of an SUV with plenty of other people. I doubt she knew anything more," said Nick, and Bel shot him a glance of gratitude as Leo started summing up.

"All right, Andréa. Good work. Send us your list of potential sites right now and then get on your way. Let us know if you find out which it is or if, God forbid, you find yourself ruling them all out. We'll see if we can get the coastguard excited about trying to intercept them."

"The Turkish Coastguard helping the Greeks? Good luck with that," said Andréas.

"We're helping them control their borders. This is how we put it across," said Leo.

"But do they *want* to control their borders – or is it just the rest of us who want them to?" asked Bel.

"The coastguard has a job. We're helping them do it. This is not macro-politics, Bel."

"I guess we'll find out, Leo," she said, but Nick heard lingering cynicism in her voice.

*

As soon as the email with the locations came through, the three of them got together as Leo plotted them on the white board. He then drew a large island, some distance off the coast.

"What's that?" asked Nick.

"It's Cyprus."

"Oh, I forgot about Cyprus. I didn't realise it was so close to Turkey."

Leo stood back from the board.

"The first question we have to answer is: would they go around the north of Cyprus or the south?"

"It's a no-brainer, isn't it?" said Nick, getting to his feet. "If you're heading west anyway, you'd go across the north. If you head south, you'd have to make a big detour around this pan handle, the north-east bit of the island. It wouldn't make sense. And you'd be straying into Syrian waters down here, which is the last thing you want with a boatload of escapees on board."

"I agree, Nick, it does *appear* to be a no-brainer, but I can think of three reasons why it may not be. There may be seafaring or navigational aspects we are unaware of that make the southerly route more appealing. They might wish to escape Turkish waters as soon as possible, which they can do by heading south, or they might just want to do the unexpected, to avoid detection. If it *is* a no-brainer, then do the other thing."

"I'm sorry, Leo. We're in danger of overthinking this. Let's get the seafaring factors checked out, but otherwise let's assume they would cross above Cyprus, heading west."

"Actually, I agree with you, Nick. I was just playing the advocate of the devil again."

"Yeah. Whatever."

"Because it's important that we are right about this. If you look at the northern tip of Cyprus, here, it's less than seventy kilometres from the Turkish coast. I've been talking to the Greek Coastguard in Iráklio. If we could get two boats with good radar equipment positioned here and here …" He drew two crosses between the coast and the island … "then we'd have the channel covered. Even if they switched off their AIS, one or other of our boats would pick them up on radar."

"AIS?"

"I'll explain later. Do you see what I'm saying?"

"I do, and it makes a lot of sense, Leo. But picking them up on radar, if we can, is not the same as catching the bastards, is it? They must have a fast boat and we'll have limited resources, as always."

"I know, but if they can pinpoint the boat, we might be able to track her, at least. We'll be on their trail, Nick. I think we need to talk to the coastguard, see if they can get the Turks to work with them."

*

There was little to choose between the remaining four locations in terms of weighted scores, so Andréas decided to tackle them west to east, starting with the one furthest from Mersin. Why would they go further east than necessary if they were heading back west after the pick-up?

A fine rain was falling as he set off for Yaprakli Koy. *It won't have rained since spring*, he thought, *and now the Turks seem to be in mortal fear of it, crawling along like idiots.* Andréas did not have time for that, so he found himself overtaking long lines of cars with his windscreen wipers on fast, the car barrelling through the spray. He glanced at his watch. It was already twenty minutes to one. Time was tight and he was hungry again.

Twenty-five minutes into the drive, an ageing pick-up truck, piled high with vegetables and trailing blue smoke, pulled out, right in front of him, just as he was about to pass. He was doing a hundred and five kilometres an hour and the truck was doing sixty, if it was lucky, so he had no choice but to brake hard. He knew the brakes were good, but he had not allowed for the road surface. The rain had made it greasy as all the summer's oil was released and now he was skidding, wheels locked. Within a split-second, he knew he was going to hit. It was just a question of how hard. He sounded the horn, made a grab for the handbrake, glanced in the rear-view mirror, but then the crunch came. A loud bang and Andréas felt the seat belt grasp his shoulder but thank God, the airbag did not inflate. He saw vegetables tumble across the motorway. He saw the truck put on its hazard warning lights and all the traffic slow in unison, allowing the driver to limp across to the right, and the relative safety of the hard shoulder. Andréas followed suit. Through the blue smoke, he could see damage to the rear of the truck. The bumper was badly dented, the offside-rear light assembly destroyed. The guy must have lost a quarter of his precarious load. *Oh, shitty shit, shit!* he thought. *I don't need this.*

He got out and went over as an old man with a white moustache hauled himself out of the truck, looking furious. Andréas raised his hands in apology, though he knew it was not his fault. He just needed to sort this out and get on his way. The old man let loose a string of Turkish invective, waving his hands at the rear of the truck and the produce strewn across the carriageway. Andréas saw that his own vehicle was almost unmarked and made apologetic noises. Soon after, he reached for his wallet.

The old man could see that he had money and was anxious to get away. The longer things went on, the more he dug his heels in. The noise from the motorway, the rain, and trying to negotiate with someone who doesn't speak your language – and might refuse to speak it, even if he did – were all getting Andréas down. And there were bigger issues at stake. Much bigger issues. After twenty minutes, he took all fourteen of the five hundred lira notes from his wallet and held them out, eyebrows raised, at the old man. Just as the old boy was tilting his head in grudging acquiescence, the police vehicle arrived and tucked itself close behind Andréas's car.

From the outset, they took an aggressive line with him, demanded to see his papers, asked him what speed he was doing, what allowances he had made for the rain. And, by the way, what are you doing in Turkey? What is your business here? The old man, a Turk, was presumed to be the victim, but Andréas was not going to get into an argument about it. Although nothing was said, there seemed to be a reluctant acceptance of the validity of Mr Kappas's identity card, driving licence and hiring documents. Finally, after a long talk with the old man, one of the policemen approached Andréa:

"The other driver will accept your money as compensation, but we have told him: he does not surrender his rights by doing this. If he has injuries, whiplash for example, which become apparent later, or if he finds the cost of repairing his vehicle and replacing the stock to be greater than the sum you have paid, he or his insurers will be entitled to bring a further claim against you. Do you understand?"

Andréas doubted if the vehicle itself was worth as much as seven thousand lira and how much could a few potatoes and cauliflowers be, for Heaven's sake? In any case, in the unlikely event of the old man having *any* insurers, they would have a hard job of it, pursuing the imaginary Mr Kappas.

"I understand, and I regret the incident, officer. Now, if I may pay the gentleman and get on my way, it would be much appreciated."

The old man took the money with a sly grin. *He'll be laughing all the way to the bank,* thought Andréas, *the crafty, old sod.*

It was almost three by the time he got away, and he still had half an hour's drive to get to his first destination. He would have to grab something to eat there, before exploring.

*

Leo and Nick were sitting around the speaker phone when the call came through, as arranged. Leo explained what they needed from the coastguard.

"Well, I can ask," they heard Iphigénia say. "The Turks will do as they see fit, of course, which may be nothing."

"Can you get a Greek boat there?"

"Not for tonight. Sunday night, maybe, but we would need their permission to enter Turkish waters."

"Isn't that just a formality, though?"

"Nothing is a formality between the Greeks and the Turks, Lieutenant. You know that."

Leo and Nick exchanged exasperated looks.

"Just tell me what you *can* do," said Leo.

"I can ask them to put boats where you ask. I can offer a Greek boat to help from Sunday night. I will point out the international kudos for them in helping break a people smuggling ring and I can promise them a prominent mention in any publicity we attract if we succeed. I don't know what else to suggest."

"You could tell them it's their responsibility, if migrants are being picked up from the Turkish coast, and they need to deal with it."

"I'm not going to do that, Lieutenant."

"Why not?"

"Because it won't work. It's not how they see it. Refugees have entered their country illegally. They were not welcome, but now they are leaving, thanks to the smugglers. I'll be pleased if I can persuade them to intervene at all."

"Iphigénia, this gang has murdered at least two people and attempted to smuggle heroin along with the refugees. The Turks have a duty to help us bring them to justice."

"And I will stress all this, Lieutenant, believe me. Leave it with me. I'll see what I can do."

The line went dead, and the two men stared at each other.

"She's not going to push very hard."

"Why do you say that, Nick?"

"There are a lot of things we don't know. Like what boat it is or where and when they are picking up their passengers. If she bullies the Turks into a full response and we don't come up with the goods, there'll be egg on her face."

"Egg?"

"Egg."

*

The snack failed to put Andréas in a better frame of mind. The kabak mücveri was nice enough – zucchini fritters not dissimilar to kolokíthokeftédes – but his pide, meat on dough pie, was dry, and far too spicy for Andréas. He left half of it.

Yaprakli Koy was a public beach. A headland separated a small cove from a much longer beach. It was a quiet, but developed resort, packed with hotels and four- or five-storey apartment blocks. Now his stomach was full, Andréas turned his back on this and drove a couple of kilometres back down the main road. This was the place he was looking for. He pulled onto the hard shoulder, hopped over the crash barrier, through white-trunked trees and a patch of wild, prickly pears, then scrambled a few metres down to a rocky shore where a concrete wall had been built.

There were steps down to a shingle beach. But the place did not feel right. It was too close to the road and not well hidden from it. There were a few lights positioned along walkways and there was a hotel, he saw, on the far side of quite a large cove. Not a very big hotel, but its sun loungers and tables with parasols extended along a concrete plinth, built onto the rocks, with steps down to the water and a small jetty. There were not many people around, despite the still warm weather and the inviting green water. It was a pleasant spot, he concluded, and the little jetty would be very handy for a RIB, but it was just too exposed, not the place to embark migrants without being noticed. He took a couple of photographs with his phone to remind himself and, perhaps, to show the rest of the team, and then struggled back up to the car.

He drove further back along the D400 until he found a crossroads, just beyond a blue sign for Narlikuyu. A handful of hoardings advertised the doubtful charms of a restaurant and a couple of small hotels in the village to his right, which must be very close to the sea. He turned and drove a hundred and fifty metres until a scattering of houses appeared and he noticed a sandy track, off to the right. It would be fine for a 4x4 but not for the hire car. His gut was telling him to explore, and he needed exercise anyway, after that pie, so he parked up and started walking down the track. It must lead to the sea, he figured, and just maybe the cove he was looking for. Ten minutes later, he was on the shore. It was an indentation in the shoreline, but it was not a cove, as such. And it was rocky. He was not sure about the RIB, but it would be very difficult for the people to get across the jumble of boulders making up the shoreline. As he made his way back, he began to wonder if he would be able to draw any conclusions at the end of his surveys or would it just be a list of possibles, all of which had advantages and disadvantages. He told himself to stick to the plan, see it through, try not to get discouraged.

He decided to drive on through the village before turning around and spotted a tarmac road leading off to the right. He took it and found himself in a wooded area which must lead down to the shore once again. When the tarmac road petered out, he got out again, took his binoculars from the boot and started walking down the track. He had seen no signs of habitation for at least six hundred metres when he came upon a tiny, unspoilt cove. Checking his iPad, he reckoned this must be Kizlar Hamami Koyu. Here, though the coastline was still rocky, there was a tiny beach. It was hidden from the west, and the coastline between here and the previous spot seemed deserted and barren. Around that headland, to the west, would be an ideal place for the main boat to remain out of sight.

With mounting excitement, he scanned the coastline to his left, the east, then swore under his breath. A small development started less than two hundred metres away. True, they would struggle to see the beach from there, but they would hear a boat engine. It was all together too close for comfort. Andréas scanned west but the headland prevented him from seeing much. He was trudging back to the car, when he noticed another track, leading off to the left. He started walking, reckoning it would be driveable for a 4x4. It hugged the coast for around five hundred metres before dropping left, to another small, sheltered cove. There were a couple of buildings here, but they were derelict, he discovered. There were boulders, but there was an easy enough route through to the shallow water. That development could still be seen, but it must be six hundred metres away, across the bay. It was enough, he reckoned.

Andréas made his way onto the beach and looked for evidence of recent use. There was nothing. He scanned the other side of the bay through the binoculars. It was quiet. He stood and watched and listened for a full minute before taking more photographs. He was excited about this spot, he decided, on the walk back to the car. The lay of the land was ideal, access for a 4x4 from the main road was not difficult, access to a RIB from the beach would not be too daunting, the main vessel could remain out of sight and there was nothing within six hundred metres to observe their activities. It took all Andréas's strength of character to stop himself calling in, there and then. Places like this were few and far between along this busy coastline. Back at the car, he felt calmer. He checked his watch. Twenty past five. It would be dark from seven and there were three places yet to explore. Damn it. He would not make it through tonight.

*

The Calamie Beach Club, he remembered, was just a couple of kilometres further round, to the east, in the small but busy resort of Narlikuyu. But it was not the resort itself that interested Andréas, but a cove just east of the place which, from Google Earth, looked more secluded. Here, the D400 passed very close to the sea. At an interchange, where rocky scrub gave way to a patchwork of cultivated fields, Andréas pulled onto a slip road that swung down to the sea, overlooking a natural harbour where he saw twenty or thirty small boats. Following the road around, he found the beach club itself and parked near the entrance. It looked to be a chalet-style hotel, built on the small promontory which extended from the eastern side of the harbour. He made his way to the far side, where the road swung back, along the edge of an inlet to a small, sandy beach at the end. This was the place, but now he saw it was not suitable at all. The road was too close and worse, it re-joined the A400 almost directly behind the beach. Why had he not spotted that on the computer? Also, while the cove and the beach looked suitable, and there seemed to be no habitation on the far side of the inlet, the entire stretch of water could be observed from the chalets on the eastern side of the hotel complex, and it looked like at least some of them were still occupied. He returned to the car and motored along to the beach, but it only confirmed his doubts. This was not the place.

After driving several more kilometres east, he came to the busy resort of Akdeniz and made his way through to the main beach. A few people were still swimming in the shallow, turquoise waters leading out to Kiz Kalesi, a castle built by the crusaders just one hundred and fifty metres off the beach. The left-hand side of the large beach featured the ruins of another castle, which he learned was Korykos. But Andréas had no time for tourist attractions. The sun was nearing the horizon and he needed to get away from the tourists and find his hidden cove.

He drove east from the town, passing signs for Korykos Joy Beach. A few hundred metres further on, he spotted the Cheers Café and had to resist the smell of frying kebabs as he swung right, onto the slip road he was looking for. He followed the road for perhaps a hundred and fifty metres before turning right onto a small, but still tarmaced, road which meandered down through trees to another cove. He got out to look for ways down to the beach and saw the colours draining from the sunset. Darkness was falling quickly now. He shone his phone onto what he thought was a path, then slipped on a rock and fell on his backside. He could make out the shape of the cove and saw the castle ruins away to his right. No lights were appearing on the headland to his left, so that was a good sign, but it was too dark already to be sure about access to the beach and the water. It might have some of the advantages of the earlier place, but it was hard to be sure, and there was still the fifth place yet to see, near the Queenaba Beach Club. With a heavy heart, he decided he would have to find a bed in Akdeniz and finish up in the morning. As he made his way back to the car, it occurred to him: there was no need to drive past the Cheers Café, now it was dark. Armed with a full stomach, he could update Leo and then go find a room.

*

An hour later, Leo found Nick and Bel talking, as he put his head around the door:

"Just had a call from Andréas," he said. "He's quite excited about a couple of spots, but he hasn't been able to finish. He'll have to do the rest in the morning."

"That's a bugger. Did we ask too much of him?" asked Nick.

"Just bad luck, I think. He had a minor accident on the way that held him up."

There was a pause as they stared at each other, each wondering if Andréas might be a weak link. Then Leo dismissed it.

"He's a good man, Nick. He'll have done his best. There just wasn't enough time. So, look. Until we hear more from him or from the coastguard, there's not much we can do. Might as well take a break, get some food and rest. Things will move quickly after that, I suspect. I'll let you know as soon as I hear anything."

Leo withdrew and closed the door. Nick stood and stretched.

"Well, I don't fancy jeeping it back to Saktoúria just to get woken up in the middle of the night and dragged back here. What say we go back to that hotel in Chaniá?"

"Why not?"

"We can save on expenses by getting a double room this time."

"How romantic you are, Nick Fisher," said Bel, standing up and giving his arm a wicked squeeze.

*

The hotel was just east of the harbour. As soon as they were checked in, Nick asked the receptionist for a good restaurant.

"I think Pallas is the best," she said, "but I'm not sure I can get you in."

"Whereabouts, is it?"

"It's at the beginning of the main harbour. I will show you." She punched some keys and then gabbled in Greek for a minute before pulling a face as she covered the receiver with her hand.

"You must go now. Right away. They are booked out later but, if you can get there in fifteen minutes, they will squeeze you in."

Nick and Bel glanced at each other. A drink before would have been nice, but it was getting late anyway, and they were hungry.

"Okay. We'll take it," said Nick.

She showed them where to go on a large, paper map, but fifteen minutes was a challenge, as it turned out. They hurried through the gardens, then along behind the town beach, past shops and cafes to the second harbour and then past the luxury yachts and the old Venetian arsenals until the lighthouse came into view and they found the restaurant on their left, with its own bakery and bar area.

"We have a cancellation, Mr Fisher," said the maître d'. "I can offer you a table on the roof terrace, if you wish."

Nick grinned at him in response, and they followed him up.

"I am sorry, you are too late for the sunset," the man said, over his shoulder.

"Don't worry. They make me sad, anyway," said Nick.

The others looked at him, confused, as they reached the table.

"I don't know why," he added, with an inconsequential smile, though he did know why, and there was nothing inconsequential about it.

It was a romantic setting. The views over the harbour and the lighthouse were quite beautiful, with the lights from the tavernas dancing in the black water, and the murmurs of conversation reassuring, somehow, as if these people were all like-minded friends. Music drifted up from below. And the food, when it came, was delicious.

"I seem to be following in the steps of Ali Pasha," said Nick.

"Oh, I hope not. His treatment of women was appalling, and he came to a sticky end."

"I know. I was in Ioánnina not long ago, staring at the island where he was assassinated and now, here I am, eating dinner in his old palace."

"Ah, so that's why it's called *Pallas*."

"No, in fact. Pallas is not Greek for palace, it's the name of one of the Titans."

"You are a strange man," said Bel, "but I feel lucky with you."

"Lucky?"

"Yes, like getting a table up here. Fortunate things happen when we're together."

"You think someone is watching over us, Bel?"

"I don't know. Maybe. Or it's *kismet*."

She gazed into his eyes, and he saw warmth and passion there, maybe even a touch of vulnerability. *That must be a recent addition,* he thought.

"And there was I, thinking we were *just friends having sex*," he reminded her, with a wink, and was rewarded with water flicked from her glass.

*

They had breakfast in bed the next morning, at eight thirty. No-one had called. By nine, Nick could wait no longer and reached for his mobile just as it started ringing.

"Good morning, Leo," he said, putting it on speaker for Bel's benefit.

"Where are you, Nick?"

"Just ten minutes away. I stayed over in Chaniá."

"That's good. Do you know where Bel is?"

"I think she was going to do the same, so I imagine she's nearby."

Bel snorted into her napkin and Nick pretended to slap her.

"Do me a favour, Nick. Give her a ring and get yourselves into the police station as quickly as you can. I need your input."

"Has there been a development, then?"

"I'll tell you when you get here."

The line went dead, and Nick was shaking his head in frustration.

"You're going to give me a ring?" said Bel, a wicked grin on her face, enjoying the double entendre.

CHAPTER 21
AN UNEXPECTED FIND

Andréas woke with a cloud of doubt in his head. His brain must have distilled his thoughts while he slept and now, he worried that he had made a mistake the previous day. He had favoured diligence over instinct, due process over gut feel, but now he remembered that you must never ignore your gut.

He checked out soon after seven. In the car, he viewed the map. It was less than fifteen kilometres. He could be there and back in well under an hour. Then, if he was wrong, he could resume the process as planned. Twenty minutes later, he was turning left at the blue sign, driving through the village again, then turning right. Like before, he parked where the tarmac ran out, but this time he hurried along the track to his right. He sensed something different at once. Were those new tyre marks in the sandy track? Had the empty cigarette pack been there yesterday? He was not sure, but he was worried. As he followed the track down to the little beach, it became obvious. There were cigarette ends and footprints in the sand. A plastic water bottle had been discarded. Behind a boulder there was scrunched up kitchen roll and signs of defecation. None of this had been there the day before.

"Dammit!" he yelled. The migrants had been and gone, sometime between seven pm and seven thirty am, most likely in the early hours. They could be two hundred kilometres away by now, maybe more. Andréas felt hot tears of frustration and a pit forming in his stomach. He should have gone with his gut and made that call. They could have staked out the cove and caught the gang red-handed. *Shit!* His process had worked. He would have been a hero. And now he would have to explain to the rest of the team how he had let them all down.

*

Nick and Bel arrived at the police station at nine thirty-five and Leo ushered them into the same meeting room as before, ordering coffees from a young constable. As soon as they were seated, he started without preamble:

"I had a call from Andréas just a few minutes ago. Seems he had a strong feeling about one particular spot yesterday and almost called in, there and then. Almost, but not quite. It had all the attributes he identified, and it just felt right, he says. But, like a well-trained policeman, he tried to suppress his excitement and avoid jumping to conclusions, so he didn't call. Instead, he carried on checking the other sites until darkness fell."

"And he didn't mention this on your call, yesterday?"

"He said he was excited about a couple of possible sites but he wanted to finish the process. I didn't press him."

"So, Sod's Law tells me one of them *was* the beach," said Nick, and Leo tilted his head in sad acknowledgement.

"This morning, his gut dragged him back to double check before he went on. When he got there, he found evidence that a group of people had been on the beach last night."

"So, they've been and gone – on the *Saturday* night?" said Bel. Leo nodded. "God, they don't hang about, do they?"

"Did Andréas interview any locals to confirm the suspicious activity, put a time on it?"

"There *are* no locals, Nick, unless someone saw them driving through the village. But I'm guessing they'd choose very early morning when everyone's asleep. Perhaps between one and four am?"

"I think Paksima reckoned between one and two, for her pick-up," added Bel.

"What about the boat? Someone must have seen it," said Nick.

"Not according to Andréas. There's a headland they could have hidden themselves behind, then sent in a RIB to pick up the migrants in two or three batches. There are some houses on the eastern headland, he says, but they're at least six hundred metres away and at night, in the dark …"

"And he's sure it was the migrants, not just some random beach party?"

"He's sure. And, from what he found, I agree with him."

"So, they've been and gone, dammit. Where the hell are they now?"

Leo stood and moved to the white board which still showed his sketch of the Turkish coast and the island of Cyprus. He picked up a red pen and drew a blob on the Turkish coast, some distance west of Mersin.

"This is our cove. It doesn't have a name, as far as we know. Andréas is calling it: *Beyond KHK.*"

He wrote the makeshift name on the map, drew a red line south from the cove, then swung west through the sea to the narrowest point between Turkey and Northern Cyprus, where he drew a cross.

"This is where we asked the Turkish Coastguard to be. The distance is eighty-five nautical miles. Assuming they went that way at a cruising speed of twenty knots, it would take them just over four hours to get past."

Nick glanced at his watch.

"So, if they left before six am, Turkish time, they're already through?"

"That's what I'm afraid of, Nick. When I put the phone down on Andréas, I called the coastguard at Iráklio and asked them to tell the Turks the boat could appear at any moment."

"And?"

"They've seen nothing on their radar so far was the message that came back."

At that moment, the phone started ringing and Leo picked up.

"Okay, good. Put her through," he said, raising his eyebrows at them as he pressed the speaker button.

"Good morning, Leo. It's Iphigénia. I'm sorry I wasn't here earlier."

"Eight thirty on a Sunday? You are allowed to sleep sometimes."

"Thank you. But I don't have good news for you, I'm sorry."

"Go on."

"The Turks saw nothing on their radar, but when I questioned them, I discovered they sent only one boat and positioned it in the middle of the channel. They said only one was available and, as we couldn't get there till the following night, it was the best they could do."

"Oh, for God's sake. What does that mean?"

"They could not scan the whole of the channel effectively from one boat. It will cover, at most, the central twenty to thirty nautical miles, but the channel is almost forty miles wide."

"So, if the smugglers hugged the coast of Turkey, or more likely the coast of Northern Cyprus, they would have avoided detection?"

"Right. Either by luck or judgement. And honestly? If I had been their skipper, I would have stayed within sight of the Cypriot shore, once I'd seen it, until I was through the channel. If he was within five miles of the shore, he would not have been caught on radar."

"Why would you have done that?"

"You told me the boat was making for Crete. So, it makes sense to be on the south side of the channel, and I always prefer to be in sight of land if I can; it's best practice, adds an extra measure of safety. Once through the channel, I could set a course of two hundred and sixty-eight degrees, almost due west, for Crete, which, from there, is about three hundred and twenty-five nautical miles."

"So, only sixteen hours or so, if they average twenty knots."

Leo thanked her and ended the call.

"We must assume they got through the channel," he said. "If they left the cove as early as midnight, Turkish time, that could have been more than six hours ago. They could reach the easternmost point of Crete by this evening."

"Can't we get the Turks to give chase?" asked Bel.

"Do you think they would respond with alacrity to such a request?" asked Nick.

"Also, they'd take a bit of catching, if we're right about their speed and the head start," added Leo.

"What about the Greek Coastguard intercepting them?" said Bel.

"It's a possibility," said Nick, "but if they're not following that exact route, it would be easy to miss them. Anyway, I think there's a better idea."

The others turned to him, expectantly.

"A while ago, you mentioned refuelling, Leo. Have you given any thought to where that might happen?"

183

"How on earth would we know?" said Bel.

Leo was shuffling back through his notes.

"I made some assumptions about speed, size of fuel tanks and fuel usage, after looking at a range of similar boats online, if I can find them," he said.

"They could have extra fuel on board though, in containers," said Bel.

"Maybe, but not enough to avoid refuelling somewhere. These things use a vast amount of petrol – or diesel. Ah! This is it."

He tore a sheet from the file and placed it on the table where they could all see it.

"As you can see, I looked at four different boats, all between twenty and twenty-five metres in length."

"Why that? How do we know?" asked Bel.

"We don't. It's a guess. Paksima told you it had a few cabins that could accommodate around twenty people at a comfortable squeeze. So, I've assumed a three or four berth motor yacht capable of doing at least twenty knots. Take this first example. The boat is twenty-two metres long and has three large cabins. It has twin, nine hundred-horsepower, diesel engines. I've learned that each horsepower uses about one hundred- and eighty grams' weight of fuel, every hour, at cruising speed."

He took the paper and walked over to the white board.

"So, with a total of eighteen hundred horsepower, this one would use about three hundred and twenty-four kilos' weight of fuel every hour. As a litre of diesel weighs about seven-tenths of a kilo, that's four hundred and sixty-three litres an hour. This model has a fourteen-hundred-gallon tank, which equates to six thousand, three hundred and sixty-four litres, so that would give it a range of six thousand, three hundred and sixty-four divided by four hundred and sixty-three: about thirteen- and three-quarter hours at its cruising speed of twenty-four knots. So, the maximum range between fuel stops works out at something like three hundred and thirty nautical miles. At lower speeds, though, this would be much higher."

Bel was looking baffled, but Nick was catching on.

"But there are so many variables, Leo. We don't know whether it's petrol or diesel, the real engine size, the weather conditions, the average speed, the tank capacity or whether they have extra supplies over and above a full tank. Isn't it all just a wild guess?"

"It's all we have, Nick. Petrol engines burn even more fuel, but they tend to have larger tank capacity as the manufacturers want to give them a comparable range. Anyway, most of these larger boats run on diesel; it's more economical and the engines are more reliable. I've done the same calculation on the other three examples here and there's much less difference than you might expect in the ranges. They are all between two hundred and seventy and three hundred and eighty nautical miles, even the petrol one."

"I suppose that makes sense. The boatbuilder would see range as an important selling point. He'd want to be competitive."

"Right. So, despite all the variables, we do have a guideline of sorts. Now, we need the computer."

They regrouped at the table, and Leo brought his laptop over and called up Google Earth.

They saw him tap in Mersin, Turkey and watched as the software pulled them across the globe before plunging like a meteorite. The familiar shapes of Turkey and Cyprus materialised as they zoomed in to the coastline.

"Now, if I skip along the coast here to Narlikuyu. This is the cove Andréas says they used."

They saw Leo call up the ruler function and drop anchor on the cove, starting a line that he ran out into the ocean, twitching left past the northern coast of Cyprus and away across the Mediterranean to Crete. At the eastern edge of the island, he clicked again, and a box appeared. He selected nautical miles as the measure of choice.

"There, do you see? By the most direct route, it's close to four hundred nautical miles from the cove to the start of Crete."

"Well, so much for that theory. It's too far. You said the range was three hundred and thirty."

"At twenty-four knots, yes, but if they dropped the speed, the range would increase significantly. If my sums are right, they would have to anyway, just to make it across."

He consulted his notes and made another calculation. Bel and Nick exchanged doubtful glances.

"At the lower average speed of eighteen knots, the range rises from three hundred and thirty to four hundred and seventy-five miles. More than enough, even allowing for the bit along the south coast here."

He moved the cursor again and the line extended around Crete and up to the Peloponnese.

"The mainland is almost six hundred miles. Cyprus is way too soon, Turkey is too far north, too much of a diversion."

He stood back from the table in triumph, like a professor who had proved his theorem, and when he spoke, there was a glint of pure, schoolboy excitement in those brown eyes:

"They have only one option: to refuel on our island. And they must do it tonight. This is our chance, guys."

"And how long would it take them, at eighteen knots?"

"A minimum of twenty-two hours plus the bit along the south coast to wherever they refuel."

"Wow," said Nick. "So, they're likely to get here between midnight and four am. Clever stuff, Leo. I hope it works. But where the hell do you buy a thousand gallons of diesel on the south coast of Crete, in the middle of the night?"

"That's what we need to find out, and quickly."

Nick looked at his watch. It was already coming up to eleven am.

"Maybe the coastguard will know," he said.

"Good point," said Leo, picking up the phone and punching keys.

While he was busy, Nick took over the controls of the laptop and zoomed out and across until he had a full view of Crete.

"There are only two places of any size on the whole south coast," he said, "Ierápetra and Paleóchora. Of those, Ierápetra seems more likely. Paleóchora is just a tourist resort, but Ierápetra has some industry."

"Would they want to be so visible, though? A boat like that, in one of those harbours, would be a rare thing – very noticeable," said Bel.

"True, but what choice do they have?"

Leo re-joined them.

"I've asked for her to call me," he said.

"Don't you know of any likely places, Leo?" asked Bel.

"I'm from Athína. I don't know the south coast well."

Nick had left the table and was staring out of the window. Then he turned back and spoke:

"I was thinking about the boy, Yasir, and where his body was found. Maybe there's a clue there?"

He crossed the room to Bel.

"If I remember right, Paksima told you, when she came back from swallowing the pills, that Yasir was not in the cabin. Someone said he'd gone for help, right?"

"Yes. The other man in the cabin said that."

"It seems likely that *going for help* got him into trouble. Maybe he'd seen something of what they were doing to Paksima? Maybe he tackled the skipper or the minders about it or started shooting his mouth off to the other passengers?"

"Could be."

"Now, it seems to me they would want to have refuelled *before* filling their mule with capsules. There could have been a problem or a delay at the refuelling site. Waiting removes the uncertainty and reduces the risk of Paksima digesting too soon."

"That makes sense, too."

"Now, unless there are other gang members on board we don't know about, we know of only three. Remember, Wilhelm the Norwegian saw two in the RIB, but one of those was fair-haired, which didn't match Paksima's descriptions of the guys that were with her. So, we have three – one fair-hair skippering the boat while two dark-hairs are shovelling capsules into poor Paksima. Perhaps Yasir shows up at that point, but they would need her back in the cabin before they could deal with him. Then, they would move quickly, to stop him blabbing."

"Couldn't the skipper put the boat on autopilot and do it himself? Maybe Yasir went straight to him when he found out what was going on," asked Bel.

"That's possible, too, but rather than trying to nail down exactly what happened, my point is that Yasir was not killed until about the time Paksima was dosed up, probably soon after. And they didn't start working with Paksima until *after* the refuelling."

"Which means the refuelling point must be at least half an hour, maybe an hour, *east* of where Yasir's body was found," said Leo.

"Exactly."

"Ierápetra, then."

"You'd think so."

The phone rang and Leo walked with it to the other side of the room. They heard snatches of conversation as Nick zoomed in on the city of Ierápetra. He soon found the small marina right in the town and learned it could accommodate up to a hundred boats.

"It's not very big," said Bel. "Does it have fuel?"

Before Nick could reply, Leo cut in. He was back, looking over their shoulders.

"Most marinas have diesel, but not always petrol," he said. "The coastguard believes there is fuel to be had at the marinas in both Ierápetra and Agía Galíni, but they are small operations, so it would be wise to call ahead if you needed a thousand gallons."

"Well, it could be either of those, I suppose, though Galíni is very close to the islands. But, thinking about it, I can't believe they would be comfortable being so visible. Think about the precautions they took in Turkey."

"What choice do they have though, Nick? If it was dark, they could creep in without causing too much of a sensation. Anyway, I'll get a couple of constables to contact the marinas, find out if they've had any visitors spending large amounts."

After Leo left the room, Nick felt deflated.

"You don't buy this, do you?" said Bel.

"It seems such a risk for them. I know it's only Crete, but still …"

He was still sitting at the table, toying with the laptop, when he saw Leo had left his folder behind and noticed a business card tucked into the corner, under a plastic flap. It said *Daric Hassan, General*

Practitioner, and an address in Mogadishu. Absent-mindedly, he slipped it out of the folder and wandered over to the photocopier, then took a photocopy of the card, folded it, and tucked it into his trouser pocket before replacing the original.

"What are you up to?" asked Bel.

"Nothing. Just desperately sorry for the guy, from what I've heard. Might drop him a line, one of these days."

"I didn't realise you'd met Yasir's father."

"I didn't," he said. "Leo was telling us about him. So tragic."

Bel looked at the file and then at him, as if seeing a new side to his personality.

Nick turned back to the laptop and scanned the harbour at Ierápetra for fuel dispensers, but the images were not clear enough to be sure. He knew Agía Galíni quite well and could not remember seeing any there either. He would take a look. He moved the cursor west, along the coast, past the small resort of Mýrtos and then a remote and mountainous area, ripped by gorges, sometimes leading to hard-to-reach beaches like Kamináki and Trís Ekklíses. Eventually, he reached Léndas, which he knew a little, having visited for a weekend once. Then, a few moments later, he spotted something looking like a weird sea creature. It was just a glimpse, before the software caught up with the cursor and tagged on a name which all but obscured the image. He went back and forth again and again, each time catching a glimpse that was then obscured by lettering.

"What are you doing?" said Bel.

"What the hell is it?" said Nick. "It looks like some sea insect with legs and a white back. I'm going to take a look."

"Where is it?"

"Just offshore, near a place called Kalí Liménes," he replied. The name on the screen changed from Mikronísi to Saint Paul Islet as he zoomed in, and then the image of a small island filled the screen. One of the *legs* was a natural promontory on the seaward side, but the other three were jetties pointing at the mainland. One had a small tanker docked at the end. The white *back* was a string of four round, white storage tanks of various sizes, gleaming in the sun. A small road led from the jetties around and up to the tanks.

"Well, I'll be buggered," said Nick. "We'd better get Leo back. It's an oil terminal for Christ's sake! There, of all places – I had no idea."

CHAPTER 22
A NICE LITTLE EARNER

It was forty minutes before Leo was able to return. There had been a vendetta killing in a village just south of the White Mountains. These things happen from time to time, he explained. Grievances going back decades. He had to review the facts and initiate an investigation, but decided to send Thaní and a constable, rather than going himself, at this stage.

"I should be there, of course, but this is more important. These guys will go on killing each other long after I'm gone."

He shot a resigned look at them.

"We've found an oil terminal," Nick said.

"You've what?"

"Right here," he pointed at the Google Earth image, "just around the coast, east of the islands where Yasir's body was found."

"Good Heavens."

"That's what I said, more or less."

Nick pretended to look guilty, and Bel sniggered for a moment.

"What the hell is it doing there?" asked Leo.

"While you were tied up, we've been researching. The business has been there for sixty years, in fact. It's what they call a bunker station. Supplies oil and other services to visiting ships. The tank farm itself was built in 1966."

"Aren't they a bit out of the way?"

"Actually, no. The site is well situated. It's just seven nautical miles from international shipping waters and handy for the sea route coming out of the Suez Canal."

"What's that got to do with anything?"

"It was very important; a key fact in the early stages and the main reason it made a fortune for the guys who set it up."

"Go on, Nick."

"Well, a huge number of ships come through the canal, of course. Knowing they could fill their bunkers at Kalí Liménes gave them the opportunity to go through the canal with stocks low. That meant a significant saving in canal fees."

"Quite a selling point."

"Not half."

"But these are commercial oil tankers we are talking about, Nick, filling their bunkers with crude oil. This is not the same thing as a motor yacht buying a thousand gallons of diesel for its fuel tanks."

"No, it's not, but these are smaller, product tankers, not mega tankers carrying crude. They carry refined products, so it is usable fuel of various sorts that the terminal stocks. It's just a question of whether they'd be prepared to sell to smaller retail customers or not. And, if you look at the Google Earth image, you can see a small oil tanker at the right-hand jetty, but there are a couple of smaller boats at the other jetties. What would they be doing there, if not getting fuel?

"Also, I found the accounts for the company that owns the place, online. They've been hit hard by the pandemic. Turnover was down by more than half, compared with last year. My guess is, they'll sell to anyone they can get."

"Hmmm. Maybe. Or the local guy is running a sideshow. Who owns the site? Who do we contact?"

"The business was set up in the early 1960s by a guy called Vangélis Ioánnidis."

"Ah." Leo gave a cynical chuckle. "*That* figures."

"What, Leo?"

"The Ioánnidis family is one of Greece's great oil and shipping dynasties. Two of them set up an oil company about fifty years ago. I think one of them married an Onassis – you'll have heard of *them*."

"Of course. Jackie Kennedy married Aristotle Onassis, didn't she?" said Nick.

"Right. Well, it's become a huge oil refining business. They also have interests in shipping, finance and media. They even own a couple of football teams, I think. Or used to. The founders must be getting old now, assuming they're still with us."

"Was Vangélis one of them?"

"I don't think so, Nick, but he'll be related, of course."

"Was related. Vangélis is dead now. Died quite young, but he'd already made zillions. Someone called Tásos Ioánnidis is described as the key principal these days and there are three other signatories to the accounts, other than the auditors. I assume they are the other directors and perhaps a company secretary."

"What's the company called?"

"It's Enka S.A., based in Athens. According to Dun & Bradstreet it's made up of four companies with a combined turnover of one hundred and thirty-five million dollars, but it has only ninety employees."

"That's very small, in terms of the family interests, I'd have thought."

"It must be. The net worth of the family is around one point four billion dollars."

"Okay. Good work, you two. I'll warn the coastguard we might be needing their services tonight, somewhere on the south coast, maybe in the Kalí Liménes area."

"No *maybe* about it," said Nick.

"I need more than your gut feel to deploy a contingent of the coastguard, Nick. At the very least, we need to talk to this company, find out if fuelling a motor yacht there is a practical possibility."

*

They decided to adopt a low profile with Enka and use Bel as the initial contact. There was no answer at the number they had for Theodóros Diamántis, but Antónios Thánou picked up on the fourth ring.

"Kýrie Thánou?" she queried.

"Ne, ne."

He sounded irritable already, she thought.

"Miláte aggliká?"

"Of course, I speak English. What is it you want?"

"I am very sorry to disturb your Sunday at home, sir, but it is an urgent and important matter. My name is Bel Saidi. I am a freelance journalist, and I am investigating the smuggling of illegal immigrants in the south-east Mediterranean."

"I have heard of you. You are Syrian, aren't you?"

"Actually, no, but never mind."

"What can I do for you, Ms Saidi?"

"If I may speak to you in confidence? The police and I are on the trail of a motor yacht which we believe is transporting migrants. We expect them to refuel in the south of Crete tonight, as they have in the past on other such trips. I'm calling you as a director of Enka to ask if they are using your bunker station at Kalí Liménes."

There was a pause. Bel heard him light a cigarette and then exhale.

"We have a capacity of over thirty thousand metric tonnes of oil, Ms Saidi. The operation was built to fill the bunkers of oil tankers, not the fuel tanks of private yachts."

"I realise it's not your target market, sir, but if they asked for, say, a thousand gallons – four and a half thousand litres – would you accommodate them, nevertheless?"

"You'd have to ask the local chief. It would be his call, but I'm sure the answer would be no. It's not his remit and would be highly ir-regular. And I follow the sales records closely. I can't recall seeing an invoiced amount under ten thousand euros, as it would have to be. It would be an obvious anomaly and I would query it. Our invoices are in six or seven figures, as a rule."

"I appreciate you would not normally do this, sir, but times have been hard of late, I know. Maybe the site has been struggling to meet its targets? Perhaps the local man has been bending the rules?"

"As I say, I would have spotted it in the sales records. And he'd have had to set up an account for this buyer."

"What if it were a cash sale, not recorded locally?"

"Then the sales records would not match the computerised inven-tory records. Any oil sold has to come out of the tanks. There would be a shortfall in the inventory."

"Are your inventory records so accurate? Would you spot amounts as small as that being syphoned off?"

"Absolutely. Accurate to the litre. We adjust for evaporation, but that's a small, calculated amount. Anything else would be obvious, not only to us, but also to our auditors, in due course."

"You seem very confident in your systems, kýrie Thánou."

"I should be. I designed them myself, to be failsafe. Now, have I answered your questions? Can I get back to my family lunch?"

"If I might take contact details for your man on the ground? I'd like to speak to him directly, if you don't mind."

"I'm sure you'll get the same response, but all right. Just one moment."

Bel raised her eyebrows at the others and clacked her dark red fingernails against the receiver. She heard Thánou yelling back at his wife, presumably, who was berating him in Greek. Then he was back, breathing heavily.

"All right. Are you ready? His name is Aléxandros Lékas. He has been the manager of the facility at Kalí Liménes for more than eight years."

He went on to read out a mobile phone number which Bel wrote down.

"Tell him I said to answer your questions. He can call me if he needs confirmation."

Bel thanked him and asked him to convey her apologies to his wife for disturbing their Sunday. She put the phone down.

"What do you make of that?" she asked.

"He didn't quite say no, did he?" said Leo. "More that it was not possible, due to the excellence of his systems."

"These things can be gotten around, as a rule," said Nick. "After eight years, this Lékas knows how everything works, up, down and sideways. I bet he's got some fiddle going on."

They agreed Leo would remain behind for now, to coordinate an operation with the coastguard and the police in Iráklio, the prefecture where Kalí Liménes was situated. Bel would call the man Lékas and arrange to meet him at or near his home. Nick would tag along and ask the difficult questions while she kept him sweet.

*

It was a long drive, halfway across the island and passing very close by Saktoúria. Nick could just about make out his little house gleaming on the mountain slope as they drove past on the Agía Galíni road. It was almost four by the time they made it to Moíres.

"What a shithole this place is," grumbled Nick as they drove through a town that seemed to have come together at random. Ugly, modern buildings, many half-built or half-finished, sprawled in the outskirts. The centre of town was chaotic. Pick-up trucks stopped in the middle of the road, motorbikes weaved between vehicles, horns honked, and the smell of cooking meat wafted from cafes amongst the billowing dust and flyblown paper and plastic. Conversations were shouted from a distance and on the move, so it was hard to tell who was talking to whom.

"It has an excellent market, I was told," said Bel.

"If I were him, I'd live in Kalí Liménes. Not much wrong with that, by the look of it."

"He does, during the week. But it's deathly quiet there, Nick. He comes home to civilisation at weekends."

"This is civilisation? God help us."

"Maybe conviviality would be a better word."

"Hmmm. Plenty of *that* here, I grant you."

The house was a newish, concrete villa set back from a quiet, side road on the eastern edge of the town. It was not an attractive house, Nick decided, but the lush gardens and the intertwined white and lilac bougainvillea that grew across the facade gave it a welcoming look. There was a new-looking, silver-blue BMW in the car port, he noticed. Aléxandros Lékas was doing all right, thank you very much, he concluded.

The woman who opened the door was younger than they expected, in her late thirties, with a girl of perhaps five entwined around her legs. Behind her, in the living room, they could see a pair of teenage boys, feet on the table, watching television.

"Kyría Léka?" said Bel. "We are here to talk to your husband."

"Ah yes. You are Bel Saidi. I have seen you on the news. And this gentleman?"

They had not discussed how to describe Nick. Bel improvised.

"He's working with me on this. Nick Fisher."

Nick beamed, thinking that would seem least like a policeman. She smiled back at him.

"Come on in. Please excuse the mess. Usual Sunday chaos. Alex is in his office, in the garden."

They followed her through, past the boys and their football match and out of the French doors to a pleasant, leafy garden with a wooden structure at the end, next to a spreading fig tree. As they approached, a man of about fifty with a greying beard stood up and came round from behind a desk. His wife smiled and retreated.

"Come in, Ms Saidi. I am Aléxandros Lékas. And this is?" He was gesturing at Nick.

"Did she forget to mention me? I'm sorry. I'm Nick Fisher."

"Another journalist?"

Nick decided to do some ad libbing of his own.

"No, I'm a private investigator working with Bel on this one."

"I see," he said, though he looked as if clarity was eluding him.

"Let me explain," cut in Bel, as they took seats in front of the desk. She went on to describe her exposé and how their investigation had led them to pursuing a suspected motor yacht carrying migrants from Turkey to Italy.

"And you think this route of theirs takes them along the south coast of Crete?"

"We're pretty sure about that. The last time, they left a corpse behind. Murdered. Not far from here."

She had his attention now.

"We've calculated that a boat of this size would have to refuel, and Crete is the only option for that. We doubt they would want to be visible in the small harbours at Ierápetra or Agía Galíni, so we reckon your oil terminal would be ideal. Somewhere they could buy perhaps a thousand gallons of diesel in a quiet spot."

197

"Except they could not."

"Why do you say that?"

"The company services account holders only. These are owners of smaller, coastal oil tankers, or something bigger from time to time. These customers buy between one hundred and five hundred *thousand* gallons."

"This is a firm rule?"

"It is company policy."

"Meaning you would turn away a motor yacht that was desperate for fuel and able to pay in cash?" asked Nick.

"If that is a theoretical question, Mr Fisher, I will give you a theoretical answer. I would not want to turn them away; running out of fuel on such a vessel is dangerous. We have a small amount of stock for our own boats – just runabouts, you understand – so I would sell them some of that, perhaps fifty or a hundred gallons, not more. Enough to take them to Galíni or Ierápetra to purchase more in the normal way."

"But this, or something like this, has never happened?"

"If you were running out of petrol in your car, would you go to the oil refinery? We are a commercial enterprise, and it's obvious. There are often tankers at our jetties. I don't think the average boat owner would expect to buy retail diesel from us."

"Could someone else at the plant be accommodating them, when you're not there?" asked Bel.

"I doubt it very much. They all know the rules and they know me. If anyone felt they had to do something contrary to company policy, they would come to me, beforehand."

"So, to be clear, you're certain your oil terminal has not been supplying one or more private motor yachts with diesel at any time over the last year," said Nick.

"I think I've said as much already."

"I'd like to hear a *yes* or a *no*, Mr Lékas."

"I don't appreciate being interrogated, Mr Fisher. Against my better judgement, I've allowed you into my home on a Sunday afternoon and I've answered your questions to the best of my ability."

Bel decided to intervene.

"I'm sorry if you find us overly direct, Aléxandre, but we've been tracking these people for some weeks. We know they smuggle both migrants and drugs and that they've caused at least three deaths. We know they are headed to Crete right now and we expect them to re-fuel hereabouts, because they will have to. And, despite what you've said, we believe your oil terminal to be the most likely place."

"Have you spoken with the harbourmasters at the other places?"

"There has not been time," said Bel.

"Then I suggest you make time, rather than jumping to the con-clusion that Enka has some underhand deal to fuel smugglers' boats for cash."

"Oh, I don't think Enka knows anything about it. Or that anyone involved understands the true nature of this boat's business," said Nick, before softening his tone. "We are not interested in punishing anyone for bending the rules or even pursuing a little self-interest, Mr Lékas. Times have been tough, I know. Sales are down massively. Which must mean your personal commissions or bonuses have been destroyed. Maybe your job is in jeopardy, too? After all those years of loyal service to Enka. Who could blame you for augmenting your income a little?"

"What are you suggesting?"

"I've seen it before, Mr Lékas. It's one of the closest things to a vic-timless crime. One can understand and almost admire the perpetrator."

"What crime?"

"You start by short-delivering one or more of your large custom-ers. Just a little. Mustn't be too greedy. The guy wants two hundred thousand gallons. He gets one hundred and ninety-nine thousand. Only the ones who don't do the proper checks, of course, because they've worked with you for years. They know you're an honest guy. They trust you. And, once you've done this once or twice, you have more oil in inventory than you should. You know exactly how much more because you keep secret records. Or maybe you syphon it off to one of the smaller tanks. This becomes your personal stash, wherever it is, and you sell it off the books for cash, or by transfer into your own bank account, not Enka's. No record of the sales, of course, and the inventory goes back down to where it should be, as if by magic. Sound familiar?"

Lékas was saying nothing, but he had folded his arms across his chest and his body was twitching as his knee jigged up and down. He was looking angry and worried.

"Whether you do this only for the boat we're tracking, or for all comers, I don't know and I don't much care. You know what you can get away with. But, if it's only our boat and they pick up a thousand gallons every six weeks or so, then you have what we Brits call *a nice little earner*. If I have it right, a *litre* of marine diesel costs about one and a half euros, so a gallon would be getting on for seven. Eight or nine visits in the year at seven thousand euros a visit? That should put your earnings back to where they were when you were getting all those commissions and bonuses; the ones that helped you maintain this expensive lifestyle."

Nick finished with an expansive wave of his arm, taking in the smart office, the house, the gardens, and the BMW.

"And I said *victimless* earlier. Well, there's no such thing, of course, but this comes close. The big customer gets a smidgeon less oil than he was entitled to or, to put it another way, he pays a fraction more for what he does get. But it's miniscule for a tanker company. A rounding error, no more. Lost in evaporation. Your employer has its customers short-changed and its policies circumvented, but it's such a minor infringement, isn't it? And yet it makes such a big difference to you, their loyal employee of so many years.

"We're not here to judge you or get you into trouble, Aléxandre. We have no intention of telling your employers, though we would expect you to stop this practice in short order. What we really want is for you to admit that you have a large motor yacht visiting tonight, Sunday night, or very early Monday morning, with a skipper who will be looking to buy diesel from you, as he has in the past. Help us with this and your secret is safe with us."

There was a long silence then. An uncomfortable silence. Bel seemed about to speak at one point, but Nick nudged her with his knee and shook his head very slightly. Lékas was fiddling with an executive toy, swinging a silver ball into a row of other balls, and watching the last ball fly out on its string to repeat the process, on and on. *It's not any kind of perpetual motion machine and that clacking is deeply irritating*, thought Nick. And Lékas did not seem to be enjoying it much, either. In fact, he looked close to tears. Eventually, he pushed it to one side and leaned forward, elbows on the desk, fingers cradled, and stared at Nick.

"How did you know?" he asked.

"I didn't," said Nick. "But I was a policeman for many years. I suppose I've developed a nose for a scam."

"Let me make it clear at the outset, I know nothing about any migrants or drugs. As far as I was concerned, this was just a pleasant man with a yacht who was desperate for fuel. That's how it all started."

"What happened, Aléxandre?"

"They turned up one evening, just after dark. I was alone at the terminal. They said they were desperate, running very low on diesel, and could I help? I asked where they were headed, and they said west. I said, I can't help you, but I think you can get diesel at Agía Galíni. He said he didn't think he had enough to get there, so I said okay, if he brought the boat to the jetty, I would let him have a top-up. It would be dangerous for him to run out, you understand?"

They nodded.

"When he was berthed, he came ashore and asked how much diesel was in the tank – the small one near the jetty. I said only two or three tonnes. He said: why don't you sell me the lot? He didn't want to go to Galíni if he could avoid it. It would be an unwelcome diversion and he might have to wait till morning to get the fuel, which would be a problem for him. Well, I wanted to ask him what kind of a skipper sets course without a clear refuelling plan, but he was taking money out of a saddle bag thing, slung around his neck. I saw him take out four packs of fifty-euro notes. It was six thousand, he said.

If I gave him eight hundred gallons, he would give me the cash. No questions asked. It was about ten percent over the odds, he said, but that was okay. It was worth it to him to pay a little more and keep on the move. Well, the extra could go in my pocket, I realised. And you're right, times have been tough. Five hundred or more euros for nothing would be very welcome."

"So, you agreed," said Nick.

"I did. I was planning to record most of it as a cash sale at the regular price and pocket the surplus cash. I'd explain the circumstances to my boss. He would understand. Then the guy tells me he'll be coming past every few weeks and it would be very helpful to him if this could be a regular arrangement. I told him it was against company policy, and I could get into trouble, maybe even lose my job. He said it would only be a thousand gallons at most and he was happy to continue paying ten percent over the odds. I asked him to let me think about it for a few days and he took my number and said he would call in a week or two."

"And then they left?"

"Yes. And I had the six thousand euros in my hand, five hundred and fifty of which was mine. It was all very easy."

"But you wanted it all."

"It wasn't until the next day that it occurred to me. I had not yet recorded the transaction and now, one of our largest customers was arriving to take an enormous quantity of oil from us. I think it was four hundred thousand gallons. And I knew the guy well. We had a chat and a rakí every time he called. I knew he never checked the pump gauges to verify the quantity billed."

"Because he trusted you."

They saw Lékas wince at that.

"I shut the pump down eight hundred gallons short. He didn't notice. That night I moved the eight hundred across from the main tank to replenish the smaller, diesel one by the quay. It's not the same oil, of course. The customer was buying LSMGO – low sulphur marine gas oil. It's quite like marine diesel, but it has a higher viscosity level.

But I figured I could get away with mixing it with the marine diesel if I kept the concentration below five percent. I didn't think that would do any harm and I knew I was getting a delivery of diesel the next day that would fill the tank and bring the concentration way down. Anyway, now the inventory in each tank was as it should be, and I could keep all the cash. When the guy called, about ten days later, I said yes, we could make it a regular arrangement."

"I see. So, assuming no diesel buyer came back with damaged fuel pumps or worse because you'd contaminated their fuel, your risks were that the customer spotted they were short-changed – but in your example the delivery was just two-tenths of a percent short, something they'd never detect after the event – or that your employer did a spot inventory check before you had time to get everything back in balance."

"There are no spot inventory checks. They're carried out semi-annually on dates I'm asked to agree in advance."

"Because the directors of Enka trust you, too."

"I suppose they must. I've been here a while."

"And have you expanded your little scam? Are there other boats you sell to?"

"No. It's too risky. I have to be there, so it has to be arranged in advance. I don't want to let any of my people know what I'm doing."

"I bet you don't."

"All right, Mr Fisher. I feel bad enough about what I've done. Please don't make it worse."

Bel spoke for the first time in quite a while.

"Thank you for telling us, Aléxandre," she said. "I know it wasn't easy for you and – quite honestly? – it's not that big a deal. You helped somebody out, and then you saw a golden opportunity to earn a little extra in such a way that no-one would really suffer. And you took this opportunity to support and protect your lovely family. We understand."

He looked at her gratefully, for a moment.

"Though, of course, Enka and its customers most certainly would not."

"But you said you would not tell them!"

"And we won't, so long as you play ball with us. Now, you said *they* earlier. Who have you seen on this boat?"

"Just a man and his family – a wife and son, I assume, though I thought it was a daughter, at first."

"Why did you think that?"

"He had long hair, like a girl, and was very good-looking."

"Can you describe the parents?" cut in Nick.

"She was quite dark, about forty to forty-five, attractive. Arab blood, I would guess. He was different. Quite tall, blond-haired, thin but wiry. He looked younger, but he was probably forty or so. A handsome man, charming."

"Did he give you his name?"

"He never told me his name, but he knew mine, somehow."

"What nationality was he?"

"He spoke to me in Greek, but I could tell he was not Greek. I would guess German or Scandinavian?"

"Could he have been British?"

"I suppose he could, but they so rarely have any Greek."

"But you saw no-one else on the boat. No helpers, no migrants?"

"No-one. Just family."

"And the name of this boat?" Nick already knew the answer, but he wanted Bel to hear it from this man.

"It was called Destiny."

Bel gave Nick an old-fashioned look.

"And now the million-dollar question, Aléxandre. Have you had the call? Is Destiny expected this evening?"

He lowered his head as if a great weight were bearing down on him and sighed. *He's trapped and he knows it,* thought Nick. *Between a rock and a hard place.* When he looked up, they saw both resignation and dread in his eyes.

"They called me yesterday. I am to be there from ten pm tonight."

"Then, we will come with you."

CHAPTER 23
KALÍ LIMÉNES

Leo had three calls to make. The priority had to be the coastguard again. They would need time to get an operation approved, get organised and get their boats in the right places. He spoke to Iphigénia at Iráklio once again and told her what he wanted.

"This is above my pay grade, Lieutenant. I will need to speak with my boss and then he may want to talk with you. Okay? We still have a few hours before dark. With good luck we can help you."

Leo did not want to be relying on luck, but he knew this was just a turn of phrase. This was one very efficient, well-trained woman and he knew she would do her best for him.

The second call would be more difficult, and, for a few seconds, Leo wondered if it would be sensible to ask his captain to make the call. More diplomatic, perhaps. More courteous, being the same rank? Leo had barely met the captain of the Iráklio prefecture, but he knew he could not run an operation on the man's turf without, at least, informing him. More likely, he would want to be involved, take all the credit if it went well, blame him if it went wrong. Hopefully, he would not try and run the thing himself at this late stage. That would not be helpful.

No, he decided. He would handle it himself, involving his captain only if the Iráklio guy proved difficult. It was Leo's case, after all. The captain had delegated every aspect to him and his involvement to date had been limited to fawning over the undoubted charms of Bel Saidi.

"We may not know each other well, Christodouláki, but I hear about you," said the Iráklio captain, "and I hear good things. They say you are in pole position for Réthymno, when Chrístos fades away, as he surely will. And, from what I hear, you deserve it. It will be good to have you next door, so to speak. But what can I do for you today?"

"I need to stray onto your turf, sir," said Leo. "We are tracking a motor yacht we believe to be carrying migrants and maybe drugs, too. We expect it to refuel tonight, somewhere between Ierápetra and Agía Galíni, very possibly at Kalí Liménes."

"I thought migrants travelled in overcrowded, inflatable boats, not motor yachts, and way north of here."

"This is a very different kind of operation, sir. High end, fast, comfortable service. And it's expensive. For those who can afford to get out at speed, and in safety."

"What is it you want to do, Leo?"

"I want to set up a joint operation between the police and the coast-guard, intercept the craft while she is refuelling and arrest the suspects. We believe them to be guilty of murders on a previous outing."

"And the migrants?"

"Will be taken to one of the camps to be processed."

"Along with the poor people from the inflatable boats."

"Yes, sir. Their money will count for nothing there."

"You sound quite pleased about that, Lieutenant."

"Not really, sir, but I will admit to not being entirely comfortable when those with money are able to buy a luxury route to freedom while the poorer migrants drown in their thousands."

The captain was silent for a moment. Leo wondered if he was about to get a bollocking.

"You can't change the world, Leo," he said, with what sounded like a touch of regret. "So, you have just a few hours to set this up?"

"That's correct, sir."

"Then you don't want me getting in the way. When are you expecting them?"

"It could be any time after ten or so. Most likely, early morning tomorrow."

"Sounds exciting, but my days of waiting in the dark in the back of beyond, are over, I'm happy to say. However, the Iráklio team must be represented, Lieutenant."

"Of course, sir. I expected you to say that."

"I will ask Lieutenant Anna Vasilákis to spoil her weekend. Do you know her, Leo?"

"I don't, sir."

"She's a tough cookie. Challenges everything. And she just completed a firearms refresher. I think you'll find her useful."

"Thank you, sir," said Leo but he was wondering if this woman would try to assume control of the operation. He was not having that. The captain asked for Leo's contact details.

"I'll have her call you within the hour," he said. "I assume you've alerted the harbourmasters at Ierápetra and Galíni?"

"I will, very soon, sir."

"And the oil terminal? We need to be careful there. It's part of the Ioánnidis empire, I believe."

"I'm aware of that, sir. Two of my team have gone to the local manager's house to enlist his assistance."

"All right, but you need to make sure his bosses are also aware, especially if one of the family is on the management team. I don't want the first thing they hear about this to be a splash in the press about drug traffickers being arrested at their oil terminal. Or worse, not being. It would not go down well."

"No, sir. Good point. We already spoke with one of the directors, Antónios Thánou, but I think there is a Ioánnidis as well. I'll make sure he's informed."

"Talking of the press, have you tipped them off?"

"No, sir." Leo was shocked. "Never crossed my mind."

"Could be great PR for us, Leo, if you pull it off."

"But not if we've got it wrong or screw up. I think I'd prefer to involve them after the event, Captain."

"All right. Your call, Lieutenant, but make sure we win some kudos. It'll be one up on the bloody Turks and a major boost for the Cretan police. And it could take you from pole position to shoe-in at Réthymno. We don't want to miss out on that, do we?" he chuckled.

"No indeed, sir," said Leo, without enthusiasm.

The third and final call was to his long-suffering wife. The operation was going down tonight. He would not be home until the morning.

"You be careful, Leo. These people are drug dealers and killers. You try to corner them like this, they'll be desperate and dangerous."

"I know that. I'm not a complete idiot, darling. There's a whole team involved. Try not to worry," he said, gently.

"I can't help but worry. We've been together twenty-three years; I don't want to lose you now."

She did not say *after losing our daughter, too*, but Leo sensed it, nevertheless. The pain never left them, and the years of suffering had brought them closer, made them even more dependent on each other.

"That's not going to happen," he said, "at least, not tonight. I'll see you in the morning, just as soon as I can get away."

*

As soon as Aléxandros Lékas admitted the rendezvous, Nick realised they would have to stay with him, watch him like a hawk, make sure he could not warn the smugglers. The guy would be in several minds about that, Nick figured, and it depended on who he feared most: the smugglers, the police, or his employers. It was a close call, but only one of those groups was known to kill people without compunction, so Nick figured he would warn the smugglers if he got the chance.

After a few minutes, Nick stepped out into the garden to make a call. It was well after six now and he needed to update Leo. He heard engine noise in the background. Leo's voice was louder and shriller than normal.

"Are you on your way?" he asked.

"I've just left with two constables on board, and I have to meet up with a Lieutenant from Iráklio on the way. We won't make Kalí Liménes until eight forty-five or so. The coast guards are meeting us there. The local boss is a guy called Darius Savvídes. They're bringing two boats, each with a crew of four, but they'll be out of sight, he says. How are you getting on with Lékas?"

"He's admitted to a scam and agreed to help us, not that he had much choice. But we're keeping our eyes on him. Says they're coming sometime after ten tonight, which seems early, from the timings we worked out, but we need to be ready, in case."

"Are you still in Moíres, then?"

"We are ..." At that moment, he saw Mrs Lékas emerging through the French windows with a tray. "... and it looks like we're about to eat something, thank God."

"All right, Nick. Get it down you, then get on your way, will you? It might take you an hour and I'd like you there to review the coast-guard's plan while there's still some light. Can you do that for me? And brief me before we arrive?"

"Sure. Okay."

Nick held the door to the garden office open for Mrs Lékas to go through. In all innocence, she had prepared a selection of savoury and sweet pastries with bowls of ripe tomato with red onion, cucumber in lemon, fresh figs, and a jug of freshly squeezed orange juice. Her husband looked irritated and embarrassed at this show of hospitality for the couple who were blackmailing him, but Nick was delighted.

"This is kind of you, Mrs Lékas. I was wondering where our next meal was coming from."

"It is nothing. You are most welcome," she said, lowering her head as she turned to go.

"We'll be leaving in a few minutes," said her husband.

"So soon?"

"I have to take these two down to the plant."

"And then you will stay?"

"Yes, they have their own car. They will follow me down."

After the door closed behind her, he explained.

"I normally go down on Sunday evenings and stay there during the week. The company rents a small village house for me; it's easier. We're just leaving a couple of hours earlier than usual."

"Will there be anyone else at the plant tonight?" Bel asked.

"Sunday evening? Very unlikely, I usually have the place to myself."

Nick had eaten enough. Now, he checked his watch.

"What time is sunset?" he asked.

Bel consulted her iPhone.

"Just before seven thirty," she said.

"Then we should leave in five minutes," said Nick.

"I need to say goodnight to the kids, pick up my bag," said Lékas, standing up.

"All right, we'll do it. Quick as we can."

"Thank you, but I don't need your company, Mr Fisher."

"Think of it as a bonus, then. Like the ones your company used to give you."

*

They arrived at Kalí Liménes just before seven, the trip from Moíres taking only thirty-five minutes. Nick sat with Lékas in his BMW while Bel tried to keep up in the Jeep. He clearly knew the road very well.

"Seems hardly worth staying down here during the week," said Nick. "It's not so far, is it?"

"I go home some nights, but I like to be here to keep an eye on things and, as you can see, it's a nice place to be."

Nick suspected he needed to be there for his own reasons rather than for the good of his employers: to keep his scam in order, or perhaps to have time away from his wife and kids.

They parked by a T junction and got out. Nick saw a collection of perhaps fifty houses grouped around a small, shingle and sand beach with a scattering of beach umbrellas but no people. The beach was only seventy metres across. A concrete bar had been built to the left-hand side and a few small boats were tied up there. A couple of flatbed trucks were parked on the hard standing behind, waiting to load something, Nick supposed. Today, tomorrow, maybe next week. It was that kind of place. Sleepy and with limited charm, though the sea looked beautiful in the evening sun. Across the water, less than a kilometre offshore, the island of Mikronísi was clearly visible; a small, symmetrical island dominated by four gleaming white oil tanks perched on top. At the lower level, behind three jetties, Nick could see buildings and a few, smaller tanks. There were no ships at the jetties, just a handful of smaller boats.

"How did they get permission to build that – here?" said Nick.

"It helps if your name is Ioánnidis. You can get things done," said Bel, walking up to join them.

"To say it's a bit off-putting for the tourists, must be a massive understatement," said Nick. "Do you get any here?" he asked, turning to Lékas.

"As you can see, there is hardly anywhere to stay, but people do come, mostly foreigners, day-tripping from Mátala, or Greeks taking a break from Moíres or Tympáki. And there are some who bring camper vans to the long beach."

Nick looked askance.

"The beach, east of town is beautiful, well over a kilometre long and there's another beach, between here and the harbour, as you'll see. As for the plant, remember it's been here for some sixty years now. The locals are used to it. They know we take great care not to pollute the seawater – you can see how clear it is – and the comings and goings of the ships provide a point of interest for some."

"One I could do without," said Nick. "I reckon this place would have been a major resort by now, but for those tanks."

"Perhaps, but we are out of the way down here, and it's only in recent times that the roads have improved."

They made their way back to the cars and drove around the beach to the west of town, to a small, man-made harbour containing perhaps twenty boats. None was more than ten metres long and most were smaller, observed Nick.

"Where are you meeting the coastguard guy?" asked Lékas.

"I don't know," said Nick. "I guess he'll find me. The harbour seems a fair bet."

"Or the oil terminal?"

Just then, Nick's phone beeped. There was a text message from Darius Savvídes. *Leo must have given him my number*, Nick realised. He read:

I thought we might discuss tonight's plans over a beer. I am at the old harbour, Taverna Pálio Limáni.

Bel saw Nick's face crease into a smile.

"What is it, Nick?"

"A man after my own heart," he said, showing her the text. "Where's Pálio Limáni, Aléxandre?"

There were just two tavernas in the town plus one out on the long beach, Mákria Ámmos. Pálio Limáni was not the best, according to Aléxandros, but, for a beer, it was a good place, just at the back of the sandiest part of the beach.

"And that's all we need, I think, after your wife's excellent pastries," said Nick.

The taverna was mostly outside, on a stretch of decking. A collection of square tables with blue and white checked tablecloths, laid under heavy glass tops to counter the wind, no doubt. For once, it was not the paler blue of the Greek flag, Nick noticed, but a darker, royal blue. Each table was surrounded by four white, painted chairs with rattan seats. From here, the terminal was imposing. There was no escaping its omnipresence. But Nick had to admit that the turquoise water lapping the sand looked inviting, nevertheless.

As their shoes hit the decking, a solid man in a short-sleeved, white shirt, damp with sweat, swung round from the only occupied table and got to his feet. It was a little hard to tell, with the bushy brown beard, but he seemed to be smiling. Nick saw it in his eyes, and then spotted the coast guard's jacket hanging on the chair and the crossed anchors in gold above the three gold bands.

"You must be Darius," he said, extending his hand.

"Hello, Mr Fisher."

"And this is my colleague, Bel Saidi, and o kýrios Lékas, who runs the little island over there."

Darius looked impressed. He very nearly bowed to Bel.

"I am familiar with some of your work, Ms Saidi," he said. "You are a brave woman. It is an honour to meet you."

Bel almost blushed as her hand disappeared into his bear paw.

"And o kýrios Lékas. I think we met a few years ago. I attended one of your presentations. Business was booming then, you were looking to expand, I think."

"Very different now, I'm sorry to say."

"Of course, but it will pass. You are fuelling private yachts now, I hear?"

"More in the nature of a private arrangement," said Nick. "Not a policy change by Enka, as I understand it."

"No," confirmed Lékas, "it's something I was persuaded to do, to help someone out. Then I was inveigled into making it a regular arrangement."

Inveigled? What a great word, thought Nick. *It sounds so much better than bribed.*

Darius looked confused for a moment. Maybe he was unfamiliar with the word, but he must have decided it was none of his business anyway and moved on.

"And this particular yacht is expected tonight, I understand."

"Yes," confirmed Lékas, "the boat is called Destiny and I was told to expect her sometime after ten pm."

"Told by whom?"

"The skipper. He will want to refuel – something close to a thousand gallons of diesel."

"Why does he come to you, and not one of the ports?" Nick cut in.

"He wants a low profile and is prepared to pay over the odds to get it. We suspect them of running illegal migrants and maybe hard drugs from Turkey to Italy, every few weeks. A boat like his would cause a stir in these little harbours. Not easily forgotten."

They sat then and ordered drinks, then went on to discuss the boat and its crew. Nick said they believed there to be three crew members, but it could be more. It must be assumed they were armed, at least with knives, and dangerous. He went on to tell Darius what had happened to Yasir, Paksima and Lohani and how they had treated Bel.

"And these bastards are Turkish, did you say?"

"We know one of them is, but we don't know if he's on board. The skipper is a Brit, I'm sorry to say. The others we don't know. Maybe another Turk, maybe an Albanian or a Serb."

"You British have a long tradition of seamanship and piracy, Nick, but he would be a rare specimen in these waters."

"I'm sure you're right."

213

"So, we hope to seize this boat and arrest the crew, yes?"

"This is the plan, yes, but bear in mind there will also be migrants on board, so we can't go in with all guns blazing."

"When they refuel, do they let the migrants off?" Darius asked.

"I've never seen any migrants, nor any other crew members for that matter," said Lékas. "It's just him – the English guy – and his wife and boy. I had no idea what they were up to, if you're right about it, that is."

"The man seems to be using his family as a front," said Nick. "Below decks are up to twenty migrants and their minders, keeping them quiet. We think they let the migrants take the air in turns when they are at sea, but they wouldn't want or need to do that while refuelling."

"Hmm. That could be a problem for us."

"Hostages?" said Nick.

"Yes. If these guys are as ruthless and unpleasant as you say, they could respond to any attack by threatening to make hostages of their fee-paying passengers."

"Cue a long-drawn out process of negotiation and a messy ending."

"We sure as hell want to avoid that."

They spent the next ten minutes exploring different approaches they could take. Nick said he would need to discuss things with Leo before they were finalised.

"This is Christodoulákis, right?"

"You know him?"

"We've come across each other once or twice. I don't know about migrants, but if he catches these guys with heroin, they're going to regret it. He's insane about that stuff."

"I'm sure he has his reasons."

"Maybe, but we might need to keep him on a tight leash." Darius gave Nick a long look, but Nick was non-committal. If Leo wanted to give drug dealers a hard ride, he was not planning to stand in his way, within reason. Satisfied his message had been received, Darius took out a marine chart. "Could we move the drinks over here? Thanks. I want to show you what we plan to do."

He mopped up a couple of small spills with a paper napkin, then spread the chart on the table.

"I have two boats waiting with their crews. Each has four men on board. The closest is here, hidden behind this island, Megalonísi. It's just a thousand metres or so west of the oil terminal. The other is about two thousand five hundred metres east, close by the island of Tráfos, off Lasséa Beach, here." He pointed to what looked like a large rock. "They will wait on this side, so they can't be seen by vessels approaching from the east. When your boat appears, this boat will alert the other, then follow at a distance, without lights. When Destiny starts refuelling, both boats will move to block the exit routes here and here. Then we put on the searchlights and use the loud hailer."

"What about me?" said Lékas.

"What do you mean? You will have started the refuelling and now you will pretend to be shocked by this sudden intrusion."

"They'll think I set them up. They could take me hostage, even kill me!"

"Go on the offensive," said Nick. "Accuse *them* of allowing themselves to be followed and putting you in the shit. You've been doing them a favour and now they're going to cost you your job, maybe even get you a prison sentence, all for a few lousy extra euros."

"That's a good approach, Nick, I like that," said Darius. "Put them on the back foot and they won't suspect the truth."

"They'll have radar on this boat, won't they? They'll know they weren't followed."

"Our boats have a very low radar profile, kýrie Léka, and it's probable they would not be looking at the screen anyway. They had no reason to suspect they were being followed. It has not happened on previous trips. I would guess they weren't paying much attention, which means they would not be able to deny the possibility that they were followed."

"Your guess ... my life."

"You'll be okay, Aléxandre," said Nick in his best reassuring voice. "They need you to fill the tanks."

"And after that?"

"By then, you'll have company. We'll have a small, armed team hidden on the island with you. They'll emerge when the searchlights go on. Fait accompli."

Lékas said nothing. He knew he had no choice but to go with it, hope he could blindside the skipper about the involvement of the coastguard and hope the police would do a decent job of protecting him when the lights came on. But doubts lingered in his mind: how much would the police care about whether he lived or died? In their eyes, his scam cast him as a minor criminal, too. Their first objective was to capture the criminals in a bloodless coup. Second, they would want to save and protect the migrants. If he was lucky, he was third on the list. But maybe he was not on the list at all.

"All right, Aléxandre? Can you handle it?" asked Nick.

"I'm going to have to, aren't I? Just remember, guys, I have a wife and three kids. Please don't punish them for my sins."

"We will look after you. Don't worry," said Darius.

Lékas looked less than convinced. The sun was a fireball now, sinking towards the sea to their right. Nick checked his watch. It was ten past seven. He turned to Darius.

"We need to use the remaining light," he said. "Can you run me around your boats' locations and the oil terminal? I'd like to get more of a feel for the set-up. And we need to decide where to position ourselves on the island."

*

Bel stayed behind to make some calls, but they took Lékas with them in the RIB with the twin sixty horse-power outboards on the back and slipped out of the harbour with less than fifteen minutes to go till sunset. As soon as they were clear of the harbour, Darius let it rip and the boat went up on the plane at over thirty knots, bouncing over and buffeting the waves. They swept past the little town and along the long beach. As they approached the tiny island of Tráfos, the coastguard vessel could be seen, lying along the west side, facing out. Nick's heart sank. From what he remembered of Destiny; this boat did not look up to the job. It looked old and ill-equipped. It was black or very dark blue-hulled with salmon pink superstructure, on the side of which the characters SAR 519 were painted. It would be close to twenty metres long.

"How fast would she be?" yelled Nick, over the noise of the engines.

"Not so fast. This is a lifeboat, not a patrol boat. Maybe twenty knots at a push?"

"Destiny is quicker, I think."

"Sure, I'd expect that, but we're not anticipating a chase, are we?"

"No, I suppose not."

"You gave us very little notice, Nick. We brought the boats that could make it in time."

The small crew were saluting them now, as they closed in, and they waved back. Then Darius swung the boat around to the eastern side of the little island.

"It's not possible to go all the way around," he called, pointing at a chain of rocks and boulders that linked the island to the small promontory at the end of the beach. "Seen enough?" he shouted, and Nick nodded, glancing at the sky, where the sun was about to touch the horizon.

They raced back across the face of Mákria Ámmos beach, past the town and then the strange little island with its collection of oil tanks. Soon after, a somewhat larger island appeared. It would be three or four hundred metres across, Nick reckoned. Darius beckoned and cupped his hand against Nick's ear.

"I think you will like this boat more," he said.

They slowed sharply as a second boat appeared, moored close to the western side of the rock. It would be about the same length, but this one was lower, sleeker and looked altogether more modern. The words Liméniko Sóma and the English translation: H for Hellenic and then Coastguard were painted on the dark blue hull along with the crossed anchors insignia and the characters L-E 192. The ubiquitous Greek flag flew from a short mast.

"This one is a CPB, a coastal patrol boat. It is called a Javelin, and for good reason. It can do fifty knots. No problem."

Nick whistled in approval. The crew must be inside, he thought, as Darius sounded his horn and received a deeper blast in response before swinging to port and accelerating away.

The oil terminal was less than a kilometre, so they proceeded more steadily through the darkening water.

"Which jetty? Does it matter?" Darius asked Lékas.

"Use the middle one," he said. "There's plenty of room, as you can see, and it's closest to the offices."

Nick was already scanning the island, looking for places to hide.

As soon as they were ashore, Leo called again, but Nick put him off, saying he needed the light to explore and would call back in half an hour or less. Lékas wanted to open up the office, check the oil stocks and test the pumps in readiness. Nick asked Darius to go with him and keep his eyes on him.

The four largest oil tanks were gleaming pink-white in the blaze from the dying sun. Up close they looked bigger still. The largest ones would be the height of a three-storey house and twice as wide, Nick reckoned. The lower level was already in shadow, but, when his eyes adjusted, he could make out administrative buildings and smaller tanks. He followed the others along the jetty towards them.

CHAPTER 24
A RUSH OF BLOOD

Bel would have welcomed a short boat trip. It looked rather thrilling as they pulled away, in a swirl of surf, and would be invigorating after what felt like a long day already. But she wanted some time to herself and to think about how recent events would shape her series of articles. A specific example of a smuggling operation – how they did it, the characters involved, the motives behind the actions and the movements of money, people and drugs – would give her piece real power; take it from theory and statistics to raw drama and human conflict. She was interested in the skipper, the Englishman. What had turned a minor member of the landed gentry into a drug and migrant trafficker? What kind of man would use his young family as a front in this way when there were dangerous criminals below decks, not to mention desperate migrants? It was to disguise the true nature of the trips, of course, but who would actually *do* that? He must be one callous bastard, she thought. But then *why* was he doing it? He had money, he had his idyllic charter business, so why get himself caught up in this? It was a mystery she was keen to explore. She would try to get some pictures as well. Character studies as well as action. They would not be press quality, but they would do.

Lost in her thoughts, she had wandered away from the taverna, through part of the town and onto the long beach. She watched the boat speed back across the bay and waved, but they did not see her in the fading light. She sat on a rock then and contemplated the sunset. It was something she often did. It helped her put things in perspective and relaxed her. Normally. But not tonight. She found her hands gripping each other, her heart thudding against her ribs. Excitement was natural, she told herself. This was a big deal. But it was not just excitement, she realised. It was fear. But how could that be? How could a former war correspondent be spooked by a minor smuggling operation when she was just an observer in a police and coastguard operation that seemed pretty much wrapped up? It did not make any sense.

She smoked rarely, but now she took the pack of Sobranie Cocktails out of her handbag, selected a pink one to match the sky and lit it. Was it intuition? Some premonition about the operation? She drew the pungent smoke deep into her lungs, then exhaled. And then, with sudden clarity, she knew. It was about Nick. He would be putting himself in harm's way. And there would be no holding him back. He would want justice for Yasir and Paksima and their families and he would not be denied. But she did not want him in danger, no matter how noble the motives. She wanted him safe. She did not want to lose this man. And it surprised her, this revelation from deep within herself. Perhaps the physical closeness had changed their relationship in ways she did not yet understand. She was not sure she wanted this. It amounted to vulnerability, dependence on another human being. She pushed the half-smoked, golden cigarette stub into the beach grit and swore to herself.

*

Leo was irritated by Nick putting him off, though he understood why. He had hoped to catch up with him before letting this stranger into his car, but now there would be no choice. He would be in Moíres in less than fifteen minutes. It had been a busy trip, most of it spent on the phone. First, Anna Vasilákis called to confirm she could make the party and to arrange the pick-up point. She sounded brisk and business-like and asked if he had enough police resources. Leo assumed she meant people.

"There will be just four of us, but I think it is enough, because we'll have the element of surprise, we will all be armed and we will also have a former British policeman, a coastguard officer and several coastguard crew members to assist us."

"Are the coast guards also armed? Do they have gunboats?"

"This I do not know."

"Then I think we need to find out. If not, we might be a bit light, don't you think?"

Leo did not appreciate being told how to do his job by someone he had not even met.

"When I've picked you up, we'll get the latest from Kalí Liménes and review the situation together. Okay?"

He could tell from the pause before the reluctant *okay, then* that she was far from happy, but he ended the call anyway.

Soon after, a captain of the coastguard called. He was Iphigénia's boss, he said. He assured Leo everything was in hand. One of his best men, Darius Savvídes, was already in the area with two boat teams. And Darius had already contacted this Nick Fisher character, as Leo requested.

"Are these gunboats? Are your guys armed?" asked Leo.

"They are not gunboats, no. We have nothing like that close enough. However, we are a paramilitary organisation, as you know, so there will be a cache of small arms we can bring into play, if need be. I'm not sure what they have, but Darius can brief you on all that."

That gave Leo some comfort. He could tell Lieutenant Vasilákis to mind her own damned business. He got the constables to call a harbourmaster each, at Agía Galíni and Ierápetra. He did not see why they should be just sitting on their arses staring out of the window when he was doing everything.

"Just let them know there's an operation going down, as a matter of courtesy. We're pretty sure it's all happening at the oil terminal at Kalí Liménes, but there's just a chance they might see this boat, Destiny. If they do, I want to know about it, right away. Clear?"

They chorused *Sir* from the back seat.

"And when you've done that, I want you to find the names of all the directors of this outfit, Enka. E-N-K-A. Make a list of them with contact details. I'm especially interested in anyone called Ioánnidis."

There's nothing like a little delegation to make you feel better, Leo chuckled to himself, but his joys were short-lived as the sign for Moíres appeared and, along with it, the stocky and unsmiling form of Lieutenant Anna Vasilákis raising her chin in acknowledgement as they drew up. *This is going to be a whole lot of fun*, he thought.

*

Just as Darius and Lékas were about to turn right at the end of the jetty, a thought struck Nick and he called out:

"Aléxandre! Hold on a minute."

As he drew closer, he shouted, "Which jetty will they come to?"

Lékas jabbed a finger at the middle one of the three, the one they had used themselves.

"You're certain?"

"This one is for larger tankers," he said, pointing to the right-hand, easternmost one. "The one over there has no diesel. Anyway, they always come to the middle one. They know how it works here."

That seemed definite enough for Nick. The others continued to make their way towards the two-storey, white building to the right, which was midway between the middle and right-hand jetties. Dead ahead was an orange-coloured, single-storey building. It might have been a parts store or a warehouse of some kind, but it was not the building itself that interested Nick. He walked fifteen metres down the left-hand side and found he could get behind it. Here, he saw that the lower level of the oil terminal had been hewn from the island's natural stone. A vertical rock face backed all the buildings and tanks on the lower level, and this now confronted him. It was sheer, and at least ten metres high. He saw four substantial pipes dropping from the higher level where the giant oil tanks were based. He slipped to his right between the orange building and a concrete, cube-shaped tank to another, smaller, grey building which was perhaps ten metres wide by eight metres deep. Rusting shipping containers and a detritus of former flotsam and jetsam surrounded the building. *Perfect*, thought Nick. There was a gap of about a metre between the grey building and the orange building and the whole of the central jetty could be seen from there. The grey building was closer to the rock face but there was still room to fit a team of people and some equipment behind it.

They would be hidden from view. He circumnavigated the building, looking for any disadvantages. The scrap took a bit of negotiating, here and there, but it would also provide some cover, if it came to it. Pleased with himself, he turned to see the others returning from the administrative building in the gathering dusk.

"Found somewhere?" called Darius.

"Behind here. It's ideal," said Nick. "Good visibility, great cover and about as close as we're going to get."

"Well done. We still have a couple of hours," said Darius. "If you're all done here, let's get back onshore and find Bel. When the police team arrives, we can brief them, then get things set up over here."

"Okay," said Nick, thinking he would telephone Leo as soon as they had crossed the three hundred metres of water between the island and the harbour.

*

The awkward silences started right away. They were the same rank but different prefectures. Different sexes. Leo was the man who thought he was running the operation. Anna, the woman who was the sole representative from Iráklio. It was her turf and she wanted to be sure everything was done right; a well-planned, smooth operation not a ragged, embarrassing cock-up. And she sensed from his incessant smoking and the way he drove, that there was something cavalier, even reckless about Leonídas Christodoulákis. Or maybe it was just the adrenaline pumping. She could not be sure. For now, the drone of the constables on their phones allowed them to assume a respectful silence and avoid talking to each other.

As soon as the constables ended their respective calls, Leo barked:

"What about Ioánnidis? Got anything yet?"

"Nearly there, Lieutenant," one of them called.

"What *about* Ioánnidis?" said Anna. "Are they mixed up in this?"

"People smuggling and drug trafficking? Ha! I wouldn't put anything past that lot, myself, but no, we have no reason to suspect them."

"Where do they fit in, then?"

"There's one on the board of Enka, the company that owns the facility. Your boss wants us to make sure he knows what we're up to before we go in."

"Not unreasonable."

"We already told one board director, as he knows. I'd have thought that would be enough, collective responsibility being what it is."

At that moment, one of the constables reached between the seats with a piece of paper torn from a notepad.

"The Enka directors, sir," he said.

Leo glanced at the clock. It was approaching eight twenty.

"I'm going to hold off for a minute. I think Fisher is about to call," he said.

"I can handle it, as you're driving," said Anna.

He shrugged and handed over the paper and Anna took out her mobile right away.

Leo had to admit. She handled it well. *She was informing him as a courtesy. It was a police operation in conjunction with the coastguard. It will be carried out with a minimum of fuss. And yes, o kýrios Lékas is working with us.* His outrage was given time to dissipate, his protestations stonewalled, his questions fielded with courtesy, but no answers whatsoever provided. *We are not yet aware. We are not in a position to reveal. We will let you know as soon as we know, sir.* It was a masterclass in saying as little as possible. At this rate, she would make Astinomikós before she was fifty, he thought, with just a scintilla of chagrin. He had never wanted that, after all, had he?

The call came in from Nick just as she was finishing up with Ioánnidis. Leo put the call on speakerphone, to her obvious irritation.

"Hello, Nick. I have Anna Vasilákis with me – my equivalent in Iráklio – and two of our constables. You might remember Dimítris and Valádis? We're only twenty minutes away from you now, but you might as well bring us up to speed anyway. We haven't anything else to do."

Nick greeted the group and went through the set-up.

"So, all of us will be concealed on this island," said Leo.

"That was my thinking, yes."

"And, when the coastguard has both boats in position and Lékas is ready to refuel, they switch on the searchlights."

"Yep. And, when they do that, you emerge from the shadows, pointing your guns at them, one of the searchlights picks you out for a moment, so the smugglers can see you, and then Darius will call on them to come out on deck, unarmed, hands raised and make their way off the boat and onto the quayside."

"So, this Darius guy will be on one of the boats."

"He'll be on the Javelin, yes, with four others."

"And the boats can be positioned so escape is impossible?"

"That's the idea."

"And you will be with us, Nick?"

"Nearby."

"What does that mean?"

"I will be concealed towards the front of the jetty. Someone has to make sure Lékas plays by the rules. And I'll ask the coastguard to give me a five-minute warning before they switch on the lights."

"Five minutes to do what?"

"Get on board Destiny. I can swim around, use the stern ladder."

"Are you mad? It's far too dangerous, Nick."

"Actually, I'm quite a good swimmer."

"I'm not talking about the swimming, as you know. There are three of them, all a good deal younger than you, and they might well be armed."

"Yes, but unless I screw up, I won't appear until just after the lights go up. My job is to get to them before the thought of hostage-taking enters their heads, get between them and the migrants, keep them safe."

"That's all very well if they do as Darius asks, but suppose their reaction is to start shooting?"

"Why would they do that? They'll be hemmed in and outgunned. Hostages will be the only way to force our hand, but I'm guessing it'll take them a few moments to figure that out. And I intend to deny them those moments. I'd better have one of your guns, though."

"When did you last fire a gun, Nick?"

"It's been a while, but I still know which way to point the bloody things."

"I'm coming with you," said Anna. "I'm a good shot and I think it's a sensible strategy. If they grab a couple of migrants and put guns to their heads this could all get very messy. And I don't know about you guys, but I was hoping to get some sleep later."

"Very heroic, you two, except now we'll be shooting at you, as well as them. Terrific," said Leo.

"There isn't going to be any shooting. We're going to nip all that in the bud."

"This is not the time for your word games, Nick."

"Wrap it up. We're going to wrap it up before anything happens. Just like that."

The words brought a face to mind. The wacky fez, those manic eyes. Nick remembered watching the comic with his dad. But the audience was not right for one of his impressions, apart from everything else wrong with the idea. He put it down to over-excitement.

"All right, look," said Leo. "We're just ten minutes away. Let's all think a bit more about this. When we get there, we can talk it over, with Darius and Lékas too. Then we'll decide."

Leo disconnected, shaking his head in disbelief.

"Ballsy guy, this Fisher," said Anna. "You might need to tell me more about him."

CHAPTER 25
NICK GOES OUT ON A LIMB

It was now pitch dark and there would be no moonlight to speak of to-night, with the new moon due. The security lights from the oil terminal were shimmering, pale reflections in the black water. That was good, on balance, he thought, but the wind was picking up again. Not so good.

He heard her shoes on the beach grit, more than saw her, and then he felt her arms coiling around him from behind and her chin resting on his shoulder.

"You okay, big guy? Where's Lékas?" she said.

"Darius has him. Don't worry."

"I want you to be careful tonight, Nick Fisher."

He felt her squeeze his waist.

"I'm always careful."

"I don't have many friends, but each one is precious to me, do you understand?"

He turned to face her and hugged her, stroking her hair, and placing a hand on the back of her neck. *Friends,* he thought. *That was the word she used.*

*

The arrival of the police team triggered an immediate meeting; a meeting with four bosses. Leo was trying to assert his authority but was less informed than Darius and Nick. Anna wanted everyone to remember, this was her prefecture. Voices were raised. People talked over each other. It was Réthymno versus Iráklio, police versus coastguard, even male versus female. It took Bel to intervene:

"For Heaven's sake!" she shouted above the din, and they all turned towards her. "We are here to catch some serious criminals, not fight among ourselves. The task force that uncovered this was set up by the captain at Réthymno, at *my* request. And he put Leo in charge."

She saw that Darius and Anna were both going to interrupt and held up her hand.

"Leo is not in charge of the coastguard, and he is not in charge of the Iráklio prefecture, any more than he is in charge of what I write. But he *is* in charge of this operation. I'm sure he will be grateful for your input and your support insofar as it relates to your discipline or expertise, but that's it. He's the boss and what he says goes. That's the only way this is going to work, folks. And we're running out of time. They could be here in an hour."

There was a stunned silence. Leo looked embarrassed and fumbled for a cigarette. Nick said:

"Thank you, Bel. You're quite right. We need to get things agreed and start moving ourselves and our kit into position."

And, with that, Nick started taking charge, in effect. Before decisions were made, he deferred to Leo, but he was defining the questions, setting the agenda. Even when he clarified his own role, there were no objections this time, although Bel was horrified.

At one point, Lékas's phone rang, and they all turned to him. "It's Ioánnidis," he said, staring at the small screen, transfixed.

"You're going to have to answer it, man," said Nick. "We don't want him haring down here and getting in the way."

He looked sick and did not move, then Leo strode over and grabbed the phone.

"Hello? … He's not here right now, I'm afraid. I'm Lieutenant Christodoulákis. This is my operation. Can I help you? … He might be in the control room at the terminal. I'm not quite sure."

Lékas shot Leo a grateful glance.

"I know who you are, kýrie Ioánnidi … I think he will have to explain that to you himself, sir … I can't stop you from doing that, sir, but it would not be helpful … We'll try to avoid damage to the installation, of course, but I cannot guarantee it … Yes, I can, but it might have to wait till morning."

Leo held the phone away from his ear as a stream of diatribe could be heard. Nick ducked his head in mock terror, Bel sniggered. Lékas looked panicky. Finally, there was silence again.

"If an opportunity presents itself, rest assured I will do that, sir. Now, if you'll excuse me, I have a police operation to run … Well, we thank you for that." Leo disconnected to a smattering of applause.

"He wished us luck, in the end," he said. "He wants you to call him back at the earliest opportunity, Aléxandre, but I told him it might not be till morning. As you will have gathered, that did not go down well."

"Nothing goes down well with that bastard. He's not coming down here, is he?"

"He threatened to, but no, I don't think he will now."

"Thank God for that," said Lékas, but he knew he was heading for big trouble when the time came.

Leo seemed to have grown in confidence from the exchange with Ioánnidis. Now he clapped his hands three times to call everyone to attention.

"All right, everyone. Listen up. I'm going to go through this one last time so there can be no misunderstandings. Then we're moving. Okay?"

*

Before they split up, Darius asked for all their phones, except for Lékas who would need his to communicate with the smugglers. He switched them off and placed them in a plastic bag, then handed out two-way radios in their place. "I have five of these," he said. "One for Leo, one for Nick and Anna to share, one for Bel and one for each boat. I'll be in the Javelin with one and my fellow officer, Michális, will be in the lifeboat with the other."

"Don't I get one?" asked Lékas.

"I have only five, but Nick and Anna can keep you in the picture. It's just a precaution, but these don't depend on the weak mobile signal," Darius said, "and they work better in a team situation. Press here to transmit and we'll all hear you. If you're not transmitting, you'll be mute, so you can talk among yourselves without being heard. Don't press this button unless I ask you to, as it will switch your set off, stop you receiving. If that happens, this green light will go out, so make sure it remains on at other times. Is that clear, everybody? Great. As soon as we're finished here, you can have your phones back."

The radio just looked like a chunky phone, battle-ready, thought Nick. He handed it to Anna, and she hooked it onto her belt.

"Can we get them wet?" he asked.

"They're reasonably waterproof. You should be okay."

"And range?"

"Just a few kilometres, but plenty for our purposes. Don't worry, Nick."

Leo then called on everyone to take up their positions and confirm by radio when they were in place. Darius took the seven of them destined for the island back out on the RIB before swinging away in the direction of the lifeboat.

Lékas headed for the control room and Leo signalled for Valádis, one of the constables, to escort him.

"Look, I'm not warning them, all right?" Lékas called back. "The only way I come out of this with *any* chance of keeping my job is if this goes well and they all get locked up. Then Ioánnidis will be taking all the applause and might just forget to fire me."

You'll be lucky, thought Nick, and Leo shook his head at Valádis who took Lékas's arm, saying:

"Come on, mate. Think of me as your bodyguard if it helps."

*

Nick and Anna remained with Leo and Dimítris, tucked in behind the grey building with the view of the central jetty. Bel remained with them, for the moment. As soon as Destiny had been sighted, Nick and Anna would creep forward to assume their positions at the front of the jetty itself and Bel would set herself up as an observer, away from the action.

Something Nick had failed to notice on his recce was the smell, not that it would have made any difference. Now, it was obvious that people used this spot as a casual toilet. There was a stench of stale urine mixed with creosote or tar, and even some discarded toilet paper that did not warrant too close an inspection. They were all grateful when Leo lit a cigarette.

Last to call in was Darius. He had taken the radio out to Michális and then swung back to the Javelin behind Megalonísi.

"All in position. Now we wait," he said. "Over to you, Micháli."

Nick checked his watch but found he couldn't read the face. It was so dark. Bel pulled the lighter out of her bag and held it for him. It was twelve minutes before ten.

"We could be here for hours, of course," he said. "I can't believe we left those pastries with Mrs Lékas. We should have brought a doggy bag."

*

For the next two and a half hours, nothing happened. Every fifteen minutes or so, the radio would crackle, and Darius would ask: "Anything yet, Micháli?" and Michális would respond: "Nothing to report, sir," or "Still nothing, sir" or "Nothing yet, sir." It amused Nick how careful Michális was to choose a slightly different set of words each time, as if his audience would howl with boredom if not only the message, but the words too, were the same. In any case, it struck Nick as a pointless exercise. Surely the man would tell Darius the minute he saw something. Was Darius worried that he might fall asleep? Was the man prone to narcolepsy? The fifth time it happened, Darius went on to say: "Is everyone still awake out there?" which gave everyone a chance to push their buttons and confirm their continued presence. Nick noticed a growing collection of white dog-ends in front of Leo. Young Dimítris, meanwhile, *was* asleep, head back against the wall, snoring softly. Leo seemed content not to wake him, though he was on duty. *Being paid to catch up on the shuteye. Not a bad deal,* mused Nick. *I could go for that right now.*

At twenty-three minutes after midnight, they heard the crackle again and then Michális's voice:

"I think we have something. They must have been further out than we thought, not hugging the coast at all. And now they're coming in from the south at about fifteen knots."

"How far away?" asked Leo.

231

"If they keep up this speed, they'll be here in just over five minutes."

"Jesus," said Nick under his breath, without pressing any buttons.

"You've got them on radar?" asked Leo.

"Actually, no. We haven't picked up much at all on radar, but they switched on their AIS a couple of minutes ago."

"So, they must have no idea we're here."

"Looks that way, sir, and, as they get close to the coast, it would be prudent to switch it on to reduce the risk of collision."

Something didn't sound right to Nick.

"Can you see the boat yet, Micháli?"

"Who's asking?"

"It's Nick Fisher. Can you see her with the naked eye?"

"Negative. They must be sailing without lights, and, at that distance, they would be below our horizon, so no silhouette."

"Darius – didn't someone tell me these AIS systems can be switched to incoming signals only? I don't understand why they're choosing to transmit, as well."

"Not all AIS systems have a silent mode feature, so both transmitting and receiving may be their only option. In any event, it's safer to do both, then you're alerting any other boats to your presence, as well. He doesn't suspect we're here, so he's playing it safe."

"With respect, we're in a remote part of the south coast of Crete and it's after midnight. How safe does he need to be?"

"We're close to an oil terminal, remember. Tankers are coming and going."

"But he has radar and his own eyes. It's a dark night but it's clear. Other boats and tankers will have lights on, one would imagine."

"I think you're making too much of this, Nick. It would be an automatic thing for the skipper to do. We're coming to the coast, let's flip on the AIS."

"Perhaps. But we need to think like smugglers. Turning on the AIS when they don't really need to – that's like screaming *here we are*. Why would they do that? They're desperate to remain hidden. The whole reason we're here is because they chose the privacy of the oil terminal rather than the local ports – and paid over the odds to get that. And what about the radar? *Why* are they so invisible? Could it be that they've done everything they can to prevent signals bouncing back to you?"

"We believe it's a GRP hull. That doesn't help."

"True, but there are other things they can do. You know that. Cover up or remove metal, introduce baffles and angles to divert the pulses."

"Sir, they're three minutes away, now," cut in Michális.

"Look, Nick," said Darius, "I'm sorry, but this isn't your expertise, and we need to get moving now."

"Don't do it," said Nick.

"What the fuck?"

Leo had been listening and knew Nick would not go out on a limb like this without good reason. Now, he cut in:

"Give us a minute here, Darius. What's your thinking, Nick?"

"It may not be Destiny."

"Who the hell *else* is it going to be?" argued Darius.

"Those AIS systems, they're just laptops, aren't they?" said Nick.

"More or less," confirmed Leo.

"Suppose they moved the AIS to the tender, then switched it on, and it's their *tender* that's heading this way."

"Why would they do that?"

"To do a recce and flush us out if we're here. We respond to the AIS, thinking it's Destiny, the tender sees us, tells the mother ship and whoosh, they're out of here."

"Leaving someone behind to be arrested? Who'd volunteer for that?"

"I don't know. Maybe a migrant found himself volunteered for it."

"*One* minute to go, guys," said Michális.

"I'm suggesting we do nothing," Nick went on. "Keep hidden, keep quiet. Let's see what appears at the terminal. Lékas can tell us what he sees under the terminal lights, or we might see them from here. If it's Destiny, we move. Anything else, we stay where we are."

"Are you okay with that, Darius?" said Leo.

"All right. But if it's Destiny and they get away, it'll be down to you, Nick Fisher. Now, I suggest radio silence for the next few minutes. Use your eyes and ears, everybody."

"There's only one problem with your plan, Nick," whispered Anna, when they were off air.

"What's that?" he demanded.

"Lékas won't have heard any of that. They don't have a radio up there."

"Holy shit. You're right."

"I'll go," she said.

Bel had caught the drift of what was going on.

"Here, take mine. I don't need one."

Anna nodded, grabbed the radio, and moved deftly through the detritus towards the control building.

*

As Anna entered the control room, she saw Lékas reaching for a switch.

"Wait! Don't do that. What does it do?"

"It's just the jetty lights, ma-am," said Valádis.

"Leave them off." She went to the window and opened it, then raised her hand for silence. The wind was ruffling the dark water and whining around the tanks, but she could just about pick up the sound of an engine, throttling down as it neared the coast.

"Can you hear it?"

"They're coming," said Lékas. "I need to switch on the lights."

"Have they called?"

Both men shook their heads.

"Then we wait."

They were silent for a few moments, the sound of an engine floating back and forth on the wind, getting more definite.

"It doesn't sound right to me," said Lékas.

"Sounds more like an outboard, doesn't it?" said Anna.

"Yes, it does."

"Let's turn off the lights in here and just watch for a while."

Lékas crossed the room and turned off the lights, leaving just the security lights glowing softly.

"Do you have binoculars?" asked Anna.

"Not here, sorry."

The three of them were staring out into the night, ears straining to catch and place the sound of the engine. It was Valádis who spotted it first, over to the right.

"Is that something?" he said, pointing east. It was the surf from the bow wave that first caught his eye.

"The water looks disturbed, for sure," said Anna, "and wait, yes, I think I can make out a hull. It's grey, I think, not very big."

"It's a RIB," said Lékas, "and there's just one person in it."

As they watched, the boat slowed again, to about five knots, Anna reckoned, and started making its way around the front of the island, staying back from the jetties and the pale pools of light from the security lamps, but it was still quite clearly visible. Anna saw a flash of reflected light.

"Get down, everyone. I think he has binoculars or a camera."

"But I'm *supposed* to be here," said Lékas.

"So you are. Okay, we'll stay down while you put the lights back on and wander around a bit, looking busy."

She watched Lékas do as he was told, putting on a white coat and picking up a clipboard, seeming to check and note readings from various meters and dials. It would all be very reassuring for any observer, Anna thought. She just hoped to God the man did not spot the coastguard boats. The Javelin should be out of sight unless he decided to swing around Megalonísi to check. The lifeboat was exposed, but it was more than two kilometres away and backed by the larger silhouette of Tráfos. As long as Michális was showing no lights, not even a lighted cigarette, they might just get away with it.

"Is he still there?" she asked Lékas.

"I think so. It's hard to see with the lights on."

"Well, you've completed your performance now. He'll have seen you, I'm sure, so you could turn them off again."

He did so and then joined them at the window, but he remained standing.

"He's still there but he's not looking any more. I think he's using a phone. Now he's sitting down again."

A moment later, they heard the engine note change.

"Is he going?"

"I think so."

"Can you see him at all? Is it a he? Is he light or dark, tall or short?"

"I'm not sure."

"Does he have blond hair?"

"No, I'd say not, and he'd be around average height."

The others got to their feet as the boat disappeared back the way it had come. They heard it accelerate until it was biffing the waves, heading south. Anna reached for the radio.

"Lieutenant Vasilákis here – Anna. The vessel was a RIB with one person aboard. It was a male, dark, average height. He seemed to be checking us out. We let him see Lékas going about his business while we remained hidden."

"Did he see the lifeboat, do you think?" asked Darius.

"No way of knowing. He left after making a call, moving fast – whether he saw no reason to be slow and careful, because he knew all was okay, or he was getting the hell out because he'd spotted the lifeboat, it's impossible to say."

"We were very careful," said Michális. "Dark and silent mode here."

"Well, we'll soon know," said Leo. "Good call, Nick. You read that one right."

There was a pause while everyone waited for Darius to echo those sentiments, but he said nothing. *A proud man* thought Nick.

"What happens next?" Nick asked.

"We wait."

This time though, they did not have long to wait. Less than five minutes later, Lékas's phone started ringing. He looked at Anna, eyebrows raised, and she nodded.

"Ne? Lékas here."

It was the same, languid voice he recognised from before, the same, strangely accented Greek.

"Hello again, Aléxandre. How are you today? Are you ready for us?"

"All ready," he responded, his mouth drying as he spoke.

"We need a little less this time. Just eight hundred and fifty. Okay?"

"No problem."

"Good. Then we'll be with you in twenty minutes or so."

Lékas went to acknowledge that, but the line was already dead.

"They're coming," he said.

Anna used the radio to warn everyone.

"They can't have seen the lifeboat," said Leo. "So, back to Plan A. Anna? You three need to get back here and get yourselves set up on the jetty. I have guns and vests for you."

CHAPTER 26
AN ASS OF YOU AND ME

Nick felt exposed. He and Anna were in the water now, along the inner wall of the right-hand jetty, tucked behind a small boat for cover. As soon as Destiny was in position, stern facing them, they would receive a five-minute warning message from the coastguard, and then their task would be to swim across the sixty-odd metres of water and attach themselves to the boat, ready to climb the stern ladder. Meanwhile, Lékas would be distracting the smugglers on the central jetty, greeting them, taking payment, and organising the attachment of the fuel lines. At the same time, the Javelin and the lifeboat would be creeping into place, blocking their escape. Bel had elected to camp out on the left-hand jetty, away from the action, but close enough to get some good shots. Leo and the two constables would stay undercover behind the grey building until the coastguard switched on their searchlights. Then, they would run to the end of the central jetty, firearms raised.

Nick's mind was racing with *what if* scenarios as they waited. It all seemed well planned but so much could go wrong, even so.

"Are you sure the guns will work?" he whispered to Anna.

"The Heckler can do immersion in water. We'll be okay," she replied.

Nick was not reassured. She might have one of the Heckler & Koch pistols, but he had been given a revolver. It would be more than em-barrassing if he pointed it at some serious desperados and only got a soggy click. And what about the stern ladder? He had assumed it was a fixed feature. It looked like it, he remembered. But what if it was not? What if it could be pulled up, like a drawbridge, or detached and removed? Mounting the transom of a sixty-foot boat without a ladder would be next to impossible, he imagined, even without soggy, bulletproof gilets weighing them down. He decided to keep that thought to himself, for now.

238

The main jetty lights were still off, he noticed. That was good. The darker, the better, but whether the smugglers would insist on more light – or worse, smell a rat – only time would tell.

As he watched, he saw Lékas make his way to the end of the jetty, holding his mobile phone. He was looking across to his right and gave a short wave. He must have sighted Destiny.

"Here we go," said Nick. "Are you okay?"

Anna gave a thumbs up and suppressed a shiver. Her mouth was a thin line now, her short, dark hair plastered against her skull. *She looks determined – and angry, somehow*, thought Nick. *Or maybe that's how she does scared.*

Within a minute, he was picking up the throb of an inboard diesel. Lékas was talking on his phone and gesticulating. *If he warns them now, things might get hairy*, thought Nick. But he seemed to be going through the normal routines, guiding them in, side on to the central jetty.

The clean lines of the white hull slid into view now and Nick sank a little lower in the water, making sure the boat was between them and Destiny. It was no more than forty metres from them now. He heard voices calling out, saw Dunham at the wheel and another man handling the ropes, leaping now from yacht to quayside, looping a rope around the bollards, pulling the yacht tight against the jetty wall, the fenders creaking and squeaking under the pressure. Having secured the bow, the man turned his attention to the stern, pulling with all his strength until the stern came around and nestled tight against the quay, then looping the rope around the bollard and securing it with what looked like a mooring hitch. *Ideal for a fast getaway*, thought Nick. The man was medium-height and dark. Nick wondered if he was the recce guy. The other one would be below, guarding the migrants. He saw that the cabin areas were curtained. No clues there as to the secret cargo. Of course, the smugglers thought Lékas was unaware of their trade, and they would want to keep it that way.

"Not brought the family this time, then?" he heard Lékas call, as Dunham stepped down from the wheelhouse and made his way over to the gunwale.

239

"Actually, I have. Not the wife and boy, but this gentleman is family, too." He indicated the darker man who was just standing up after putting the gangplank in place. He gave a curt nod at Lékas and then glared at Dunham, before walking over and hissing something in his ear.

Nick and Anna exchanged raised eyebrows.

"As I've been reminded, I'm afraid we're behind schedule, Aléxandre my old mate, so we'll have to give the rakí a miss this time and get pumping, if you don't mind."

"No problem," he said, and started dragging the heavy fuel line aboard, assisted by the darker man, who had already lifted the cover to the fuel inlet.

Nick's radio was in the small boat, under a tarpaulin. Now he heard it crackle and a hushed but perfectly clear voice said: "Five minutes."

They saw Dunham's head whip around and he stared in their direction for a moment. They froze.

"What's up?" said the darker man.

"Thought I heard something, for a moment."

Now they were both staring until Lékas, *bless him*, said:

"I thought you were in a hurry, guys. I need your help to get this attached."

The dark man said: "Probably a rat," and returned to his work.

Dunham continued to stare for several more seconds before turning away. Anna started to move, but Nick grabbed her arm.

"Wait, give it thirty seconds."

"But we only have five minutes!" she hissed.

Nick waved his hand as if calming the waters. "Thirty seconds," he said, setting the stopwatch on his wristwatch to four and a half minutes.

Dunham did not look again and seemed preoccupied now, counting out notes. If they were fifty-euro notes, Nick reckoned there would need to be about one hundred and twenty of them.

Nick reached into the boat and switched off the radio. He did not know if the thing was one hundred percent waterproof and anyway, he was not about to risk another crackle or one of the others speaking at the wrong moment. He glanced at Destiny and saw there was no stern ladder whatsoever. Where did that false memory come from? It was a quite different arrangement. After the initial shock, he realised it might be better. A broad platform extended just above the water behind and below the aft deck. It was called a swim platform if Nick remembered right. If they could get themselves onto that, it would be a simple matter to vault the metre-or-so-high transom.

Now, he signalled to Anna, and they slid into the water. It was not pitch dark. A glance in their direction, and they might be spotted. Nick was hoping the security lights and the lights on Destiny itself would impair the smugglers' night vision. He guided Anna along the jetty wall to the very end, rather than swimming across the diagonal. This put them in a different line of sight to the one Dunham would remember and, as they reached the end, Nick could see that, as hoped, they were almost hidden from the smugglers now by the bulk of Destiny herself. They pushed out across the stretch of water between the jetty and the stern. The water was not cold. They swam a steady breaststroke, taking care not to break the surface with their legs. From the halfway point, they started to believe they would make it.

Another minute or so and Nick reached the edge of the GRP platform and grabbed hold. Relief was fleeting. There was still a mountain to climb. He checked his watch. Just over two minutes remained, and he hoped to God it was enough. Anna was just a few seconds behind him. She gave him a nervous grin. He jerked his head, then put a finger to his lips, indicating they should climb on to the platform as quietly as possible. Then he winked at her. *Here we go.* He would try to keep his actions smooth, but swift. Any sudden moves and the weight shift from his body would send an alarm signal through the boat. He allowed his body to float up to the surface, positioned himself parallel to the platform edge, then part heaved, part rolled himself onto the platform. He could feel the yacht absorbing his weight, but it was a smooth movement, like the swell. He was confident no-one would notice. Now he helped Anna up and signalled her to stay put. He saw now that there was a little door in the transom, leading from the swim platform to the aft deck. He took out the four adhesive, fluorescent orange patches Darius had given him and handed two to Anna.

"Stick these on your upper arms," he whispered.

"What for?"

"Stop you getting shot by our guys."

"Makes us a target though!"

"That's why I said arms, not chest or back. Hobson's choice, I know. But they need to know where we are."

Reluctantly, she complied. He kneeled on the platform and raised his head above the transom. The square, aft deck area was accommodating the still-wet RIB, he saw. Beyond, was a raised seating area where the aft part of the upper deck provided a canopy, and beyond that, the entrance to the interior. Nick could see that the seating area was empty and there was no-one on his end of the upper deck, but, other than that, it would be potluck, as he could not see into the darkness of the interior or the front of the upper deck. Logic told him Lékas was keeping the two men busy near the fuel tanks and the third would be down in the cabins, guarding the migrants, but logic is not enough when your life depends on it.

He searched for corroborating evidence and found none. He listened hard and could hear muted exchanges between Dunham and Lékas, but nothing from the darker man and no sounds from below. It was hard to believe perhaps twenty people were living and breathing, just a few metres away. They would need to get themselves close to the migrants before the lights came on. It was now or never.

He nodded to Anna, then, eschewing the little door, he vaulted over the transom and landed on the aft deck, soft as a cat. Anna did the same and then they drew their guns and moved forward, keeping low. The steps leading to the upper deck looked tempting. If the whole of that deck were empty, it would be a good vantage point, but it was not what they were there for. Their job was to protect the migrants, prevent hostage-taking, and that meant heading down to the cabins.

Nick raised his revolver and used his left hand to pull open the door to the salon area. It was empty. He nodded to Anna, and they crept in, keeping low. They could hear exchanges between Dunham and Lékas just outside and could even make out some of Dunham's crisply enunciated words. They would have to assume the other guy was with them. The salon area was polished wood with orangey-brown, cushioned seating for at least six in an L shape around two solid-looking, square tables on wooden pillars. To Nick's immediate right, near the entrance, was a paler, striped armchair. Beyond the salon gleamed a compact galley. They made their way through without a sound, past the metal staircase leading up to the fly deck, and on to the wheelhouse. To the right-hand side, a short passageway led to a staircase heading down. Nick signalled to Anna and pointed. That was where they were going.

When they reached the top of the staircase, Nick paused. It would be impossible to be silent, descending those metal stairs, he realised. He leaned over the stairwell and then reared back. A dark-skinned man in battle fatigues was sitting on a chair at the foot of the stairs. He had an AK-47 assault rifle in his lap. Nick checked the stopwatch again and saw just six seconds remained. Quickly he cancelled it before the bleeper started. He turned to Anna and mimed holding a machine gun, then pointed down the stairwell. Then he brought his mouth right up to her ear.

"We'll have to be super quick," he whispered, and she nodded, frowning with concentration.

They heard the flick of a Zippo-style lighter, and blue smoke started drifting up from below. Inside one of the cabins, someone was complaining, but the smoker hissed, and silence resumed.

Nick had been counting. Now he raised both hands with the fingers splayed and started dropping a finger each second. Anna got the message and readied herself. At five seconds, Nick lowered his hands, and they released their safety catches with audible clicks. The guy must have recognised the sound, because they heard the chair scuff the wooden floor but, at the same moment, the deck was flooded with brilliant, blinding, white light.

"Go!" yelled Nick and hurled himself down the stairwell, colliding feet first with the man in fatigues before he could raise his gun. He fell back over the chair and Nick threw himself onto the man's legs and pressed the revolver barrel against his forehead as Anna appeared behind him and reached for the AK-47 and pulled it from him. They became aware of Darius's voice, booming from the loud hailer and the roar of the coastguard boats revving hard as they closed in. They also heard men running on the jetty.

"This is the Greek Coastguard," they heard Darius call. "Your exit routes are blocked."

There was a pause and the light vanished for a few seconds. Nick tightened his grip on the man's collar as he imagined each boat's searchlights swinging across the water to illuminate its sister ship and reinforce the message.

"And armed police are directing firearms at you."

This time some light returned as the other searchlight swept the jetty. Through the cabin portholes, they saw Leo, Valádis and Dimítris, each five metres apart and crouched on one knee, pointing their pistols at the boat. They were lit for a moment and then both searchlights were once again focused on Destiny.

"Escape is not possible, so please, put your hands behind your heads and make your way towards the gangplank."

Nick and Anna had no idea whether the smugglers on deck were complying, but then what choice did they have? The timing had been impeccable.

"All right, son. Take it easy now," Nick said in an avuncular voice tainted with underlying menace, moving his body weight from the man's legs and into a crouching position. "You heard the man. Your mates are surrendering, as we speak. So, take it easy now. It's all over."

As he rocked back, he became aware of several sets of eyes staring at them from the cabin. They still looked terrified. A nut brown, older man in Arab dress was glaring at him urgently, his eyeballs flitting to and fro, but it was not until Nick felt the cold metal against the back of his neck that he grasped what he had been trying to tell him.

"Put down your guns," said a heavily accented voice.

"Do as he says, Nick. This one has an AK-47 too," said Anna, as she put on the safety and laid her Heckler & Koch pistol on the floor. Nick followed suit with his revolver.

"And you," he said, turning to Anna, "will return the gun to my friend."

She reached for the pistol, but he kicked it away from her hand.

"The assault rifle, I mean."

With great reluctance, Anna reached over and passed the AK-47 to the man as he scrambled to his feet. Immediately, he thrust the rifle butt hard into Nick's stomach, winding him. Then, he took a step back and trained the rifle on them both. His colleague then collected both handguns, checked the safety catches and tucked them under his belt.

We are so fucked, thought Nick. *You'd think by now I'd remember never to assume anything. Why, then, did I assume the man on deck was one of the three the Norwegian saw and not a fourth man? I might regret that for the rest of my life. But there again, that might not be so very long, now.*

They heard Darius on the loud hailer again.

"I need you to move *now*. Make your way to the gangplank." It must have been one of the policemen, probably Leo who fired into the air at that point, to reinforce the message.

"Wait, boss," called one of the guards, softly. "We're coming up."

Nick watched helplessly as they locked the three cabin doors and then prodded Anna and him up the stairs, at the end of the gun barrels, through the wheelhouse and onto the side of the boat to join the others, who had gone nowhere, despite Darius's commands. The light was so bright on deck, it took Nick's eyes a minute or two to adjust. Then, he saw that one guard had thrown his AK to the dark man and taken Nick's revolver from his belt, and he was now pointing it at Nick's head. He did not throw the Heckler to Dunham, who appeared to be unarmed. *That's interesting*, he thought.

Now, the dark man started speaking:

"As you can see, two of your team are now our hostages. We also have eighteen people locked up below decks. And we outgun you. As you may know, these Kalashnikovs fire up to six hundred rounds per minute."

245

He paused to let that alarming statistic sink in.

"You will have your police team stand down right away and, while we refuel, you will have your coastguard cutters move aside to allow us free passage."

Nick's heart was sinking. It was all his fault. That one little word – *assume*. It went right back to training, centuries ago. He remembered the police trainer at the blackboard, dividing the word with two sweeping, chalk lines, saying: *This is what you do when you assume; you make an ass of you and me.* He even remembered the chalk screeching and the class wincing as he underlined those three words before turning back to them, saying: *So, don't do it, all right? Ever. Not even once. Never.* The words echoed in his head now. Had he learned nothing in thirty-odd years? Leo would have no choice now but to do as they asked. And, as soon as they had their fuel on board, Nick and Anna would be joining them on a boat trip to God knows where; a trip they would be unlikely to survive.

CHAPTER 27
CONFRONTATION

The dark man was speaking again:

"You will leave your weapons there, on the jetty, and you will walk back to the quayside and stay there. Do it now. You have thirty seconds, or this man will die."

Nick saw the man pointing the AK-47 at him and felt a rush of uncontrollable sadness. He almost burst into tears. It was not the emotion he expected or wanted, but the threat of imminent death made him instantly aware of just how much he wanted to live. Despite all the pain of the last few years: the death of his father, the divorce, the sour taste of losing his job, the problems between him and Jason, he had survived, picked up the pieces and made a life for himself, here in Crete. He thought of that and the people in the village he had come to care about. He thought about his daughter, Lauren, and he thought about Bel. He did not want to die. Not now. Not like this.

He saw Leo give him a short, sad wave as he and the constables walked away from their pistols and retreated the length of the jetty at a trot. Pretty soon, they would restart the refuelling, the coastguard would back off and then it would be too late. They would be alone, at the mercy of these known killers.

Realising the assault rifle was no longer pointing at him, Nick found himself able to think again and now he was thinking hard. He became aware of Dunham, looking at him steadily. He seemed to be trying to communicate something, unable openly to express it, but there was an intensity in those blue eyes and Nick found himself staring back. He had felt some strange affinity with this man since their first meeting. He felt they were bonded by a certain Britishness, an innate sense of decency, of right and wrong. It was a weird notion, to feel that way about a well-heeled wastrel who was smuggling people and drugs, but the feeling was there, for some reason. And it was strong. Undeniable.

As he watched, he thought he saw Dunham's eyes flit to the guard's midriff and then they were back, staring. Had he imagined it? In the bright, artificial light, he could not be sure. And then it happened again. This time it was followed by a raised eyebrow. And Nick twigged. Dunham had spotted the Heckler in the man's belt and that look could mean just one thing. *Get hold of that gun and I will help you. I'm on your side.* To test the theory, Nick raised an eyebrow himself, as if to say: *Really?* And this time, Dunham blinked in slow motion. It was almost uncomfortably seductive, but it amounted to a nod. *Okay, game on.*

Nick surveyed the scene. Lékas was neutral, he figured. He did not think he would fight with the smugglers, but he might not fight against them either. So, if he could count on Dunham, it was three against three. The only problem – and it was a big one – was the other three had all the guns. He would stay alert, bide his time, look for an opportunity. And before that, he would have to try and let Anna know Dunham was with them, not against them. But how to communicate it, and would she even believe him?

*

Bel crept down from the jetty to a ten-metre boat on the starboard side. Here, she was that little bit closer to the central jetty, and the boat's cabin provided some cover. She fitted her zoom lens and knelt on the deck, laying the camera on the gunwale, pointing at the end of the adjacent jetty, some thirty metres away.

When the searchlights came on, she adjusted her lens focus and then she heard Darius make his demands as the lights darted about, but then, for a good minute, nothing happened. *What's happening?* she thought. *Why are they not complying? Are they playing for time?* She heard Darius speaking again and saw Leo fire a single gunshot into the air. And then a sick feeling formed in her stomach as she saw Nick, pushed and prodded out of the wheelhouse and onto the deck, followed by Anna. A man followed with a machine-gun and then another. *So, there were four of them. Holy shit.* And then one of the smugglers was talking, but it was not Dunham.

She could not quite hear the words. Instead, she zoomed in on him and took a string of photographs. The last two showed him pointing a machine-gun at Nick's head. Soon after the man stopped speaking, she saw Leo's team put down their guns and retreat to the quayside. Now she focused on Nick. He looked strange, motionless, pale in the blaze of light. She was afraid for him and wondered if she should return to the group. But what good would it do? How would she be able to help? No, she decided. She would stay professional, detached, and focused. Record the events. She hoped to God one of those events was not Nick's head exploding from a high velocity bullet, fired at close range. She did not want to see that. She never wanted to see anything like that again.

*

A few minutes later, the searchlights were switched off and the sound of the lifeboat's engines kicked in as it chugged across the front of the oil terminal to line up alongside the Javelin, leaving an escape route, heading east from the terminal to begin with, but then south, then west when clear of the shore. Nick saw Lékas pulling the heavy fuel line across the deck. He tried to attach it, but it did not quite reach.

"Will you feed me a bit more line. A metre or so should do it."

The dark man put down his AK and did as he was asked, then Lékas said:

"Now, will you give me a hand, please?"

"What is it?"

"I need someone to take the weight of the line while I attach the coupling."

Nick glanced at Dunham. There was something in his face. Both eyebrows raised with a minute inflection of the head. Nick understood: *such a request for help had never been made before.* This was Lékas trying to help, giving them a chance.

And now, Dunham was speaking:

"Should I go check on the passengers, Razmik?"

It was a redundant question, but it was enough to distract Nick's minder for a moment.

"Perhaps I could come with you," said Anna, joining in the fun. "I need to use the toilet."

"Nobody goes nowhere," said Razmik, flustered, but he had turned towards Anna. Nick saw his chance and spun himself anti-clockwise, ducking his head and whirling his arm, his hand in a karate chop. As Razmik turned back, his gun hand collided with Nick's flailing arm. He did not drop the revolver, as Nick might have hoped, but his grip was loosened. Now, Nick grabbed the man's wrist with his other hand and twisted the gun up and away from his face. He saw Anna grappling with the other guy and his AK-47. She had done well. The gun was straddled, crossways between them, both wrestling for control. She was a tough, solid woman, but he doubted she could win that battle. Maybe she could hold on for a few more precious moments.

Nick came to full height now as he fought with the man and then, seeing his chance, kneed him in the groin as hard as he could. *One for Paksima*, he thought, as the man groaned and buckled. Dunham was there, quick as a flash, whipping the Heckler from the man's belt, flipping off the safety and putting it to the head of the other guard, who froze, allowing Anna to tug the machine-gun from his grasp. Nick heard men running on the jetty again. The police team must have seen what was going on and decided to assist, but at the same time, the dark man was throwing himself to the deck and rolling towards the other AK, but Nick was still locked with Razmik. He brought both hands into play, trying to wrest the revolver out of his hand while the man clawed at his face and eyes. They were on the deck now, Nick sitting up, pulling back his head to protect his eyes while gripping Razmik's neck. Now Anna was covering the other guard, Dunham tried to repeat his trick, putting his pistol hard against the man's temple and hissing:

"Freeze, Razmik, or you're dead."

Now, at last, Nick was able to wrench the revolver from Razmik's hand and roll himself away. Then all hell broke loose.

Leo was shouting:

"Do not pick up the weapon, or we fire."

But the dark man had already grabbed it and kept on rolling to the gunwale, despite the shots coming from the jetty. Nick saw that he was not hit and was about to fire back at the police. He glanced at Dunham and Anna and saw they had their charges under control, then threw himself forward onto his elbows on the deck, grasping the revolver with both hands. He loosed off a couple of rounds at the dark man. He thought he must have winged him, at least, but it failed to prevent him spraying the police with around thirty rounds in a three-second burst. Nick got in one more shot while that was happening but missed, and now the man was turning on them, as a pool of dark liquid formed around him. For a moment, Nick thought it was blood but there was too much of it. Far too much. It was diesel. And now he could smell it as it ran across the deck. Someone must have shot a hole in the refuelling pipe.

Nick knew diesel liquid was not so dangerous. Technically it was flammable but getting it to burn was not easy. *Was marine diesel different? More dangerous?* From the man's reaction, *he* seemed to think so, or perhaps he thought it was petrol. He looked horrified as he found himself sitting in a spreading pool of the stuff. He was pointing the AK at them now, but he was hesitating. Nick was flat to the deck, not offering much of a target, while Dunham and Anna were staying close to their respective guards. He might be confused about what was happening with Dunham and anyway, he would need him to sail the yacht. And he would not want to kill his own men. Instead of firing, he tried to get to his feet but slipped in the fuel and crashed onto one knee. *If he succeeds in standing*, Nick was thinking, *the police should have a clear shot*. He saw Lékas hovering at the hatch entrance, staying low, but he was unarmed. Even if he wanted to atone, somehow, there was little he could do.

Now, he saw the man try again. The lower half of his body was smothered in oil, but he managed to place his left boot on the deck without slipping and then lever himself up. Nick saw him glance in the direction of the police and then stoop, but no firing came from the jetty. He started walking gingerly across the deck towards them.

Nick found himself in a position to take the man out, but would he still manage to press the trigger? Just a couple of seconds from that brute of a gun could take them all out. Nick had fired before, of course, but that was to protect the police. Now, as a civilian, he was conscious that killing this man in cold blood could earn him a murder rap. Leo had not given him *carte blanche*, he had just lent him a weapon with which to defend himself.

As Nick hesitated, it was Anna who spoke, in a clear, calm voice:

"That's far enough."

"Or what?"

The dark man could see that neither she nor Dunham were in a position to shoot without giving their guards an opportunity to overpower them. He took another step forward. He would be no more than six or seven metres away. Nick was acutely aware of the widening angle eroding any cover he might have had. But his revolver was pointed at the guy's head, and he knew he still had three rounds in the chamber.

"Or I will ask my colleague to shoot."

"He's not going to do that. He knows I would get several rounds off, even if he got me right between the eyes, which at this distance is not likely."

"You would still be dead."

"Perhaps, but I'm a desperate man, Lieutenant. It's all or nothing for me. Always has been."

It was an impasse. The man stopped moving forward. They stared at each other in silence as the wind rattled the shrouds and waves slapped the hull. Nick thought he heard something bump the side of the boat, but he could not be sure. *Where the hell are the police?* he wondered.

Nick had squirmed around so he could see the others while keeping his gun trained on the man's head. Now, out of the corner of his eye, he saw Dunham move very slowly, his pistol still pressed against his guard's head, but he was turning, pushing the two guards together, side by side, while he was now to the left-hand side, but still very close to the man he was guarding. Nick saw that this change enabled Anna to cover both guards with the AK. Risky, but doable. She herself would be more exposed, so she would need to stay as close to them as the weapon allowed. She realised what was happening and jerked her gun to chest level to emphasise she was covering them both now, though Dunham continued to press his pistol against his man's head.

The dark man must have seen what was happening, but perhaps he failed to grasp the significance of it. Certainly, he was not prepared for what happened next. Dunham dropped to the deck, rolled three hundred and sixty degrees to his right, and adopted a firing position on the deck. The man seemed to be trying to work out what the hell was going on. Nick took his chance and fired twice. One bullet struck him in the chest, near the left shoulder, the other grazed his head. He tottered, more in shock than mortal injury, then Dunham made his decision. He did not want to shoot this man, but he did want to stop him. He wanted all this to stop. Right now. He leapt to his feet, put his head down and charged.

Nick watched, horrified. It was an act of extreme bravery, and it was sheer lunacy. It was Captain Oates leaving the tent. It was The Light Brigade at Balaklava. As soon as the man heard him coming, he brought the gun up, already firing. Nick saw chips fly off the deck as three holes in a diagonal line ripped into Dunham's body before the gun appeared to jam or maybe the clip ran out. Nick did not care which it was, he was over to him in a second. The force of the impacts had knocked Dunham back, but his momentum brought him in a diesel slide to the dark man's feet, where he lay face up, bleeding. His hands were drenched in the diesel and so was the pistol he still held in his right hand.

Nick searched the guy's face for remorse but found none. He was trying to replace the AK's magazine but saw he was out of time. Instead, he wielded the gun like a club. Nick wanted to take him alive, if he could, but he would shoot if he had to. He was acutely aware of having just one bullet left. He dodged the swinging gun, then heard Anna cry out and saw her wrestling with the two men and the

AK. They must have seen the way the wind was blowing and rushed her just at the moment Dunham's heroics distracted her. Nick made a split-second decision. He was less than five metres from them. He aimed carefully and shot the larger of the two guards in the body. That would give Anna a chance. But now the dark man was advancing on him. He pointed the revolver at him and said:

"Stop right there. And drop the gun, or I'll shoot."

The man stopped and stared at him for a moment, as if trying to work something out, then raised his hands and took a couple of steps back, before laying the now useless AK very slowly on the deck, along-side Dunham's body. Nick continued to point his empty gun at the man's head. He heard Anna still struggling behind him and hoped to God she did not lose control of the other AK. Then, as he watched, he saw the man groping in the diesel for Dunham's hand and the spare pistol. But now he was struggling to free the gun. Nick did not want to press the trigger and produce a revealing click. He glanced behind him to see Anna still struggling with one of the men. The AK must be somewhere beneath their wrestling bodies, dammit.

He looked back at the man. He had his hand around the gun now but still had not freed it. Maybe Dunham was holding on somehow. Maybe he was alive, maybe rigor mortis had already set in. Nick had no way of knowing, and he had no idea what to do if the man freed that gun, except say his prayers. That would be it. For him. For Anna. Every second the man was wrestling for the gun in the oily slime seemed like an eternity. Nick was frozen with inertia, waiting to die when, suddenly, the deck was ablaze with light again and a crisp, young Greek voice he did not recognise was calling, in English:

"Lay down your weapons, all of you. Or we will shoot."

As if in a dream, Nick became aware of four fresh faces at the gunwales, each levelling a pistol. He lowered his own weapon, sank to a crouch. Behind him he was aware that the scuffling had stopped. He glanced around and saw one man on the ground, dead or unconscious, the other standing, as was Anna, the AK on the deck in front of them. He turned back to the dark man just in time to see him finally tear the weapon from Dunham's hand. Seemingly in slow motion, he turned to face Nick, a rictus smile creasing his oil-smeared face, a slippery arm extended, the hand gripping the Heckler. Nick was locked in a nightmare, feet in thick treacle, brain racing ahead of a comatose body. He braced for the impact.

The young men did not hesitate for a second. Three bullets hit the man simultaneously and he catapulted backwards over Dunham's ankles and into the oil slick. Nick saw a dark hole where his left eye should have been, while the right was locked in a fixed stare, but he went on looking for several more seconds while his brain caught up with events and his pulse rate slowed from drum machine to jack-hammer. Then he laid down his gun and slowly stood, hands raised. Two of the young men were already collecting up weapons. Lékas was emerging into the light, white-faced, hands raised. Anna was smiling ruefully at Nick. And he realised. It was over.

By now, the men from the coastguard, with Anna's guidance, had worked out who the bad guys were, and handcuffed them. The one on the deck – the guard Nick had shot – was not quite dead, but he had lost a lot of blood, so Nick reckoned the jury was out on him. He turned his attention to Dunham. For a moment, the arc of the bullet holes across his broken body brought to Nick's mind the trajectory of a small, flat stone, skimming across the water. He wiped his eyes with the back of his hand and seized an oily wrist. To his astonishment, there was still a weak pulse.

"This one's alive," he called to the man who appeared to be in charge. "We need urgent medical assistance here."

The man nodded and started making a call on his radio. Then he came over.

"This one – he is good guy or bad guy?"

"He is the skipper of this boat," said Nick.

"Then he is bad guy, no?"

"I'm not sure he is all that bad," said Nick. "We'll have to see."

The young coast guard looked puzzled, and Nick became aware of a familiar voice, raised in argument, and saw Bel at the gangplank, trying to get aboard.

"It's okay, Sergeant," he called. "She's with me."

When she came over, he saw the shock on her face.

"Thank God," she said, "I thought you'd been killed."

"I would have been if this guy had his way," he said, jerking his head at the body, "but Darius's boys saved us."

"Yes. I wasn't sure they would get here in time. I saw two small boats leaving the coastguard ships before they moved away. Who the hell was that, anyway?"

Nick had worked it out. "I think his name was MacKinnon."

"Who?"

"Adil MacKinnon. Dunham's brother-in-law."

"I thought he was supposed to be Syrian."

"He was half-Syrian. Scottish father, Syrian mother. Like his sister, Leila."

"Ha! When we get our phones back, I'll check with Andréa. I have pictures on my camera."

"Yes. Do. Get him to confirm it."

"How do you know it's him, Nick?"

"I don't, for certain. Just makes sense, from something he said, the way he and Dunham interacted, the similarity to Leila …"

"He wasn't supposed to be here."

"No. But no-one told him that, unfortunately."

"And he killed his sister's husband."

"Dunham's not dead yet, but no thanks to Adil MacKinnon. And what the hell happened to the police?"

"It's not good, Nick. I saw Valádis's body on the jetty. Dimítris dragged Leo to safety after he got shot. That's what Lékas saw, he told me. I imagine he's still with him."

"Leo? Oh, Christ no. How bad is he?"

"I don't know. Not good."

"We'd better go find him," he said.

*

They found Leo propped against the wall of one of the smaller buildings, Dimítris by his side, pressing a balled handkerchief against a stomach wound.

"Oh, mate," said Nick, "Sorry to see you suffering, buddy."

"I fucked up, Nick," he croaked. "Didn't think they'd have guns like that. I underestimated what we needed, big time. Anna tried to tell me. I got Valádis killed."

Nick saw tears in his eyes.

"You weren't to know," he said. "All we knew, there were three guys and a knife. Anyway, I fucked up, too. I assumed there were three, not four."

"Who was the other guy?"

"Adil. The boss. Dunham's wife's brother. I guess he was hitching a ride home. Upped the security several notches so he could get himself out of there."

"You think he closed down the business then?"

"I'm hoping so. Let's see what we find on board. Anyway, *he* is closed down. He's deader than your granddad and another of their guys is in poor shape. Dunham was hit three times. I don't know if he's going to make it. Anna's okay. She was great. And Lékas managed to stay out of the shitstorm. He's unharmed. I'm really sorry about Valádi, Leo. He was a brave lad."

"He was indeed … and the coastguard guys?"

"All present and correct. I owe Darius a very large drink. They saved our bacon."

"Bacon?"

"Never mind, Leo. Now, let me look at this."

He signalled to Dimítri to remove the handkerchief for a moment and fresh, bright blood pumped from a fleshy hole torn in his gut area.

"Is this the only wound?" he asked, and Dimítris nodded.

"One is enough, thank you. It hurts like fuck," said Leo, as Nick reached around his friend's body, probing for an exit wound, before sitting back on his haunches.

"Carry on, Dimítri. You're doing a grand job," he said, before turning back to Leo and studying his face for a moment. "Well, I reckon you'll live, as long as you don't bleed out. The bullet's still in there, so they'll have to dig it out for you. The coastguard have called in an emergency medical team. So, hang on in there, my friend."

"I don't suppose you have a smoke?" Leo said. "Mine got lost somewhere."

"I don't, Leo."

"But I do," said Bel, stretching forward with an open pack.

Leo helped himself to a green-coloured cigarette with a gold tip and Bel tucked another, for later, in his breast pocket, before joining him with one of her own and lighting them. He managed a faint smile as he exhaled.

"The prettiest smoke I've had in quite a while," he said.

*

They each gave Leo an encouraging smile and left him in the capable hands of Dimítris. As they ambled back to Destiny, they saw a small crowd of people on the deck, being directed, under guard, over the gangplank and onto the jetty, past the spot where Valádis's body still lay, now covered by a tarpaulin. Most were of Arabic appearance, but there were a few from other parts of the world, too, and one or two black faces. Almost all were well dressed. Nick saw many of them were holding on to each other. The men's faces looked grim. Some of the women were in tears. The children were silent.

"What will happen to them now?" asked Nick.

"I imagine they'll be held here until transport can be brought to take them to one of the camps," said Bel. "You saw what those are like. They'll be held in squalor for several months and then most of them will be sent home."

"Poor devils," he said.

Bel took some photographs and Nick tried to smile with sympathy at them as they were ushered past, but no-one smiled back. *We are the enemy now*, he concluded. Perhaps with good reason. Their new life in Italy or beyond, for which they had paid and risked so much, had been denied them. Now, their future was bleak and uncertain, and they were prisoners, in effect.

Just as they reached the boat, they heard the throb of the helicopters. They watched them race over the bay and then hover uncertainly over the island, looking for landing spots. Lékas had turned on the jetty lights to help, but it was either too great a slope or oil tanks, buildings or equipment were in the way. They retreated to the beach to the right of the harbour, and they saw them light up the sand, the rotors fanning the tops from the waves as they landed.

More coast guards were in evidence now, and they saw Darius amongst them, organising boats to collect the medical team. The two wounded men had not been moved, they saw, but a tarpaulin had been placed over Adil's body. Anna was kneeling at Dunham's side.

"Is he still with us?" asked Nick.

"Barely," she replied, "he keeps slipping in and out of consciousness."

Nick saw blood swirling in the diesel around his torso. He studied the bullet holes.

"This one looks messy, but it's just a flesh wound, I think," he said, "but this is close to the heart. Just below it, I'm thinking, otherwise he would already have left us. But I don't like this one at all. It pierced his left lung by the look of it."

"Survivable?" asked Bel.

"He's youngish, fit," said Nick. "If he gets some attention soon, he has a chance."

As if he had been listening, they saw Dunham's eyes flicker open for a second. Nick thought he saw a glimmer of recognition, a twitch of warmth, then he groaned softly and passed out.

"We need to get him on his side. Try to stop the lung collapsing," said Nick.

"Do we have any way of contacting his family?" asked Bel as they rolled him onto his left-hand side.

"I suspect Dunham's the only one who knows where they are," said Nick.

"Why do you say that?"

"If my theory is correct, he hid them. To protect them."

She turned to him, eyes narrowed, and was about to ask another question when Anna said:

"We need to move. Here come the medics."

*

As Bel took to photographing the medics in action and Anna was trying to contact her press officer at four in the morning, Nick spotted Lékas to one side, standing on his own. He walked over.

"Called the boss yet?" he said.

"Not yet. I'll stay on here for a while. Call him around breakfast time."

"At least you stopped the oil flow, finally."

Nick followed his eyes to the three forms on the deck, the carnage of splinters, bullet holes, blood and oil.

"And all this happened on the boat, rather than his precious oil terminal."

"There is that."

"Are you planning to confess?"

"I'd like to, in many ways, but I can't."

"How so?"

"If I admit to having made retail sales to Destiny over several months, he'll check the records and find out the sales weren't recorded. Then he'll check the inventory records and find no discrepancies. That can mean only one thing."

"You robbed Peter to pay Paul."

"Exactly. What would you do if you were me?"

"You know what? I think I'd resign up front. Admit to some vague irregularities of policy or procedure you were forced into by these guys and bow out gracefully. I doubt they'd investigate the issue further. You might even get to keep your ill-gotten gains and your pension. And your CV would still be pristine. You can tell your next employer you just got bored here, in the middle of nowhere. It was time to move on."

Lékas turned to look back at his little island.

"I've come to love this place, Mr Fisher. It's beautiful to me. My own little fiefdom. And I know how everything works, every detail. It's a good feeling, being an expert. I'll be sad to leave, but I think you're right. Resignation is the least bad option."

"You never know, they might insist that you stay on."

Nick gave him a conspiratorial grin and moved back to join Anna. They watched the medics take the wounded away on stretchers.

"Where have you put the other guard?" asked Nick.

"As soon as the migrants left, I handcuffed him and locked him below for the time being."

"Shall we interview him, then search the boat?"

"Good idea."

The man was Turkish and had little English and no Greek, or so he claimed. The fight seemed to have gone out of him now his boss was dead, his fellow guard seriously wounded, and he was facing a lengthy jail term himself. But this was a hardened professional criminal, no doubt about it. Even when he was in a position to give information, through an interpreter, it would be something to trade, not volunteer. They soon gave up on him and locked the door to the cabin before moving aft, to the separate cabin they remembered Paksima describing. Here they found two bunk beds, one above the other, and a separate camp bed. Nick figured that was where Adil had been sleeping. Beneath the bed, he found a leather holdall. He pulled it out and put it on the bed.

"I'll let you open it," he said.

Anna checked for any booby trap devices, then went to flip the catches.

"It's locked."

"That figures. I'll see if I can find the key."

He went back up on deck and rummaged through Adil's pockets. Nothing. Then he thought for a moment and undid the top buttons of the man's shirt. A key was attached to a leather thong around his neck.

This time Anna was able to unlock it, before flipping the catches.

"Bingo," said Nick.

They were looking at bundles of used fifty euro notes and started taking them out. Each bundle seemed to contain fifty notes, secured by an elastic band. They laid them on the bed, one by one.

"That's it," said Anna, placing the last bundle.

They counted seventy-two.

"Four bundles must be ten grand, so you're looking at a hundred and eighty grand," said Nick.

"Wow."

"Loose change to these guys, I suspect."

He was looking in the holdall, then he reached in and removed a thick cardboard layer.

"Aha," he said, pulling out two large, polythene packs of what looked like flour, and a small, purple bag with a drawstring. It looked like velvet, and Nick had a good idea what it contained: the currency of the rich and mobile.

"This is the real stuff," he said. "Adil's pension fund."

He picked up one of the packs and laid it flat on his upturned palm.

"About two kilos of powdered heroin in each bag, I'm guessing. Do you have any idea of the street value, Lieutenant?"

"A hundred thousand?"

Nick snorted.

"More like four hundred thousand euros, after cutting it. Not that he'd get quite that for it, mind you."

"My God."

"Not to mention these little babies."

He loosened the drawstring and upended the purple bag, letting a cascade of dull, silver-grey stones tumble onto the bed. He shook the bag to show it was empty, but he had trapped one stone between his finger and thumb and held it in the bag.

"What are they?"

"Uncut diamonds. I can't even hazard a guess at what they're worth. A lot, though."

"All this from people smuggling?"

"No. Hardly. Heroin from Afghanistan, bought at the border for not very much, taken by road to Turkey, then shipped to Italy. Normally, it would be processed somewhere along the way, cut with something to reduce the purity to thirty percent or so, made into smaller packages or capsules. But this is uncut, probably seventy percent pure, powdered, white heroin."

"So," she said slowly, "the family charter business was a cover for a migrant smuggling operation, but within that they were also trafficking heroin?"

"Yes. Not pure, like this. This is a one-off. Adil making his escape, I suspect. On the regular trips they shipped capsules of cut heroin, in mules like Paksima."

"I've never seen anything like this," she said, standing back and pulling out her phone. She took a few photographs and then Nick offered to take one of her standing proudly in front of the haul.

"Get that one to your boss and your press officer, I would," he said. "Now, you'd better count these before I put them back."

She did as she was told.

"There are fifteen," she said.

"Okay," he said, pouring all but one back into the bag and pulling the drawstring tight, before lobbing the bag spectacularly into the holdall with his right hand. As Anna's eyes were drawn to the bag's trajectory, he used his left hand to slip the remaining stone into the pocket of his shorts.

"Careful!" said Anna.

"They're diamonds, for God's sake!"

"I'm going to check them, anyway."

He watched, faintly amused, as she took the bag out, emptied it onto the bed, checked for damage and made certain there were still fifteen. Then she was content. They spent the next couple of minutes repacking the holdall and then Anna said:

"I'm going to tell the boss about all this before I get tempted to run off with it."

"You do that," said Nick. "And then we need to find a drink somewhere."

CHAPTER 28
FRIENDS

By four am, the wounded had been flown to hospital and the bodies removed to the mortuary. Dimítris insisted on accompanying his much-loved boss to the hospital. Anna had called her captain and received a bollocking for waking him until she went on to explain. That changed his mood to near ecstasy when he heard that the smuggling operation had been closed down and he saw the haul on the photo Anna sent to his mobile phone. His enthusiasm seemed only slightly dented when he heard that a constable from Réthymno had died and Christodoulákis was badly hurt.

"Great work, Anna," he said. "I'll get a security van dispatched first thing to pick that lot up. In the meantime, don't let it out of your sight. And I'll call a press conference for lunchtime tomorrow. Can you make that?"

"I was hoping to clean up and get some sleep, sir."

"You'll have time to shower and change, grab something to eat. After the press conference, you can sleep for the rest of the day if you want, with my blessing. Don't worry. I'll do most of the talking."

And take most of the credit, no doubt, she thought.

As she ended the call, they heard the sound of an outboard and a DRG bumped up against the jetty, just as the first faint light of dawn was beginning to streak the night sky. It was Darius, and he was carrying two bottles.

He strode over.

"I have tsikoúdia. It's been a tough night. But you did well, my friends." His beard appeared to be smiling again; his eyes most certainly were, as he grabbed each of them in a bear hug.

"I'm not sure we did *that* well," said Nick. "Your guys saved our arses, frankly. Their timing was impeccable."

"As the Americans say, you did the heavy lifting, my friends. I heard a scrap starting and I had men to spare. Of course, we were going to help if we could. Now, take a drink with me. I insist."

He produced four small glasses from his jacket pocket and passed them around, then offered the bottle to Anna first, then Bel, then Nick before filling his own glass.

"Yeiá mas," he said, and they repeated it, in chorus.

"This is rakí, though, isn't it?" said Nick, the familiar flavour scouring its way down his throat.

"You may call it rakí, Nick, but I am not a Turk. To me, it is tsikoúdia."

He filled the glasses again, despite Anna's attempted refusal. This time it was Nick who led the toast.

"To a brave constable, who gave his life tonight in the fight against evil. I give you Valádis."

"Valádis," they choroused, tapped their glasses twice on the bulkhead and emptied them as one.

*

By the time they reached Saktoúria, it was almost seven in the morning. The wind had died down, finally, and the sea was glittering under a deep blue sky. Nick's senses were heightened by incipient exhaustion. It was a long time since he had pulled an all-nighter, and the rakí may not have helped.

As they drifted to a halt outside his little cottage, he said:

"I'm afraid we'll have to defer our natural passions, Bel; I'm totally whacked."

She looked at him, searching his eyes. Then she stroked the side of his face.

"I'm not staying, Nick. I have everything I need now, and I must get this story out. It's important to move quickly at this point."

"Ah, yes, of course," he said, trying to keep his voice steady.

"It's been wonderful, seeing you again, sharing this adventure."

"Right."

"I mean it. And you've helped me a lot. I'm very grateful."

She kissed him softly on his cheek and squeezed his hand.

"And I adore your little house," she said, as they got out of the Jeep. "You've got yourself well sorted, Nick Fisher."

"If you ever have a holiday, come back. Spend a few days here."

"I'd like that," she said, but Nick knew she would not return. She would keep moving on. Always. That's how she was. She had bestowed her gifts, for which he must be grateful, but now she would go, before anything solidified into commitment or obligation or there was the tiniest whiff of boredom.

They were loading up the Mercedes now and Nick shut the tailgate for her.

"Are you okay?" she asked.

"I'm fine," he beamed. "It's been fun. And I hope your story goes well for you, stirs things up, makes a real difference."

"I hope so, too. Goodbye, Nick."

She stood on tiptoe to kiss him on the cheek, and, with that, she was in the driving seat and on her way, a braceleted, brown hand waving elegantly from the driver's window, her dark eyes glowing in the rear-view mirror. As Nick turned back, heavy-hearted towards the cottage, the stray cat looked at him, hesitating. Then it miaowed, turned tail, and hurtled down the lane.

CHAPTER 29
DUNHAM'S STORY

It was five days before Anna called.

"I've finally got the all-clear to interview Dunham," she said on the phone. "Leo said you should come along. We can pay him a call, too."

"How are they?"

"Leo will make a full recovery, but it'll take a few weeks. Dunham needed a pneumonectomy. They had to take out the lung that got shot, but he's expected to make it."

"Can you live with just one?"

"You can. The remaining lung expands in response, apparently. If you're lucky, you can get back to about seventy percent of the breathing capacity you had before, but you must take things easy. You can still have a long life, but it has to be a less active, slower paced one."

"What did that second bullet do?"

"Took a chunk out of the liver, just below the heart. He was very lucky. The liver will grow back. And, as you thought, the first bullet was just a flesh wound in his side. That one went straight through."

"And your guard, the guy I shot?"

"Don't worry about him. He'll live to stand trial."

"Where are they?"

"Leo and Dunham are in the same hospital, here in Iráklio. When can you get over?"

They arranged to meet there at ten the following morning.

*

As they entered the room, Leo was closing the window and looking guilty. There was a smell of fresh tobacco smoke in the air. The doctor was not happy.

"Now, Leo, you're not supposed to be out of bed, as you well know.

You're risking tearing those stitches – and just so you can poison yourself with those damned cigarettes!"

Leo mumbled something apologetic and allowed himself to be bundled back between the sheets, where the doctor checked him over briefly. While he was doing this, Leo gave them a resigned look, but there was a mischievous grin behind it, Nick thought.

They spent ten minutes with him. Established that he was firmly on the mend and would be out in a few days, then ran through what they needed to find out from Oliver Dunham.

*

The doctor paused at the door to Dunham's hospital bedroom.

"Mr Dunham is still very weak. I can give you half an hour. If you need more, I will need to check him again. Understood?"

They both nodded and he responded by opening the door and holding it open for them. Nick was surprised at how normal Oliver Dunham looked, at least superficially.

"Do come in, Mr Fisher, and who is this?"

Anna introduced herself.

"I remember you from our little skirmish, of course, but I had no idea who you were," he added.

"How *are* you?" asked Nick.

"Lucky to be alive, they tell me. Might have to give up the weeds, though."

"And a few other things, I imagine."

"Maybe one or two."

"Have you been in touch with the family?"

"Just a text to say I'm okay and I'll call soon."

"Is that all?"

"I'm getting stronger every day. I want to be stronger before they see me. And I have to tell Leila about Adil. I'm not looking forward to that."

"Let's hope she doesn't see it in the press or on TV, then."

"Not likely, where they are. I have to tell her he's dead, but I also have to tell her what an evil bastard he was. It won't be easy. Trouble is, she thinks he's a saint. Or rather was."

"How could she believe that?" asked Anna.

"She sees him as a man who risked everything to help these poor refugees from their mother's home country, Syria. He was a Schindler figure for her – the German guy who helped all those Jews? She was the one who put us together. With Destiny, he could open up a new route, from a point much closer to the Syrian border."

"Why would you agree to help, though?"

"They pleaded with me. And it seemed to be a good cause, helping these desperate people to a new life."

"But highly illegal," Anna pointed out.

"Technically, yes, but we decided to do it as a family. The refugees would remain below decks. Adil had a couple of guys who would help us. And it was a new route. We didn't think we were taking such a big risk. And frankly, Leila and I needed the money."

"I thought you had heaps of money," said Nick.

"My father has money. Heaps and heaps of it. But last year he married again, and his new wife turned him against me. Convinced him I was a wastrel, that I would never shape up while he went on supporting me, the bitch. We had a massive row and he cut me off. Cancelled my allowance. Every penny. Told me to get off my arse, put my back into the charter business, make it work, make him a return on his investment in Destiny."

"But doing this was easier."

"I didn't have reserves, and we needed money *now*, not in five years' time. It takes time to build a business. And it wouldn't be forever, Adil said. Just a handful of trips. And twenty grand a trip. That was all for me. He paid for the diesel."

"Twenty grand."

"Yes. It seemed a lot to me till I saw those pictures in the paper. But, of course, I knew nothing about any drugs."

Anna snorted in disbelief.

"Come on, Mr Dunham. How do you expect us to believe that?"

"Maybe I was naïve or stupid, but I reckoned they were making a pretty good haul from the migrants. I found out most of them were paying around fifteen grand US for the trip, so that's three hundred thousand dollars for twenty passengers. Okay, they had to pay for the diesel, the guy who forged the papers and me, but I reckoned they'd still clear close to two hundred thousand bucks each trip."

"Not enough for these greedy bastards. A couple of mules and they could double it."

"What are you saying, Mr Fisher?"

"That, in all likelihood, you've been trafficking heroin every trip, along with migrants."

"And you knew nothing about this," said Anna, her voice heavy with scepticism.

"I swear, I did not," said Dunham. "I would never have thought Adil capable of that, of using us like that, putting his family at such risk."

There was a protracted silence. Anna went to say something, but Nick's eyes darted at her and she lowered her head, remaining silent. Finally, Dunham spoke again:

"The first five trips were fine," he said, slowly. "It all went very smoothly. Dragan and Razmik handled the migrants. We'd see two or three occasionally, when they were allowed on deck for a breather. We were discouraged from talking to them, but Jamil being Jamil, did chat with quite a few. I handled the boat, minding my own business. Then, on the sixth trip, a young girl became ill, seriously ill. I didn't know what it was, but I knew we had to get help for her. But they didn't want to do anything."

"By *they*, you mean the minders, Dragan and Razmik?" asked Anna, and Dunham nodded.

"They said it was too risky, but eventually I persuaded them."

"How did you do that?"

"I reminded them I was the skipper, and I was the only one who could sail the fucking boat. If they wanted me to continue doing it for them, they had to do this for me. I was not going to have a young girl die needlessly on my boat. Well, there was an argument and they tried to get nasty, but I was adamant. I said we could sneak into Igoumenítsa in the dark. The port authorities are quite hot there on account of the ferry lanes. They are there twenty-four hours, and you have to radio in as you approach. But I said we'd lie offshore and use the tender to avoid all that. We could leave the girl on the quay, near the fishing harbour. Someone would soon find her. I think they called Adil then, and he must have reluctantly agreed."

"Which would be when Adil called Osmanek Fahri," said Nick.

"Sorry? What do you mean?"

"Your brother-in-law arranged to have that girl, Paksima, killed. They traced her to the hospital at Ioánnina and Fahri murdered her in her hospital room."

"Oh, my God!"

"Along the way, they compromised an earlier customer of theirs, a young doctor who was working illegally. He committed suicide. They also abducted and assaulted a journalist who just happened to be there at the time."

Dunham was blinking several times and shaking his head.

"Those were the unfortunate effects of your good intentions, Mr Dunham. You forced Adil to cover his tracks at all costs."

"I didn't realise. I saw people on the quayside. I thought she'd be safe with them."

"The Norwegians. They were kind enough to drive her all the way to Ioannina and get her into the hospital, but then they left her with the doctors, believing her to be safe in their care."

"As one would. As normal people would, anyway."

"And on that same trip, did you notice a young black boy? He was in the same cabin as Paksima. They were close, briefly."

"D'you know, I *did*. I remember him because he was so young and so very dark-skinned. The migrants are mostly coffee-coloured, so he stood out, rather. Seemed a nice boy, though."

"Did you see him with Paksima?"

"I did, and I remember he seemed agitated. I assumed he was worried about her condition. And then, later, when we were taking her into the tender, off Igoumenítsa, I thought of him again. I suppose I expected him to be there when we took her out of the cabin, but I didn't see him. Later, I asked Dragan and he said the boy had decided to get off when we refuelled, to make a life for himself in Crete."

"And you believed that?"

"I was surprised that he would leave Paksima. He seemed to care about her. But I guess he had his own plans. There was only that one opportunity to get off the boat, so he took it."

"Except that he didn't."

"No?"

"Dragan lied to you. They cut the boy's throat and threw him into the sea about half an hour after you left the oil terminal. He was a nice, well brought-up boy from Somalia, and he had fallen for Paksima. Then, he discovered, not only had she been recruited as a drugs mule and forced to swallow capsules containing powdered heroin, but also, she was being sexually abused by your minders. He wanted to raise the alarm, to you and the other migrants, so they shut him up."

"Oh, Jesus. I must admit, I wondered if Dragan was hiding something."

"I think you chose to look the other way," said Anna.

Dunham looked wounded at the suggestion but there was no denial, Nick noticed.

"What happened later, when the remaining migrants had been delivered to Italy?" he asked.

"How do you mean?"

"Were you happy to carry on, do more trips?"

"No. I called Adil a couple of hours after the drop. I couldn't put my finger on it, but the whole thing with Paksima had freaked me out. I'd seen another side of these guys and I didn't like it. And, if I'm honest, I did wonder how she'd become so ill, so quickly. Razmik told me it was a burst appendix, but I wasn't sure whether to believe him. And I wasn't sure Dragan had been telling the truth about the black lad. I noticed the migrants seemed even more subdued than usual. So, when I called him, I said enough was enough; I wasn't doing any more runs."

"How did that go down?"

"Like a lead balloon. He tried to persuade me. Offered to up my piece of the pie to twenty-five grand, but I said no. Then he played the refugee card. Said I would be deserting his and Leila's people at an increasingly desperate time. I said I'd done my bit, and now it was over. He got angry then. More than angry, furious. He started to threaten me, so I hung up on him."

"Then what happened?"

"We sailed back to Crete. Took a breather for a couple of days. Went to a beach near Plakiás, amongst other things."

"Soúda."

"So you said."

"And then to Chaniá, where Jamil was attacked?"

"Yes. It was a warning. Comply or else. And a new low point for Adil, arranging an attack on his ten-year-old nephew."

"Did you tell Leila?" asked Anna.

"I tried to, but she wasn't ready to believe it. We argued. She said I was jealous of him. Always had been. Can you imagine?"

"What, that you would be jealous of a violent drug and people smuggler?" asked Nick.

"Or perhaps jealous of someone who showed some real determination to make something of his life?" asked Anna. "Albeit totally misguided," she added as a dutiful afterthought.

"Ooh, that was a low blow, Lieutenant. Are you suggesting my wife thinks I'm a wastrel, too?"

"Let's stick with the story, shall we?" said Nick. "What happened next?"

"It was my turn to be furious. I called Adil and told him what I thought of men who attack little boys. He was cold and intransigent. Do what I want, or he will be seriously hurt next time, or your wife will lose her looks."

"He was threatening his own sister?"

"Oh yes. All in a day's work for Adil. He made it sound like he had a bottle of acid with her name on it. Hard to believe he would do that to his own sister, but I really wasn't sure. I was angry, but I was scared, too. He'd shown what he could do – from Turkey, mind you – and I didn't doubt he could do more, if he chose. We argued, we haggled. Finally, I said I would do one more trip – and only one – and I would do it alone, without my family on board. And I would do it for a hundred thousand. To my amazement, he agreed. It felt too good to be true.

"After that, I moved fast. I told Leila she and Jamil would have to go into hiding for a week or two. She thought I was being ridiculous, but I insisted. I bought plane tickets for Glasgow to obfuscate things, even checked them onto the flight, but then I drove them to a place I know, where they would be safe. Made damned sure I wasn't followed. I did all this from Ágios Nikólaos before your little visit, then I set off for Mersin the next morning. It was only when the last batch of migrants was being embarked that I realised Adil was inviting himself along. He was getting out, he said, and he had brought guns. Enough for a small war, it seemed to me. Now I understood why he had been so desperate for there to be one more trip."

"Did you realise he had his stash with him – the heroin and the diamonds?"

"You probably won't believe me, but it never even crossed my mind. I'm such an innocent."

Nick and Anna exchanged doubtful glances.

"And your family. Where are they?" asked Anna. "We will not share this information."

"Well, I guess that's less of a concern now, anyway. They're at a monastery on a remote part of the south coast. A quiet and beautiful place with its own small beach, maybe two-thirds of the way from Mýrtos to Léndas. It's called Virgin Monastery Koudoumá."

"So, you all would have sailed past it, in fact."

"We did, indeed. I enjoyed the irony, but I reckoned they were pretty safe there."

There was a long pause then. Nick stood up and went to the window. Anna was fiddling with her notes.

"What's going to happen to me?" asked Dunham, after a while.

"You'll be charged with people smuggling for sure, maybe drug smuggling, maybe murder," Anna said. "I will talk to the Investigating Judge with my boss, the captain, and take it from there."

"I thought you'd say that, Lieutenant. But, you know, I didn't mean any harm. I thought I was helping make the world a better place. Things got a little out of hand, but that wasn't my doing, and I fought with the good guys at the end, remember, at the cost of a lung I was rather fond of."

"Well," said Anna. "If it's believed that you were coerced into the final trip, then some mitigation might be appropriate, but you still have to convince judge and jury that you were not complicit in either murder. Also, how could you not have been aware of the drug smuggling that took place on your boat, not to mention the sexual abuse of at least one young woman?"

"You're going down for quite a few years, I'm afraid, old son," said Nick. "Jamil will be all grown up when you get out, and Daddy's not going to be impressed, is he? You see, life's really not that easy. And – if it feels easy – it's generally because some other poor schmuck is carrying the can for you. Some people are acutely aware of that, whereas others turn a blind eye to it. You'll have time now, won't you? Time to reflect on which camp you chose and whether to adopt a different approach in what's left of your life."

Dunham stared at him for a long moment, the hot, bright anger and wounded pride in his eyes slowly solidifying into a non-reflective wall of emptiness.

"I'm not your son, Nick Fisher," he said.

CHAPTER 30
THE LIFELINE

On the longish drive back over the mountains, Nick had time to reflect. Perhaps he had been too hard on Oliver Dunham. The man was a privileged prat and a naïve fool, but, worst of all, he had allowed himself to be used by a manipulative and deeply unpleasant character within his own family. A man who would stop at nothing in his pursuit of wealth and power. But Ollie had hoped for the best, ignored the worst, and he had done so relentlessly. He had hoped this man had the noblest of intentions, hoped he didn't traffic hard drugs, hoped he didn't have people threatened or killed. Until, suddenly, it was all staring him in the face and then, finally, he swapped sides. Had he done that because it was the right thing to do or because he thought it was the best chance of saving his own, wretched skin? Who knows? *I certainly don't,* he thought.

And then, as he drove on, he remembered the beach at Soúda. The father and son. The stone skimmer and his young apprentice. How envious he had been of the easy warmth and trust between them. The exemplary father and his adoring son. But now Jamal, too, would have to learn that life is not easy, after all. That there is a price to be paid and someone has to pay it.

*

Instead of turning left onto the Spíli road, Nick turned right and headed into Réthymno. He worked his way around the one-way system to the central car park. His destination was just across the street. Inside, he found an A5 padded envelope, scribbled out some guidance on a piece of paper without leaving a signature, folded it and tucked it inside, before pulling a folded sheet out of the pocket of his shorts, which gave him what he needed to print the address. Finally, he took something from the bottom of his other pocket, wrapped it in tissue,

276

then slipped it between the sides of the folded sheet before sealing the envelope. He tested the seal to make sure it was secure.

At the counter, the woman expressed mild surprise:

"We don't get many for *there*," she said. "Is the item worth more than twenty euros? I can insure it for you if it is. And what shall I say it is – for the customs form?"

Nick smiled.

"It's sentimental value only – it's just a letter with a pebble my friend's son left behind. I thought he'd like to have it."

The woman smiled back.

"That's kind of you. I'll put: *small rock, no value* then, shall I?"

"Perfect," grinned Nick, thinking that half her description was spot-on, funnily enough, even if the other half was spectacularly wrong.

Just across the end of the street from the post office was Barrio, one of his favourite coffee houses. He treated himself to a cappuccino and a pastry and sat for a few minutes. He imagined the package arriving if it got through. There would be astonishment and curiosity, then delight, and ultimately, relief. From what Leo had said, the guy knew his way around the black market. He would be fine. He might choose not to use it yet, but he would have it there: a lifeline, a means of escape for them both.

*

It was late afternoon by the time he made it back to Saktoúria. The sun was low in the sky and there was a slight chill in the air. He knew the cupboards were bare, so he splashed his face, changed quickly, and wandered down to the kafenío.

"O Níko," bawled Kóstas, "where the hell you been, man?"

"Working. What do you think?"

"Here, I have package for you."

He handed Nick a chunky A4 envelope, postmarked Athens. He recognised the writing. It must be a copy of Bel's article, already.

"Where is that beautiful creature you were with last time?" asked Kóstas.

"Back in Beirut by now, I should think."

"Beirut? What the hell she do there?"

"That's where she lives, Kostí."

He made a face.

"Who want to live there, when you can live in Kríti?"

"She wants to change the world."

"We thought you had found your new wife, Níko."

Nick saw Lena and Yiórgos, drinking beer together, waved and started walking towards them.

"We're just good friends," he called back over his shoulder. Kóstas responded with a doubtful snort, but Lena appeared to brighten slightly, he noticed.

"Let me get you a beer," said Yiórgos. "I want to hear about this case. You brave man, Níko, fighting these bastards. I see in the paper. What a stash! Did you get any diamonds?"

"What do *you* think, Yiórgo?" he said, raising an eyebrow as he pulled out a chair, "but I did get paid a little this time, so the beers are on me tonight."

There was a small cheer, and Yiórgos drummed the table as Kóstas lumbered over with a tray of bottles and glasses.

"Now, where would you like me to start?" asked Nick.

THE END

LEAVING A REVIEW

If you have enjoyed reading my book, it would be wonderful if you could find a minute to complete a short review of *The Stone Skimmers* on your chosen retailer's website. Thank you!

Alex

THANK YOU

Special thanks are due to my good friend Leonie Carter McMahon. She helped me devise plot outlines at the outset of the series and the back story for *Nick Fisher*. She also provided a detailed critique of the final draft of this novel and came up with ideas and changes, many of which I was happy to adopt.

I would also like to make special mention of Barry Hunter who, despite having great difficulty reading at all (he was recovering from a detached retina) managed to work his way through all the marine scenes, gave me the inside track on marine technology and generally corrected the landlubber in me.

I would also like to thank my brave beta readers, especially the thoroughly eagle-eyed Sarah Toonen, but also Terri Jones, George Schrijver, Alexandra ("Sandy") Smithies, Roger Collins, Christine and Bob Hoare, Denise and Peter Simon. I found this a more challenging book to write, and your encouragement, feedback and support not only got me through the process, but also, without doubt, helped me improve the quality of the novel.

Thanks also to my newsletter subscribers and all those who have been kind enough to leave reviews or make comments on Amazon, Facebook, Goodreads, or anywhere else. It's challenging for a new author without the marketing muscle of a major publisher to achieve any kind of visibility in today's fiercely competitive marketplace and letting the world know that you enjoyed my books is extremely helpful and important to me. I read every comment and review and am very grateful to those who have taken the trouble to do this.

And lastly, but by no means least, thank you for buying and reading this novel. I hope you enjoyed it and will seek out more Nick Fisher novels and perhaps also give my short stories a try. You can see all my published writing at www.alexdunlevy.com.

ABOUT THE AUTHOR

Alex abandoned a career in finance at the age of forty-nine and spent a few years staring at the Mediterranean, contemplating life and loss. Finally, he accepted what his heart had always known. So, he joined some writing groups and he began to write.

He has now completed three novels in a series of crime thrillers set on the island of Crete and featuring British protagonist Nick Fisher. *The Unforgiving Stone* was the October 2020 debut. *Beneath the Stone* followed in 2021 and *The Stone Skimmers* in 2022. All three have been awarded medallions of quality by B.R.A.G. (Book Readers Appreciation Group) and Amazon UK readers rate them 4.5 or 4.6 (out of 5) on average.

Alex has also published a collection of short stories, *The Late Shift Specialist*. These are quite different from his crime writing. Uniquely personal - they are quirky, funny or sad – but always written straight from the heart.

He has been toying with other ideas. These include a black comedy set in the world of corporate finance and a bitter-sweet coming-of-age story, set in the 1960s. But he expects there to be more Nick Fisher novels before too long.

Born in Derbyshire, England, Alex now lives in Crete, Greece, where he has an old, stone house in the central south of the island, between the Amari Valley and the Libyan Sea.

CONTACT

If you would like to get in touch with Alex, please visit his website: www.alexdunlevy.com where you can join his mailing list, if you wish, and find out about any special offers, or just drop an email to alexdunlevyauthor@gmail.com

He can also be found on Facebook and Twitter.

ALSO BY ALEX DUNLEVY

The Unforgiving Stone
(the first novel in the Nick Fisher series)

Beneath the Stone
(the second novel in the Nick Fisher series)

The Late Shift Specialist
(a collection of short stories)

Printed in Great Britain
by Amazon

37165069R00169